MEGACITY

MEGACITY

EDITED BY
KATHLEEN McCAUL MOURA

BOILER HOUSE PRESS

9   Introduction
By Kathleen McCaul Moura

35   1–WHAT IS A MEGACITY?
A conversation between two Lagos architects
With Kunlé Adeyemi and Dele Adeyemo

47   2–MANILA
Lamentations 5:23
By Jessica Zafra

61   3–KINSHASA
Mr. Fix It: Troublesome Kinshasa
By Richard Ali A Mutu

76   4–DELHI
Mangosil
By Uday Prakash

100   5–MEXICO CITY
The Water Was Drained
By Diego Gerard

106   6–TONGJIANG
Glorious City of Forgetting
By Emily Ruth Ford

123   7–MOSCOW
       The Broken Doll
       By Liza Alexandrova-Zorina

141   8–DELHI
       Driving in Greater Noida
       By Deepti Kapoor

170   9–LAGOS
       Shuffering and Shmiling in Lagos
       By Ayodele Olofintuade

181   10–SHENZEN
       Metro Line Five
       By Wu Jun

205   11–PARIS
       An Attempt at Exhausting a Place in Paris
       By Anna Pook

220   12–MEXICO CITY
       Planes Flying Over a Monster
       By Daniel Saldaña París

230   13–TOKYO
       Slow Boat
       By Hideo Furukawa

247   14–CAIRO
       Using Life
       By Ahmed Naji

258   15–SÃO PAULO
      Margins of Error
      By Ferréz

265   16–KARACHI
      The Scatter Here is Too Great
      By Bilal Tanweer

272   17–SÃO PAULO
      Desesterro
      By Sheyla Smanioto

287   18–CAIRO
      The Bridge
      By Montasser Al-Qaffash

291   19–MANILA
      Somersaults
      By Jeffrey P. Yap

325   Acknowledgements
326   About the authors
332   About the translators

INTRODUCTION

BY KATHLEEN McCAUL MOURA

It was the megacity that taught me to hustle. In 2011 I arrived in São Paulo, pregnant, on the arm of a local who was neither rich nor poor. We needed to find some health-care but, because I was already expecting, none of the insurance providers who cover the middle classes and a good part of the working class in Brazil would take us on. Filipe, my husband, did not panic. He simply found what locals in that extraordinary city of twenty million people call a *jeitinho* – a little way.

Working things out with a doctor friend of his, based at the São Paulo's only well-respected public hospital, he told me we needed to fake an emergency. I was to go to the hospital's A and E and tell them I was eight weeks pregnant and that I had been bleeding heavily. They would register me on the computer system, then, before I was seen, Filipe's friend would collect me and sneak me onto the maternity services system a few floors above. Job done, free public healthcare for the next nine months. My husband leant back over the balcony of our tiny nineteenth-floor tower-block apartment smiling, pleased with his plan. I gawped back in horror. To do this seemed immoral, full of risk on so many levels. In the end, faced with no other choice, I said I would do it.

Things went wrong almost immediately. Our friend was held up with a real patient and, as a result, I ended up on an examining table with my legs apart and my feet in stirrups, a plastic-gloved hand coming towards me. It was too much. I jumped off the bed and started shouting, pretty hysterically, at my husband. The doctor was confused, worried, until Filipe explained what we were here to do. The doctor sent us up to the maternity unit himself. The matron on duty told us three other mothers had already been in with the same ruse that day so we should come back early the next morning. Megacities such as São Paulo are difficult places to navigate – geographically, psychologically and administratively – and no local, I realised, would be surprised by an individual making their way any which way they could.

My antenatal care involved hours leant up against raw concrete pillars, avoiding very sick patients left in public corridors and throwing up into black plastic bin bags after particularly difficult blood tests. The doctors, however, were very good. My daughter and I survived and then flourished in São Paulo. Over the years, I came to see myself as a megacity local. I could navigate the opaque bus system with a buggy but learnt from experience never ever to take a baby into the rush-hour metro. I knew to avoid streets favoured by local crackheads on my way to the beautifully restored world famous concert hall, Sala São Paulo. I learnt that the best nights were not to be had on glamorous rooftops with endless glittering views, but in the squatted, graffitied night-clubs of crumbling, pockmarked downtown. The freshest sushi was not prepared by five-star hotels but in a small garage with no windows down in Japan-town. As a journalist, I interviewed world-famous architects in their own glass towers, favela poets performing at local bars stacked with beer and books on philosophy, wealthy art collectors, mutinous teenagers from the margins.

I mostly relished these adventures into the megacity, until the night my husband and I had one of the most common São Paulo experiences. Clopping obliviously along at one in the morning, down a dark street on the way to a new club, I found a small gun pointed at my stomach. Two short, tubby men in football shirts and board shorts grinned at us and made us hand over our wallets and mobiles. They motioned for us to turn away from the bright lights of the bar where people were drinking and chatting just a few metres from us, back into the black street where we had carelessly parked our car. This was bad. I gave a small moan. One of the guys told us not to worry, they weren't going to kidnap us or kill us, just take our car. We were lucky, said friends and family, shrugging; there were so many stories that ended differently, brutally. For days afterwards, gruesome tales were told to us with the lightest humour in an effort, I think, to make us feel better. Just like back in the hospital, I realised that locals here thought differently, accepting armed robbery as just another megacity hustle, just another guy trying to make their way.

I was never able to muster this nonchalance and we left São Paulo not long after the hold-up, ending up in the small English city of Norwich where I was to study creative writing at the University of East Anglia. But the megacity never really left me. I wrote about spaghetti highways thick with cars, thudding helicopters, sky-high towers, stolen guns, parties of champagne and blood. I wanted to get inside the megacity mindset, the matter-of-fact survival instinct, the nose for black humour that I never really achieved myself. All of this led me to embark upon a creative writing doctorate exploring the way in which the infrastructure and architecture of massive urban hubs affects the way we live, and the way we write. This anthology, which gathers brilliant new writing from megacities across the world, is a happy and gratifying product of that research.

Megacities are defined as cities with over ten million residents. In developing countries particularly, they operate differently to the cities which flourished in the nineteenth and twentieth centuries. Whereas the construction of the great European capitals was a triumph of 'public planning' and 'co-ordinated public enterprise'[1], the rising megacities of Asia, Africa and Latin America herald the collapse of these civic structures. These new megacities have grown rapidly and without apparent control, spreading outwards, often illegally, and with little thought given to the public space so valued by European urban planners of the nineteenth century. Contemporary megacities are vaster than any urban landscape previously imagined; the biggest have populations of over twenty million people – the estimated urban population of the whole world at the time of the French Revolution.[2]

In many of the newer megacities, infrastructure has struggled to keep pace with sprawling immigrant peripheries and ambitious new building projects. Because of this, everyday life in Lagos, to take one example, is very different from that known to a Londoner. This is both obvious and the result of complex factors, as Kunlé Adeyemi makes clear in his introductory conversation with Dele Adeyemo, two megacity architects very much preoccupied with the questions of how these cities function:

'...from a morphological point of view, one could argue that Lagos and London are similar cities as they are settled along water, however, the population of Lagos with an estimate of over twenty million people is actually more than twice of that of London. Ironically, the physical infrastructure supporting the city of London is staggeringly much larger than that of Lagos... Seeing how people have adapted to those conditions both socially and also politically is really fascinating – to see how the city survives through very, very difficult developmental times.'

Very difficult, but really fascinating. This could be said to encapsulate the attitude towards megacities for a whole generation of urbanists, geographers and economists who have been studying these urban hubs for years. Megacities emerged as a hot topic of conversation amongst architects at the turn of the millennium and that interest is now enjoying a powerful second wave, not only amongst researchers such as Dele Adeyemo but also in the popular imagination, in part as a result of the growing and related issues of climate change, global migration, population explosions and rising inequality.

Have writers and readers kept pace with the swell of interest in megacities? Whether mega or not, big cities provide more than impressive statistics and research opportunities. They have been, and remain, a source of inspiration to writers across the world, the place to go to symbolise and explore the complexities of contemporary life. In this tradition, the work of Baudelaire is of central importance. Marshall Bermann argues that Baudelaire's reaction to the reconstruction of Paris in the mid-nineteenth century crystalised the idea that the city was integral to the experience of modernity – 'the intimate unity of the modern self and the modern environment'.[3]

Baudelaire was inspired by Baron Hausmann's redevelopment of the city centre between 1853–1870. The construction of wide avenues allowed public life to flourish and for Baudelaire himself to explore the full tableau of Parisian life. The 'poetic prose, musical without rhythm and without rhyme, supple enough and rugged enough to adapt itself' came, according to Baudelaire, mostly from 'the exploration of enormous cities.'[4] and was central to the development of the poet's style. The changing city provided not only a modern voice for the poet but also concrete subject matter. The demolition of central slums, which allowed rich and poor to take a good look at one another for the first time, inspired 'Eyes of the Poor'. The introduction of macadam – meaning faster, more treacherous, roads running through the centre of the city – brought with it a new a sense of speed, movement and danger, captured in 'Loss of Halo'. Walter Benjamin wrote that the introduction of covered arcades, gas-lights, boulevards and squares, made Paris an inviting, safe place in which to wander at any time of day or night; it was an urban landscape that gave rise to the flâneur, a character such as Baudelaire who made it his occupation simply to walk and observe the city around him.[5]

The influence of Baudelaire – and the figure of the flâneur – continues to be felt. The narrator of Teju Cole's 2011 novel *Open City* is a typical urban wanderer in this tradition. The action has been transferred to twenty-first century New York, but the title of the novel gives a clue to reading the setting in much the same way as Baudelaire read nineteenth-century Paris: an open landscape which invites exploration. A feminist reading of Baudelaire's flâneur inspired one of 2016's most lauded and exciting books on the city – *Flaneuse.* Author Laura Elkin reclaims the flâneur for women while describing 'the creative potential of the city, and the liberating possibilities of a good walk.'[6]

The writer in many of today's megacities, however, often faces a different urban landscape to that of Hausmann's Paris, or even the streets of contemporary Paris and New York described by Elkin and Cole. In many of the newer megacities, 'a good walk' is virtually impossible. São Paulo, for example, has an increasing number of neighbourhoods without any pavements at all. The infamous shopping mall Daslu could only be entered by car or by helicopter, a form of transport so popular in the city that Uber now have their very own helicopter fleet.[7] Where it is possible to walk, security concerns and the increasing privatisation of public space makes the idea of a stroll in the contemporary megacity far less appealing, less 'creative' and certainly less 'open.' Teresa P. R. Caldeira notes:

'How could the experience of walking on the streets not be transformed if one's environment consists of high fences, armed guards, closed streets and video cameras instead of gardens and yards, neighbours talking, and the possibility of glancing some family scene through the windows? The idea of going for a walk, of naturally passing among strangers... are all compromised in a city of walls.'[8]

In the light of the megacity, the modern landscape of Baudelaire's poems can begin to appear somewhat dated. The slums which were destroyed by Hausmann, scattering the disadvantaged amongst wealthier citizens, are back with a vengeance. Almost one billion people, around thirty-two percent of the world's population, now live in urban poverty.[9] In 'Eyes of the Poor', Baudelaire is enjoying a drink with his lover in a new boulevard café when he is confronted by a staring, ragged family. Whilst the narrator is drawn to the plight of these desperate souls, embarrassed by his own fortune, his companion is irritated and wants the waiter to turn the family away. The narrator exclaims that he hates his lover that day. Tensions between rich and poor, strong feelings of guilt, fear and envy, exist in the contemporary megacity, but if Baudelaire were having the same drink today, in Mexico City perhaps, it is unlikely this encounter would have taken place. These days, the megacity poor mostly occupy periphery neighbourhoods, far from the glitzy bars, which are protected by security and often housed in air-conditioned malls instead of on the street. The smooth and speedy rides through central neighbourhoods depicted in 'Loss of a Halo' are also a thing of the past. Population explosions, increasing car ownership and failing infrastructure mean that a ride through the centre of almost all megacities means hours stuck in gridlocked traffic. In São Paulo, traffic jams are an everyday conversation topic and there are those who believe in the 'imminent total collapse' of the city because of the intensity of the traffic problem.[10]

These significant changes to urban life and landscape are happening across the world. In 1975 there were only three megacities; the UN predicts that by 2030 there will be forty-three. By 2050, two out of three people will live in a city setting.[11] It seems ironic that, just as an understanding of cities is becoming ever more essential to our sense of what it means to be modern, one of the most timeless and enjoyable ways of knowing our cities – by strolling their streets and taking the time to stop and look, practiced not only by Baudelaire, but by many of the great city writers – Walter Benjamin, TS Eliot, Jane Jacobs to name just a few – is becoming impossible. This does not mean, however, that flânerie is dead. The writers gathered here all prove, in different ways, that the essence of flânerie – of observing the city and digesting its fruits – is very much alive and being practiced with creativity and verve in megacities around the world.

When we talk of the millions that are now living in these megacities, when we look out upon vast cityscapes, when we read criticism of the 'demographics, economics, sociopolitics, infrastructure, morphology, environment and resources'[12] related to megacities, it can be hard to imagine the individual amongst this teeming mass. This is perhaps what the literature of megacities can give us back; a sense of the individual, their stories and their settings.

One example of this is the significant change in the mental outlook of a typical megacity resident that this anthology reveals. Georg Simmel famously defined the mindset of the twentieth century metropolitan as blasé, sophisticated, intellectual, overcome by an ennui created by the endless pleasures of the modern city.[13] None of the characters that people the pages of this anthology are blasé about their surroundings and none of them are bored. Many of them display quite opposite mental states, being disoriented, even traumatised by the speed with which the cities they call home are changing. The shop-keeper narrator of 'Somersaults' has his world turned upside down when the city of Manila announces plans to put a high-speed railway in the path of his grocery store. He fights to defend his historic neighbourhood, but is left, literally, in the gutter by the juggernaut that is megacity development. In 'Glorious City of Forgetting', set in a fantasy Chinese megacity, factory worker Li Xifan revels in this rampant progress, delighting in the hypersonic railway that replaces the old station: 'the most ancient in China, a traditional wooden relic, without any particular charm.' However, the subconscious damage done in the construction of a new city without any respect for the past begins to haunt Xifan, who finds, to her horror, that in this particular megacity it is not only buildings that can be so easily erased, but people too.

The confusion that characters in this anthology often feel is not only caused by the speed, but also the disorderly manner in which megacities have been constructed. Whereas Baudelaire's Paris was the work of a single visionary, Chinese megacities have sprung up with little thought either for overall structure or public values. Shenzen, the youngest and fastest growing megacity in the world, inspired the term 'generic city', coined by Rem Koolhaas to describe a city without history that develops randomly, without planning, regulation or public vision. The effect of all this is shown clearly in the story, 'Metro Line Five', which follows the unhappy Shenzen housewife Shi Yu through a turmoil of unmarked roads, towering cranes, and construction sites as she unsuccessfully tries to navigate her way through the confused cityscape and develop a sense of her own place within it.

Megacity infrastructure is not only disorderly but often ineffectual too, harming not only the mental well-being of residents but also their physical health. In 'The Water was Drained', a non-fiction piece from Mexico City – a place which spends more on its water supply than any other city in the world – the twenty-four million inhabitants are routinely subjected to often grave gastrointestinal illnesses due to the practice of dumping waste water directly onto the surrounding farms supplying the city's produce. Despite this, Mexico City continues to function; its citizens have developed immunity from particular *helicobacter pylori* bacterium, unique in the world, that thrive in their water supply and routinely floor visitors. This highlights another trait of the modern megacity resident: their toughness, their adaptability. In 'Lamentations 5.23', Manila's taxi drivers have developed a new way of working in response to the gridlock which is ubiquitous to megacities across the world: it is the drivers, not the customers, who decide which direction they are heading – bad luck if it doesn't suit your day. A particular grim megacity humour pervades this hot, stinky, cloudy story, where housewives rent corpses to make extra money from a wake and radio presenters exclaim that the Armageddon is coming 'right after the commercial break, but everyone will get a free beverage.'

Traumatised but tough, confused but resilient; these are among the ironies of the megacity mentality. Perhaps the most paradoxical reality to find its way into these pages is the way in which, despite living in such densely populated cities, megacity residents can become so easily isolated. In 'The Bridge', it is the very proximity of one Cairo woman's neighbours that forces her to close herself off from the world. When a new flyover blocks the formerly expansive view from her balcony, she starts seeing faces from stalled cars gaping at her whilst she is watching television. Soon the barrage of faces suffocates her to such an extent that she must hide herself away completely inside her flat. 'The Broken Doll' describes a megacity isolation so complete that when Moscovian social psychologist Iva Nova locks herself out of her apartment she can find absolutely no one to help her. She ends up sheltering in the local railway station before finally being led into a gruelling, shocking life of indentured labour.

How has the city space, formerly understood by critics such as Benjamin and Simmel to be synonymous with individuality and liberty, become a symbol of confinement, entrapment and isolation? One reason might be found in the fact that the public parks, avenues and squares, which brought people together in the old capitals of Europe, are increasingly rare in the new megacities. Teresa P. R. Caldeira argues that the privatisation of public space in the megacity has severely damaged the liberal ideal of a free and equal society. 'Openness, indeterminacy, fluidity, and coexisting, unassimilated difference have found some of their best expressions in the public spaces of modern cities,' she says. But cities such as Los Angeles and São Paulo 'display a strikingly different type of public urban space' that makes no gestures towards openness, indeterminacy, accommodation of difference, or equality, but rather take inequality and separation as organising values.'[14]

The new difficulties in accessing the rewards of the city are well expressed by São Paulo writer Sheyla Smaniato, herself from the poor periphery of that enormous city. It took twenty-four years, she writes in the introduction to her novel extract featured in this anthology, to make the twenty-kilometre journey from the margins of São Paulo to its centre, to feel as if it was hers, not only in geographical terms, but in terms of her identity as a female citizen and a writer: 'It wasn't just a case of taking three buses. Before that, I had to understand who I was. I had to understand that being a woman and from the periphery meant taking three buses in order to speak, five buses in order to be heard, seven buses in order to be respected. There is no train for this journey. You have to set out on foot, taking it step by step.'

But whilst the poor of the megacity are striving to be part of an open society, the rich are moving away and closing their doors. Private, secured condominiums – referred to by Caldeira as 'fortified enclaves – in which residents can avoid the city's social problems whilst emulating the kind of public space that is now missing from the megacity, have become increasingly popular across the world. The essay 'Driving in Greater Noida' showcases Delhi's answer to this new kind of lifestyle. Deepti Kapoor flits deftly about one residential utopia, amongst tennis players, children riding safely on their bikes and pedigree dog walkers, all symbolic of a 'well-earned, tranquil and personally gratifying existence.' She does not find the compound inspiring, however, exhausted 'by the unreality of it... the long stretches of anything approaching society... by the desiccated, stark, unforgiving luxury.'

Sterile fakes of true city life they may be, but it is nevertheless easy, when faced with the apocalyptic vision of poverty and crime that surrounds them, to see why the megacity rich flock to these closed condominiums. Since 1970 the growth of slums in the Southern hemisphere has completely outpaced any other kind of urbanisation. Much of the twenty-first century urban world, Mike Davis says, 'squats in squalor, surrounded by pollution, excrement, and decay.'[15] Dog-nappings, car-jackings and muggings are all dangers circling the Delhi compound of which Kapoor writes. The walls, she says, 'increasingly feel like those built around an island, buffeted by a treacherous sea.'

Life is much harder, of course, for those on the outside, for the men, women and children who must navigate the seas of megacity poverty, living in circumstances which are often extremely difficult and very violent. In an extract from the novel *Margins of Error*, translated here into English for the first time, the typical feelings of a middle-class megacity dweller – confusion, disorientation, isolation – take a back seat to the more pressing problem of staying alive. Set in a fictional São Paulo, it is based on the experiences of its author, Ferréz, who grew up in one of the poorest and most dangerous parts of the city's South Zone, where the neighbourhood of Jardim Ângela was at one point declared by the UN to be the homicide capital of the world.[16] Jacaré is running to save his life after an altercation in a bar. He escapes those hunting him down but ends up dead anyway. Perhaps most shocking is not the actual murder but the blasé attitude with which Jacaré's friends greet news of his murder. It's an approach to death which is a necessary rite of passage in violent megacity peripheries, as the hero of *Margins of Error*, Rael, learns in the very first chapter of the novel: 'His losses were constant and seemingly interminable: when his first friend died it was an enormous shock, but the deaths of the other two affected him less; Rael was finally growing up.'[17]

Squalor, violence and murder on one hand, secured ivory towers on the other. It could certainly seem, in the light of many of the extracts in this anthology, that megacities and the people who live within them are in crisis. Many analysts would agree with this: Brazilian critics have argued that megacities such as São Paulo have returned to the dark ages and now operate under a medieval feudal system.[18] However, at least one of Simmel's observations remains true over one hundred years later, that the metropolitan type of man 'exists in a thousand individual variants.' In other words, one man's megacity hell could very well be another man's heaven.

Dangerous and violent they may be, but for countryside immigrants, megacities represent opportunity and advancement. Edward Glaesar argues that poorer people are not 'mad or mistaken' to migrate to megacities, rather they 'flock to urban areas because cities offer advantages they couldn't find in their previous homes.' Slums are densely packed, Glaesar points out, because 'life in a favela beats stultifying rural poverty.'[19] The hero of the Delhi novella *Mangosil*, Chandrakant Thorat, lives in a neighbourhood built on a molten mix of plastic and petrol products, where 'dengue fever, black magic, criminality and disease' are rife. Despite these shocking conditions, moving to a Delhi slum represents survival, freedom and, at least for a time, miraculous happiness for Thorat and his wife, with the small rug in their tiny half-flat transformed into a magic carpet.

Megacities represent opportunity for the wealthy too. The oldest and most functional of the world's big cities have become playgrounds of high-end culture and Michelin-starred restaurants for a booming class of super-rich. London, for example, has become the site of the largest concentration of 'ultra-high net worth individuals' on the planet[20] with property developers concentrating on super-high-end, two million pound-plus residences. Although this confirms that megacity living has become, for those who can afford it, an essential part of an elite global lifestyle, the non-fiction essay, 'Shout Out to My Ex', reveals the inevitable flipside. 'An Attempt at Exhausting a Place in Paris', paints a kinder picture of the world's more glamorous megacities. Following in the footsteps of Georges Perec, observing the streets from a Parisian café window, Anna Pook finds a globalised city of immigrant cultures that still conforms, in its own way, to the ideals of the open city which critics such as Teresa P. R. Caldeira believe have been lost. A fellow customer at the cafe, originally from Africa, strikes up a conversation with the author. The pair discuss their roles as teachers, trust each other enough to exchange numbers, order drinks for their friends. When the man points to their respective tables, both covered in pens and paper and tells the British-born author 'we have the same culture', it feels like the truth.

The pleasure and excitement that megacities can offer is not restricted to the richest residents or the most well-functioning cities, as Ayodele Olofintuade's memoir 'Shuffering and Shmiling in Lagos' proves. A famous supporter of enormous cities, even Edward Glaesar admits that, in Lagos, the suffering can seem 'so extensive and extreme that observers can't help but see the whole city as hellish.'[21] Through Olofintuade's eyes, however, we discover a city populated by folktales and mythical beings that turn the city of her childhood into a land of fantasies.

Despite her long and often fruitful relationship with Lagos, Olofintuade never displays the ennui with which Simmel characterised the average city dweller, jaded by endless attractions. This is perhaps because the thrills of the megacity must be enjoyed on a sharper knife-edge than in the cities of the past. Olofintuade never forgets that Lagos is not only the scene of endless, dizzying fun, but can also be a death-trap, the city where her beloved brother lost his life. An extract from the Cairo novel, *Using Life*, shows just how dangerous the megacity can be, even in its pleasures. Ahmed Naji describes with licentious glee the fact that even in a religious country of strict moral laws such as Egypt, in the capital Cairo anything goes – from all night parties of drink and drugs to graphic post-breakfast sex sessions. But even writing about these pastimes comes with real peril: Naji was famously thrown into jail for inciting immoral behaviour when an extract of his novel appeared in a prestigious literary magazine, causing one man to claim that reading the steamy Cairo scenes caused his heartbeat to fluctuate and his blood pressure to drop.

Absurd, extreme, pleasure-filled, crime-ridden; sky-high meccas of opportunity and vast swathes of squalor; it is not an easy task to encapsulate or to sum-up the megacity and its people. But there is one thing that remains constant in these quickly mutating, rapidly growing urban masses and that is their newfound ubiquity. One in eight of the world's population now live in thirty-three megacities, with many more predicted to arrive and make these places their home in the coming years. In 1950, thirty percent of the world's population was urban, by 2050, sixty-eight percent of the world will live in cities.[22]

'Homely' is not a word often used in relation to cities that can, to an outside observer, appear a 'hellish mess,' but perhaps this is the motif which, surprisingly, binds this anthology of megacity writing together. Questions of home permeate all these stories and essays – whether it is the search for a home, a home that is in danger, or the satisfaction of finally being able to use the word 'home' in relation to an inhospitable megalopolis. After three attempts to escape the oldest and still the largest megacity in the world, Tokyo, the narrator of Hideo Furukawa's novel *Slow Boat*, gives up, realising that what he needs to survive is simply a place of his own, 'a stronghold right in the heart of the city. A place with the power to keep Tokyo out.'

Perhaps the best example of the power of home comes from one of the most dysfunctional megacities, Kinshasa in the DRC. Along with Dhaka, Kinshasa is the poorest megacity of them all, a city where formal state institutions have completely collapsed, where two thirds of the population are malnourished, where one in five adults has HIV, where tens of thousands of children run wild on the streets. Kinshasa is described by locals as a 'cadaver, a wreck.' The horror of local's daily lives reaches its nadir in the practice of labelling certain children as witches, many of whom are then sacrificed.[23] This chillingly common practice is not avoided in Richard Ali A Mutu's novel *Mr. Fix It: Troublesome Kinshasa*. For his narrator, Ebamba, it is part of his everyday life – but so too are parties, rhythmic Congolese music, cold beer and the beauty of the sunset setting on a city river. In common with many who make their homes in megacities – and practically all the heroes and heroines who populate these pages – Ebamba has astonishing reserves of resilience and a deep appreciation of the urban aesthetic. His love of his city, his belief in his home and its beauty is all the more incredible, and, in some ways, admirable for its ability to exist alongside such grim reality. In a world in which practically every corner has been explored, it is megacities such as Kinshasa, seen through Ebamba's eyes, which now provide us all with exciting new frontiers:

'A cool breeze is blowing, the sky is darkening. The sun is setting near the Congo River, round like a ball of fire, red as blood. The surface of the river is untroubled. The wind is getting colder and passerbys shiver. Night sets in, the sun vanishes from the horizon. In the sky, several types of birds are noisily rushing back to their nests, while the trees are slowly swinging their branches in the breeze. The wind is humming a song as if to say it is going to rain soon...

'It's Saturday, the day when Kinshasa is at its most hectic. Kinshasa full of joy, Kinshasa home to life and its troubles. Kinshasa home to beer of all kinds: Nkoy, Mo-prima, Turbo, Skol... Kinshasa, the land of bursting joy in all its forms... It's true, you may live to be one hundred years old, but if you have never seen Kinshasa, you cannot say that you have truly lived.'

Books

Benjamin, Walter, *Selected Writings: 1938-1940 Volume 4* Eds. Howard Eiland and Michael W. Jennings, (Cambridge MA and London: The Belknap Press of Harvard University Press, 2006)

Berman, Marshall *All That is Solid Melts into Air* (New York: Simon and Schuster, 1982)

Caldeira, Teresa P. R. *City of Walls: Crime, Segregation and Citizenship in São Paulo* (Berkeley and Los Angeles: University of California Press, 2000)

Cole, Teju *Open City* (London: Faber and Faber, 2011)

Davis, Mike *Planet of the Slums* (London: Verso, 2006)

Glaesar, Edward *The Triumph of the City* (London: Pan Books, 2011)

Graham, Steven *Vertical: The City from Satellites to Bunkers* (London: Verso, 2016)

Graham, Steven and Marvin, Simon *Splintering Urbanism* (New York and London: Routledge, 2001)

Simmel, Georg 'The Metropolis and Mental Life' in *Classic Essays on the Culture of Cities* ed. Richard Sennet (New Jersey: Prentice-Hall, 1969)

UN-Habitat *State of the World's Cities Report* (UN World Habitat, 2006)

Articles

Miraglia, P. 'Safe Spaces in São Paulo' in *Urban Age* (2008) https://urbanage.lsecities.net/essays/safe-spaces-in-sao-paulo-1 [Accessed 02/04/2019]

Rolnik, R. and Klintowitz, D. '(Im)mobility in the city of São Paulo' in *Estudos Avançados* Vol.25 No.71 (São Paulo: Jan./Apr. 2011) www.scielo.br/scielo.php?pid=S0103-40142011000100007&script=sci_arttext&tlng=en [Accessed 02/04/2019]

Scholes, L. 'Flâneuse by Lauren Elkin review – wandering women' in *The Guardian* (2016) www.theguardian.com/books/2016/jul/25/flaneuse-women-walk-city-paris-new-york-tokyo-venice-london-review-lauren-elkin [Accessed 02/04/2019]

Schmidt, B. 'Uber Lets You Hail a Helicopter in Brazil for $63' in *Bloomberg* (2016) www.bloomberg.com/news/articles/2016-06-21/uber-lets-you-hail-a-helicopter-in-brazil-for-63 [Accessed 02/04/2019]

United Nations '68% of the world population projected to live in urban areas by 2050, says UN' in *UN Department of Economic and Social Affairs – News* (2018a) www.un.org/development/desa/en/news/popue lation/2018-revision-of-world-urbanization-prospects.html [Accessed 02/04/2019]

United Nations '2018 Revision of World Urbanization Prospects' in *UN Department of Economic and Social Affairs – News* (2018b) www.un.org/ development/desa/publications/2018-revision-of-world-urbanization-prospects.html [Accessed 02/04/2019]

NOTES

1. Graham, S. and Marvin, S. *Splintering Urbanism* (New York and London: Routledge, 2001) p.302
2. Davis, M. *Planet of the Slums* (London, Verso: 2006) p.2
3. Berman, M. *All That is Solid Melts into Air* (New York: Simon and Schuster, 1982) p.132
4. *Ibid.* p.148
5. Benjamin, W. *Selected Writings: Volume 4 1938–1940* ed. Howard E. and Michael W. Jennings (Cambridge (MA) and London: The Belknap Press of Harvard University Press, 2006)
6. Scholes, L. 'Flâneuse by Lauren Elkin review – wandering women' in *The Guardian* (2016) www.theguardian.com/books/2016/jul/25/ flaneuse-women-walk-city-paris-new-york-tokyo-venice-london-review-lauren-elkin [Accessed 02/04/2019]
7. Schmidt, B. 'Uber Lets You Hail a Helicopter in Brazil for $63' in *Bloomberg* (2016) www.bloomberg.com/news/articles/2016-06-21/ uber-lets-you-hail-a-helicopter-in-brazil-for-63 [Accessed 02/04/2019]
8. Caldeira, T. P. R. *City of Walls: Crime, Segregation and Citizenship in São Paulo* (Berkeley and Los Angeles: University of California Press, 2000) p.298
9. *State of the World's Cities Report* (UN World Habitat, 2006)

10. Rolnik, R. and Klintowitz, D. '(Im)mobility in the city of São Paulo' in *Estudos Avançados* Vol.25 No.71 (São Paulo: Jan./Apr. 2011) www. scielo.br/scielo.php?pid=S0103-40142011000100007&script=sci_arttext&tlng=en [Accessed 02/04/2019]

11. United Nations '68% of the world population projected to live in urban areas by 2050, says UN' in *UN Department of Economic and Social Affairs – News* (2018a) www.un.org/development/desa/en/news/population/2018-revision-of-world-urbanization-prospects. html [Accessed 02/04/2019]

12. Kunlé Adeyemi lists these seven factors as tools with which describe urban dynamics in the introduction, below.

13. Simmel, G. 'The Metropolis and Mental Life' in *Classic Essays on the Culture of Cities* ed. Richard Sennet (New Jersey: Prentice-Hall, 1969) p.55

14. Caldeira, T. P. R. *City of Walls: Crime, Segregation and Citizenship in São Paulo* (Berkeley and Los Angeles: University of California Press, 2000) p.304

15. Davis, M. *Planet of the Slums* (London, Verso: 2006) p.19

16. Miraglia, P. 'Safe Spaces in São Paulo' in *Urban Age* (2008) https://urbanage.lsecities.net/essays/safe-spaces-in-sao-paulo-1 [Accessed 02/04/2019]

17. Ferrez *Capao Pecado* 2nd Ed. Trans. Meadowcroft, V. (São Paulo: Planeta, 2016)

18. Davis, M. *Planet of the Slums* (London, Verso: 2006) p.119

19. Glaesar, E. *The Triumph of the City* (London: Pan Books, 2011) p.71

20. Graham, S. *Vertical: The City from Satellites to Bunkers* (London: Verso 2016) p.200

21. Glaesar, E. *The Triumph of the City* (London: Pan Books, 2011) p.70

22. United Nations '2018 Revision of World Urbanization Prospects' in *UN Department of Economic and Social Affairs – News* (2018b) www.un.org/development/desa/publications/2018-revision-of-world-urbanization-prospects.html [Accessed 02/04/2019]

23. Davis, M. *Planet of the Slums* (London, Verso: 2006) p.193

MEGACITY

1

WHAT IS A MEGACITY? A CONVERSATION BETWEEN TWO LAGOS ARCHITECTS

WITH KUNLÉ ADEYEMI AND DELE ADEYEMO

The fastest growing megacity in the world, Lagos, is also one of the most notorious, often described as an urban jungle of slums and towers, corrupt police and charming con-men, thick with traffic and the wildest of bus drivers. A city on the brink, where 'if you sit down you will die of hunger' it has also been celebrated as an 'announcement of the future,'[1] a mecca for writers, urbanists and artists striving to understand the new urban landscape of the megacity.

One of the most famous students of Lagos is architect and urban theorist Rem Koolhaas. His study of the future of cities with local architect Kunlé Adeyemi and the Harvard Graduate School of Design led him to write extensively on the city over several years. Koolhaas has praised Lagos because, like many megacities in the Global South, the city defies Western ideals of what a city should be and how it should function. Lagos, Koolhaas has said, is the ultimate dysfunctional city made beautiful, almost utopian, by the independence and agency of its residents.

Since working with Koolhaas on the future cities project, Kunlé Adeyemi has become an acclaimed urbanist
and researcher in his own right. He runs the architecture,
design and urbanism practice, NLÉ, which means 'at home'
in Yoruba, focusing on the rapidly developing cities of the
Global South as well as other regions.

One of his most famous projects is the floating school
in Makoko, designed for the residents of Lagos's enormous water-borne slum, where thousands of people live
in houseboat dwellings next to the Third Mainland Bridge.
The school has won design awards throughout the world
and turned the perception of the ever-precarious Makoko,
under constant threat from government slum-clearance
programmes, into a model megacity neighbourhood, ear-
marked for regeneration and praised for its innovative
approach to the environment.

Thinking creatively about megacities is what Kunlé does
extremely well. To introduce readers of this anthology into
the world of the megacity, he talked to fellow architect,
urbanist and Lagos-phile, Dele Adeyemo about urban narrative, architectural story-telling and our rapidly urbanising
global landscape.

DELE: I guess the conversation we're about to have is between two architects who know Lagos well and can operate in that city, but also are engaged in questions around megacities. This anthology is one of fictions and non-fictions from megacities. It's from megacity writers as opposed to architects. So, we have the responsibility of bringing the architectural perspective to this anthology – our conversation will be the introduction for many readers to the whole concept of the megacity.

The subject of the megacity is trending again but as you know ... it was around about the beginning of the new millennium that studies – such as the one made by Rem Koolhaas and yourself on Lagos – that made megacities into a really big conversation amongst architects and urbanists. I think now, because we see the effects of climate change unfolding, population explosion, as well as global migration and rising inequality, people see, all over, that the issue of the megacity is really critical. As a concept now discussed in popular culture as well as by architects, it would be good to start off with what you think constitutes a megacity.

KUNLÉ: The classical definition of a megacity is a city or an urban conurbation with a population of over ten million people. Cities with populations of over ten million people have different living conditions – in terms of infrastructure, demographics and the environment – but technically a megacity really is just a metropolitan area of over ten million people.

DELE: It seems relevant here for you to explain your concept of the Seven Desimer Factors that you use to define the megacity...

KUNLÉ: The way we analyse urban dynamics is that we look at them through seven lenses or seven factors of development, using the acronym DESIMER: demographics, economics, socio-politics, infrastructure, morphology, environment and resources. Of course, the classical definition of megacities focuses on demographics as the prime factor and doesn't really refer to the other complexities, which might make some cities more interesting or more complex than others.

DELE: In that light, is there a difference for you between the megacities of the South, such as Lagos, and the traditional megacities of the North – such as London and New York?

KUNLÉ: Well yes, in some senses. From a morphological point of view, one could argue that Lagos and London are similar cities as they are settled along water; however, the population of Lagos, with an estimate of over twenty million people, is actually more than twice that of London. Ironically, the physical infrastructure supporting the city of London is – staggeringly – much larger than that of Lagos.

DELE: Lagos is a city with its own particular rhythms, its own rules. In Lagos there are universes within universes. You turn one corner or look through a window, and you have a view onto a whole other world of activity. The city has often been associated with the cliché of sprawling urban slums, but I want you to expand on what you feel are the characteristics of Lagos – how is it a unique megacity and what are the ways you work within that context?

KUNLÉ: What makes Lagos unique as a megacity is, of course, the fact that it is the largest city on the continent, Africa, and Africa is the second most rapidly urbanising continent in the world. So, in a way, Lagos is the epicentre of that urbanisation. It's also one of the largest economies on the continent, in its own right, as opposed to Nigeria as a whole. That in itself makes it very relevant when you are talking about megacities. But I'd say more importantly that being on the ground – and having really lived through a period when the city had a much more rapid population growth – has been fascinating. There were periods when the infrastructure was clearly unable to match the population growth. Seeing how people adapt to those conditions both socially and politically is really fascinating – to see how the city survives through very, very difficult developmental times.

We are now maybe at a point where the city has most of its head above water and we are beginning to see some of the more interesting or more beneficial aspects of that survival process, where art and culture and social dynamics are beginning to improve. It's becoming a much more liveable city, not without some challenges but definitely much better than it was ten years ago. For me, that is what makes Lagos unique – its resilience, its capacity to adapt. Its people, specifically, are just completely driven. They are committed to a level of, let's say, ambition that drives them to keep surviving. They have got the city to a point where – the country as a whole is another thing – but Lagos specifically is in a much better condition than it was. In a way, Lagos feels like a much larger narrative than Nigeria in some aspects.

DELE: I think that's something that's come up a lot in urbanisation and global architecture conversations: the separation between the global megacity, and the rest of the country. We are past the point now where most of the world's population live in cities and by the middle of the century that will be the condition of at least three quarters of the world's population. So, in some ways Lagos has potentially more to do with New York or London or Shanghai, because these cities are dealing with, as you were saying, the same issues of globalisation, continuous urbanisation and rapid population growth. Do you think that global megacities like Lagos are becoming more important than the countries they are based in?

KUNLÉ: Yes, in some ways. We've seen that socio-politically in London and the UK with Brexit. And we know that economically Lagos is the commercial capital of Nigeria. As cities and rural areas or countrysides continue to evolve, there are increasing questions about, and interests in, geo-political redefinitions.

DELE: One of the things that I wanted to ask you is how your work inserts itself into the narrative of the megacity. A project like Makoko, the floating school, is a beautiful concept well-realised: you used the skills and tools that architecture has to expand the question of slum-housing in Lagos into a bigger conversation about designing for climate change. With the purpose of this anthology in mind, I thought it would be interesting for you to explain to readers how you use architectural projects such as Makoko to tell stories about Lagos as it responds to the specific challenges of a megacity.

KUNLÉ: The Makoko project basically started from the physical challenge of housing. I went into the floating Makoko community looking to tackle this challenge whilst researching affordable housing. We realised the problem was beyond one of simply providing a solution for building. There are also the environmental conditions of tackling climate change, in this particular case flooding: the project happened at a time when the city started to flood more frequently.

We realised that the people who live in Makoko were already dealing with those conditions and so we asked ourselves: how do we learn from them, whilst improving those conditions? We had to understand their limitations – in terms of resources, materials, building techniques – maybe improving and taking them one step further but not necessarily erasing all of them completely. How do you develop and take what is absolutely considered poor quality to an international standard without losing some of the essential values that allow it to be propagated by everyday people? That's essentially what we were looking at in that circumstance. Most importantly, we were learning from the environment.

DELE: And also, as someone who knows a little about the politics of Nigeria and everyday life in Lagos, navigating that with the local community and local government and other interests must be a challenge in itself?

KUNLÉ: Yes, it is. One of the things that made the project so relevant is that it sits right in the middle of issues of urbanisation. Part of the drive for the city when Makoko was being demolished was the pressure of urbanisation.

The city wanting to grow and take up slum-land that they thought was valuable as prime real estate. The question was, how do we make best use of the land or water? Do we follow our normal ways of slum clearance and land reclamation and building towers? Is that the solution for addressing the growth of a city like Lagos?

What we tried to unpack was the fact that the narrative is a lot more complex because there are other factors that in today's world we have to take into consideration – it's not just economic drive. Environmental issues are very important, social issues, how people live, how people want to live; in particular the type of people that live in a way that is mostly not seen to be plausible, which is on water as opposed to land. I think in a way this is really just a question about how we see the cities of the future. We need to start thinking about them differently. We need to start thinking about how to live differently, how to build differently.

DELE: I think that is something that really comes across in the Makoko project. A new culture for living on water is what you've said previously. The architectural visualisations that you've created are very compelling and present an alternative way of being, an alternative image of what a home could be in a megacity.

KUNLÉ: I think the most compelling and visual experience is going to a place like Makoko itself. What we show and what we present is always fictional – at the same time it is also slightly idealistic. But it also provokes what could be. We are basically just trying to provoke questions about how to think differently.

The fundamental premise is that a large proportion of our cities that are growing rapidly – and that are so-called megacities – are by water, with a large number of them being affected by climate change. The question is simple: how do we learn to live with that condition as opposed to fighting it?

DELE: This brings us to the question about the role of the architect evolving from someone who's primary focus is on building buildings to becoming an agent of change. In a way, a big part of being an agent of change is storytelling. Architects surely need to become better storytellers. One fine example can be seen in the works by the architecturally trained artist Olalekan Jeyifous and his fantastical stories about the future of Lagos told through incredible futuristic visualisations; in a similar way you are doing that yourself through your research and your built projects. Do you think it is important that we – the architects – claim the narrative for the megacity?

KUNLÉ: We need to claim our narrative of the megacity and our narrative of the role architecture has to play in the issues of urbanisation, ruralisation and the issues of – basically – human movement. It comes down to how humanity shifts and cultivates its environment. The economists will have their narrative, the sociologists will have their narrative, the environmentalists will have their narrative, what is our narrative, our role?

I think an architect is trained in a way to orchestrate a number of complex disciplines, to provide solutions that are both manifested in form and space – and that, I'd say, is the strength that we have. So, for me, the narrative is also about the extent to which we can understand the complexity of the megacity and get ourselves involved, without necessarily being focused on materialisation and form production. We have to be more involved, be more engaged, in issues a little bit beyond our traditional construct of what design is. That's the way I see it. It just means you need to acquire knowledge and collaborate a lot more and really understand what drives issues of design around the world. It's not just aesthetics – it's much more compelling and urgent and need-based.

DELE: So, do you feel that the architectural propositions and stories you tell about a potential project change the narrative within the city?

KUNLÉ: I honestly don't know. This is all work in progress. My team and I just try and put our best foot forward. And we have learnt a few lessons along the way. There are two important pillars that sort of shape the work that we do. The first pillar is humanity – fundamentally, people. What people are, their backgrounds, their interests, their social and cultural issues and needs. The other pillar is the environment. These two are almost completely equal. You have to understand that the environment itself has a completely different dynamic that can overpower humanity. The question is how we make these co-exist: how do we ensure that ourselves as human beings – and the products and the artefacts and the things that we produce – facilitate the co-existence of these two pillars? When we produce architecture and design, we try to benchmark them against these two things: how do they sit properly with people and how do they sit properly with the environment? It's quite simple so far.

DELE: I want to bring us back to Lagos. You mentioned that Lagos is becoming a very creative place and you know there is this real, emergent creative culture – it's been going on for at least ten or fifteen years and there's a real confidence now. So, my question is how does working in the context of Lagos help you to create this kind of narrative and architectural language which is attractive and desirable both in the city and beyond?

KUNLE: One of the most powerful effects that anyone who experiences Lagos will tell you about is the fact that there is a lot of resistance and a lot of friction in everything. There is a challenge in achieving anything. It's almost a sort of high-risk, high-return environment. High-risk, in the sense that you need to overcome everything. Just getting from one place to another, there is traffic; you want to make a call, there is no network; you try to charge your phone, there is no power; you want to turn on the power generator, there is no gas. But, somehow, you simply have to overcome these challenges. So, it's an environment where resistance and friction constantly make you think in multiple ways, to develop ways of being extremely versatile and open, extremely innovative and extremely competitive – with everyone trying to get ahead of the next person. Working in an environment like Lagos, I would say, definitely makes one more agile.

Architecture should hopefully become more agile, especially if it is rooted in real values. For me, Lagos is a great place to cultivate architecture and some form of development if you can reduce the level of corruption. But that is a real challenge. How often can you keep it really authentic and really rooted in values? We've done a lot of projects and we've had different levels of success and some levels of failure. You learn from your failures and you get better and better at it. I find it a great place to work *because* it is challenging, but it is also very frustrating. Sometimes it is the worst – the last place I want to be working! The dichotomy is huge; there is a huge polarity between what is possible and what you actually achieve.

1. Packer, G. 'The Megacity' in *The New Yorker* (2006) www.newyorker.com/magazine/2006/11/13/the-megacity [Accessed 02/04/19]

2—MANILA

LAMENTATIONS 5:23

BY JESSICA ZAFRA

The city of Manila yawns, coughs, and awakens to the crowing of roosters, the sputtering of tricycles, and the screams of 'WATER!' as naked citizens covered in soap turn on their showers and get... nothing. The artery-clogging smells of pork sausages and leftover rice fried in grease and garlic waft from open windows and mingle with the grey exhalations of cars and factories. The sun comes out, but a big dark cloud in the shape of a suckling pig hangs in the sky — it may rain or it may shine, probably at the same time.

Announcers bellow from AM radios, their voices full of cheerful foreboding: Armageddon is coming right after the commercial break, but everyone will get a free beverage! 'Good morning! In the news! Hostilities in Mindanao enter a new phase as Army troops and Moro rebels trade insulting text messages by cell phone!'

Housemaids and tough-looking guys in 'Espirit' and 'Hello Kitty' T-shirts line up for hot *pan de sal* at a bakery, while the last remaining stragglers at a neighbour's wake put away their cards and make their way home. What's a Filipino wake without a little friendly gambling? What's a Filipino funeral without keening relatives threatening to leap into the freshly-dug grave? This is a wake alright, but there will be no funeral: the dead man is not related to anyone on the premises. The 'widow' – the enterprising woman who rented the corpse – counts the proceeds from her business venture.

A lone teenager who should be getting ready for school is practicing free throws in the makeshift basketball court – a hoop nailed to a lamppost. When a basketball game is in progress the street is effectively closed to traffic. Meanwhile the radio announcers cry, 'Television personality Alma Aranas denies that she is romantically involved with basketball player Boyet Bola. 'We're just good friends,' declared Alma, who has a two-year-old daughter by shopping mall tycoon Charlemagne Chan.'

Maximilian Ubaldo, University of the Philippines College of Music '91, emerges from a hotel and flags down a taxi. He vaguely registers the name on the side of the taxi: Lamentations 5:23. He tosses his guitar case and backpack onto the back seat and sits in front. 'Cubao,' he tells the cabbie. A plastic statuette of the Santo Niño, the Infant Jesus of Prague, is glued onto the dashboard. It is flanked by miniature liquor bottles.

The cabbie scratches his head and makes clucking noises. 'Boss, I'm going toward Baclaran,' he says, for in Manila you do not tell the driver where to go – he informs you of his desired route, and if you happen to be travelling in the same direction, he might do you the honour of letting you ride his vehicle.

'I'll add fifty bucks to whatever's on the metre,' Max says. He's not in the mood to assert his rights. His reserves of patience have been depleted by the tireless silver jubilarians of Something or Other High School, with their endless requests for the greatest hits of Barry Manilow. If Max had to play 'Mandy' one more time, he would beat himself to death with his own bass.

'Cubao it is,' says Quintin Maalat, forty-six.

Max leans back and closes his eyes. For the thousandth time he resolves to decline gigs at class reunions. He resolves to finish writing a song. He resolves to form a jazz band. He falls asleep with his mouth open, drooling onto the cracked upholstery.

Quintin presses the rewind button on his cassette player. He made this tape for his wife Mameng, a domestic helper in Hong Kong. The tape whirs, then Quintin's voice blasts forth, tremulous and off-key: 'Ohhhh my luuuuuv, my daaaarling, I hunger for yoooour touch...'

Max's skull cracks against the window, and as Quintin lifts his voice in a duet with himself, Max is fully awake.

In the long line that snakes in front of the United States Embassy, Rowena Dipasupil, twenty-six, nervously re-reads her answers on the visa application. Purpose of visit, there's a tough one. To seek better career opportunities? To be in a place where, if you worked hard, it wouldn't matter that you had no influential relatives? To get the hell out of this city where each day felt like a kind of punishment for sins she didn't know she'd committed? Maybe to meet a guy who would regard her as an equal, and not the inadequate replacement for his mother? Good thing only a short blank space was allotted for the answer. There wasn't enough room for melodrama. 'Vacation' would have to do.

Someone taps her on the shoulder. 'Is this your first time to apply for a visa?' says a middle-aged woman with blonde streaks in her hair. She doesn't wait for an answer. 'This is my third application. I want to visit my daughter. She lives in Wisconsin. Her husband is a retired army man. She's doing very well.'

'That's nice,' says Rowena, who does not possess the Filipino trait of congeniality, or even the ability to feign interest in the lives of total strangers.

'Oh yes,' the woman continues breathlessly. 'I hope I get a visa at last. I brought all sorts of documents. Why are you going to the States? Are you marrying an American?'

'No,' says Rowena.

'I'm sure you'll find a husband easily,' says the woman. 'You're very... uh... you have a good personality.'

Rowena flinches, recalling the last time she'd heard that description. She was auditioning to be a TV news reporter. Her incisive reportage was no match for the California accent and mestiza looks of the girl who got hired. What did it matter if Miss Fil-America's IQ was lower than her bra size? How naïve of Rowena to think that the news was about, well, the news.

Inside Baclaran church, the priest delivers a fire-and-brimstone sermon. 'Adulterers should be denied Holy Communion!' he thunders, while the faithful bow their heads in rapt contemplation. It is not the sermon they're contemplating, but the words appearing on the tiny screens of their cellular phones. 'C U L8R AT STRBKS K?' reads one message. There are dirty jokes, jokes about the President, invitations to street parties and 'underground' raves sponsored by multinational clothing manufacturers, greetings, gossip and, occasionally, useful information.

Before a Station of the Cross ('Jesus falls for the second time'), a young woman kneels and asks God to send her more customers, preferably Japanese. It is a known fact that prostitutes are among the most fervent churchgoers. This makes perfect sense, for who needs forgiveness on a regular basis? When politicians go to church there are cameras to record their piety.

Veronica Fulgoso, thirty-one, actually listens to the sermon and ponders its practical applications. How is the priest supposed to identify every churchgoer who cheats on his spouse? Will scarlet letters be tattooed on their foreheads? Veronica's mother Consuelo, seventy, has been to church nearly every day of her life, except for sick days and the worst parts of World War II. Veronica considers herself a DIY Catholic – cut out the middleman, talk to God direct – although she once had a religious phase. It was back in the third grade, when she had seen a documentary on the Blessed Virgin Mary's apparitions at Garabandal. She had believed that if she did not go to church daily, the world would end. When she got the measles and the Apocalypse didn't happen, she was seriously disappointed.

'Give me your arm,' says Consuelo, who has grown more fragile by the day since Veronica announced her intention of taking her master's at Harvard. 'However am I going to survive without you? I'm too old to be alone.'

'You won't be alone,' Veronica points out. 'You have a cook, a gardener, a driver and a nurse. Your son lives next door to you.'

'But he has his own family,' Consuelo says. 'It's not the same. And I don't like the thought of you living alone. God knows what sort of men you'll meet. How do you know they can be trusted?'

'Mom, I'm thirty-one years old,' Veronica says. 'I'm not an idiot'

'Don't be impertinent,' says Consuelo. 'I know what men are like. They're after only one thing, and when they get it, they leave.'

'Really?' Veronica says. 'And what would that be?'

'Gruesome Sacrifice!' scream the tabloids in red letters three inches high. A freelance journalist has appealed to the terrorist group, Abu Sayyaf, to release their twenty-one foreign hostages. The woman lopped off the top of her ring finger and sent it to the terrorists, along with a note written in her own blood. Beside the headline is a photograph of the amputated digit, preserved in a jar of rubbing alcohol.

Dressed in a white shirt and white trousers, Arcadio Pamintuan, forty-two, boards a bus and stands next to the driver, blocking the TV screen showing a pirated copy of the movie *Gladiator*. Boos and hisses from the passengers.

'Brothers and sisters,' Arcadio begins, 'I've come to share good news.'

'Shut up!' someone yells. 'We're watching the movie.'

Arcadio is undaunted. He has been booed, spat on, insulted, threatened with a gun, and twice shoved out of moving buses. 'I understand your fascination with movies, for I was once an actor. You may remember me as Arnel Azcarraga.' Two or three passengers recognise the name.

'Yes, I was a movie star. A bomba star. I appeared in smutty movies. I took off my clothes and fornicated for money.'

As Arcadio launches into the tale of his iniquity and eventual enlightenment, Hector Ronquillo, nineteen, tries not to look at the couple across the aisle. Tourists, from the looks of them: the ratty T-shirts, dirty shorts, sandals, greasy ponytails, the huge backpacks shoved into the luggage rack, the gamy aroma. They are kissing so avidly that, from where Hector sits, the man appears to be devouring the woman. 'Don't look,' Hector tells himself. His fingernails dig into his palms.

Arcadio is getting warmed up. 'When they told me to strip, I said, "Why not? I come from a poor family. We needed the money."'

Hector is in trouble. He didn't return to The Residence last night, and for that he will be punished. When his adviser finds out that he spent the night with a girl he met in an online chat room, he may even get expelled. For a moment he considers making up some story about an accident. That's it, an accident. Wait, he doesn't have any injuries. Maybe he could throw himself off the bus...

'Later I needed the money. For drugs,' Arcadio says. He's really getting into his speech – there's a slight quiver in his voice, and his volume is just right. The audience is turning away from the computer-generated Roman Colosseum on the screen and watching him. It's like being a movie star all over again, except that he gets to keep his clothes on. This time he gets to be on the side of righteousness. 'To overcome my shame at being a whore, I took drugs.'

Or a family emergency, Hector thinks. That would be more believable. But why didn't he call The Residence to inform them of his whereabouts? Well, he couldn't get to the phone because his father's condition was serious...

'I sank deeper and deeper into the pit,' Arcadio says. 'And when I thought I had hit the bottom, I was arrested and thrown in jail.'

Hector shakes his head. In the corner of his eye, he sees the man swallowing the woman's face. He can't lie. He's done enough of that already. He knew that the chat room was an occasion for sin, and still he flirted with Marimar. A complete stranger. When she asked for a meeting, he said yes. And when she suggested that they check into a motel...

'I thought my movie friends would help me, but they left me to rot in prison,' Arcadio cries. 'Then in the depths of my despair, I found Him. He forgave my sins and washed me clean.'

Everyone staying at The Residence has to swear to remain chaste until they marry; then they do their duty and raise as many children as the Lord sees fit to grant them. But Marimar was so alluring, even if she wore too much make-up... Two months ago, Hector had been to a play where the lead actress took off her shirt. The sight of her small, perky breasts had troubled him. He reported this to his adviser, who prescribed a course of self-mortification. Flagellation, ten strokes a day, and as the bits of glass ground into his back he was to contemplate the weakness of the flesh. Chicken wire around his right thigh, once a week, and as he bled onto his pants he was to beg the Lord for forgiveness and the strength to resist temptation. Sometimes, as he wielded the whip, he was overcome by such a powerful sensation that he would forget to count the strokes. He forgot everything – his sin, his guilt, the sharp pain as the whip bit into his flesh – as his body was wracked with ecstasy. The pleasure was so intense that he would cry out. His neighbours thought he was flogging himself too hard. Hector did not report these occasions to his adviser.

'The Lord will smite the sinners, as He did Sodom and Gomorrah,' Arcadio says.

Hector pushes the 'Stop' button and glances across the aisle, where the woman's head is disappearing into the man's gaping mouth.

Arcadio produces a large plastic envelope and waves it above his head. 'Brothers and sisters, in order to save the sinful I need your help. Your love offerings will go a long way in aiding my mission. Remember, God loves the cheerful giver.'

The bus jerks to a stop. As Hector lurches off the bus a taxi hurtles past him, missing his foot by two centimeters.

'I know a shortcut,' declares Quintin, and Lamentations 5:23 careens into a narrow street.

'Isn't this a one-way–' Max starts to ask, just as the taxi hits a deep, wide pothole. Max is thrown forward, and the last thing he remembers before losing consciousness is the scepter of the Infant Jesus coming toward his eye.

'Meanwhile!' bellows the AM radio newscaster. 'A manananggal has been seen on a rooftop in Fairview, Quezon City! The monster, a woman with huge wings and no legs, was reportedly attempting to suck the fetus from the womb of a pregnant woman named Luz Cruz! The manananggal had lowered its tongue through a hole in the roof and was preparing to attack the woman's stomach, when it was spotted by neighbours! They shouted and threw stones at it, scaring it away! The flying monster was said to be heading towards the Senate Building!'

Sherilyn Adapon, thirty-five, examines the dark circles under her eyes and wonders if the time has come for cosmetic surgery. She still has the face and figure – give or take ten pounds – that won her the second runner-up crown in the 1985 Pearl of the Orient beauty pageant, but one can always use a little help. She would've been crowned the Pearl of the Orient Princess, too – she was definitely prettier than the winner – if she hadn't gotten such a tough question in the interview portion. 'If you had to give up one of your five senses, which one would you give up, and why?' It was hard enough standing in a skimpy bathing suit in front of a thousand drooling strangers without having to remember all five senses. What did that have to do with real life anyway? Real life meant looking after her aging parents, putting her brothers and sisters through school, supporting assorted relatives, and staying beautiful so her boyfriend wouldn't complain about paying her bills.

She takes the tube of Preparation H from the medicine cabinet and smears it under her eyes. Just an emergency measure, in case Wally shows up without warning. He's in Manila on official business, and while that battle-axe he married squanders his money at the casino, he may drop by. Maybe, if he's in a good mood, she can ask him about finding a job for the nephew of the wife of the cousin of the godfather of her parents' next-door neighbours in Leyte. She looks at the mirror and giggles. The things you have to do to look good: treat your face like a hemorrhoid.

It's Baby Girl's fault she hasn't had any sleep. Baby Girl

promised she would come to the house at 8 p.m. for her fortnightly tarot card reading. Baby Girl has never been punctual – her perception of time is different from other people's, that's how she can see the future – but who knew she would arrive at 3 a.m.?

Baby Girl, age unknown, hasn't been the same since her nineteen-year-old boyfriend Jomari shot her in the head. The bullet ricocheted off her forehead and buried itself in her bedroom wall, right next to the poster of dogs playing billiards. Baby Girl declared that if she hadn't been wearing the magical amulet, which her late grandfather had dug up on Good Friday fifty years previously, the bullet would've shattered her skull. Instead, it left a noticeable dent on her forehead, which she conceals with a red bandana.

'I will prepare a charm for you,' Baby Girl announces, shuffling the cards. 'A special charm. I have to wait until the moon is at its fullest. The charm will protect you from people who have evil intentions.'

'Which people?' Sherilyn asks, alarmed. Baby Girl might not have all her marbles, but she is the best fortune-teller Sherilyn has ever had.

'A woman,' Baby Girl says. 'She is wearing dark blue. Her hair is... brown. Her gums are... black.' Her speech is slurring and slowing down – she sounds like a tape recorder running low on batteries. 'Her name... has the... letters 1, A, and... D...' She slumps face forward on the table.

'Baby Girl? Are you alright?'

'Huh?' Baby Girl says, lifting her head. She blinks several times. 'It was a black dwarf. It tried to take over my body.'

Suddenly someone is banging on the gate. 'Sherilyn Adapon!' a woman screams. 'Come out here, you slut!'

'What the...' Sherilyn goes to the window and draws the curtain.

A woman in a dark blue dress is standing outside her gate. 'I am the wife of Walter Palomaria,' the woman shrieks. 'Bring him out right this minute! Walter! You cheating bastard!' She pounds on the gate and starts wailing like a police siren.

Max wakes up with the worst headache he has ever had. He is slumped on a hard plastic chair in a strange room. His face feels wet, and when he touches his forehead, he realizes he's bleeding. He's in some kind of clinic.

'Excuse me?' he says to the nurse at the counter. 'Where am I?'

'A taxi driver brought you,' the nurse says. 'He says you were drunk, and you cut your face on the Santo Niño in his cab.'

'What?' Max cries. 'That bastard, it was his fault.' He remembers the pothole, and the Infant Jesus moving toward his eye. Good thing Baby Jesus didn't put his eye out, but he does have a giant gash above his left eyebrow, and it's bleeding like hell.

'Can I see a doctor?' he asks the nurse.

'In half an hour. He's attending to another patient!' She hands him a piece of paper. 'You need to buy this at the pharmacy before you see the doctor!'

'What's this?' Max asks.

'Medicines. Anaesthesia, thread for your stitches. The pharmacy is on the ground floor.'

Max continues to look bewildered.

'This is a public hospital,' she says briskly. 'We do not provide free supplies or medication.'

Holding his bleeding forehead, Max staggers to the pharmacy.

Edgar Saturnino, twenty-four, pulls his shiny fuchsia mini over his muscular thighs and darts from behind the lamp-post where he has been trying, unsuccessfully, to conceal himself. 'Taxi!' he cries. The taxi roars past him. Stupid, stupid, stupid, Edgar berates himself. You shouldn't have overslept. You shouldn't have spent the night with that boy. But Hector was so sweet, so naïve. He actually believed Edgar was a woman named Marimar. 'Taxi!' he calls. Why won't they stop? By the time he gets home the neighbours will be awake, and if they see him dressed like this'

A taxi pulls up at the curb. On its side is painted the improbable name, Lamentations 5:23. 'Where to?' the driver says, looking him up and down.

Edgar ignores him; he is desperate to get a cab. 'San Juan,' Edgar says.

'Three hundred pesos,' our old friend Quintin says.

'What?'

'Three hundred pesos,' Quintin shrugs. 'You won't be able to get another ride at this hour. Certainly not dressed like that.'

Something in Edgar snaps. Years of being derided and misunderstood come to the surface all at once, dredged up by a mean cabbie who wants three hundred bucks for a trip that usually costs sixty. I'm not a bad person, Edgar tells himself. I don't hurt other people intentionally. I have a decent job. So I like to put on high heels and a little dress. Does that make me a monster?

'Are you riding or not?' Quintin says.

Edgar opens the cab door and drags Quintin out onto the sidewalk. Forgetting his long, fake, red fingernails, he starts beating the crap out of the taxi driver. The city swirls around him: the honking of car horns, the shrieking of sirens, ringing of cellular phones, bellowing radio announcers, easy-listening muzak, and ten million stories all happening at once.

MR. FIX IT: TROUBLESOME KINSHASA
A Novel Excerpt

BY RICHARD ALI A MUTU
TRANSLATED BY BIENVENU SENE MONGABA
AND SARA SENE

'...Write this down too: three bags of rice, four bags of beans, one restaurant-size pot, one brand new long-sleeved shirt – still in its packaging – one red tie for her father, one tie bar, one belt, a pair of sunglasses, one pair of shoes and a set of jewelry for her mother – don't forget the earrings, please!'

'But...'

'"But, but..." What are you arguing for? Are we going to haggle over this? Is this the market?'

'No, but...'

'What do you mean, "no but"? You have a problem with this? We aren't even finished yet. The girl's uncles haven't spoken, or her mum. Her older brothers and sisters have yet to state their demands...'

Ebamba's uncle sits there, speechless. The rest of his family, and Ebamba himself, are gesturing to him to just stop talking. There's no point. They'll just have to wait for the girl's family members to finish detailing their demands. Ebamba's uncle can't help muttering to himself. *Alright, I'll stop talking. At any rate, what else could I say? I just can't stand what they are doing. Are they doing this on purpose or what? This just isn't right! Hell no!*

Just after Eyenga's dad stops talking, her mom immediately adds, 'Thank you, my husband. As far as I'm concerned, I am not going to ask for much. Apart from what my husband has mentioned, I'll just add a stove and three pairs of shoes... And, well, I'll stop at that!'

Then it is Eyenga's uncles' turn to speak.

'We thank you, our brothers, for approaching us honorably through the main door of our compound instead of stealing in through the window. On behalf of all of Eyenga's uncles here, as well as those who got stuck in Kinshasa's traffic and those who've stayed behind in the village, we are content to ask you for these few items: two baskets of kola nuts, one bag of salt, one motorboat engine, four bicycles, five buckets of palm wine, and, finally, a small envelope for Uncle Antoine from the village, because he is very ill and we urgently have to buy some medication for him. We will just end here.'

The sky has clouded over, and the first raindrops are already beginning to fall, so the guests are ushered into the house from the patio to continue the marriage negotiations. As the rain suddenly comes crashing down, the guests begin to hurry but, small as the house is, there is not enough room for everyone, and Ebamba's friends have to find shelter inside the neighbours' house, while a third group rushes into the landlord's home.

'Uncle, we are very sorry, could you maybe just move over your chair a bit? You are sitting right beneath the crack in the roof, right where the rain seeps in the most.'

'Sure, I can see some raindrops on my sleeve already.'

'We are really sorry...'

'Not at all, it's like that in most houses in Kinshasa these days...'

'What are you implying now, huh, uncle? What are you trying to say?'

Eyenga's father angrily jumps into the peaceful conversation between his wife and one of Ebamba's uncles.

'Come on, Filipo!' soothes his wife 'Why do you always have to take things that way, huh? What did he say that was insulting in the first place? It is true, these days all houses in Kinshasa have leaking roofs...'

Now Eyenga's father gets really angry. 'So, you find it normal to get those remarks?'

'What kind of remarks? Did he say anything out of the ordinary?'

'How dare he talk like that? I will not allow anyone to make those remarks about my house, ever!'

Eyenga's father is really furious now and starts yelling at his wife, while Ebamba's uncle keeps apologising.

'I didn't mean to be disrespectful, dear father-in-law. I have the same thing in my own home, you know. When it rains it leaks through the roof, and when it really pours down, the rain even sweeps in from beneath the door. I'm really sorry. Don't be offended, please.'

The rain keeps pouring down stubbornly, and it seeps through the roof in more and more places. People are running out of dry spots to sit in. The rain comes down as if someone had opened a giant faucet and the family frantically puts out more and more buckets to protect the carpet. And then, as the living room is so small and people have to shift around to stay out of the rain, the decision is made to resume negotiations once the rain stops.

7:30 in the evening. Time keeps ticking away. The rain will not relent, it's still pitch dark, mosquitoes are out in force too – and the bad smell remains strong. In the living room, the heat is unbearable. Ebamba takes off his jacket and tie, and sits down next to his uncles. They are still waiting for the rain to subside, so that the roof will stop leaking. They have been given some beer, which they sip slowly, while they patiently wait for the rain to stop. The family has rolled up the curtains to let in some air. The rain finally seems to subside, it's just dripping now. It will certainly clear up soon.

The rain stops. The power comes back on. The bad smell goes. A soft, cool breeze sweeps into the house. But it really is impossible now to sit outside; the whole yard is flooded over. The water drains slowly, but it will take buckets and sweeping to get rid of it all. The neighbours come in to help, with pails and squeegees.

The street is flooded too. It has only been two months since the Chinese finished paving it and building the sewers, but the sewers are already beginning to get blocked up by all the rubbish the locals are throwing out: plastic bottles, all sorts of bags, leaves and assorted garbage.

Some people say that the Chinese did not do their job properly. The road already has potholes here and there. Others say it's the handiwork of the neighbourhood's witches, and in particular the witches on that street, who are opposed to the President's 'five chantiers' for the country's development. Those witches claim nobody had asked for their permission before getting started with the construction, and they hadn't received their due, so the ancestors, who own the land, couldn't approve. The road is certainly going to get worn out very fast if nobody comes around to pay what is due. That's what they promised, just like in that story by Sene Mongaba, 'Bokobandela'.

The locals were more and more afraid of the curse: in just the past month, there have been six accidents, and last week a little child was even run over as he was crossing the street near the Shell gas station. He died instantly.

That sad matter had been brought before the mayor, who, as usual, laughed it off and simply promised to come and visit the good citizens of the street. The locals were still waiting for him to make good on his promise, but that's another story for some other time.

Knock knock knock! Bang bang bang!

Inside, nobody stirs.

Knock knock knock! Bang bang bang!

'Who is it?' No one replies, but the knocking on the door resumes.

Knock knock knock!

'Who's there?!'

'Open the door! And don't keep me waiting!'

'Who are you? What do you want? Stop banging on that door!'

'Hey, Ebamba, don't play with me! Hurry up, open the door!'

Ebamba rushes out of bed, his heart beating madly. He suddenly recognises the voice of Mama Mongala, his landlady. He stands up, puts on his shirt without even taking the time to check himself in the mirror, and opens the door.

At first, he only opens the door a crack to look outside. Then he peeks out to see if it really is Mama Mongala, his landlady. The sizzling hot sunlight blinds him, so he can't see right away. He squints and opens his eyes as wide as he can. He sees that it is indeed his landlady, Mama Mongala, but she has turned her back to the door and can't see him. Ebamba stares at her. He really is astonished that she has come to knock on his door so early in the morning. His head starts spinning from thinking and he tells himself that it's not the first time she has come to see him, after all, difficult and hard as she is. Fine then, he is going to find out what it is all about.

He opens the door wide, draws open the curtains and calls out to his landlady, 'Mama Mongala, good morning!'

Mama Mongala turns around to face him, looks right at him, and sucks her teeth aggressively. 'Oh, go to hell! Good morning, alright! Today is the day you get out of my house!'

Ebamba is taken aback. 'Why? What is the matter?'

'You are surprised? You haven't seen anything yet! I'll show you surprised, boy!' Then, less loudly, she adds, 'This world is funny! You would think that people just don't like to receive acts of kindness!'

'What have I possibly done, Mama Mongala? What is so awful that you can't even wait to sit down and explain it calmly? It's still early morning, on a Sunday. Can't we just sit down and talk about it? So that you can tell me what the unforgivable thing I have done is for you to kick me out of your house, all of a sudden, with no notice?'

'No notice, you say? You want to intimidate me with your laws and regulations, in my own house?'

'No, that's not what I meant. I just wanted to say that we could peacefully address the situation...'

She has been talking so loudly that all her other tenants have woken up and gathered to see what is going on. Mama Mongala is not the kind of person who can talk softly. Whatever the matter at hand, she speaks with a booming voice. Hearing all the commotion, the dogs in the courtyard start barking along and everyone is buzzing with surprise. What can possibly be the problem?

There are these kinds of days, when the will to live just escapes you. You find yourself wondering what you could possibly have done wrong on this Earth. Why bad things always befall you. The answer is simply that you are a human and this is the lot of humans in this world. The six o'clock sun is shining as brightly as if it were already noon. A slight breeze softens it.

Yesterday's rain was really something: on Ebamba's street, three houses have been completely flooded and the roof was blown off another. In other compounds, several trees lost their branches. Yes, the downpour had been truly terrible, and Mama Mongala's compound hadn't been spared either. She had been pained to discover that her beloved avocado tree had been thrown to the ground.

On the next street over, the wind had blown down walls. A pair of twin infants had died. Their mom had lit a petrol lamp because the power was out. Sadly, she had neglected to blow it out before going to bed and the kids had burned to death. In the morning, that version of events left people unconvinced. How was it possible that only the kids had died, and the parents had been spared? Others even added that the house had plainly not burned, and that even though the kids had burned to a crisp, the bed they were sleeping on had been left intact. That definitely looked like an act of dark forces. Things don't happen that way. It was clear that things never happened that way. People were really in an uproar that morning because of it, and some had even gone to confront the twins' father about it. They had come with sticks, spears, machetes and several other makeshift weapons to kill him, as it was clear to them he had brought about his kids' death with his sorcery.

Sunday is the day that business is taken care of. As the poet says, fair weather returns after rain. What is amazing, though, is that in this city that's not the way things go. The rain always leaves disaster in its wake. Here you have a flooded house, there someone was shocked to death, on the next street a tree was felled or its branches broke off, the ground caved in, roofs were blown away, people are left homeless or trapped and have to be helped out of their homes. Others hide in their homes to protect themselves from the sewer's stench and so on.

Since people are used to the situation, this state of things has become the new normal. But it is certainly not normal. As some news-people shout: *Eza normal te!* It's not right!

The sun shines warmer, the sky is clear again. The rain has cleared all the previous night's clouds. But it's the kind of heat that brings back rain. Now, during the rainy season, it pours down for two or three days in a row. On the news, some people like to play the scaremongering game, they claim that it's a sure sign that the end of the world is approaching. To them, Armageddon will take place right at the end of the rainy season. The public's fears grow every day: what is going to happen? Will it all come to an end?

This morning, though, the sun scorches the earth. In the compound, Mama Mongala has stopped shouting, but she still looks furious. Ebamba drags out two chairs and offers a seat to Mama Mongala so they can talk things through, but she angrily refuses.

'I'm not going to sit down!' The chair remains empty and she stands there, arms crossed. Ebamba sits down in silence. Mama Mongala barks down at him. 'You think you can treat me like a fool, Ebamba, don't you?' Wagging her finger at him, she goes on, 'You think you can play with me? Answer me!'

Softly, like someone who's weary of loud noises, Ebamba replies, 'What have I done to you?'

'What have you done? What have you done, is that what you are asking me?'

'For God's sake, Mama, yes – what have I done to you?'

'So, you pretend you don't know! You don't know what you have done, you say. Where were you last night and what time did you get back?'

Ebamba looks puzzled, he's now truly surprised. What's the matter? He opens his mouth to speak. 'So, is this the only reason you got me out of bed at the break of dawn to shout at me?'

Mama Mongala shoots back, 'Does it surprise you?'

'Why wouldn't I be surprised?'

Mama Mongala moves closer to Ebamba, who is still rooted to his chair. She loosens the knot in the fabric wrapped around her left hip, shakes the cloth a bit, and ties it back on tighter. Hands on her hips, she takes a deep breath and snorts. Twisting her mouth, she says, 'Ebamba, I asked you a question. Where were you last night?'

'I went to meet my girlfriend's family to ask for the dowry list, so we can get married.'

'Huh. And you say it with no shame, you are planning to marry.'

'What, why would it be a problem? Why should I be ashamed of getting married? Do I need to ask you if I can get married? Are you joking?'

'Let me ask you, when you moved in, didn't you see that there are plenty of girls in this compound already?'

'Of course, I saw them alright...'

'So then, how did it get into your head to go chase girls elsewhere?'

'Mama Mongala, I really don't understand what you are getting at. I came here to rent an apartment, not to date girls from the compound. When I moved in, I was already dating my present girlfriend. What was I supposed to do?'

'You already had a girlfriend? Do you know how many people I turned down as tenants before you came along? Do you know why I took you in? Look, I am going to be clear with you. My daughter Maguy is waiting for you. You are going to marry her, or I'll kick you out of the compound!'

'What are you talking about? When I moved in here, did we sign a paper saying I would marry her?'

'Well, we are signing it now. I'm telling you, from this moment on, Maguy is your wife! I don't even want to see your girlfriend's shadow around here or you'll see what I am capable of.'

'God almighty!'

Ebamba's mouth is wide open with amazement. He is petrified. Mama Mongala turns around to leave, then thinks better of it and walks back up to him. 'Now that you know, be careful what you do. I'm dead serious. If you try to deceive me, you'll see.'

Having said that, she turns her back to him and leaves, leaving Ebamba there. Ebamba remains in his chair, frightened and sad. His problems are crushing him. What is he going to do? What has he done wrong? What is going to happen to him? Where can he possibly go? He is already two months late on his rent. Same thing for his electricity and water bills. Until today, it hadn't occurred to him that his landlady hadn't chased after him to get her rent money.

Some days, when he comes home from making the little hand-to-mouth deals he comes up with to survive, tired and broke as he is, Maguy, the landlady's daughter, brings him nicely cooked meals. Sometimes she even gives him money, or hands him enough for a drink, or brings over some other small gift. Now it dawns on him that those were all signs that he was supposed to date and marry her.

A cool breeze blows and the sky darkens. The sun sets near the Congo River, round like a ball of fire, red as blood. The surface of the river is untroubled. The wind is getting colder and passers-by shiver. Night sets in, the sun vanishes from the horizon. In the sky, several types of birds rush noisily back to their nests, while the trees slowly swing their branches in the breeze. The wind is humming a song as if to say it is going to rain soon...

It's Saturday, the day when Kinshasa is at its most hectic. Kinshasa full of joy, Kinshasa home to life and its troubles. Kinshasa home to beer of all kinds: Nkoy, Mo-prima, Turbo, Skol... Kinshasa, the land of bursting joy in all its forms... It's true, you may live to be one hundred years old, but if you have never seen Kinshasa, you cannot say that you have truly lived. You have to see Kinshasa at least once. You have to see the Congo River.

We're approaching 6:12 in the evening. The bars are already crowded. In Niangwe, in Kimbondo, in Tshiban-gu, in Super, in Beau Marché, at Muguylaguyla and, topping it all, in Matongé Oshwe, the party is in full swing. Goat and chicken are roasted and eaten as enthusiastically as candy, drink is overflowing. Dance is everywhere. Kinshasa is the land of music, the land of *ndombolo*.

We're approaching 9:05 in the evening. The snake-girls are beginning to come out. You look at them; their beauty will bring tears to your eyes. They shine like gold. Some wear miniskirts, others just leggings, some wear super-wax wraps, others skin-tight pants. They roam everywhere, looking for someone to bite, or someone who'll take a bite at them. You can find them along Avenue du Stade, around Inzia, at Yolo Nord, at Boulevard... The nameless girls, the givers of joy, the horse-girls whom anyone can ride. The girls from Bongolo...They come in all shades of colour: black, chocolate brown, white, mixed, albinos... In all sizes: short, tall, medium-height, dwarves... And some are mute, disabled...

At a bar called Muguylaguyla, Ebamba and his friends are dancing to the notes of Ya Jossart: as they say, walk on the turtle's back, and then swell your chest. They dance Mama Siska... Beer has taken hold of them, they are getting drunk and they are starting to do things they can't really control. Ebamba finds himself feeling up his friend's girlfriend, who slaps him and brings him back to reality. Thankfully, he snaps back to a normal human state right away.

Ebamba's girlfriend, Eyenga, had also come along, but she had already left because she wasn't feeling well. Ebamba had walked her to her house and then, since it was his old friend's birthday party, had gone back to join his friends who were dancing and drinking at the Muguylaguyla.

The party goes on and on, and it gets better and better. The rain has disappeared, carried off by the wind, leaving behind a cool breeze. You dance and dance and you don't even break a sweat. The few raindrops have only boosted everyone to keep the party going and people are dancing away and having fun.

It's 1:05 in the morning.

Knock knock...

Knock knock...

Ebamba is standing at the door to his compound, the gate is already locked for the night. He knocks in the hope that someone will hear him and let him in. He can't even call some neighbour to open the door because his cellphone is missing. He lost it at the party, dropped it from his pocket while he was dancing. Its new owner had picked it up and hurried away with it.

No one is coming. He is beginning to lose patience, but the beer is taking its toll on him, and he just doesn't have the strength to climb over the wall. He just wants to crawl into his bed and sleep. Discouraged, he sits down, his back to the wall...

1:30...

He hears someone's steps approach, someone's opening the door. The gate squeaks open, he stands up to let himself in.

His eyes focus on the person standing there. It's Maguy. She's just wearing a revealing wrap, barely covering her chest.

As they politely exchange a greeting, Maguy can smell the scent of beer all over Ebamba, as he walks past her toward his apartment.

It's pitch dark in the compound. Everyone's sleeping soundly. That night, they had forgotten to unleash the dogs in the yard, so the silence is complete. No one stirs.

Ebamba skulks to his door, gets out his keys, and lets himself in. Maguy stays behind to lock the gate and then rushes back to her home.

It's 1:40... A cool, smooth hand is caressing Ebamba's penis. Ebamba feels his pleasure rise. Those same hands then unbutton his shirt and go on to play with the hair on his chest. A wave of desire and pleasure engulfs Ebamba.

The hands pursue their work. Ebamba, still shrouded in sleep, feels as if he's going to die. He feels the touch of a pair of juicy lips sucking the skin on his chest, biting him lovingly. His body starts burning up. All the hair on his body stands up. It feels so delicious he has goosebumps all over.

Desire wins over sleep. He begins to realize that this is definitely not a dream. He opens his eyes and he is truly startled to see a woman there.

'What?' he begins. Maguy lets go of his body and takes a step back. Ebamba comes back to his senses and is taken aback with what is going on. 'What the hell is this? How did you get in?'

'What are you afraid of?' Maguy asks, so sweet that any ordinary man would just surrender, no questions asked. 'What is so worrying, huh? Am I killing you, am I hurting you? You left your door open and I have come in to make you feel good...'

'Make me feel good?!'

'Hush, stop talking,' Maguy says, untying her wrap. To Ebamba's eyes, Maguy looks just like Eve in the Garden of Eden – her soft, brown body, with its round, firm breasts, standing there, her gaze fixed upon him.

Maguy draws closer to Ebamba, who's already trapped in her net. He is mute, his body shakes a little. He opens his mouth, but nothing comes out. Maguy takes off his shirt and kisses his lips.

Maguy slips down Ebamba's pants and she takes them off him completely. He just lets her. Then they fall back together on Ebamba's bed. The bed squeaks beneath them. The effect of the booze has completely worn off, now. Ebamba starts sweating everywhere, as their naked bodies come together.

There is no going back. Ebamba feels like he's going crazy, bloodshot eyes and all. He surrenders, he gives his everything, he lets Maguy play with him in any way she wants. The girl does to him all that she can think of. Everything spins around him, he's losing his mind completely. Never seen anything like that.

4—DELHI

MANGOSIL
A Novel Excerpt

BY UDAY PRAKASH
TRANSLATED BY JASON GRANEBAUM

This story is dedicated to
Laghve, Paul and Shailendra

A preface to the end of time
(Reading this preface is mandatory)

This is the story of Chandrakant Thorat. It's also my story.
And it's a story that takes place in the present day, in our own
time; a tale with the sights and sounds of this day and age.

A few of the characters have been cast out of their own
space and time, and now stand in wait for the destruction at
the end. I am one of them, living outside of my proper space
and time, in a filthy quarter far from the finery and culture
of the city.

The efforts of human beings to lead lives in the shanty
towns that circle the city on grabbed land eventually take
shape, one unfortunate day, on the maps of a town planner,
or property dealer, or urban coloniser. Then, the engineers
of the empire of money send out the bulldozers – they fan

out, non-stop – until even a dirty sprawl of shacks is transformed into a Metro Rail, a flyover, a shopping mall, a dam,
a quarry, a factory, or a five-star-plus hotel. And when it happens, lives like Chandrakant Thorat's are gone for good.

Chandrakant Thorat is a friend of mine, and he's one of the
characters of this story. My life is bound to his as if by decree
or fate. Even if I didn't want it to be so, it would be.

You ought to know the truth: there are only two reasons
lives like ours are stamped out.

One: our lives are left over as proof of past and present
sins and crimes against castes, races, cultures; they always
want to keep this as hidden as they can.

Two: our lives get in the way of the enterprising city,
or act as a road bump in the master plan of a country that
thinks of itself as a big player on the world stage. Our very
humanity threatens to reveal the wicked culture of money
and means as something suspect and unlovely. That's why
whenever civilizations once developing, now on the brink
of prosperity, decide to embark on a program of 'beautifica-
tion', they try to root out such lives, the same way the mess
on the floor is swept outside.

Suppose we fled these megalopolises to an exurb, or to the
mountains, or into the forest, or to a small town? There, too,
lives like ours would one day be inundated and swept away,
just as the Harappan or Babylonian civilizations you must
have read about in archeology books were also wiped out.

The memory of the destruction at the end of time lies in
the psyche of every community of every people, including
ours. There is something else you should know. Whenever
our lives are steamrolled in the name of cultural progress

and cultural beauty to profit the rich city or state – or when lives drown for power and energy – it's not just us. The deer, butterflies, birds, elephants, peepal and teak trees, the flora (divine beings all) are also washed away from this earth. Beings that descended from heaven, thousands of years ago, in the ancient treta or dwapar epochs; beings that settled into rocks and books so that our suffering might be eased. To allow us to endure our pain and desolation. To light our way like a candle or firefly or light bulb in the darkness. When violence permeates everything, and reality has become a nightmare, these creatures carry us into a dream.

You know the truth: none of it is meant for us. Not the medicine of rich, developed nations that give relief from suffering, or the energy that creates the illusion of light and wind and words and dazzle – none is meant for us. Top-tier hospitals, banks, institutions, parliaments, courts, airports, and wide boulevards aren't for us. We're chased away from these places or crushed underfoot.

Only they may inhabit the buildings and institutions built by civilizations of wealth. Their constitutions only serve to protect their interests. Their language of poetry and legend is covered with our blood, sweat, sorrow, and tears.

Their poems and epics aren't ours. They want to keep us out of everything: poetry, prose, music, cities, work, industry, the marketplace. We're the drudging, untouchable, poor, unemployed, dissatisfied, anxious, and hungry people who, to them, are utterly unknown. They despise us each and every moment; each and every moment, they wish to do away with us.

Jahangirpuri bylane number seven

Buttressed by what is said to be the largest fruit and vegetable market in Asia, lies a neighbourhood in Northwest
Delhi – Jahangirpuri. If you're travelling between India and
Pakistan on the Goodwill Bus, you'll see what looks like a
residential area right before the bypass road on the left-
hand side: rising up from the mud and the muck, that's
Jahangirpuri. But from a distance the land between the highway and the settlement doesn't seem to be made of simple
blackened ooze, dirt and water, but instead from a chemical
mix consisting of a molten solution of motor oil, grease, gas-
oline and plastic. Might as well throw in the rotting organic
matter from the fruit and vegetables as well. Jagangirpuri
was most assuredly settled without a planning map. Over
many years, people showed up, built a house wherever they
found some space, and settled down. In the surrounding
area you'll find what looks like ancient ruins, giving the
impression that this area has been gradually inhabited over
a period of centuries. If you're flying overhead and glance
down, you'll see a mishmash of half-built houses. It's as
if someone took the waste material from wealthy Delhi's
architectural nest, and swept it clean out here into a pile: a
trash heap of higgledy-piggledy brick houses tossed in the
middle of a black chemical slime bog that exudes the stench
of rotting fruit and vegetables. There are exceptions – a few
multi-storied, modern houses – but this is like what Delhi,
Bangalore, Hyderabad and Bombay look like from way up in
the sky compared to the rest of India: incongruous tokens of
priceless, shining marble stuck in the mire and mud of the
subcontinent's swamp of chilling poverty.

Narrow alleys or bylanes, no more than ten to twelve feet wide, wind through the rows of houses that are built right on top of one another in Jahangirpuri. In some places, they are as narrow as eight to ten feet from one side to the other. You can traverse these bylanes, without fear of collision, only on foot or by cycle. During the hot season, people bring their cots outside and sleep; settlements like these are the hardest hit by the capital city's frequent power and water cuts. Gossip, STDs, dengue fever, black magic, criminality and disease spread most vigorously in places like Jahangirpuri. This summer, the channels built for water drainage were all running open, and every morning, the young and the old and infirm squatted above them and did their business. The smell rising from the ditches after the water is turned off gives the neighbourhood its unmistakable stamp.

It's half past ten at night right now in bylane number seven, where a fat, dark-complexioned man of forty-five or fifty tiptoes down the alley loosely clasping a bag in his right hand. It's dark; all five lampposts in the streets are dark. The bright light shining in the eyes of the people sleeping outside bothered them, so they unscrewed the bulbs. At the end of the bylane was (until just a few months ago) a working light, but Gurpreet and Somu from bylane three broke it because they were running around with Deepti and Shalini from E-7/2 of bylane seven, and liked it dark when they brought the girls back late at night on the back of their Hero Honda motorbikes. Deepti and Shalini were C-list models; aside from appearing in cheap ads for underwear and hair removal products, they were also available at nights in five-star hotels, or for private parties. An older lady of the night lived in house E-6/3. Her husband had been run over by a bus in front of the Liberty Cinema three years before. Since then, she has been supporting her three kids and elderly mother-in-law with the help of the kind-hearted men who visit her after hours. She has full sympathy from the residents of bylane seven, and even if the bulb at the far end hadn't been removed, no one would have batted an eye.

The man with the bag in his hand walks ten steps down the darkness of bylane seven and, halting in front of the ditch, removes a pint of Bonnie Scot, and downs it in one go, before tossing away the empty bottle and pissing in the ditch. The man is Chandrakant Thorat. Even though he was middle-aged, Chandrakant enjoyed new Indy Pop like 'Jhanjar wali hoke matvali' and 'Channave ghar aa jaave.' It was funny that the favourite music of Chandrakant, who spoke pidgin Marathi and just passable Hindi, was Panjabi pop music. And whenever love stirred in his heart for Shobha, his wife, the emotion found expression in Panjabi: *Baby, baby, what can I do? My heart's horn honks when I see your pretty face! You oughta hear it, baby! You gotta hear it, baby!* Shobha responded, chiding him, 'Coming home drunk again? How many times have I told you, drink as much as you'd like, but do it at home. If anything ever happened to you, I'd end up like our lady of the night! Then what?'

These words sobered him up instantly. He certainly didn't want to die and force his wife to rely on kind-hearted men.

'You just doused my Bonnie Scot with bitter herbs. Make me some food. I've got to go to work early tomorrow.' Then Chandrakant was silent. He hung his head low as he ate, stretched and yawned, then lay down to sleep on the mat on the floor. His wife ate afterwards, then did household chores late into the night, washing dishes, chopping vegetables for the morning, ironing Chandrakant's pants and shirt, until finally, at midnight, she sat by the outdoor tap and bathed. By the time she finished her work, humming some old song while she adjusted the fan on top of the trunk, Chandrakant was already snoring.

Running off with Shobha

Shobha and Chandrakant had been living together for some thirty years. Chandrakant had fled with her from Sarani where she had been living with her husband, Ramakant.

Ramakant had no job and no skills: he ran around wherever he could to try and get a small piece of the action. He was addicted to playing the market, and also worked part-time for the police as a false witness. Those days, the eyes of a certain police inspector had fallen on Shobha; every night, the inspector came over to their house to drink and eat. Every night for three months, the middle-aged inspector's lust fell on Shobha. Those three tortuous months in Shobha's life were worse than hell. He arrived at the house around nine at night; as soon as he stepped in the door, he took off his uniform and hung it on a peg. Then – down to his sweaty, smelly, dirty undershirt and brown, greasy shorts – he took a seat on the little mat on the floor and forbade the outside door to be closed because then there would be no breeze to cool him down. Ramakant served the inspector as if he were his butler, running back and forth to the kitchen and market for salty namkeen snacks, hard-boiled eggs, and, whenever the need arose, another bottle of hooch. Ramakant also kept his glass nearby, so whenever he had a free moment after running around fetching things for the inspector, he sat down next to the inspector and joined him for a shot. He was proud of those moments, they were a real honour and treat. He laughed and joked with the inspector, and chided his wife Shobha: 'Hurry up, squeeze the lemon, bring the snacks! Inspector sahib likes green chilies. Thinly, cut them thinly!' Or, 'Don't just toss the dish on the floor! Place it in the man's hand, nicely, gently, that's it. And what happened to the coriander? Didn't I just buy two bunches for inspector sahib to enjoy?'

'Ramakant, how about one more?' the inspector said. 'And give your better half something to drink, too. Tomorrow a friend of mine is coming. We'll have a party!' the inspector said. Ramakant's face lit up at the mention of a party. A party meant he would get to eat mutton or chicken, with plenty of snacks, too, plus more good booze. On top of that, he was always able to ferret away a few rupees from the money the inspector gave him for the food and drink.

'Consider it done, sahib! So, will it be mutton or chicken? Should I have her make fish or pakoras to go with the drinks? She's a fantastic cook. How much meat, four pounds or five? And how much whisky d'you think'll be necessary?' He grinned shamelessly and added, 'See, if there's any food left over it'll be a big help the next day. After a big party, Shobha's in no shape at all until two or three in the afternoon.'

After getting drunk, the inspector might launch into song, or start hurling vile curses. He had convinced himself that Shobha was thrilled to have found such a robust specimen of a man as he, and one with money, too – particularly after playing long-suffering wife to the penniless, shiftless, good-for-nothing Ramakant. The inspector also came to accept that in her heart of hearts, Shobha fancied him indeed. And once the inspector understood this, he stepped up his abuse of Ramakant, chastising and reprimanding him at every word, pausing to fasten his gaze on Shobha, to whom he started sweet-talking. It transpired that since she was little she had a soft spot for dark gulab jamun, not to mention her other favourite sweet, rabri-ilichi kul. How was this loser going to procure such sweetmeats for Shobha? The inspector at once sent Ramakant out to fetch the delicacies. As soon as he was out the door, the inspector drew her near.

His hairy potbelly poked out from a filthy, stinking undershirt, underneath which he grabbed Shobha's head and brought it to his sweaty, soiled crotch. Her every breath caught a second stench of the raw sewage rivulets that criss-crossed the neighbourhood. She nearly retched on the spot. The inspector stroked her hair as he swigged from the bottle. Sounds issued from her mouth as if she were getting the sour taste of a lemon and the hot part of a chili both at once. The door to the outside was left open, a fact that late-night pas-sers-by often noticed. Moreover, the little vacant patch of land in front of the house was a popular spot for people to stop and answer the call of nature. Here, in perfect darkness, a crush of young nogoodniks, out for a midnight stroll, gathered by the house of police flunky Ramakant to watch live porn.

'Party night' meant that the inspector brought a buddy. Those nights, Shobha endured inhuman torment and suf-fering. After getting well drunk, the men let loose the beast within. And in that room, Shobha fell victim to the violence of the wild animals and the frenzy they unleashed. Once they got going, they sang, drank more, praised the fish pakoras to high heaven, laughed and giggled, groped and fondled Shobha, squeezed and pinched. Ramakant encouraged them in all this.

A fat and flabby fair-skinned contractor was brought to one such party by the inspector. He was in his late fifties, early sixties. That night they had even set up a VCR to watch porn; back then, VCRs had just come out and could be rented in the bazaar. Leering at the stunning Shobha, he casually let slip that this year he was going to be elected as municipal councillor, having locked up all the votes from this neighbourhood and the surrounding ones.

That night Shobha was taken to the gates of hell. The contractor and inspector committed unnatural acts, including the contractor inserting a beer bottle in her rectum. The inspector laughed, 'What the heck are you doing!?'

'What am I doing?' The contractor over-flowed with delight. 'Just a little drilling from the back side to bore a big hole so that the motor'll hum from the underside! I've got a twenty-horsepower tractor!'

Shobha gasped for breath, blood dripping on the rug and floor, while porn flashed on the TV. Unconsciousness relieved her from the torments. It was nearly four in the morning when the inspector and contractor finally made their way home. Shobha was greeted with splitting pain when she came to; she wanted to get up and get dressed and wash off the blood and semen. She found Ramakant mounting her. She gave him a kick. Then, in fits and groans, she found the bucket of water kept just outside the front door and began washing herself, not a stitch of clothing covering her body.

As she sat groaning and washing off her blood and the spit and semen of the contractor, inspector, and Ramakant, she had the feeling that at four in the morning she had been ogled by the eyes of many men in the darkness from across the bylane. Bloodletting, blood-soaked, bestial violence: these people stayed up all night to watch this? Not a wink of sleep, smelling the shit from the sewage all night long? This was their idea of fun?

Almost a week later, the contractor showed up one afternoon in his car. The inspector was with him. They brought all sorts of goodies for Shobha: saris with matching tops, lingerie, teddies, lace panties, salwar-kurta, bangles, jewellery, and more. The contractor seemed very pleased and, between sips of chai, informed her that he had appointed her Director of the All-Women's Welfare Association, meaning that now he would take her with him on tour to Mumbai, Nagpur, Pune, Kolhapur, and other cities.

That day, Chandrakant, a servant in the contractor's employ, was introduced to Shobha.

Six weeks later, at a government rest house in Jalgaon, the contractor took her to the VIP room. There, party underway, Shobha slipped out under the pretext of needing to change her clothes and, bag packed with everything she had, ran off with Chandrakant to Delhi, where they rented a ground floor flat for five hundred rupees a month at house number E-3/1, bylane number seven, Jahangirpuri. He found part-time work as a helper at a department store in Vijaynagar and she began making food and snacks and pickle and preserves for neighbouring households.

Fleeing from Jalgaon with Chandrakant that night had rescued Shobha from a terrible crime; Chandrakant had masterminded the escape. Fifteen days had passed since the last party, when the contractor had announced they were going to Jalgaon. He had been busy with some construction project. Only the inspector had come in the meantime, two or three times. Shobha waited quietly for the next party, for which she had purchased thirteen rupees worth of rat poison kept hidden in her secret bundle. She mixed it into the goatmeat dish, and was ready to serve it to the inspector, contractor, and her husband, Ramakant. After she did, Shobha faced a dilemma: eat it and herself perish, or don't eat it and run off with Chandrakant? She kept her plan hidden from Chandrakant; he seemed so guileless and honest that she was sure he would never allow her to go through with it. Chandrakant finally acceded to them running away together from Jalgaon, though he was clearly scared.

Shobha in the half-flat

E-3/1 was a four-story house. There was space underneath the stairs that, with a little imagination, formed something like a room. Ten feet long, seven feet wide, not exactly a room, but a half flat, and thus with no proper front door. Chandrakant and Shobha fastened two planks of wood over the opening. The first they nailed to the top with scrap metal and hung a blue plastic curtain. The second served as a sliding door leaf. On cold winter days when both Chandrakant and Shobha went out, they kept the door closed. In front of the door, or wall, or board, or whatever you want to call it, was an additional space that measured about four-and-a-half feet. On the left side was a little tap where Shobha and Chandrakant did all their bathing, laundry, and dishes. They called it 'the balcony'; two feet below was an open sewer. A strong, sour smell continuously wafted upwards, along with a buzzing swarm of flies. A few days ago, Chandrakant had found another board to cover it up.

They slept on a coarse little mat spread on the floor of their half-flat, which they called, in English, the 'room.' Chandrakant and Shobha also owned a banged-up tin trunk in which they kept items used infrequently. Also kept in the trunk were the bangles, jewellery, saris and salwars from the inspector and contractor; stainless steel and glass pots and plates from her parents when she got married; a pair of silver anklets; her mangalsutra wedding thread; a toe ring; armlet; a sari of silver thread. A half-inch strip of plywood was fastened above the trunk, on top of which perched the household's most valuable and necessary item, a fan. It was because of the fan they were able to sleep in the heat, without harassment from flies and mosquitoes. When it went on the blink, the despondent pair would go out to fetch the electrician and wouldn't rest until he'd fixed it. But it rarely stopped working. Flip the switch and it purred to life with a loud whoosh. The strong flow of cool air made Chandrakant and Shobha very happy.

In the corner of the room was a little stove that ran on wood scraps. That's where Shobha cooked, and no food was more delicious than Shobha's. Chandrakant had been hooked on Shobha's cooking since the days of Sarni when he went in the big car to the parties at Ramakant's with his boss, the contractor.

He used to pull right up to the door, making it a little difficult for the passersby who liked to peer inside the house. The contractor would turn up the tape deck as loud as it would go, drowning out both the noise of the 'party' and the shrieks of Shobha. Chandrakant was right there, stretched out in the back of the car, listening to the music issuing from its sound system. He had no idea what was going on inside. He never even peeked.

His eyes opened to find Shobha banging on the car window. She brought him food, a thali with roti, meat curry, onions, and more, sometimes a bit of rice. He liked her meat curry so much that it seemed there was never enough. This happened two or three times, and Shobha began to sense his fondness, maybe because the two were around the same age. This was thirty years ago, when Shobha was nineteen or twenty, and villagers didn't pay attention to age differences between bride and groom. Ramakant was between thirty and thirty-five. The inspector who those days raped Shobha daily couldn't have been younger than forty-five, and the contractor, boss of servant Chandrakant, must have been nearing sixty.

Chandrakant, a young man of nineteen, was utterly different from these middle-aged, savage, stinking men; he stretched out in the back of the car, eyes closed, quietly listening to music, never asking for seconds, never taking a peek inside the house to see what went on during the 'party.'

That night she quietly crept to the car door window and, peering inside, saw Chandrakant mopping up the last of meat sauce with a roti, two more still on his thali.

'Do you want some more meat and sauce?' she asked, startling Chandrakant.

'No, no, this is plenty!'

Shobha met his reply with a smile. 'Then what's the use of the other roti?'

Chandrakant didn't have an answer.

She brought another katori dish full of meat and sauce, and two more roti as well. It pleased her as Chandrakant silently took the bread and lowered his head to begin eating. She watched him as he ate. He suddenly lifted up his head: his hair was a mess, his mouth full of food. He stared at Shobha and blushed as he broke into a kind of giggle.

It was like the end of a lifesaving rope that dangled in front of the black hole of her hellish life. She decided to grab it and run away, not knowing whether it was out of love or from an intense desire to be free.

The next party, Shobha informed the inspector, contractor, and Ramakant, who were busy eating fish pakoras and drinking, that she was going outside to serve Chandrakant his food. Once there, she got in the car and told him everything. She showed him her legs, back, chest, and neck for him to examine. 'Someone might come, I can't show you the rest here,' Shobha began. 'But mark my words, one day I'll be dead and they'll throw my body away. Save me however you can. Take me anywhere. I'll do your laundry, clean and dust, cook for you every day, wash the dishes. You like my meat curry, right? I can cook better. I can put a masala into the dish that'll fill the whole house with the most unbelievable fragrance you've ever smelled. If you want me to sleep outside, in the courtyard, on the stoop, I will. I don't need sheets or blankets. I can live with the clothes on my back. When you're not making money, I'll make it for you.'

The tape deck was still blaring music; twenty-year-old Shobha hiccupped between her little sobs. 'You can do to me what the inspector and builder do to me and I won't say a word. If it hurts, I won't cry, I won't scream. I'll stop the blood, I won't allow myself to bleed. I'll clean everything up without a fuss, no one will know. I'll just keep smiling. You can tear me to bits and I'll keep smiling. I'll stay by your side and serve your every need. I'll nurse you when you get sick, soothe your body with massage. Do with me whatever you want, your heart's desire – I won't stop you. If you bring someone else I'll serve her too. Just get me out of this trap.' Shobha had gripped Chandrakant's shirtsleeve as if she would never let go, as if it were a root on a riverbank she suddenly found and clung to, like life itself, in spite of being swept under by the current.

Listening to twenty-year-old Shobha, nineteen-year-old Chandrakant felt for the first time he wasn't just a servant in the contractor's employ. He could be more, and this thought gave rise to a kind of self-confidence he'd never had. Just then, Ramakant appeared. He saw Shobha attached to Chandrakant's sleeve, sitting close in the back seat of the car, telling him things, crying. In one fell swoop he opened the door, seized Shobha, and dragged her out. 'Did you come out here to feed him or fuck him, you whore. Haven't had enough yet?'

This was that same violent night when the contractor shredded Shobha's rectum with a beer bottle and she passed out from the bleeding. That night was also the first time Chandrakant heard her scream. A scream that carried so much pain it pierced the closed car window and even Chandrakant's eardrum. He panicked, sat up, and switched off the music. And for the first time he rolled down the window and stuck his head outside.

Inside, they had switched off the light; all there was to see was shifting shadows in the dark. He listened, but the only thing he could make out was the fearsome growling of wild animals issuing from inside the house, and it sounded as if they had found their prey and were tearing it to bits in a frenzy. For the first time, he despaired of Shobha's fate, she who had just a few minutes ago clung to his shirtsleeve, whose tears still moistened the same sleeve, whose curry and roti he had just finished eating. The image of her tearful face flashed before his eyes, and he felt as if she were still there with him. Chandrakant thought, I will absolutely help her out of that trap and lift her out of the pit.

Fear, however, reared its head inside of nineteen-year-old Chandrakant. The inspector and contractor were very powerful. He had seen their acts of barbarity with his own eyes. He knew from conversations with them and by the way they talked about places like Lucknow, Bhopal, Bombay, Delhi, and Calcutta that their influence stretched far and wide. They could get to wherever they wanted to go. And they would get to wherever he took this girl: the inspector, the contractor, their flunkeys – they would find them, there was nowhere to hide.

Chandrakant was in a tangle of fear and nerves and worry. That's why when he fled the house in Jalgaon with Shobha, he had wrapped a towel around his face and covered his body with a sheet. Shobha, however, beamed non-stop with a joy that bordered on rapture. As the train left Sarani station with the two safely inside their compartment, Shobha stowed her trunk and bundle and Chandrakant's bag underneath the berth with such delicacy and care it was as if she would make her new home right there on the train with Chandrakant – as if she was going to light a little cooking stove on the floor of the train and start a household. The carriage in which the two passengers rode rumbling along the iron rails wasn't made of wood, glass, and steel, but was transformed into a simple courtyard of fragrant adobe, where sweet spicy smells mixed with the rising smoke of the cooking stove, where a twenty-year-old girl, leisurely humming a song, rolled out the roti, fully absorbed in her work.

Something in this was quite pleasing to Chandrakant; time and again he wanted to break into song. What that pleasing something was, however, he wasn't able to fully comprehend.

The nest and eggs of a bird

Ah ha! So this is what had been so pleasing to Chandrakant that day on the moving train, the thing he wasn't able to fully understand. It was some ten days after they found the half flat in the Jahangirpuri neighbourhood of Delhi at E-3/1, bylane seven. The two of them had spent the first few days purchasing household goods for their mini-place, cleaning and setting up house. Chandrakant had found work as a shop assistant in a department store in Vijaynagar, which is also known as Kingsway Camp. Vijaynagar was no more than six kilometres from Jahangirpuri, with plenty of buses at the Azadpur bus stand headed that way. He set off for work at six in the morning, came back at two in the afternoon for lunch, and returned to work at three thirty. It was nearly nine at night by the time he came back for good. Shobha had no idea how much money she had run off with from Sarani – it had easily covered the stove, fan, curtains, tarp, tin trunk, sheets and blankets, cup and saucer sets, pressure cooker, thali dishes, glasses, food staples, tea and sugar, and all other household necessities. Smiling, she plunged her hand into her rainbow flower vinyl purse (a treasure-chest as bountiful as Tutankhamen's), and withdrew as much money as she pleased. Day three after their arrival in Delhi, Shobha began calling Chandakant 'Chandu' while he continued calling Shobha 'Shobha'. Chandrakant began to get a little worried watching Shobha buy so much stuff, but she just scooped her hand into the flowered purse and said, 'Don't worry, Chandu! No worries at all! I hit the big one with Ramakant and inspector's and contractor's cash.'

It was a Monday, when the bazaar at Vijaynagar was closed and Chandrakant had the day off. He stretched out on the ground in the little room and began listening to the radio. *Oh don't shake down the apples from my tree! A little thorn will break the skin in a flash!* Every once in a while he joined in. As he sang along, Shobha's voice rang in from outside, 'Nice voice, Chandu, it's like you're Kishore Kumar singing along with Lata Mangeshkar! Today's a singing kind of day!'

Chandrakant gazed outside, transfixed. Shobha was sitting next to the tap on the 'balcony' bathing, rubbing the soles of her feet with a little pumice stone, her sari bunched up to her thighs. As she poured water over her head with the red plastic mug, it was as if her sari was dissolving in the water, the sari turning to liquid and washing over her skin in glistening colours, clinging tightly to her body, revealing more and more of her wet form.

Chandrakant felt a lump in his throat, his voice began to crack, and so he stopped singing along with the radio and started staring at Shobha. His gaze must have burned into her backside because she turned around suddenly. 'What happened, Mr. Mohammed Ra crooner man?' she teased. 'Lose your voice? Cat got your tongue, Chandu? Feeling shy?'

He didn't say a word, but just kept staring. Lather ran down her face, little white soap bubbles popped on her closed eyelids, she couldn't see a thing. This was the first time Chandrakant could observe her the way he wanted for as long as he wanted to. Beneath the folds of her sari, she lathered her chest, bar of soap in hand.

Chandrakant realised for the first time how huge her eyes were, just like the actress Hema Malini's, but bigger, even bigger. They had been living together in the half-flat for ten days, and he had known her even longer, from before, in Sarani, but he had never really looked at her body and her eyes as he did now. Chandrakant felt embarrassed for having spent so much time with Shobha – for having lived so long – without ever having been as close as he was now to the kind of body and shape of eyes that this girl had.

And how this girl looked though the soap lather that glittered like dewdrops, how it took his breath away, this was a new sensation. Shobha stood up in her dripping wet sari and began drying her hair with a towel. The magnetic field that originated from the water tap and enveloped him was also something new. It was like a zap from inside inducing him toward her with full force. His mind was in a bad way. He could see only colours swimming in front of his eyes, like the soap bubbles that floated in the air.

He walked up behind Shobha and clasped her around the waist, then lifted her back into the half-flat, the ten-by-seven 'room' that, for the moment, was the Delhi home of these two winged creatures.

Shobha said nothing. She was still wet; her hair too, eyes closed, face flushed with a flame that slowly let its heat seep over her body, and into her blood, until heat rose from her skin and met Chandrakant's lips. Not a drop of dew escaped his waiting mouth while hands explored every place on Shobha's body, tracing her wet skin.

The little mat on the floor beside the trunk, in the cramped half flat, was wringing wet. And atop that wet rug Chandu and Shobha seized one another as if at the epicentre of a consuming blaze. Soap bubbles of all hues seeped through the room, while outside on the balcony it wasn't water that gushed from the tap and noisily filled the bucket, but a rainbow of colour.

Shobha felt as if she was sinking into a deep dream on a magic carpet, not just lying on a rug. Her wet sari lay to the side, while atop her body was a blushing nineteen-year-old boy, smiling nervously, rather than the old, savage inspector, or contractor, or the husband she had been made to marry. That night in Sarani, she had grabbed hold of the edge of the rope that sprang from the boy's smile, a smile born while eating her homemade curry and roti. And now it looked as if she might make it out alive.

It was as if the mouth of nineteen-year-old Chandrakant, whom she had begun to call Chandu, was still stuffed with the bits of her food, hungry and blushing as he smiled. Overcome with love for Shobha, he gathered her tangled hair in his hands and kissed her feverishly.

After that Monday, some thirty years ago, and a mere ten days after the two of them had moved to their half-flat at E-3/1, bylane number seven, Jahangirpuri, Shobha had begun referring to the covering on the floor as the carpet rather than a rug. She hummed while she worked, and after Chandrakant left for work in Vijaynagar, she sang duets with Lata Mangeshkar and Asha Bhosle on the radio. Shobha prepared food for the two of them, peeled and chopped and sliced the vegetables, did their laundry, took naps, while Chandrakant swept her up and onto the magic carpet where the two of them would make love in a blaze of heat.

Like this, years passed, Shobha grew plump, Chandrakant's hair thinned and turned grey, both of them sometimes fell ill, then got better, all the while and for thirty years playing the nonstop game of fanning the flames atop their magic carpet. Shobha got pregnant seven times. She registered with the government hospital in Aadarsh Nagar, stitched and sewed clothes and booties and a bed for the baby, and ate and drank with great precaution. But either she miscarried, or the baby succumbed to an illness a few months after birth – each and every time. Chandrakant and Shobha were devastated. They decided that the mosquitoes and bacteria from the sewage gutter in front of their house had infected the babies with some illness; a thick, damp, and often strong stench came through their windows from the gutter. During the monsoon season, earth-worms, centipedes, millipedes, snails, and frogs would crawl or hop from the gutter into their flat. One time when Shobha and Chandrakant were deep in the middle of playing their favourite game on the magic carpet, Shobha screamed when she saw a baby snake slithering on the ground off to her left. Another time it was a boa constrictor that sprang out from behind a box. Things got even worst during the rainy season – spiders were everywhere.

Both of them wished to move somewhere else, somewhere clean and tidy. But as time went on, rents began to soar.

Chandrakant had always been on the lookout for another job or additional income, but nothing ever materialised. His boss at the shop, Gulshan Arora, was a good man, and no other shopkeeper would have paid a better salary. Over the thirty years, Arora had become an elderly seventy-year-old. Both his daughters had been married off, and he had one son who ran a small travel agency in Paharganj. Father and son didn't get along, and the son didn't care about the father's shop. The son, too, was already married, and had for the past several years waited for his father to die so he could sell the Kwality Departmental Stores. Gulshan Arora seemed to have an inkling of his son's wishes: time and again after a serious illness he returned from the brink of death, as if to dash his son's hopes. Gulshan Arora placed great faith in Chandrakant, since he didn't have any other option. The store limped along, but Arora still had to pay expenses.

Gulshan Arora was by then totally alone; his wife had died a dozen or so years ago. He had detained Chandrakant at his house on several occasions for late-night rum-drinking and chicken-eating sessions. He told Chandrakant not to worry about his inevitable death: he had left the store to his younger daughter and had made a provision in his will for Chandrakant to the amount of 200,000 rupees. After the third or fourth drink, Gulshan Arora got animated and waxed philosophical. Chandrakant was aware that his boss, in spite of his age, brought home call girls, and was continuously taking herbal supplements and vitamin boosters called 'Lion Life,' 'Shot Gun,' and 'Hard Rock Candy Man' – these were the days before anyone had heard of Viagra or 40–60 Plus.

Chandrakant, while listening to his seventy-year-old boss's elaborate stories, would often begin to long for the man's death – and just then, Gulshan Arora by some means sensed his thoughts, smiled from ear to ear, and said, 'Chandu! Enough with your dreaming of my death. My father was eighty-two when he came here from Lahore in '47, and when he died in '74, he was over a hundred and ten. The neighbourhood had a huge celebration for his funeral procession, and we even hired the Daulatram Band and gave away endless sweets.'

It was then he showed the palm of his hand to Chandrakant. 'The astrologer told me that I've got at least thirty-five more years. Then, after I turn one hundred and five, I'm gonna get me on that morning train, loud and high right up to the sky! But don't you worry, Chandu. Your job's even more secure than a government one.

'Wrap up the rest of this chicken for your wife and be on your way,' he said to Chandrakant in a hushed voice. 'I've got a working girl on her way, and she'll be here any second. You get to work over there in Jahangirpuri, and I'll get to work over here in Model Town.'

But the children of Chandrakant and Shobha never got as old as Gulshan Arora's. One after the other, the babies born to them in that half-flat in bylane number seven kept dying. None lived longer than four months. Not one or two, but seven babies in a row.

5—MEXICO CITY

THE WATER WAS DRAINED

BY DIEGO GERARD

The water was drained, yet the city is still sinking...
The water was drained and now we must pull it uphill,
for miles on end...
The water in this city drives it to its ruin...

I

Water, in its geological nature, belongs where Mexico City now stands. The valley, home to over nine million people, used to be the lacustrine system of Texcoco, a body of water extending over one thousand two hundred square miles, the core of which became the heart of the Aztec empire, namely its capital, Tenochtitlan. In hindsight the obvious question arises: why build right on the lake and not around it, taking full advantage of the pristine resource?

Recent excavations suggest that Mexicas – the first Aztec tribe – settled on the lake with strategic military purposes, using the water around them as a defensive barrier. It is believed that the official myth of Tenochtitlan, which states that the Aztec empire would be built where an eagle perched over a cactus was found devouring a snake – an image forever captured on the Mexican flag – was an embellishment created to eclipse the gruesomeness of their own military actions.

Regardless of the myths, legends, or actual military strategies, the empire began to grow right on the lake, becoming one of the most powerful in Central America. The first technological hydraulic efforts were perfected under the lifespan and reign of Moctezuma II, the last Aztec emperor, circa 1500. The city developed an agricultural method called chinampas – superficial parcels nurtured by the lake beneath them – which became the city's building blocks, enabling Tenochtitlan to thrive above the surface of the water. The city continued to grow, leading to increased placement of land on the water, and gradually sucking in more of the diminishing lake.

Moctezuma II's death at hands of the Spanish conquistadors and the fall of his empire led to the complete draining of the lake and its tributaries. Through conquest and the new Spanish rule, Mexico City's landscape began to resemble what it has become. The lake was gone, but its trace remains as an eerie reminder of this unnatural path to progress. It is believed that Moctezuma II had plans to sustain the city's growth and preserve the metropolitan system that relied so heavily upon the lake. His death, though, and the consequences of the dry cityscape of his former, sacked empire, would make his figure return via the city's contemporary vernacular.

II

Mexico City's water supply system is the costliest and, probably, the most absurd in the planet. Sistema Cutzamala, developed in the 1940s, is the engineering project responsible for the water supply of the city and the rest of the metropolitan area, which is populated by nearly twenty-four million people.

A few facts to illustrate its absurdity: water is hydro-elevated from dams in neighbouring states for at least seventy-five miles, then treated at chlorination plants, and finally dropped into Mexico City's valley through more pipes and aquifers – collecting pollutants as it travels, and being chemically modified in its treatment plants and throughout the trajectory, before gushing from taps or travelling further in tanker-trucks. This system renders Mexico City's water as the most expensive in the world, providing a quality that hardly matches the investment, since the majority of the cost goes to propelling it uphill to make it available.

To make matters worse, the draining of the Texcoco Lake is not only directly linked to poor supply, but has presented a grimmer problem: getting the waste water – the infamous aguas negras (black waters) – out of the city. Once the questionable water is used, discharging it has become hazardous and expensive. Since there are no natural bodies of water left – no natural escape routes – the government has implemented pumping stations and a sewage system best known for its impossible blockages (I wonder which other city employs waste-divers to unclog sewers blocked by everything ranging from fecal matter and electronic waste, to animals carcasses and the occasional dead human body) to drive the water away.

As capitalism and our obsession with urbanism has taught us, the dirty water – once freed of the blockages by the divers – is tossed into the outskirts of the city, into underdeveloped, rural communities that have historically earned a living from agriculture. Their produce, sold en masse in Mexico City's markets, has been cultivated by black waters in which unique specimens of bacteria have settled, and which have therefore seeped into the food.

As writer and photographer Kurt Hollander discusses in his book *Several Ways To Die In Mexico City* (2012), the cultivation of food in waste-waters causes grave gastrointestinal illness, cholera, and salmonellosis as the clearest examples (source of inspiration for a photographic series of his, shooting a variety of bathrooms throughout Mexico, all of which were used to violently discharge what he previously ate).

Yet, best known as 'Moctezuma's Revenge', one of the severest consequences of the foul water affecting mostly tourists and visitors is a lack of acclimatization of the immune system to the bacterium that swims in our black waters, a type of helicobacter pylori unique in the world, that has managed to thrive in the city's water supply. Moctezuma's figure is thus summoned to the present.

It is thought that Moctezuma, dead at the hand of foreigners, represents the loathing of outsiders, and to some extent he has been reduced to this image. But what if – to fully understand the source of his mythological revenge and the appropriation of his name by a severe stomach ailment – we trace back to the draining of the lake after the downfall of his empire?

The first misstep in this horrid spiral is the treatment of water since conquest, of going against nature's ways.

But of course, diarrhea, salmonellosis, or even Moctezuma's Revenge may not be powerful enough evidence to seek a reversal towards sustainability. For further arguments, let us examine how the vestiges of the lake manifest themselves in a variety of ways.

III

On 19th September, in both 1985 and 2017, the land, appealing to its geological knowledge, reminded us that its power leaps far beyond Moctezuma's ghost.

Merely weeks ago, a 7.1 earthquake struck Mexico City – on a day when we were not only commemorating the deadly earthquake of 1985, but also performing simulacra across the city to be reminded of how we remain at nature's mercy, and even perhaps, of how we are enslaved by our past mistakes.

The earthquake's shockwaves ran into the lacustrine area, now overtaken by a superficial layer of pavement and buildings. Below this layer, the lake continues to bemoan its captor. The foundational base of a large part of the city is an unstable sediment of compressible sands saturated in water, where the alleged eagle once chose to devour the serpent, or where Mexicas found their concept of military safety. According to seismologist Victor Manuel Cruz-Atienza, who has studied the effects of shockwaves in the lacustrine area, what the soft, sandy matter beneath us does is exponentially amplify the oscillatory potency of the earthquake's waves. In the case of this recent earthquake, the shockwaves reached a potency of at least three hundred

times their actual strength in the lacustrine area alone –
the highest case of amplification documented in the world.
We saw buildings crumble to the ground, all of which were
erected where there was once water.

As me and many others hurried through the city in the
earthquake's aftermath, offering the little help we could, it
took only the naked eye to see the surviving slanted buildings lazily leaning and resting on each other as the soft
terrain continues to sink. What treacherous personification
– for it is only when they are toppled and reduced to rubble
that buildings seem to convey true alarm.

As I write this, running a hand over the smooth surface
of my desk, feeling for absolute stillness, I attempt to avert
my eyes and mind from the depleted state of our streets and
our communities, from our post-traumatic symptoms, and
try instead to zoom back in the mind's eye, picturing the
lake extending over the valley, the hills and firm ground in
the surrounding areas. But the image ultimately vanishes
and is overtaken by what I've endlessly seen through the
ready-made screen of an airplane window during approach:
buildings as far as the eye can see... no water.

6—TONGJIANG

GLORIOUS CITY OF FORGETTING

BY EMILY RUTH FORD

I remember the date clearly: 25th September, 2020. I left Factory Seven at 6 a.m., just like I do every day, breathing in the cool dawn air. A white sun zag-zigged across the empty sky. It takes fifteen-and-a-half minutes to walk across Tongjiang Intelligent Manufacturing Park to the metro station, down green paths lined with green trees, past creamy factory buildings where inside, edge-cutting machines work twenty-four hours a day. The air in the park hums with the energy of new things coming to life: cameras, toys, watches, lamps...

As the sun rose that morning, I crossed the park, descended below the earth and took the red line east. Commuting was the best part of my day. Our metro was only five years old then, with fifty lines, and in other cities across China, they were looking to Tongjiang as the model for a hyper-connected future. That morning, the station had more lines than passengers. The long platform stretching into the tunnel was completely deserted. Inside the train, the carriages gleamed like space-rockets.

When I arrived at Gaoxi, I took the escalator back up to earth, exited the station and stopped at the zebra crossing. My apartment building was on the opposing side of the speedway. In my nose and mouth I tasted wood dust from an old house being destroyed behind the station. The crashing of diggers filled my ears like flies. A pair of identical yellow Ferraris stared at each other, ahead of queues of stationary taxis, and revved their engines. I remember thinking it was unusual to see two copies of this costly car in the same spot, like car-twins. I glimpsed my reflection in the dark windows of one Ferrari as I crossed the six-lane speedway. My long fringe was matted from the hairnet I wore on duty at Factory Seven.

The apartment I shared with my husband was in a sky-rise situated in Gaoxi, on the outskirts of the city, thirty stories high and fifteen years old. Creeping smog stains had turned most of its pink façade grey. Some micro-bloggers on Weibo say pollution is a big problem in Tongjiang, but Mayor Wu says the air is actually getting cleaner on average, because more people are coming to live here. Across the street from our building was a fish market that smelled of rotting kelp and an underground liquor store selling pretend-label whisky bottles. Our building was not one of the new sky-rises in Tongjiang, the ones most people wanted to live in. In fact, fifteen years old was kind of ancient for the city. But we liked it well enough.

'Good morning, Mr. Yi!' I said to our doorman, who sat in his slime green plastic chair.

He stared up at me as I entered the hallway. He didn't say anything back. I wondered if he had just woken up from a nap. He was usually pretty friendly, for a doorman. Mr. Yi didn't have many people to talk to in the mornings, as my neighbours were rushing off to work or school. But because I was coming home from my shift, I always had plenty of time. Most days, I set my backpack down as I went in and we chatted, although sometimes he was too engrossed in mathematical puzzles and just nodded his head. When he was in a good mood, he'd offer me a steaming bun from a string bag, black sesame or chives, and growl at me in thick Tongjiang dialect, which always sounded to me like old people, like the past. Ten years before, Tongjiang had been a tiny speck on the eastern seaboard, just another unknown city somewhere north of Nanjing. Everyone spoke dialect in those days.

I shrugged off his strange behaviour, scooped a few letters from the cold metal mailbox and took the even-numbered elevator upwards to the twenty-second floor. I was looking forward to getting inside and practising my English. Even now, before I go to bed each morning, I study for half an hour.

Making a speech to a tape recorder like this, it's uneasy for me, but I'm more confident than I've ever been. I learned the basics at school – English grammar is pretty simple – but my pronunciation was strange back then and our textbooks were American primers from the '70s, so I must have sounded very out-fashioned. I don't know if an English person would have understood me, then. Now I work on my English by watching British shows on the internet video channel YouKu. My favourites are *Downton Abbey*, *Come Dine With Me* and *Robot Wars*. Especially *Robot Wars*. I learn a lot about British culture from watching these shows.

That morning, after I returned from work, I took the elevator upwards to the twenty-second floor. I came out onto our landing, which despite my efforts to clean it, always stank of mould. Piano notes trickled down from the floor above, Chopin or Schubert, I forget now. I remember thinking, 'The little girl at number 10A is getting really good.'

I turned left to go to our apartment, number 8C, yanked open the creaky metal lattice that cross-crissed the door and inserted my key into the lock. I tried to turn the key rightwise as usual, but the lock was stiff, as happened sometimes. I pressed hard on the buzzer and stepped back two paces. Our red New Year monkey charm swayed in the hallway breeze, its bells pealing like little bursts of monkey laughter. After a few seconds my husband Yan opened the door. His face was still pillow-creased from sleep. His expression was slate-blank.

'May I help you?' he asked.

'Ha ha, very funny,' I said. 'Don't play games now! I'm exhausted and I need to eat something before I pass out. And I have to study.'

'I'm afraid I don't understand,' Yan said. 'Do I know you?'

'What do you mean, "Do I know you?" Why are you being like this?' I said, annoyed by the cold in his voice. Then, I had a realisation. 'Oh Yan, you're sleepwalking again!'

Yan stared at me.

'Sleepwalking?' He pinched both arms with his fingers and rolled his neck around. 'I don't think so. I feel completely awake. Who did you say you are again?'

'What on the earth are you talking about?' I said.

A light stirred in his face. 'Is this about the electricity bill? You're the new inspector?' he said. 'I'm sorry, I know, I'm behind with payments. I've been a bit disorganised lately. So much paperwork these days! I promise I'll pay it today.'

'Why are you saying these things?' I said. I must say that at this moment I felt a fear rising inside me, although I knew there must have been some undermisstanding. 'What's going on here, Yan? Let me in!'

My husband rubbed his forehead with the back of his hand. He needed to cut his fingernails, I noticed, making a mental note to remind him about it later. His nails were long and the ones on his left hand were stained golden from where he held his cigarette. This did not seem like the time to bring it up.

'I'm afraid we haven't met before,' Yan said, adopting the polite tone he uses when dealing with a person he suspects may be crazy, or trying to sell him something. 'I've never seen you before in my life. There must be a mistake happening. Are you in the right building? Are you positive you're not the electricity inspector?'

'What do you mean, you haven't seen me before?' I said. 'Yan, I'm Xifan! Your wife! Since nearly five years, feels like longer. For goodness sake, let me in!'

Whatever this game was, I wished he would knock it out. We had been below-staffed at the camera factory that night, and I'd spent the whole shift running around, restarting machines and complaining at junior workers for not tying their hair back. I could feel small blisters forming on my face from where the plastics furnace had burned my skin. My eyes stung from the chemicals we poured onto the camera lenses. Inside my canvas plimsolls, my sockless feet were rubbed raw.

Puzzlement twitched in Yan's face. I know all his expressions, much better than my own. He's a car mechanic who likes to work things out in a very orderly and methodical way. He's not usually a trickster.

'I have a wife,' he said slowly. 'Xifan. She works night shifts in the factory park over in the western district.' He looked at his watch. 'She should be coming home right about now, actually.'

I felt tears bubble up behind my eyes. I clenched my teeth together and took a breath.

'I'm sorry,' Yan said, and moved to close the door. 'I hope you find who you're looking for.'

I stared at my front door, waited a minute or two, then rang the buzzer again, several times, like a crazy woman. The lift dinged. Our neighbour got out and gave me a strange look, going quickly inside Flat 8B.

My husband opened the door again, wearily. 'Yes?' he said. 'I told you before, I don't know you!'

'Yan,' I said. 'I have no idea what's going on here. But I wish you would cut it off. It's me, Xifan. Li Xifan! I am twenty-five years old. I am your wife. I can prove it to you! Ask me anything you want!'

Yan rubbed his eyes wearily. 'I'm not really sure–'

'Your name is Liu Yan.' I interrupted him, trying my hardest to sound patient and not hysterical, as I was beginning to feel. 'Your favourite food is fish ball soup! Each night before we go to bed you swallow fat yellow Yaoyao pills for back pain!'

By this point I was effectively yelling. 'You pretend to fix Volkswagens for a living but really you're swapping the engines for fakes. You phone-call your mother in Suzhou at 8 p.m. every Sunday and complain about her for the rest of the night. Let me in and I will show you photo albums with a million pictures of us together!'

My husband shook his head and I felt the inside of my chest turn to frost.

'I'm so sorry,' he said, closing the door. 'There must be some kind of mistake. I honestly have no idea who you are.'

I like my job at Factory Seven well enough, but in private, I have other dreams. In my spare time, I am studying to be a tour guide. Sometimes, I show visiting German groups around the factories when they come to China to buy ball bearings or rubber tyres. The Board for the Promotion of Glorious Tongjiang says our city is one of the most under-rated metropolises on China's eastern seaboard and it is the responsibility of all residents to change perceptions.

That's why studying English is so important to me. I don't mean to brag, but I've always been good at languages. My father is from Wenzhou, and the Wenzhounese are famous for their devilish dialect with eight different tones, so perhaps that gave me an ear for sounds. My mother's family doesn't know where they are from. The government moved them across the country in the 1960s, back when many Chinese were strangers in new places, and my grand-mother could not remember her home village to tell us before she died. There are many memories in my family's history that I do not know. I suppose that's not so unnormal.

That morning when Yan didn't recognise me, I felt despair like I had never felt before. After he closed the door the second time, I pressed the buzzer and rattled the lattice, but he didn't answer. Inside, I was crying. Yet I still believed there was an undermisstanding. We argued sometimes, but mostly we had a good marriage. We first met as nursery pupils, then when we were nineteen, we saw ourselves again and talked in love with one another. My mother used to say she could see my father in Yan, and that was a compliment, because she loves my father like an angel. I knew that Yan would never hurt me deliberately. He would be horrified if he knew what he had done.

'Xifan, you are a rational woman,' I reminded myself that morning. 'Most likely, he will simply go back to sleep, wake up again and everything will return to normal.'

I took the elevator back down to earth, as I tried to figure out what to do. 'Hello Mr. Yi,' I said to the doorman, who was sitting in his plastic chair. Mr. Yi frowned, and it struck me then why he had looked at me so strangely before. There was a feeling building in my stomach, like a terror yet to be born.

I left our sky-rise and crossed over Gaoyu Lu to the neighbourhood café selling tea and congee. It was a tiny place, with four tables covered in yellow plastic tablecloths and a halogen strip-light in the ceiling with bugs trapped inside. I am not sure, but at least one bug in there always seemed to be alive.

The café served congee from 6 a.m. until 6 p.m. Sitting at any one of the four tables you could see directly into the kitchen, where an overfat, dimple-faced chef from Dong'an, whom I secretly nicknamed Pork Chop, stirred huge pots and sang tunelessly under his breath. I went to this café at least twice a week, so I knew all three workers by their faces – the café owner, the waitress and Pork Chop. We were about as friendly as you can be to another person without knowing their name.

I walked into the café. It was empty. I sat down at a table and smoothed out the sticky creases in the yellow tablecloth while I waited. Through the window, I could see the Gaoyu Lu youtiao-seller handing out fried dough sticks to customers. The Tongjiang authorities have cleared away most of the street hawkers, because they feel they're non-hygienic for such a modern city, but on my street there were still one or two left. The waitress came over and set down a glass. She was young and slender with thick hair that fell to her waist. The waitress reminded me of how I looked once, before I went out to work at the factory. She must have served me congee with dried fish flakes a thousand times. When she bent down, her skin smelt like talcum powder and lilies.

'I'll have the usual, please,' I said.

The waitress frowned, her soft forehead creasing like a spider-web.

'I'm so sorry, I don't recall ever seeing you in here before,' she said, tipping her chin downward in embarrassment. 'I must be having a complete memory blank! You know how it is, so many customers, some days I have trouble recognising my own face! What would you like to eat?'

'Fish-flake congee and lemon tea, please,' I said quickly, so she wouldn't hear my panic.

After a few minutes, the waitress brought my food, then sat down at the neighbouring table and opened a gossip magazine. A minute later she yawned, then she took out her phone and selfied. I ate the hot, salty congee in silence and listened to the muffled sound of the kitchen radio as I thought what to do about my situation.

The radio was reporting a news broadcast from Beijing. A chemical explosion had struck a battery plant in China's interior, killing four hundred workers. The radio said the factory owners had bribed safety inspectors to give them a good report, even though the machines were non-functioning. President Huang says corruption is a cancer we all must help destroy. I agree, although I am not really into politics. It mostly feels very distant from my life.

A few strangers had gathered outside the café, darkening the glass and making my face seeable in the window. I swept my fringe to one side and looked at my reflection to see if I could tell what had changed. I'm not what most people would call pretty, but I've always liked my face. I have sleepy eyes that remind people of my grandmother, fairer-than-average skin, and a button nose. I looked hard at my face in the window. I looked tired, but apart from that, nothing seemed different.

I went back over the events of the morning, just as I have recounted them in this speech. Three people had not recognised me at this point: Mr. Yi, Yan and the young waitress.

'What's happening?' I whispered, as I replayed the morning's encounters in my mind. I felt like I was trapped inside an impossible puzzle. Or perhaps nothing was happening and I was stuck in a dream. I swept a few fish flakes off the tablecloth, put my head on my arms, and fell asleep.

When I awoke the young waitress was nudging me, a look of concern lifting her long eyelashes into her eyebrows. I raised my head reluctantly, unsticking strands of my hair that had got glued to the congee bowl.

'Are you okay?' she asked. 'You were talking in your sleep!'

'I'm sorry,' I said. 'I'm just tired, that's all. I work night shifts, so usually I'm in bed by now.' She crinkled her eyes as if to say, no problem. I beamed at her vigorously, in case going to sleep had changed something and she recognised me this time. She nodded her head and turned away, her long hair swaying at her back. I fished a two hundred yuan note out of my backpack and folded it under the sugar shaker, along with a few scattered copper mao.

I should mention a little about Tongjiang. Tongjiang today is a much more glorious city than when I was growing up. The authorities have made so many improvements that it is almost impossible to describe how much better our lives are. Last year the Tongjiang government tore down every building older than twenty years and built them all back up again, taller and completely uniform, with dormitories that can fit twice as many factory workers as before. There are sixteen million permanent residents in Tongjiang and five million migrants from the villages.

This causes problems, sometimes. For example, the countryside workers at my factory speak mostly in dialect. Sometimes I cannot understand my team, who come from just a few hundred miles away. It's a little unefficient. I look forward to the day when dialects are gone for good and every Chinese speaks perfect, standard putonghua.

What else should I mention? Last year the government diverted the river with a hyper-electric dam so that the water no longer has to go through the city but flows directly to the ocean. They built a super-high speedway where the river used to run. They replaced the confusing old streets with five huge ring roads that made it much simpler to drive around town. And since people stopped going to the temples decades ago, they have been turned into 7/11s and online shopping portals. That's just a few examples of progress. Some Tongjiangers say our city is changing too fast and they don't know it any more. They look out of their bedroom windows in the morning and a sky-rise has gone up overnight, disrupting the view. GPS doesn't work here, because the streets are multiplying so quickly the maps can't update fast enough. Taxi drivers get so frustrated, they toss you out onto the sidewalk. I can see how all that is annoying. But mostly, I find the change exhilarating.

I walked out of the café onto Gaoyu Lu. It was raining, fat black drops crying themselves out of the sky. As I stood outside the café, looking up at the rain dancing in the trees, a man in his forties whom I had never seen before stopped walking and gaped at me. He carried a Louis Vuitton bag and smiled a smile that seemed too wide for his face. His receding hairline drew back from his temples, like the sea going out. I always feel slightly sorry for bald men, even though I feel baldness can be quite handsome, sometimes.

'Xifan?' he said. 'Li Xifan? Oh my gosh, is it really you? I was beginning to think I would never see you again!'

He moved in to hug me and I felt my muscles tense up. His embrace was tight, like a distant elderly uncle. I put my arms heart-halfedly around him.

'We must have dinner, old friend! What do you say?' he said, clasping my arm. 'There's a great new hotpot place on the corner of Changping Lu and Huaile. They import the beef direct from Mongolia. The grass is different up there on the plains and it makes for incredibly tasty meat. What if I call you later in the week and we get something in the diary?'

I wanted to shout out to this man through the rain, 'I don't know who you are! Stop touching me!' But I felt so stung from Yan's cold towards me earlier that morning that I hesitated. Who knew, perhaps we did know each other from somewhere and I had forgotten this man, unlikely as that seemed. After all, he must have had my number if he was planning to phone-call me.

'That sounds great, old friend,' I said, with all the fake enthusiasm I could find. 'I'll wait for your call.'

I stood on the sidewalk for a few minutes, even more con-fused than before, until the rain dried up and the morning sun warmed my cheeks. September in Tongjiang is a glorious month. The heat of high summer has left, but it's still balmy and welcoming. That year, in July, temperatures hit a record for our province, forty-three degrees at night. The tarmac on the roads melted in coaly puddles. It was so hot that teenagers sizzled eggs on the sidewalk and BBC journalists came to film it.

The heat sparked accidents, too. Glass panes the size of cars started falling out of sky-rises onto the streets below. A girl who worked in Factory Eight had her body crushed by a pane. It was frightening: she was exactly the age of me. An investigation found the sky-rise architects had paid crooked middlemen to give them cheap glue, so they could steal the rest of the money, but the glue wasn't safe at high temperatures and melted, making the glass fall out. The authorities put the architects on trial, and they were sentenced to death, quite correctly.

I left the congee café and began walking east, towards Tongjiang Mainline Station. Our new railway station is my favourite place in the city, maybe the world, and sometimes I go there just to relax. The old station was the most ancient in China, a traditional wooden relic, without any particular charm. This one has thirty magnetic levitation platforms in a hall as huge as five aircraft hangars. There is a viewing deck where I like to look out over the tracks, lined up as far as the eyes can see. Right now, only three are in use: Tongjiangers can go direct to Shanghai, Guangzhou or Nanjing. But soon hypersonic rail will arrive and then, those tracks will take us all over China.

This kind of improvement is something I struggle to describe in English. One Chinese word I teach to the

German groups who come to Tongjiang is 'fangbian'. Fangbian literally means convenient, but its meaning goes a lot deeper than the English word. Fangbian is something that transforms the quality of your life. Imagine a giant 7/11 that opens twenty-four hours a day and drone-flies any product you want directly to you, just whenever you imagine it. I've heard that in Europe, shops and buildings are very old and services don't work so well. If my groups take home anything from China, I hope it is this concept of fangbian. I believe it is a truly life-altering idea.

As I walked, the traffic on the road bridge above me sounded like rushing sea waves. I went right to head down to the station, turned the corner and stopped dead, astonished. Si Lu, the street that led to Tongjiang Mainline Station, was gone. In its place stood a giant, mirrored sky-rise, staring down at me like a glass god. I felt a sting of sad for the old street that had vanished. Even though new buildings are glorious, they can be rather upheaving when you are not expecting them.

I took my phone out of my backpack and phone-called my father. I knew he would have good advice. My dad doesn't like how fast things are changing in Tongjiang. When I was growing up, we lived in an old-China style home, where families shared joined-up apartments, using the same hallways and bathrooms, so we saw our neighbours many times a day. Now he and my mother have their own flat in a sky-rise, but he leaves the front door open because otherwise he feels too private. We were very poor when I was a child, but because of all the progress my life has jump-frogged my dad's. I bought my first mobile phone before he even had a landline. Soon I will be able to afford a car, although he has never owned one.

'Hello, baba dear,' I said, as I heard him ask my mother to bring him a glass of water. It made me happy just to hear his croaky voice. I looked up to see the white sun directly above me. Midday. The sun had vanished my shadow. I tried to keep my voice controlled and feelingless.

'Baba, I just thought I'd say hi. How are you this morning?'

'Leilei!' he said. 'It's so wonderful to hear from you! But a bit early for phone-calling, isn't it? Shouldn't you be at work? And why are you calling me baba, silly.'

'Who's Leilei?' I asked, confused. 'You mean cousin Leilei? Baba, it's me, Xifan. Your only child!'

I longed with every part of my body for him to be joking.

'I haven't heard from Xifan in a little while,' my dad said, thoughtfully. 'She usually calls on Sundays, though. How about you come visit this weekend, Leilei dear? We'll ask Xifan too, and your aunt can make jiaozi and garlic greens. How's your mother by the way?'

I looked at the screen to check I had dialled the right number, but I knew it was my dad's voice in there, loud and transparent. I let my phone fall down to the street where it cracked like a stupid egg. I didn't care. I could hear his voice in there, still chatting away. I sank onto the warm tarmac and cried.

There are many ways to be forgotten. But I did not choose my fate. The events I have described in this speech occurred three years ago today. The International Memory Inquiry says that since then, at least four million forgettings have been recorded in Tongjiang. People wake up and their families, their friends, their workmates do not recognise them. We tell someone our names and are forgotten again, instantly. It is as though our faces have simply been deleted from the collective memory bank. Because of this, many people are frightened of us. There is a non-spoken stigma around being forgotten.

Since the epidemic broke out, I have talked to oral history researchers, medical professionals, memory scientists. The Inquiry thinks I was Patient X, or one of the first. That's an honour, I suppose. No one has yet been able to explain the forgettings, but I know Harvard has put its best scientists on the case, and I hope this account will help understandings.

I had to leave my job and find a new home in a dormitory, although once the forgettings became better understood, Factory Seven allowed me to return, and now I wear a badge with my name and title on it, so people know who I am. It is not easy to manage workers when they do not recognise you, however.

Yan has not dealt with what happened well. He is a proud man and I imagine he does not like to think he is a victim of a forgetting, even a sideways one. Some days I take the metro to the Volkswagen garage where he works and ask him a stupid question, like how often I should change the oil in my pretend car, or where the cheap place to buy diesel is. Once, I overheard him telling a customer that his wife died in a factory fire.

I have not been home since I was forgotten. I don't want to scare my parents. I saw my dad on the metro six months ago and although I would not usually do this, I ran over to hug him. I couldn't control it. 'Baba!' I shouted, and he shrieked like he was being attacked by wolves.

Despite everything that has happened, I try to look to the positive side. I am twenty-eight years old, and have many years of living in front of me. I run a support group for forgottens where we talk about what's happened to us. We write down our names and stories and wear identifying hats, so we know we are dealing with the same friends as before. Not everyone copes, though. An elderly neighbour in Gaoxi jumped out of a sky-rise and the criminal rate has gone up too, because forgottens have nothing, and no one remembers who we are.

Some days I dream that the change will go backwards and I will reclaim my old place in life. In the meantime, I try to look on the bright side. I have no responsibilities, no duties; not to my parents, not to Yan. Some of my former friends live in unhappy marriages where they feel the other person does not know them, but because they are remembered, they cannot escape. On the contrary, I am free to live my life just as I like. These days, when I take German groups around the factories, sometimes I tell them my name is Xifan. Other times I make up something completely different. Just however my mood takes me.

THE BROKEN DOLL
A Novel Extract

BY LIZA ALEXANDROVA-ZORINA
TRANSLATED BY NATASHA PEROVA

A person's fate descends on him in various ways: attacking
him from around the corner as a killer, or gripping him
mercilessly as a migraine. This time it shuffled towards Iva
in the shape of a lame old woman with a grey face and faded
eyes. She examined Iva hanging over her crouched body on
the station floor.

'Where're you from?'

Iva ignored her but she wouldn't leave her alone.

'Your papers okay?'

Iva shook her head.

'D'you need work? What can you do?'

'I locked myself out of my apartment...'

The old gimpy led Iva to a nearby construction site, fenced
in with cement blocks and barbed wire. Inside there were row
upon row of two-story metal bunk-huts for builders, which
you could only get to the upper floor by using a wobbly lad-
der. Some of the huts were occupied by construction workers
– swarthy, short-legged men with gold teeth – while others

were up for rent. Inside were narrow cots and bedside tables, a dim, battery-operated lamp kept winking and crackling.

'You can spend the night here and we'll start tomorrow. Are you hungry?'

Iva dropped on the bed, her whole body aching, colic scraping her insides as if she'd swallowed a handful of nails.

'I've been watching you at the station. I thought to myself, this girl's a goner. I've seen so many go downhill there.' The old woman put the kettle on to boil. 'You're lucky I kept my eye on you.'

'I locked myself out of my apartment... Can you help me?' Iva muttered.

'I'll help you, but it'll cost you something...' the gimpy chuckled.

In the morning the old woman took Iva to a basement full of apathetic women with faces like bread soaked in milk. They washed her hair under a tap, gave her a sloppy haircut, dyed it with some nasty-smelling stuff that tickled her nose, then rinsed and dried it. Iva looked in the mirror and cried out in horror.

'Now you're Olga Golub.' The old woman introduced the carrot-haired image in the mirror to Iva.

Iva stroked her short-cropped, peroxided head and thought that her double now looked much more like Iva Nova than herself.

'Here, take your papers.' The old woman gave her a passport, work-record card, and medical certificate.

The girl looking at Iva from the passport photograph was visibly younger than she and had a peasant's face.

'Where is this Olga now? What has happened to her?' Iva asked, but no one answered.

Then they took a suburban train from the same station. Riding in a half empty car Iva watched the landscapes flowing past: construction sites in progress, apartment blocks looking like termite mounds, abandoned warehouses, garbage dumps topped with rusted car skeletons and smoking bonfires, shabby little houses perched along the roadsides, goods vans loaded with black ore overflowing on the rails, and the seemingly unending fences, covered with graffiti, stretching along the railway. Somewhere far away there was her past life, her new apartment, her training sessions and book launches, but the train was carrying her away from the Iva Nova she used to be only recently.

They arrived at the station and went towards a seven-story building surrounded by a wall, with a gate guarded by a shaggy old mongrel. The ground-floor windows were curtained so tightly that sunlight never penetrated them. The railway bridge rattled loudly when a train passed over it, making the windowpanes vibrate like birds with broken wings.

'I've brought a new one,' the old woman nodded at Iva and they were let in.

Autumn was eating the trees like rust and despite the warm weather there was a breath of cold wind in the air. Iva looked at her reflection in a puddle and stepped on it to destroy the image.

'Are you nuts, or what?' The old woman shouted and started wiping off dirty drops from her skirt.

It was quiet in the hostel, as if nobody lived there. Iva lowered her voice to a whisper:

'Won't I get into trouble with the false papers?'

'These are your papers. Don't be a fool.' The old woman raised her voice and gave her a push.

In a crowded room with windows facing a concrete wall there was a young woman behind a computer, her eyes radiating tired anger. She looked through the papers and typed on the keys with such force that Iva had a fit of toothache.

'Packer? Stacker? Cashier?'

'Cashier,' the old woman answered for Iva.

'Twenty shifts? Thirty?'

'Thirty.'

The woman shrugged, produced some forms and pushed them to Iva.

Iva started reading them at which point the woman shrieked: 'I'm not going to waste a whole day on you.' She threw her a pen. 'Don't be a pest. Just sign it.'

The hostel's walls were papered with all sorts of warnings: 'No smoking!' 'No littering!' 'No noise!' 'Don't open!' 'For men only!' 'For women only!' And dozens of rules and prohibitions on each floor: you can't bring in strangers, you can't stay here without registration, no drinking on the premises, music only with earphones, no washing your clothes in the sink, et cetera, et cetera.

'Toilet and shower room...' the old woman pointed to the door at the end of the corridor, making a grimace at the smell coming from it. 'You've got to get up early and wait in line for at least an hour to get in. Canteen is on the ground floor. You're not allowed to cook here. If they find a kettle or an electric stove in your room, they'll expel you right away.'

The old woman unlocked one of the doors and pushed Iva inside, where the room's six bunks with bedside tables reminded Iva of a hospital. The floor and windowsills were so cluttered with bags and things that you couldn't move without stumbling on a shoe or a plastic bag.

'Here's your bed. Bedside tables are for two. Don't touch what's not yours and keep an eye on your own things. This floor is for women. Men are upstairs.'

'That's good,' said Iva looking around.

'Nothing good about it.' The gimpy snickered. 'There's nothing more terrible than a women's prison or a nunnery. Better to be with men, if you ask me.'

At this point the room's inmates came in: gloomy, tired women with saucer-like pale faces and colourless eyes. They dropped on their bunks and fell asleep.

'Good evening,' Iva said, but nobody even looked in her direction.

An emaciated hunchback woman brought a stack of flatbreads which she started taking out of her plastic bag, holding each with both hands as if they were heavy bricks.

'May I have one?' Iva begged. 'Please.'

The old hunchback eyed her angrily and threw a flatbread on her bunk. Iva devoured it under the blanket.

Morning hung beyond the window like faded linen. Opening her eyes, Iva already felt dead-tired, as if it were evening.

'Good morning, Nobody,' she said to her reflection in the dirty mirror. Her roommates had gone out before dawn, leaving a rank smell of sweat; only the old hunchback was watching Iva suspiciously from her bunk, her feet sticking out from under a shortish blanket as if she were a corpse.

'Thanks for the flatbread,' Iva said to the old woman, but had no answer.

Iva looked out of the door and saw a long line to the bathroom: sleepy women with flabby features shifted from foot to foot, swaying and muttering under their breath. Suddenly they fell silent, as a sunray gliding between the rooftops and the railway bridge looked into the dark corridor through the half-open window and licked at the hostel inmates.

'Are you Olga?' A long-nosed girl in a blue uniform stood before Iva. 'Have your breakfast and get on the bus, quick. Don't make us wait.'

Iva went down to the canteen where a fat woman in a white coat was dispensing thin porridge. Iva rinsed her hands under a rusty tap over which she read: 'No washing your laundry!' 'No washing your feet!' She joined the line.

'If you work hard you won't go hungry,' said one woman.

'I worked at a candy factory for a week, wrapping candy, my fingers got all numb and sore. I was happy when this job at the bakery turned up. Now I pack loaves of bread, they're so soft and warm – it's good work.'

'Where's your lunch box?' the cook barked at Iva when her turn came.

Iva had nothing to say and only looked around in terror.

'Newcomer?' Someone asked. 'She's new,' they explained to the cook who cursed and threw a plastic box with food at Iva.

'What's this?' Iva asked in surprise.

'Your lunch,' the line behind her shouted and pushed Iva aside. 'Get going!'

There were no vacant seats at the table and so she squatted near the door, which struck her a few times when someone pushed it too hard. She drank the porridge from the plate and then ate up the meatball noodles from her lunch box. She stroked her full belly and suppressed a burp. It was definitely better here than at the station or under the bridge. Her lost apartment and, indeed, her past life appeared like a dream now – anyone could take her by the hand and lead her wherever they liked, and she'd obediently follow without asking any questions. She couldn't care less.

The bus was already waiting in the yard and a group of women, young and old, thin as rakes or fat as loaves, lined up to get in, while the long-nosed girl in the blue uniform counted them.

'Where the devil have you been? Get in.'

A roll-call began. The long-nosed attendant called out the names and marked them in her list.

'Olga Golub!'

No one answered.

'Olga Golub!'

'Here!' Iva remembered. The woman gave her an angry look.

The bus was so overcrowded that Iva had to sit on the steps. The women slept the whole way, hugging their bags. When the bus jumped on a bump in the road, their heads hopped like balls. The bus smelled of petrol and unwashed hair. The two-hour drive crouched on the steps gave Iva swollen legs and back pain.

They stopped at a trade centre that was covered with adverts like an old suitcase plastered with stickers from foreign hotels. The trade centre stood among grey construction sites, windowless warehouses, garages, and car parks.

The women fell out of the bus and followed the long-nosed attendant, who counted them again and prodded them: 'Get a move on!' They passed down a long corridor, climbed a narrow staircase smelling of fried potatoes, and arrived in a cold cloak room where some employees were changing into uniforms. Iva said hallo, but no one paid any attention. Iva was issued her uniform and a little key to her locker.

'Change into this. Quick.'

Iva put on an oversized white shirt and a tight red skirt in which she had to mince. She tied a red cravat around her neck and stuffed her hair under a funny bonnet. The attendant pinned a badge to her shirt that said, 'Olga Golub – Trainee', and led her to the shop floor.

'You'll have two-days' coaching at the till and then you'll work on your own. You won't get paid for the days of coaching. From time to time you'll be asked to help pack, stock shelves, clean, wash floors, whatever. Lunch break is half an hour, and so is supper. You're not allowed to leave your work station for a smoke or to go to the toilet, only with the permission of the administrator.'

At till point Number Seven, Iva was met by a young man with a pock-marked face and crooked shoulders like a broken clothes hanger. His glasses had finger-thick lenses and when he read the checks it looked like he was licking them.

'I won't stay here long,' said Iva stubbornly to herself, shaking off her stupor. She examined her work station and imagined how one day she'd stuff the money under her shirt, leave her post quietly without attracting the security guards' attention, leave the shop floor casually, discard the silly bonnet, and dissolve in the crowd.

'I won't stay here long,' she repeated out loud so that the pock-marked man raised his brows in surprise.

'I'll tell the security guards to keep an eye on you,' the attendant said by way of goodbye.

While her tutor was showing her how the cash register worked, he tried to press against her body and touch her breasts. He breathed in her ear as he spoke, tickling and nauseating her at the same time. He finished each sentence with a short nervous giggle.

'Hallo. Cash or credit card?' He giggled.

'Hallo. Cash or credit card?' Iva repeated through clenched teeth.

'Take a quick look at each customer. Watch out for those with big bags, and they may also hide small items under their jackets. Remember, if security catches a customer with stolen goods, you'll be fined, not them.'

'Take a quick look...' Iva repeated mechanically.

'Scan each item, put them in plastic bags, show the customer the sum total, and if he agrees, you print out a receipt.'

'...print out a receipt...' mumbled Iva after him.

'Have a nice day. Come again.'

'Have a nice day. Come again.'

'And then immediately to the next customer: "Hallo. Cash or credit card?"'

'Hallo. Cash or credit card?'

The shop opened and cashiers dressed in white shirts and red skirts took their places at the tills. The first customers arrived and wandered alone in the labyrinths of food shelves while the slant-eyed administrators scoured around the cashiers supervising their every move.

'Let's have a rehearsal now. I'll be a customer.' Her coach burned her neck with his breath as he spoke.

'Hallo. Cash or credit card?' Iva pretended that she was taking foodstuffs from a basket, putting them in plastic bags, and printing out a receipt. 'Have a nice day. Come again... Hallo. Cash or credit card?'

The first customers looked like ordinary human beings

to Iva, with heads and bodies, she remembered their faces, intonations and gestures, she repeated the words they said, nibbling them as a chicken bone, and saying as they left: Have a nice day... Have a nice day... Have a nice day...

But then their images started crumbling and blurred into a long series of smiles, pressed lips, wrinkled noses like shapeless tumors, mouths spitting out words, puffed plump faces, anxious fussy hands counting coins, prodding banknotes, re-packing their purchases, fumbling in their purses, wiping their necks, collecting their change and receipts. They touched Iva's hands with their coarse fingers so that she wanted to wipe off their sticky touches with a wet rag soaked in some acid solution. The wet rag was intended for cleaning the cash register once an hour and those who forgot to do that were fined by the vigilant administrators. Fines threatened them at every step.

'Hallo...' Iva said trying to smile but managing only a grimace, like a child about to break into a sob. 'Have a nice day! Come again... Hallo...'

The human line flickering before her eyes made her mix up buttons on the cash register and her pock-marked coach had to remove the spoiled receipts, pressing on her with his whole body and suffocating her with his rancid sweat. He giggled while the customers stared angrily at Iva: 'Why so slowly?'

Iva cringed but made more errors all the same, so that finally her coach had to replace her.

'Sorry, I'm just learning. This is my first day,' Iva apologised.

She was terrified of running into someone she knew – as if anyone could have recognised the former Iva in this haggard woman with a puffy face and reddish tufts sticking out from under her ridiculous bonnet.

By lunchtime the crowd had merged into one large blur as if Iva were seeing it through a glass bottle. She felt like a tart who'd been gang-raped by a whole regiment.

'Cashier Number Seven – lunch break,' her administrator announced.

Her coach heaved a sigh of relief and led Iva to the staff room. His shoulders twitched and his legs jerked as if he had beetles in his pants.

'Today you have an hour for lunch, toilet, shopping. If you take a nap let no one see it.'

The staff room was full of women hurriedly eating from their lunch boxes like the one Iva got in the morning. Iva watched in dismay how they gobbled up their food without chewing properly to be done with it as soon as they could.

She went outside where, under the sign 'No smoking', a group of sales people and security guards were smoking away while taxi drivers walked to and fro calling out 'Taxi... taxi...' The pock-marked man lighted a cigarette and offered one to Iva.

'You know, life is so arranged that every second of it costs money.' He giggled.

'I know it only too well. Would you help me?'

Her coach turned away, watching the cars parked around the trade centre.

'I'll give you an expensive car for it.'

He said nothing, looking at Iva through his thick lenses.

'I need to break the door of an apartment...'

'No, no... I won't get involved in anything like that...' He laughed and ground out his cigarette.

'Oh, it's nothing like that... it's my own apartment...

Wait...' But the man had already dived inside and the doors had closed behind him.

While Iva's body was sitting at the till and she repeated like a mechanical doll, 'Hallo. Cash or credit card... Have a nice day. Come again...' she was actually sleeping with her eyes open and seeing dreams about her past life. She could no longer distinguish between dreams and reality. In her continual nightmare, she was surrounded by masked characters from posters, their eyes covered with coins as if they were corpses, and she expected an alarm clock to ring and dispel the horror, so she'd wake up in her own apartment with the unpacked boxes. But the alarm clock did not ring. Her pock-marked coach glanced at Iva's face crumpled with fatigue, shuddered and sent her to the delicatessen section.

Giggling young women, flushed from the hot ovens, packed roasted chickens in paper bags and removed cakes and pies from red-hot baking sheets onto trays. Iva had seen so many people during the day that she could no longer tell them apart, like a prosopagnosia patient; she could now perceive the surrounding world only as a chorus of sounds: the thunder of rolling carts, coughing, laughter, crackling of oil in the frying pan, whispered obscenities, voices from the loudspeakers – 'Dear customers...' – broken glass, cell phones ringing, music from the radio in the staff room, and voices, voices, and more voices: 'Please... Thank you... Please... Thank you... A chicken and two burgers please... Shall I heat them up... No thanks... It's my turn... Hallo... Have a nice day... Come again...' The kitchen smells made her head swim. Swallowing the bile rising in her throat, she rushed from the oven with chickens roasted on skewers to the counter with a demanding faceless crowd behind it.

When the crowd dispersed, she collapsed on the floor in utter exhaustion and pressed her head to her knees. But she was immediately pulled up and slapped on the face with a dirty kitchen towel.

'Get up, fool. It's not allowed, they'll fine you.'

Pretending to be working Iva moved the pies from one tray to another, barely managing to resist the temptation of putting one in her mouth. She listened to the women around her talking. Some of them expressed themselves with only nouns and adverbs, others with just verbs, and if they lacked words, they used gestures and grimaces: 'She came over... shouted so... fined me... I cried and cried... Then said to myself, 'forget it'... get over it... I'll survive... children, school, money, husband, mistress... Tiny wages, miserable life...' They wiped their tears but also giggled all the time.

Someone took Iva by the hand and she followed obediently with eyes half-closed, avoiding the loaders dashing about, who tried to pinch her. When she opened her eyes, she found herself in a kitchen with huge stoves caked in filthy soot and sinks the size of bathtubs stretching along the walls. Someone threw a pair of rubber gloves and a sponge to Iva, led her to one of the sinks with a tower of dirty plates, miraculously not collapsing, and barked:

'They're yours.'

Iva picked off a piece of burnt dough from a sheet and put it in her mouth. For an hour it was as if she were in a trance, washing dishes and suffering terrible hunger pangs, as if an invisible hand were winding her intestines on its fist. When Iva stopped washing and raised her head, she saw other women bent over the other sinks scrubbing black frying pans and probably wondering why their lives had been ruined like a burnt supper.

The bus was waiting at the bus stop. Iva got on and took the first vacant seat. The other women protested but Iva fell asleep instantly, as if she'd lost consciousness. She didn't wake up even when the bus bumped over the pitted road and her head hit the window. The uniformed attendant had to slap her on the face, scratching her with a long blue fingernail.

'Get up, we've arrived.'

The clock struck midnight and in one of the rooms the radio played the national anthem, solemn and sinister. Iva saw a pregnant woman walking towards her down the corridor and imagined it was an apparition which would disappear if she touched it, so she poked her belly with a finger and felt how tight it was and quite real, of course. The pregnant woman screamed and jerked away, glaring at Iva.

'Hallo...' said Iva to everyone she met. 'Hallo... Hallo... Hallo.'

No one paid any attention to her, they shuffled past her, completely depleted after the day's work, and only a one-eyed old man returned her greeting, scratching his head.

'Have a nice day. Come again,' Iva answered, waving to him.

Reaching her room, she collapsed on her bunk and listened to the trains thundering over the railway bridge, the hunchback's snoring, and the Asiatic women either praying or crying in their beds. In her dream she was still in the supermarket, overcrowded with evil-looking people, while a stranger by the name of Come-Again threw coins at her and stuck out his tongue, which turned out to be a cash register tape. 'Hallo... Hallo... Hallo...' Iva muttered tossing in her bed.

'If hell exists it must be something like a supermarket,' an old man collecting wastepaper baskets said, and winked at Iva.

'What is paradise like?' Iva asked him. He didn't know and pretended he hadn't heard the question.

Stretching along the food section was a row of stalls with bright adverts, faceless dummies, and shop windows announcing, 'Sale – Sale – Sale...' Iva looked at the displayed outfits with longing: she couldn't afford them now, and she remembered her unpacked boxes at home full of expensive dresses and pantsuits which no one was wearing. She was surrounded by handsome men and pretty women laughing at her from the posters while the vigilant security cameras seemed to tickle her neck from all sides.

'Hallo... Hallo...' she kept greeting the customers, her smile more like a spasm. 'Have a nice day. Come again.'

When there were no customers, she dipped her hand into the till and counted the banknotes while the guard with a sloping forehead watched her, suspiciously screwing up his eyes.

'Why do you work so slowly?' The administrator's smile exploded into a shout and red spots spread all over her face. 'I'll report you to the manager.'

'I'm sorry,' responded Iva like an automaton. 'Have a nice day. Come again.'

Her days were scheduled by the minute now. Iva lived as a clockwork doll with a plastic heart and disemboweled soul. At six in the morning Iva got up; at 6:10 she went downstairs to the canteen, washed under the tap, ate her breakfast and received her lunch box; at 6:40 she lined up for the roll call and got on the bus; at nine sharp she was sitting at the till having hastily changed into her uniform. Her work day lasted twelve hours but she worked overtime to make a bit of extra money; she scrubbed the floors and did the dishes, at ten sharp she got on the return bus and at midnight she arrived at the hostel. She took a shower during the night: she'd get up with her eyes closed and go into the bathroom, bumping against the walls, she'd stand under a shower for five minutes, the spurt of water from a hose beating painfully at her body, and then return to her bed shivering with cold.

Her Mondays turned into Fridays, and her Sundays into Wednesdays; seconds stretched into minutes while hours compressed and flitted by like landscapes beyond a train window.

'Why's your shirt wrinkled?' her administrator towered over her. 'And the collar is dirty.' He'd open his notebook and issued her another fine.

The saleswomen ate right there on the shop floor; squatting by the shelves they'd put a sweet in their mouth or, hiding from the cameras behind customers' backs, they'd chip off a few grapes from the wooden crates. When they left in the evening, two guards searched them at the exit: they pawed them unemotionally, turned their bags and pockets inside out, but women still managed to steal some trifles, hiding them in their mouths or secret pockets. Iva stole some toothpaste and soap, squeezing them into her lunch box; she hid some face cream in her locker and applied it during lunch break; and once she changed her underwear and stockings in the toilet.

'Either you control circumstances, or they control you.' She suddenly heard this said one day as she passed the books section. She jumped and moved closer. She looked over a customer's shoulder: she was holding a book by Iva Nova.

Customers heaped their purchases onto the conveyor belt. They dropped them on the floor, sniffed them, examined them, and read the labels aloud.

Iva put the packages into plastic bags and stiffened with hate. 'When will you be done stuffing yourselves, you pigs,' she thought to herself. She was wondering what each would do in her place: for instance that fat one with the hairy belly sticking out from under his shirt, or that small blonde with such a naïve face you could almost read the name of the village she'd come from on it, or that stern-looking lady whose eyes were fixed on the cash register showing the sums. What would they do if they happened to land in a situation like hers? But out loud she repeated like a robot, 'Have a nice day. Come again,' while imagining how she'd stage an experiment on these people sending them out into the street without money, without shelter, and without any hope of help. She pictured them as dirty tramps rummaging in refuse heaps in search of something edible. 'Hallo' Credit card or cash?' Iva said for the umpteenth time, and it was getting increasingly evident to her that she was the victim of someone's cruel experiment. 'Who might be behind it?' she wondered, looking up, and the ceiling looked back at her with its hundred lamps.

'Number Seven, you're loafing again,' the administrator shouted at her. 'Number Seven, you work too slowly. Number Seven, this is your last warning. Number Seven, lunch time.' She spent the thirty-minute lunch break going to the toilet, eating her lunch, and taking a short nap while hidden in a corner.

When her heart got too tired and felt like it was about to burst, Iva would walk around the supermarket pretending she was shooting at people's heads, squinting one eye as she took her aim. Bang – a woman with a shapeless face like a lump of plasticine collapsed on the floor. Bang – a man clutched at his heart and dropped on his overloaded trolley, which rolled rattling down the aisle dragging him along. Iva emptied a whole magazine into the big belly of a fat girl looking longingly at the sweets display, then reloaded her gun and went to the fish counter with a big water tank full of suffocating half-dead carp. She smashed the water tank with one shot and the fish scattered on the floor flapping their fins, she went on shooting at the crowd and the wounded fell onto the lumps of ice and fish steaks. From behind the tray with dried fruit, a pink-cheeked child emerged and shouted: 'Buy it!'

'Get lost!' Iva whispered and fired away.

'Number Seven, are you okay?' the administrator looked in her eyes and shuddered. 'Maybe you should take a day off?'

'No problem.' Iva tried to smile but just pressed her lips, took aim and smashed the administrator's head.

'Tomorrow's your day off,' he told her and marked something in his notebook. Iva tried to protest but he waved her aside. 'A year ago, one girl who had worked non-stop for two months broke a customer's head with a can. Now we have instructions to watch out for those who look daggers at customers and send them home to get a proper sleep. What if you start killing one another? Then the administration will be held responsible.'

8—DELHI

DRIVING IN GREATER NOIDA

BY DEEPTI KAPOOR

There's a radio advert in Hindi. I don't remember it perfectly, but it goes something like this:

A young married couple in Delhi are looking to buy their first house, but property prices in the city are rising and the wife is panicking, worried that, unable to afford somewhere respectable, they'll be forced out to the margins. 'Nahi! Nahi!' she cries, as if in a horror film. 'Don't make me move to Greater Noida!' Her husband, however, is a more sensible sort. He reassures her and tells her he can take out a loan (this is what the advert is ultimately for). Everything will be okay. They won't have to move to Greater Noida.

I listen to this on the expressway in the back of my mother's car, sitting behind her driver, Dinesh, on the way to her apartment in Greater Noida.

β

Greater Noida is an extension of Noida. And Noida (correctly, NOIDA) stands for New Okhla Industrial Development Authority. It lies over the Yamuna River, a few kilometres east of Delhi, in the politically important, hugely populous, and often lawless state of Uttar Pradesh. Noida came into being on 17th April 1976 – forever known as Noida Day – as part of a master plan to shift industry out of the city. But Delhi's population grew faster than expected and spilled over into Noida. This unplanned, unregulated growth put a severe strain on its infrastructure, so in 1989, to remedy this, Greater Noida was born.

γ

Greater Noida is about thirty kilometres south-east of Noida, along the pristine tarmac of the Greater Noida Expressway. A planned city, it was zoned before anyone moved in. Its roads are abnormally wide, and its cabling and piping were laid down first and hidden underground. It had sectors, and all the sectors were named after the Greek alphabet. They were given these incongruous names so as to be as neutral as possible, the ingenious thinking being that when political power inevitably changed hands, the new party wouldn't replace one loaded set of names for another. An area named after a Dalit hero wouldn't over-night become the sector named after an ancient Hindu king, as happens elsewhere in the country, ad nauseam, ad infinitum.

For a certain kind of Dilliwala, Greater Noida is a place of exile, as Milton Keynes might be for a certain Londoner. But for others, like my mother, who used to live in a crumbling apartment block in east Delhi – an area of the city that bears the capital's name but few of its benefits – it holds the promise of the future.

δ

Her children were grown up, and she had no ties to the land – my mother is a widow who lives comfortably enough on the far-sighted investments my father made – so she wanted to leave east Delhi for a nicer environment, preferably one with a swimming pool. Some years ago, she discovered she could sell her drab apartment in east Delhi and buy two new luxury twelfth-floor apartments in a five-star gated township in Greater Noida. The developer, ATS, was selling flats at a reduced rate before completion in order to stimulate occupancy. She needed two because she also took care of my grandmother, her mother. They needed two because they couldn't live under the same roof without driving each other insane.

ε

Some parts of Greater Noida already resembled a functioning city. This was not the case in the area in which my mother's township was being built. Paradiso was in Sector Chi. The first time we went to look at the apartments, in

2010, they were part of a giant construction site, surrounded by a vast sea of fields and dirt. There were to be eighteen towers in the property; maybe half were complete that day. The thirty-two-acre complex already had its name, though: ATS Greens Paradiso. Every developer uses evocative names such as this.

I remember bare walls, scaffolding, seeing the grey sky through the skeletal frames, hard hats, cranes, JCBs, labourers, stray dogs, stray children, barbed wire, and an incredible number of birds. More than this, I remember the drive out there: the expressway from Noida as it plunged deeper into a desolate space, the highway that had no petrol stations, no dhabas, no people. We passed immense concrete monsters on either side of us, then miles of nothing, a dust storm, some women carrying bricks on their heads, a herd of buffalo. I thought: folly, hubris, private sector isolation. A tractor drove towards us on the wrong side of the road. The road was the only thing that felt real, and it seemed to lead into nothing. Then suddenly, near Paradiso, an oddly gleaming modern bunker-mansion sitting in the middle of everything. This was a farmer's house.

ζ

Greater Noida was something before it was Greater Noida. It was built on farmland that was populated, for the most part, by the pastoral-agricultural Gujjar caste. This fertile, high-yield farmland had to be acquired from the farmers by the GNIDA (Greater Noida Industrial Development Authority, or simply 'the Authority') before the city could be built. The all-but-forced acquisition of this land was, and still is, a contentious issue: although many landowners got very rich very quick, others – the landless workers who ploughed the fields, for instance – became unemployed and poor, with no compensation. Even the farmers who got rich had problems. For one, many of them saw the way in which their land was subsequently sold on by the Authority to private developers for immense profit, and the way in which these developers in turn built luxury townships, with individual units whose sales price, when multiplied, made the land value astronomical. They soon came to believe, with justification, that the price they had been paid for their land wasn't nearly enough.

There was another kind of problem, too: these newly rich farmers, who had previously been so occupied, now found they had nothing to do. They built their mansions and palaces, bought numerous SUVs and threw lavish weddings, but always with the awareness, acute or opaque, that they no longer had their land, they no longer had their work and that, one day, their fortune would end. The issues this provoked could have been tempered had the Authority fulfilled its promise to provide hospitals, schools, training facilities and other such community necessities. But neither the state nor the private developers wanted much to do with the locals once they had their land. The farmers, seen as a volatile, lazy and criminal bunch, weren't even trusted to work as guards in the new residential complexes – these workers were brought in from outside.

η

Dinesh, my mother's driver, is a Gujjar farmer. He was born in Greater Noida when it wasn't Greater Noida. He lives in Imalyaka, a village about six kilometres south-east of Paradiso. His being a farmer was relayed to me when he began working for my mother, but it made no impression then. I simply thought: how nice, he's a farmer, working the land, a son of the soil. I didn't even bother asking why a farmer was employed as a driver. Later on, I learned that he was only a farmer in name: his father, the actual farmer, died when he was a teenager, and their land was acquired soon after. He's never done a day of farming in his life.

Now I ask the question: why is a wealthy ex-farmer who's had his land acquired working as a driver? And the answer is: because he's not wealthy, not exactly. His mother, with rare good sense, put almost all the money from the land sale in the bank and told her sons they had to work. His brother is training to be a cable TV installer, because suddenly their village is full of cable TV.

θ

Dinesh is a good man. He collects my husband and me from the airport and takes us around Delhi every time we visit. He negotiates the city's notorious parking problems with ease. He memorises shortcuts and predicts traffic jams. He doesn't use the horn and he doesn't lose his temper. He's slightly shy, he talks very softly. He has a sense of the absurd. One can tease a laugh out of him on occasion. It's hard to know what he really thinks about anything, but once or twice I've impressed him, maybe earned his respect. Once: some cops tried to extort money on the highway, claiming, with no evidence, that Dinesh was an illegal taxi service. I dealt with the situation and spoke to the cops in a manner he would not have believed possible. Twice: he drove us to the south Delhi mansion of a very feared, very powerful man, famous in Uttar Pradesh. By association, I gained some of that power.

ɩ

Dinesh picks us up from the airport when we arrive and drives us from Delhi to Greater Noida. Between Delhi and Noida is the DND Flyway (Delhi–Noida Direct), a nine-point-two kilometre, eight-lane 'world class expressway' spanning the Yamuna River, curving gently away from the capital into the frontier land. As it does, property billboards begin to appear, towering out of the reeds, saying:

'Urbainia. It's All About You.'

'Color Homes. The Promise of an Enviable Life.'

'Lotus Greens. Live the Difference.'

ATS Greens Paradiso is no different. Now finished, the guards salute as we enter, the gates sweep aside. Affluent teens wearing baseball caps bounce basketballs, yummy mummies go on power walks, armies of servants assiduously wash expensive cars. There are Indian Americans, British Asians, Korean businessmen from multinational corporations. There are the middle-classes of India; the professionals, the retired people, the widows, the software engineers. There are those looking for refuge from the urban grind. There are pleasant trees and lawns. There is no litter. There is a sense of decorum, an aura of peace.

к

But recently, things haven't been panning out so well for Greater Noida. The economy has slowed, development has stalled, and crime has noticeably increased. Days before I flew in, there was a gunpoint carjacking at a large, desolate roundabout about one kilometre from the township. It was not the first; there is a carjacking gang on the prowl. For years before this, we have been warned, when returning from weddings late at night, to lock all the jewellery in the boot of the car. This is bandit country. Late at night, Dinesh avoids a certain underpass, where they are known to prey on cars. We take the long route home. And if he finishes driving for us past midnight, Dinesh sleeps over in the servant's room with Rajesh, my mother's live-in domestic. It's too dangerous for him to ride his motorbike the six kilometres to Imalyaka.

An email does the rounds on Paradiso's intra-community Internet group. Here's an excerpt:

'After the incident around ATS, the same group moved to Eldeco Circle. They followed the same modus operandi. They blocked the Verna car driven by the victim, by suddenly overtaking and stopping in front of Car. They broke the windshield by Base Ball bat and one person pointed agun [sic] on the head of the victim. They took away his mobile, purse and the car. The victim was in sate [sic] of shock but not hurt physically. He filed the FIR today in Police Station when we all were there for a meeting with Police officials.'

There are also fears within the complex: Another group email, later in December, reads:

'Last night at about 12:50 a.m., a resident of Paradiso could not park his car in his own parking slot as somebody else's car was parked there. He tried parking his car elsewhere. However, being a large car, he was unable to do so and accidentally banged the car into the boundary wall. Angered, he called the security guard and asked him to name the owner of the car parked in his slot. The car did not have a sticker and, as such, the guard expressed his inability to identify the owner. The Resident took out his revolver and put it to the chest of the guard. The petrified guard managed to escape unhurt.'

Yet it isn't always high drama. There's also a protracted email debate about the timings for use of the tennis courts. It turns heated at one point, quite uncivilised, until sense prevails. There are other trifles: one revolves around the pool, which is closed for the winter far too early, in October, when the sun is still very hot. Residents gaze out at its glassy surface, sweating in the heat, pining for a dip.

λ

People do not much venture beyond the township walls these days, at least on foot. They leave the compound in their cars for their work or their social engagements. Even Rajesh, my mother's domestic, doesn't walk outside any more. A year ago, he played cricket in the nearby playing field, and went running on the highway for exercise. But one day last year his friend, another domestic, had his mobile phone taken from him in broad daylight by a bunch of goons. He agrees it has become worse recently. All the domestics say so. They say it is known far and wide that wealth resides here, wealth which has no defence.

So Rajesh makes do walking in circles inside the complex. 'But,' he says, 'the residents look at me suspiciously now.'

μ

Greater Noida is a paranoid, fractured land. One senses the residents inside ATS – the vocal, proactive ones at least – trying to build, or just hold onto, their dream. Their emails often end with positive, Obamian 'Together we can!' exhortations. They have a lot invested in these walls, which increasingly feel like those built around an island, buffeted by a treacherous sea.

ν

Even the dogs aren't safe. Tipu Sultan was the eight-eenth-century ruler of the Kingdom of Mysore, but Tipu Sultan is also the name of a resident's dog. He is a pug, a breed more commonly known in India as 'the Vodafone Dog', on account of one being used several years back in the mobile carrier's nationwide advertising campaign. The increased popularity this engendered led to a spate of dog-nappings, to order and on spec. Tipu Sultan suffered the indignity of this one evening while his owner's domestic was walking him outside the complex. Two bike-born miscreants stopped and grabbed his leash and pulled him onto the back of the bike. But by the grace of God or some other power, the criminals fumbled at the decisive moment, and Tipu leapt to freedom.

One evening, not long after this incident, I bumped into Tipu while his owner was walking him around the complex. I was granted an audience, only to be snubbed on approach by his upturned doggy nose.

(As I wrote this, a friend's beloved pug was dognapped outside her home in Ghaziabad, not far from Noida. After negotiations with a known dognapping gang in the area, they were, thankfully, reunited.)

ξ

On this visit I am determined to know more. Not of the inside, whose gossip I pick up easily, but of the world that exists just outside. I decide to explore, to try and get a sense of this place. I decide to explore those places we choose to avoid, outside the guarded gates.

The night we landed in Delhi, Dinesh let slip he had become a father. We didn't even know his wife was pregnant. I'd said, 'How's your wife, Dinesh?' and he'd replied, 'She's had a doll.' The as yet unnamed girl is now six days old. It's the perfect excuse to go and poke around. Dinesh turns up one morning soon after, and instead of having him drive us into Delhi, we tell him we're going to Imalyaka instead, to visit his family. He calmly nods his assent. My mother, ever curious, decides to come too. We put some money in an envelope as a gift and, as we drive out the complex, fretting that we don't have the correct envelope with the one-rupee coin embedded into it, as tradition dictates. My mother thinks out loud. She says:, 'These things matter to these people.'

o

To get to Imalyaka, we have to pass through Kasna, a town one kilometre from Paradiso. Kasna is full of dust, half-finished houses of exposed brick and steel poles, loitering men, auto shops, naked bulbs that illuminate faces in the dark, piles of car tyres, veg stalls, chai shops. On the approach road, trucks with Haryana and UP plates are parked either side, forming a canyon, leaving only a small channel of road. As we emerge, rabid dogs ambush the car from the left, fangs exposed. Paradiso recedes on the horizon. We have never been this way before. There is no reason to have come: the service road to the expressway back to Noida and Delhi is in the opposite direction; the malls of Greater Noida are in the opposite direction. No resident of Paradiso has a reason to come this way.

Dinesh says Kasna is full of migrant workers. This is where the domestic staff live, the cleaners, the cooks. The population is transitory, somewhat unaccountable. A police patrol jeep is parked at one corner. On every wall of the road out of Kasna, small-scale property dealers have painted their signs and phone numbers in red and blue:

'aakashganga property. jyoti prop. subham – property'

After Kasna, the landscape becomes blasted; it has the aspect of fired clay. Driving a short distance, we come upon what looks like a fortress, but as we near, I see guard towers along the perimeter and the tops of modern houses inside, arranged in neat rows, just like a town. Dinesh says it's the new jail. Luksar Jail, I read later, is relieving the load of the old Dasna Jail in Ghaziabad. Sixty-seven prisoners were transferred in the first week. Over the following weeks, one thousand seven hundred more.

Whereas the roads around Paradiso are immaculate, the road to Imalyaka is, at times, barely a road at all. As we rise and fall at a crawl, I'm reminded of nature documentaries where the four-by-four looks like it's going to topple over. It's in no one's interest to fix anything here. It's easy to see how this can be bandit territory. I look out beyond the small mounds, hoping to catch a glimpse of one. A tractor passes by happily, several men clinging to its side.

Dinesh stops before we enter Imalyaka to show us his family's few remaining fields. They are more like allotments. One has mustard. The other – still being planted, a worker out there casting seeds around – Dinesh doesn't know.

π

On entering the village we're confronted by a beast of a house with a gleaming white suv parked outside: big gates, high, ornately decorated walls, rooms built on many levels. This is another farmer's house.

In the past, one might feel self-conscious entering a village like this in such a nice car. Small children would have come out to stare, wave and bang at the windows, run along-side shouting, as if royalty had arrived. But now our car is run-of-the-mill here; many villagers have far fancier vehicles than ours. So we drive on unnoticed, as Dinesh navigates the right-angled corners of the narrowing lanes with remarkable skill. Finally, we reach a kind of alcove, a place to park, and walk the short distance to Dinesh's home.

His family compound is still a farmyard. Buffalo lie on straw beds, tethered to poles, children run round piles of wood. The houses are unfinished one- or two-storey brick things, with plaster and flat roofs. There are charpoys (rope beds) and cakes of dung to be burnt as fuel. We're presented with milk fresh from the buffalo, boiled and sugared. My mother, who is suspi-cious of the hygiene, and I, who detest milk, find excuses not to drink it. My husband, who is of Lincolnshire farming stock, swallows two glasses, to great approval. The women come out to talk; they wear bright, traditional Gujjar clothing as opposed to the men's dull shirts and trousers. They seem stronger than the men, bolder, more vocal, less inhibited. There's some dis-cussion among them about whether it would be appropriate to smoke a pipe in our presence. At first, we think they're offering it to us, so we say no. There is a small comedy of errors, but when the matter is cleared, their hookah is prepared. We hand over the envelope. We go and see mother and child, sitting in the dark inside one of the rooms. Outside again, we make small talk. I ask a casual question: 'How often do you have power cuts?' They say the power comes on around seven in the evening and goes off at four in the morning. Every day? Yes, every day. Later on, they complain about the jail. It has come up so close to their village, without consent or even consultation, and now the area is ruined.

Everyone says it is the local Gujjars who commit the crimes. Locals who have run out of money. Locals who never had any in the first place. Locals who are jealous of their neighbours. Locals with drug habits. But Dinesh says all the criminals come from outside, from Delhi or from other parts of Uttar Pradesh, hunting the rich people. Naturally he doesn't want to make his community look bad.

ρ

Mr. Safal Suri tells us a story. He is at the local market, the one that's ugly and dirty and haphazard, with blocks of shabby shop buildings and too many cars and a couple of private hospitals nearby that look like giant plastic Nokia phones. There's also a chemist in the market, which my mother uses. Mr. Suri is visiting the same chemist in the night. The area is deserted. An alcohol shop – metal-grilled so it can't be robbed – sits next door. There is a chunky SUV parked nearby, a brand-new Scorpio, still without number plates. Four local Gujjars – 'smart, handsome guys between the ages of twenty-two and twenty-eight' – are putting cartons and cartons of whisky inside. Evidently, they are planning on having a good time. Only, they need more money. Mr. Suri eavesdrops on their conversation.

Man One: You bought the car, you have the money. Where's the money?

Man Two: We'll get the money, don't worry. We'll just kidnap someone, it's no big deal.

Man One: Okay, let's go kidnap someone first, then we'll get the whisky.

Man Two: No, let's take the whisky back to the village first, then we'll kidnap.

Man One: Okay, but where should we do it? Here, in Greater Noida?

Man Two: No! Not here. If people had money, they wouldn't be staying out here. Let's go somewhere in south Delhi.

In Delhi, especially south Delhi, even the auto drivers are millionaires. They pile into the suv and drive away.

Safal Suri is a property dealer. He lives in Paradiso and often advises my mother on matters of real estate. He's boyish, energetic, slightly tubby beneath a powerful frame, like a rugby player. We meet him in his office on a plot about two kilometres from Paradiso: a miniature version of a colonial bungalow, all red stone and small ornamental turrets, with a high-enough boundary wall to block the view from outside. On account of my husband, and the touches of his accent I've picked up, he mistakes me for British. I correct him, tell him I'm Indian, that I lived in east Delhi for many years, but he seems not to register this, so for the first half hour of our meeting he explains India to me. I sit patiently and listen. Eventually the good stuff comes. He has knowledge and gossip coming out of his ears.

He talks about many things: about the one hundred billion-dollar Delhi–Mumbai Industrial Corridor (DMIC) project that's coming up, which will run through Greater Noida, turning it into a logistics hub. He talks about the impending metro connection, how it was stalled by the previous, and legendarily corrupt, Congress government due to a conflict of private interests, and how it will transform the area completely when it arrives. He talks about the previous

Chief Minister of UP, Mayawati, the Dalit leader who hails from these parts, and how she invested heavily, wanting to see the area prosper. He talks of the way in which she would rotate civil service and police postings every six months, not allowing anyone to be posted within three hundred kilometres of their home in order to avoid officers getting their feet under the table and turning into local goons.

He talks of the Yadavs, the father-and-son Samajwadi Party (SP) chiefs who currently rule UP, reportedly diverting funds from the Greater Noida and Noida budgets to their ancestral lands in Eastern UP, shoring up support in their traditional vote banks, looking after their own. It's spooking investors. He says, 'Real estate is nothing to do with reality, it's all about sentiment.' So everyone is praying for the BJP to come into power in the state elections. Even those who don't support the BJP.

He talks about the proposed airport in the Yamuna Expressway region, south towards Agra. He talks about Disneyland, of how McKinsey consulted with him about the viability of opening a park here. He talks about the lawlessness of UP. He says that Punjab and Haryana have a law and order problem, but UP hasn't even matured to that point yet. He jokes: 'To have a problem, you have to have law and order in the first place.'

But he lauds the potential of Greater Noida, saying that, unlike anywhere else close to Delhi, it has an abundance of land. He reminds me that money will always flow to the place where free land lies in proximity to power.

At one point he brings out a map that he's had made, and lays it on the table. It shows Greater Noida. All the sectors – Alpha, Beta, Gamma, Delta. Sector Chi, where we sit.

The more recently developed land was originally designated by Mayawati to be used for industry. She went looking for investment to this end, promising sixty-year leases instead of thirty, alongside other sops. But the financial crash happened ('America sneezed and the whole world caught a cold') and the investment interest disappeared. The problem was, the land had already been acquired, loans had already been taken to cover these acquisitions. The government had to do something. So the industrial land was speedily converted to high-density residential and sold to developers. This is where Paradiso comes from. This is the land my mother lives in now, eerie, desolate, intended for industry, beloved of carjackers.

Σ

A few days later we drive to Delta sector, one of the first to be developed. It feels like a real suburb here. There are houses with gardens strewn with kids' toys, and quiet leafy roads.

We are here to visit my late father's plot, which he won in the lottery when Greater Noida was first announced all those years back. It was to be my parents' retirement, their investment. It sat vacant for years. Almost vacant: a law was passed whereby twenty-five percent of a plot had to be built on, so my mother (my father had died by then) built the most basic of houses, a brick shell. Eventually some landless people began squatting; this is a common occurrence. At first my mother tried to evict them, later it was decided they could stay. Better the devil you know.

We find the address and pull up the car, stand outside and look. A man passing on his bicycle stops to watch us watching. Inside, it's overgrown with weeds, so much so that I can only just make out the house at the back of the plot. On the boundary wall, the black marble plaque says 'Kapoor's', with an apostrophe of possession. I've never been here before, and I'm overcome suddenly. I feel like I'm visiting his grave.

We drive away, past newer houses, tightly packed together, more crowded. These are home to the less prosperous Gujjar farmers. They have charpoys in their concrete yards, and old women lying on them smoking hookahs. At a junction, I ask Dinesh to stop at what appears to be a mall. It has signs for luxury brands skirting the wall outside. There's another sign that says: 'be seen in a world class business destination'. Half the sign is obscured by shrubbery. I ask Dinesh to drive inside, and he giggles at my ignorance and tells me the mall is closed, it has been for a while. Why? I ask. He shrugs and pulls the face of a schoolboy asked an absurd question. It opens for a while, it closes again, no one knows why. That's just how it is.

We drive on. I've been meaning to look at one of the new ATS projects, in the construction-site stage, named Dolce, as in La Dolce Vita. On the way, Dinesh, who is warming to this bizarre series of drives, begins to talk freely and without prompting. He points out a small cluster of village homes that seem to rise on top of one another, anachronistic among the new roads and planned colonies. He says it's one of the original villages, which cannot be removed; no matter how much farmland is acquired, the gaons – the villages – must remain. He finds this amusing.

I push him further. I'm curious to know what he makes of the strange names the sectors have been given. He giggles some more and shakes his head, bemused. He thinks they're silly. So what does he call these places then? He calls them by their names, of course, the names of the villages. And the roads he knows by the fields he used to play in as a boy. So what about Paradiso, what's that called? That, he says, is Kasna.

τ

A visit to Greater Noida is incomplete without a visit to Jaypee Greens. Jaypee Greens is a city within the city, the jewel in the real-estate crown of the Jaypee Group, a huge conglomerate with business interests everywhere you'd expect: power, cement, expressways, hospitals, hospitality, et cetera. One hits it straight off the expressway from Noida. There's no escaping it.

In their own words:

'Jaypee Greens Greater Noida is a premium 182 Ha golf-centric real estate development with best options of properties in Greater Noida. The project is developed with the objective of integrating homes with golf course, landscaped emerald spaces, resort living and commercial developments... Jaypee Greens Greater Noida presents an option to live a life you've always cherished for...' The flats in Greater Noida symbolize the passport to a well-earned, tran-quil and personally gratifying existence. It is a 'legacy to be enjoyed from one generation to the next'.

I tell Dinesh that my husband and I are visiting Jaypee Greens today. He nods and starts to drive. But when we reach the general vicinity, the place is so big, so highly secure, with serious barrier gates at strategic points along each of its boundary walls, that it's hard to know exactly where to go. We feel intimidated by the scale of it. We drive up to one gate, to be immediately sent elsewhere: only cars with passes may enter here.

When we pull up to the correct gate, instead of asking where we need to go, we adopt the dismissively bored attitude of the rich and powerful. The guards check the boot of the car and put a wheeled mirror underneath to make sure we're not a bomb, then wave us through. We enter a space that feels like something inside a container ship, only with a hotel-style entrance on one side. Dinesh and the car are sent down a ramp to an underground car park. We pass through metal detectors while our bags go through an X-ray machine.

The lobby is casual corporate chic, large and hushed, now decorated for Christmas. Two businessmen sit on a sofa in a far corner, while an official Jaypee man sits at a desk on the other side. An affable, management school-type woman with a winning smile approaches. We make a show of looking around approvingly, as if we're prospective buyers of something, and tell her we're here to examine the golf course for my husband's uncle, an important man and a big golfer. She seems pleased. We ask to see the course. She looks troubled. For that we have to go out and enter at another gate. Ah, so what is here? Here there are two restaurants and a bar. We look at one another, pretending we're debating whether we have the time to spare. We do. So may we have a bite to eat in the restaurant before moving on? Certainly. We're shown through to the All Day Dining restaurant, a generic five-star space with many tables, only two of which are occupied.

Though we both declare how agreeable the silence is, we doubt the quality of the food. The menu is continental. It says: 'Ask your waiter for the soup of the day.' I ask the waiter. He says: 'Veg and Non-Veg.' I ask him to be more specific. He looks at me blankly then says he'll find out. Of the two other tables, one is an older English couple who appear to be tourists, maybe attached to a wedding; the other, a couple of young professionals who may or may not be having an affair. Part of the golf course is visible through the plate glass windows. A gaggle of female golfers in white baseball caps, possibly Korean, wander in and out of view. The waiter returns. He says the veg soup is cream of tomato, the non-veg mulligatawny. We order a chicken salad with brown bread. They have no brown bread.

As we pick at the salad, a couple enters, seemingly nouveau riche, possibly Gujjar. All body fat, bright clothes and gold. They sit down, examine the menu for a moment, get up and walk out again.

Afterwards we slip out to catch a glimpse of the golf course, but there's a buffer zone of gardens and pathways, men watering the flowers, and we feel like we're going to be stopped at any moment, interrogated, denounced as imposters. We catch sight of the greens. They are placid, the golfers have vanished. Jaypee apartments and towers form the hazy horizon. Directly in front of us a bush has been teased into the shape of a Formula 1 car at pit stop, complete with mechanics changing the tyre. India's first F1 Track is not far from here. But that's another story entirely.

Back inside, in a second lobby, a forlorn Christmas tree keeps watch over a cake and bakery stall. A display shelf on the right is bursting with loaves. I go to inspect them. The man behind the counter looks up and says: 'They're plastic, madam.' He shows me the real bread. A wholemeal loaf looks nice, so I buy it. When I cut into it later, it's dry and not very good.

υ

Before reaching home, we stop outside Paradiso to talk to the old woman who sells vegetables in one of the neglected plots. I've been seeing her there every time we come back in the evening. There are many semi-derelict plots surrounding the complex, their 'twenty-five percent' houses offering shelter to the labourers who are building this land. A small community has sprung up here now. In the morning, a barber puts a chair in the earth, ties a mirror to a tree, brings out his razor; a tailor sits at a desk with his old Singer sewing machine, tailoring clothes in the sun. A fire burns in the evening chill.

I ask Dinesh, who has suddenly assumed the manner of a secret service bodyguard, if he knows who these people are. 'Biharis,' he sneers dismissively. He sees no value in what they have to say.

As soon as I climb out of the car and walk towards the old lady, a group forms, complete with snot-nosed urchin. I ask the woman where she's from. Is she Bihari? She scoffs at this: she's not Bihari, she's from UP. What does she do here? She tells me that in the daytime she works as a labourer, and in the evening she sells vegetables here. Who does she sell veg to? Do the residents of Paradiso buy from her? She shakes her head. 'The residents of Paradiso don't buy their vegetables from me. They go to the grocery store in the mall.' The domestic staff, the people who work in the rich people's houses, these are the people who buy her vegetables. I ask her where she lives now, and she points to the concrete shell behind. Does she know who owns this plot? She shrugs her shoulders.

I buy half a dozen eggs before leaving. As she packs them, I ask her what she thinks of all the crime round here these days. She looks puzzled, thinks about it for a moment, and finally tells me there isn't any crime. I hand over the money and get in the car. We drive fifty metres to the gate. At home I discover there are five eggs in the bag instead of six.

φ

I tell everyone I meet that I don't like this place. Still, there's a frisson of excitement coming back at night from the city in the fog, past the dreaded circle into this no man's land. Will we be carjacked? Part of me waits for it.

χ

I'm exhausted by Greater Noida, that's the truth. Exhausted by the unreality of it. By the absence of anything approaching society. By the long stretches of nothingness. By the desiccated, stark, unforgiving luxury.

Then in the daylight, seeing the residents, their children being pushed on their small bikes, the tennis players, the plastic litter-bin frogs, I think: who am I to judge? They deserve a quiet life, a peaceful one, their utopia, their twenty-four-hour power, swimming pools, gardens, gyms, drivers, maids. They deserve the complexities of their lives that I'll never be able to touch upon. Only, so does everyone else.

ψ

Before we fly back to Goa, I arrange to meet the ATS 'President of Marketing and Sales Operations', Mr. Sanjeev Kathuria. The ATS office is on the Expressway between Noida and Greater Noida.

When I get there, there's no record of my appointment. I'm asked to wait. The waiting room has several sofas around a table full of glossy magazines. Mini bottles of good mineral water are available. The office section is cut off by a frosted glass wall that has a keypad secured door. We're surrounded by smartly dressed people, educated, professional. An inspirational video extols the virtues of ATS on a wall-mounted flat-screen TV. A modern Muslim family from the Gulf, or maybe from the UK, watches us watching them before they are ushered into a sales office. There is no old-fashioned housing-society-style exclusion here. ATS does not discriminate.

A young woman comes through the frosted glass door to tell me a meeting with Mr. Kathuria will be difficult today – he's very busy. If I want to speak to him I'll have to wait a long time. Things don't look promising. So I drop a name; my uncle's, who was a very powerful bureaucrat in his time. 'Oh,' she says. 'You're his niece?' Five minutes later we're called in.

Mr. Kathuria is avuncular. He looks like a college professor, which he was before he became the President of
Marketing and Sales Operations for ATS. His face inspires
trust, a useful asset in this business. On his whiteboard are
the words: 'The Challenge Is To Be A Good Human Being!!!'

I congratulate him on his work. Along with Jaypee, ATS
is the cream of the crop (indeed, when Jaypee conducted
an inter-community sports day recently, no other property
group but ATS was invited). He acknowledges their success;
he's proud. They've gone from one hundred crore (sixteen
million dollars) to ten thousand crore (one-point-six billion
dollars) in fifteen years. I tell him the reason my mother
went with them was down to their attention to detail, the
quality of their finishing and their maintenance. And it's
true; they really take care of their construction. So often
in new developments in the country, there's a lack of care
during construction. But ATS buildings are top-notch. 'We
build everything in-house, in a very controlled atmosphere.'
He explains all this with a smile. I like him. I'd probably buy
property from him.

I ask what kind of residents they have. Good people.
'Literate, white-collar people.' But not the locals? The Gujjars
whose land was acquired? 'No,' he says, still smiling. 'The
Gujjars don't go for the high-end communities.' They build
their own houses, or they go and buy in the smaller developments. I don't bring up the Gujjar farmer that Safal Suri,
the property dealer, told me about earlier – the one who had
bought two hundred and thirty flats alone in the new ATS
property, Pristine. He is probably a statistical anomaly.

What of their plans for the future? He talks about the
hundred-acre integrated township in the pipeline, on the

Yamuna Expressway; the super-luxury project back towards
Noida, starting at five crore ($1 million) per unit, with a dif-
ferent architecture, 'a different style of living, redefining
luxury for the very, very elite'; an entire town parallel to
Chandigarh, in Punjab, which alongside residential buildings will have schools, a golf course, hospitals and hotels.

Inevitably, we reach the matter of security. It is a concern, he admits, his voice momentarily losing its sheen. ATS
advises residents not to travel outside after dark. (At home,
my mother says: 'They never said that to me when I was
looking to buy.')

'The problem with Greater Noida,' he goes on, 'is that
it's still too lonely. There aren't enough people yet. People
haven't come because the shift in offices [from other areas]
hasn't happened. But it's getting better. Infosys has picked up
land, Mahindra too.' And of course, the metro is on its way.

But the biggest change will come when the BJP wins
UP. 'When that happens,' he says, energised, paraphrasing
an IAS officer who recently invested in an ATS property,
'Noida and Greater Noida will be on a very different tangent.
Everything will change.' Surely 'if' and not 'when'? Is he so
certain the BJP will win? He smiles indulgently. He says: 'UP
put Narendra Modi where he is. UP has given a clear man-
date already in the general elections.'

Ω

On 21st December, the day before we leave for home,
another email is posted to the ATS group. It repeats the old
familiar note of caution:

'Friends,

'Another incident of attempted carjacking reported from more or less same spot with a resident of complex... Police informed.

'Please avoid outbound travel in night if possible.

'Thanks...'

After the previously reported incident, a police patrol vehicle had been posted at the roundabout. It remained there for half an hour, from 9 p.m. to 9:30 p.m. While considered a good gesture, it wasn't enough to satisfy the residents. There were suggestions for further action: surveillance cameras installed; a regular police presence at the crucial isolated spot; private sector patrols in the area; expanding the internal security force. An increase in ATS maintenance fees was regarded by some as a small price to pay for peace of mind, if only a security force could be guaranteed. It was only a matter of implementation. A sobering voice reminded the group that private security had no jurisdiction outside the complex. Nor inside, for that matter.

ἐπίλογος

These are the birth pangs of a new Indian city. A period of flux, of creation; of change and loss. Omelettes and eggs. Life and death. It will settle. The question is, what will be here when it does? As we leave for the airport, the fog so thick we cannot see the car ten metres in front of us, I ask Dinesh what he thinks of it all. He shrugs.

And what of my mother? Would she have moved to Greater Noida, knowing what she knows now? I ask her these questions on the phone a couple of weeks later, standing on the balcony among palm trees in the Goan sun.

After much thought, she says yes, she probably would. She likes her life inside the campus. She has decent neighbours, young friends, an active social life. She gets to swim. She can walk around within the walls at night; in east Delhi she could walk nowhere. Of course law and order is a problem, but then, she says, that's just one of the pitfalls of life in North India. And she reminds me of my brother's words when she moved out there. 'You're moving to the jungle!' She knew people who moved to East Delhi in '84 and they said exactly the same thing: it was a wilderness out there. 'But people adjust.' And she has her property. The price has plateaued, it's true, but everyone knows it will rise again.

9—LAGOS

SHUFFERING AND SHMILING IN LAGOS

BY AYODELE OLOFINTUADE

My earliest memory of Lagos was the smell that hits you passing through the last toll gate of Ogun State. It's a smell of loamy soil after the first rains. The stink of waste follows at its heels, making you want to retch. Just before you actually throw up, the sea blows the smell away leaving you with fresh, salty air. After the bumpy ride on the Lagos-Ibadan expressway, that smell brings relief. It's a signal that you're about to really start enjoying the holidays. It is both the smell of rot and the smell of new beginnings. Visions of crowded streets, shiny toys, beaches and numerous cousins fill my head, and my heart races ahead of me.

We lived in Ibadan, a large city in West Africa where my mother's mother had settled. However, we still had innumerable relatives living in Lagos who we would spend the holidays with. My mother never told us which family member would host us until we got there. She had a way of keeping everything a mystery until the taxi ferrying us from the motor-park had nearly reached its destination. We could be staying with our cousins at Ajegunle, in their sprawling house full of secret nooks. They had an old fish pond which we turned into a swimming pool during the hot, dry season, and a vast library in which you could lose yourself. Or we could be going to Victoria Island, where our reserved – and extremely rich – cousins quietly showed off the latest gadgets brought back from their last trip abroad. I hated that cold house.

My favourite was my aunt's tiny bungalow, on a tiny street in the heart of Lagos Island, where I ate seafood to my heart's content, and played with wild things masquerading as children.

My most enduring imaginings of Lagos came from the stories told to me by Alhaja, my grandmother, who grew up in Arooloya Those stories changed Lagos from a mere playground into a cityscape of fantasies. She told us stories about racing her mates through the streets of Arooloya – Ita-Faaji, Idumota, Oke-Popo – butt-naked, until someone drew the attention of her mother to the fact that she was no longer a child, that she'd sprouted a pair of breasts and hair on her pudenda. Alhaja was thrown a cotton wrapper. This minor distraction did not stop her from winning all the races – against both boys and girls.

She told us stories of how she was withdrawn from school, because the schoolmaster whipped her a little too hard for her mother's liking, and was immediately apprenticed to a Sisi.

Sisi's were women suspected to be earthbound daughters of the sea, because they were educated, sophisticated and well-versed in the art of seduction. A Sisi would take in your half-wild daughter and turn her into a business-savvy coquette.

My grandmother was a storyteller, passing down ancestral memories through her words, through her gestures.
Memories of mad, bad women, who did what they liked,
exactly how they liked it.

In the evenings, she would lie down on her king-sized
bed, a gaggle of grandchildren around her, and tell us about
Yemoja, the goddess of the seas, who comes out of the waters
of Okun at night to seduce mortals. Yemoja afflicts them
with such an itch in their loins that, no matter how hard it is
scratched – with other women, parties, or even godliness – it
cannot not be assuaged.

I remember a particular story in which Yemoja stayed so
long with a man that she had a daughter with him. When
it was the agreed time for him to let his lover and daughter
return to the seas, the man ran into the hinterlands, his
daughter in tow. Yemoja took him, the daughter, and the
house where they had lived, by flooding the little town the
man had chosen as his hideout, then dragging the whole
house back to Lagos, and from there into the sea.

My holiday trips, and periodic stays in Lagos, mostly with
my mother's cousins and step-siblings, were inundated with
urban myths as well as folklore. Myths full of otherworldly
beings, like the cloven-hoofed woman that prowled Third
Mainland Bridge, ghosts that traded with human beings at
night markets, and the man with a mouth full of sharpened
iron teeth that gave 'innocent' young women rides of no return.

One of my aunts claimed an encounter with this particular
legend. According to her, the man had picked her up somewhere on the Island, offering her a ride to Yaba, around 3a.m.
After they drove off, my aunt described the silence in the car
as blanket-like, making her chatter nervously. As they climbed

the Third Mainland Bridge, she claimed she had started telling her benefactor about the legend, scoffing at the impressionable young women with overheated imaginations who usually told it. My aunt asked if he believed there could be such a man in existence, with a mouth full of iron teeth. The man turned towards her, flashed a mouth full of iron and asked, 'You mean, like these?'

My aunt, apparently of superhero persuasions, jumped out of his car while it was still in motion. For weeks after, she showed off the bruises and abrasions she got from rolling on the Bridge.

For a child like me, who lived her reality between the pages of books and oral history, as actively as she climbed trees and built mud-houses, there was only a thin line between the myths and the harsh realities of being a Lagosian. One moment you are telling your younger brother a half-believed tale of monster fishes that beach themselves as sacrifices to feed the starving masses of Eko, the next your taxi driver is pulling over because a man or woman just took a suicide jump off the Third Mainland Bridge.

Lagos, back then, was as wild as any fairytale forest. Children– who should have been in school – hawked, begging for alms or picking the pockets of the unwary. Bands of armed robbers terrorised whole neighbourhoods with their guns and oiled nakedness. Con-men took your money simply because you were fool enough to reveal your newbie status by gawking at the high rises and skyscrapers that made up Broad Street. Vagrants built fiefdoms under the numerous bridges, on and off the Island. Sex workers (male, intersex and female), trawled the streets of Ayilara, Ikeja, Ikoyi. 'Corporate beggars' were dressed to the nines, spinning sob stories that made you dip into your handbag for your last naira note.

'My pregnant wife was in a car accident. The doctor says they need to carry out an operation urgently or she will lose our triplets and die!'

There were protesters and power-hungry activists. Gun-toting policemen harassed commercial bus drivers, shouting 'Show me your particolas!'; 'Area boys', whose ages ranged from fifteen to fifty, roamed in gangs, bullying and extorting whoever they could. Then, of course, there were the one-percenters, stupendously wealthy, insulated from everyday life by triple glazed glass and air-conditioning – in their homes, in their cars, and within their heads.

Everything happened in Lagos and you saw it all riding the Molue Bus, immortalised by Fela Kuti in his song, Shuffering and Shmiling:

Everyday my people dey inside bus
Forty-nine sitting ninety-nine standing
Dem dey die, dem dey wake like cocks...
Shuffering and Shmiling...

Lagos was inside those buses, rides of bodies, piled one atop another. Old men groping young women and receiving slaps; snake-oil merchants selling cure-alls for the common cold to the not-so-common filariasis; preacher men who told you the 'one-and-only true path to heaven' only after you donated your widow's mite.

Molue bus rides made your head spin with their airlessness, literarily snatching your breath away, whilst you were squeezed between the stomach of a pregnant woman standing right behind you, and the gigantic buttocks of the woman standing in front of you. Your short arms barely reached the overhead handholds as you jostled between washed and unwashed bodies, sweat mixed with perfumes sprayed so generously that you reeled drunkenly as you got off the bus, unsure if it was even the right stop.

My brother Olawale was ten years older than me, a marine engineer and sailor, who, by the time I turned ten, spent months away at sea. Each time he returned home heavy with presents: a beautiful, multi-coloured shell; a dried-out sea-horse hung on a leather thong to be worn around the neck; books, comics, magazines. The gift I'll always remember him by was the one he gave me for my thirteenth birthday – a deep vermillion red lipstick. That red lipstick, which he also taught me how to wear, was symbolic. I was no longer a little girl but a young woman who was so beautiful she should wear red lipstick, because it complimented her earth-dark skin.

On my fourteenth birthday, Olawale snuck me into The Shrine, where I watched, for the first and last time, Fela Anikulapo Kuti, his Queens and Egypt 80 perform on stage.

I idolised my unconventional brother. His life cemented my love for Lagos and her badness. His death cemented my hatred for Lagos and her death traps. His car took a tumble on the Lagos end of the Lagos-Ibadan expressway, immortalising him; those that die young become gods.

But before he died, I moved to Lagos as soon as I finished my secondary school finals, at sixteen years of age, I packed my things and moved from Ibadan to Lagos. My first port of call was my aunt's house in Omidun, a tiny neighbourhood in the very heart of Lagos Island, known as Eko to the people who lived and loved within her uncertainties. I slept all day and played chess and Scrabble all night, with a bunch of other teenagers, mostly male. We would sit outside the home of one of the boys and watch Eko come alive. Lagos never sleeps.

It was during this period that the Lagos of my imagination morphed from a fairy-tale landscape into a grown woman. I imagined her as a woman who was raised on the tiny street of Lafiaji. This is where the true daughters of Okun thrive. They drawled their Yoruba in a manner that could fool the uninitiated into thinking they were laid back, but they were not. They picked up and discarded boyfriends, husbands and lovers as casually as they flitted from one party to another.

They were hard-headed business women with skin bleached the colour of ripe oranges, dark knuckles, knees and ankles, a couple of gold teeth flashed in insincere smiles. Women with overflowing curves, selling everything from exotic lace to spare car parts. No work was too 'masculine' or too 'menial' for the Eko woman, as long as she was making her money.

These women were raised on the streets of Lafiaji to the beat of underground fuji music, and Lagos was part of the dust kicked up by their dancing feet. Lagos was the cumulus of smoke hanging over their heads, puffed from expertly-wrapped joints,.

At some point Lagos began to appear not only as a Lafaji woman, but also a mother, watching over all her children. She was the all-seeing one that smirks as her children run to Oluwole to obtain fake WAEC results, fake university degrees and fake travel documents that would give their feet wings on adventures to the other cities of the world.

I imagined her watching, with ill-concealed glee, as these same children defied the well-buffed boots of the army and the dictators, who governed with guns and bombs, grinding Nigeria's economy to a halt, causing grave poverty. She watched her children turn the city into the cocaine capital of Nigeria when they returned from England, America and Latin America with pockets full of easily-made foreign currency.

And then Lagos became, for me, an old woman, a war-torn grandmother, revealing her wounds, her colonial past. She walked me through the foreign-built enclaves of Ikoyi and Victoria Island and taught me about Madam Efunronye Tinubu who traded in firearms and slaves. She showed me Freedom Park, a former colony prison where past leaders such as Awolowo and Nnamdi Azikiwe were incarcerated in prison cells no larger than a sugar box. The colonial gallows stand proudly, smack in the centre of the prison, where everyone who dared the authorities were hung by their neck until they were dead.

After my brother died, I left Lagos, a grieving, cynical, twenty-four-year-old, disenchanted with the city and its illusory promises. Almost broken, promising never to look back, I returned to my grandmother's home in Ibadan. I took refuge in the quiet and simplicity of a city that had little but would generously share it with you. With time, I healed.

Like a junkie, however, I was addicted to the city. I returned to Lagos as an adult who would no longer be fooled by the glitter, or so I told myself. It was then that she turned herself into my master, my playground, my mistress. Lagos was my first true kiss, the city of my awakening.

There was always something going on: arts, music, plays, parties, books – fun! I would enter Lagos, pockets bulging with hard currency, ready to jump on whichever dizzying ride I had been promised. Lagos stopped appearing as a grandmother to me. She would take everything I had then kick me out when I ran out of funds. While the fun lasted, I revelled in her parties. I loved most of all her open-air concerts and particularly the one curated monthly by Ade Bantu.

Afropolitan Vibes was full of old hands in the music industry and young, upcoming artistes. One moment you were dancing to the latest hip-hop song, exported to the rest of the world by these amazingly talented young people, who would not take a 'no' in their quest for international stardom. The next you were sunk in nostalgia and 'fandom', as the musicians you spent most of your teenage years crushing on rocked the stage. Salawa Abeni, Fatai Rolling Dollars, Abass Akande Obesere – these were the ones who had made music against all odds; terrible studio conditions, thieving music promoters, non-paying concert organisers, piracy. At these concerts I forgot politeness and self-consciousness. I forgot my 'home-training' as I danced until my bones reminded me, once more, that time had passed. I belted out the lyrics of half-forgotten songs until my voice became hoarse. Lagos wilding.

The older I grow, the more my eyes are opened to the vagaries of Lagos, although this doesn't mean she doesn't have a way of throwing you a lifeline. The more you peel back the city's layers, the more you realise you never knew her in the first place. From a childhood populated by myths, to teenage years chasing after some dreamy idea of the city, to an adulthood that tries to look at Lagos with eyes wide open. I've yet to determine how deeply I love or hate this city of desperadoes and dreamers.

Often, today, she is best when I think of her food. Lagos is a delight of crabs and other crustaceans, freshly caught that morning from the ever-generous waters of Osa, steamed in their own juices, a dash of lime, garlic, ginger and salt to taste. Tilapia, obokun, eja-osan, stewed over a low fire in tomatoes, onions and generous helpings of bell peppers that have your eyes streaming tears of joy. Alongside, there is plantain, fried to a state of golden-brown perfection, and it is all heaped on a bed of long-grain rice that will have your salivary glands working overtime.

But when I see how the homeless in the city are treated, I know she is not only about beans cooked to a state of fluffiness. Lagos is ruthless with her poor, rendering them homeless willy-nilly. Land grabbers, aided by the government, throw people out of the seafront shanties that they've occupied for so many years, sometimes centuries.

These days, I mostly like to imagine Lagos as an old sexworker that demands payment before services, her ancient eyes looking through you, down to your soul. She is like a vampire; one bite from her and you're forever hooked. She would take you and take you until there's nothing left of you and then throw you out, a husk, never looking back.

But she can also be tender, this old sex-worker. She would pick a child and nurture her until she's the perfect representation of all the good that's within her. She would present this child, with whom she was well pleased, to the world. And this child would walk the streets of other cosmopolitan cities in other parts of the globe, oblivious to the privilege that brought her there.

Her head would be held high, her intellect sharpened, her tongue fluid in the language of the powered. She would be the envy of all who beheld her. People would stare in wonder, asking from what magical place she had come. Then, and only then, would she tell them: about Lagos, Nigeria, the place her heart calls home.

10—SHENZEN

METRO LINE FIVE

BY WU JUN
TRANSLATED BY LUCY CRAIG-McQUAIDE

Shi Yu changed into a pink slip then lay down on the massage table. She hadn't seen Zhu Xiyan this time. When she closed her eyes, the beauty treatment finally began. Just as the beautician was preparing the massage oil, Shi Yu heard a vibration on her right, followed by a melody floating through the air.

'Gazing at the rising moon...' Shi Yu rushed to answer the phone before the moon could reach its peak. It was the Environmental Protection Society. Shi Yu realised sadly that those were the only calls she expected that year. There was a time when everyone had made eyes at her and told her their news, but that was over now.

Shi Yu had been notified about the Environmental Protection Society meeting two weeks ago, but she had forgotten about it. She wordlessly communicated to the beautician not to make a sound, then pulled herself together and said 'I'm on my way! I'm nearly there, don't worry. Don't wait, start without me!'

She turned over and got off the bed before she had finished speaking. She got dressed, ignoring the half-open door. Then she grabbed her expensive glasses from the shelf and put them on. As she left, she turned to fix her hair and practise a smile in the mirror. Downstairs, she didn't look up as she said, 'Something's come up, so I have to go. Save my spot, I'll be back soon!' Her attitude wasn't an act, and she didn't feel a twinge of guilt about it. She had tried to book many times before, and the reply had always been that they were too busy, that they only had a few girls working there, that they were fully booked. Try again another time. We'll let you know when we can fit you in. What bad luck that this should happen when her turn had finally come around.

There were building works for the metro everywhere jamming up the roads, so she lost time taking a detour. Cranes towered over the roads like pins in a map that just made people lose their way. They hadn't put up road signs and she ended up going down several dead ends. At first she couldn't reverse, and she sweated profusely as she tried to back out.

In the end she was late, but luckily no one waited for her at that kind of meeting. The last item on the agenda was putting forward ideas, but because she had arrived late, she thought it would be best not to say anything. She might otherwise have proposed that the city of Shenzhen stop constructing the metro. *Things weren't bad before the metro. But now it is a nuisance and it was damaging both the environment and the original landscape. Shenzhen is a must-see landmark in the progress of Chinese civilisation as well as an essential stopping point for people of distinction. Why mess that up?* Seeing everyone else speaking out confidently, she butted in awkwardly, but when it was time for her to say her piece, all she could muster was that she had no opinion.

At the end of the meeting, she was greeted by a few women stuffing imported grapes into their mouths. They were friendly but all they talked about was how pretty everyone looked, how their clothes suited them, and where they had bought them from.

Men nodded and waved at her from across the room. They gathered up their documents and left one after another. One of them, Yu Zhong, stared at her longingly, waiting to say something. Shi Yu noticed but didn't want to go over. He was fat and had some sort of eye problem, and always stared at her. He liked talking about politics and the latest hot topics of conversation. Yu Zhong asked her out to dinner every time there was a meeting. Shi Yu hung back to avoid him and watched as, one by one, everyone got into their cars or got lifts, so in the end she drove back alone. As she started the engine, Shi Yu looked back at the building. *Damn it!* She berated herself and hit the gas.

There had been over two dozen of these meetings. They had to hire out a space every time, so by now Shi Yu had visited quite a few hotel and office meeting rooms. In her opinion, most of the participants had nothing better to do; they were either retired support personnel or hung around because they were unemployed like her. The fact that they rented meeting rooms made her think that none of them actually cared about the environment, or that they had no idea about real conservation. Most of the attendees just complained and made cynical comments about the environment. Despite this, very few people ever missed a meeting.

Once, Shi Yu was put in charge of taking photographs. She did a few rounds of the room to take photos of people giving speeches. When she got back to her seat and looked at the pictures, she was dismayed. Everyone, even those sitting around the rostrum, was doodling stick figures or practising their signatures instead of taking notes.

Shi Yu was determined not to go again after that, but when they contacted her for the next meeting she couldn't resist. She berated herself again as she turned onto the overpass. Before they had started work on the metro, she could take this main road all the way to her door and be home in under fifteen minutes.

Perhaps the argument was bound to happen.

When she reached the salon, the same beautician was waiting for her. Her smile wasn't as friendly as before, though. Clearly Shi Yu had held her up and made her lose money.

'You're back,' she said with a blank expression, and went upstairs. Shi Yu didn't look at her. She put on a pair of pink slippers and followed her up the narrow staircase into the same room as before, then got changed and lay down. She was really tired this time and couldn't keep her eyes open. She heard the sound of the face mask being mixed together and screwed her eyes shut. Last time, the face cream had got into her eyes and they had gone all red. She'd had a hard time eating dinner that evening because she felt like the women at the table were all staring at her. One of them even asked her if she was okay, as though to draw attention to the fact that Shi Yu had been crying.

Some went in her eyes again this time. And this was just the start. Shi Yu didn't have any dinner plans that evening so she kept quiet. She would just wear her pyjamas or even her husband's old vest and shorts, sit in front of the television and eat as much as she wanted. In any case, no one cared what she did so she could always just pay to join a gym later. Shi Yu was used to killing time while her husband was at work. She was very rational when it came to beauty treatments and knew that they were pretty pointless. If she slept badly or got depressed, then everything would go down the drain and she would be back at square one.

When Shi Yu was a teacher, she once heard some of her male colleagues talking about a famous singer, who was a celebrity member of the People's Political Consultative Conference. One of Shi Yu's colleagues and this woman had been on the same flight. He said that when she woke up she looked just like his grandmother, with big bags under her eyes and more than a few white hairs. The woman didn't look anything like she usually did on TV, but everyone went to a beauty salon and got a makeover before going on screen. In the end, he quietly put away his autograph book. On hearing this, Shi Yu walked up and said 'You lot are too harsh. You've just downloaded her MP3 and now you're criticising her.' The woman had sent it to the school as a present for Teachers' Day.

Her colleagues smiled. 'You're right. But you needn't worry, you're still young and beautiful!' Shi Yu smiled in spite of herself, but she felt upset. *So that's what men think of women, then.* From then on, she understood that everyone gets old, and having beauty treatments and putting on makeup are just ways to lie to yourself. But sometimes lying to yourself is necessary.

Shi Yu moved even though the face mask was only half on. She wasn't happy. The beautician had clearly skipped the massage part of the treatment. She might have just forgotten, or perhaps she had done it deliberately to punish Shi Yu for wasting two hours of her time. This beauty salon was very successful. The beautician noticed that Shi Yu wasn't asleep and asked whether she had heard of French-made shapewear.

'I have,' she said.

The beautician went on about on the benefits of wearing such underwear and added that a single pair cost one thousand nine hundred yuan. From behind the mask, Shi Yu curled her lip.

'One thousand nine hundred yuan! Only an idiot would buy that. It's clearly a pyramid scheme!'

Shi Yu peered through narrowed eyes and saw the beautician glaring at her. Shi Yu didn't like her and tried to avoid looking at her. She had tried to book this appointment three times. Their response on the phone was very thorough. 'Lots of people are off on Saturdays and Sundays. People pay a lot of money for appointments at the weekend. They're all diamond level members who want the full treatment.'

The third time, Shi Yu went to the salon in person. She took no notice of the employee offering her water and walked up to the reception desk and said, 'I came to your establishment two years ago, you know. Not to get a treatment though. I was carrying out an inspection.' It was true. She and members of the Environmental Protection Society had taken journalists there to look into the pollution from beauty salons. Shi Yu noticed that, upon hearing this, the employees still looked just as indifferent. The owner sitting nearby looked up and smiled politely but then went straight back to looking over the accounts. No one paid any attention to what Shi Yu had said. To business owners, if you're not a paying customer, you're nobody.

Shi Yu was from Chaozhou, a notoriously conservative place. She had never left Guangdong province, so she was a real local. Shi Yu had played musical instruments and studied at the College of Music Affiliated School when she was young. She later gave it up, but her personality and way of thinking had changed completely. When she quit her teaching job, everyone said that she had finally got some guts. It might have only been a village-run school, but there was always a chance of becoming a fully-qualified teacher one day. And yet, she thought, or rather knew, that her personality was incompatible with that profession. Besides, teaching senior classes was tiring.

Shi Yu had heard that they were laying people off, but she didn't mind. She knew what men liked. She knew that they liked her style, which was something that other local girls didn't have. A rich man and a pretty woman make for a perfect couple, so she might as well just go home and be a full-time housewife. She had been lauded for her decision, of course. She was totally unlike a normal Guangdong girl, especially one from Chaozhou – even the director of the school board had said so – but she had lasted less than a year there and regretted it: if she hadn't left, she wouldn't have got mixed up with the Environmental Protection Society.

When Shi Yu thought about how she used to be someone of importance, she hated herself and her husband. She still blamed him for not stopping her. She couldn't tell him that she hated him, of course, but she could admit it to herself. She wanted to get in shape and have kids. She used to live life to the full and her body had paid the price. Fortunately, her husband wasn't bothered. His ex-wife had given him two children, which made Shi Yu want to have a child of her own even more, to put their minds at ease. But it seemed that the more she wanted one, the less inclined the heavens were to help her.

When the beautician started to peddle the salon's five thousand-yuan gold loyalty card, Shi Yu suddenly sat up and shouted, 'Are you done?'

The masseuse jumped but swiftly regained her composure. 'Sorry, I didn't know you were awake.'

'Why talk to me if you thought I was asleep, then? You lot are so desperate for commission that you're stopping me from sleeping.'

It was clear that the beautician had been in similar situations before. She hurried over to get the water and moved everything out of the way, as though to make room for her client's anger. She stood in the doorway and watched as Shi Yu peeled the face mask off her face bit by bit, even though it hadn't dried completely, then threw it on the floor.

'I'm sorry, Miss Shi.'

'Don't call me Miss. I'm going to get changed, so get out. Go downstairs and get me my money back. I didn't want to have to do this, you know.'

She pointed at the green mould covering the walls and went on. 'Doing facials, washing feet, and cooking all in the same room is really unhygienic and violates health and safety regulations. The other day there was water dripping from the ceiling, but it turns out it wasn't water – it was oil. It dirtied my clothes. Hurry up and give me my money back. I'm never coming back here!'

The beautician was dumbfounded. She wanted to explain

herself but didn't know what to say so she simply left. Zhu Xiyan came in as Shi Yu was straightening her trouser hems.

'Your breasts are so big, Miss! I'm jealous,' she said, beaming.

Shi Yu stood up straight and saw a very young woman. She was wearing a uniform too, but she was so short and the clothes so long that they trailed under her feet. Shi Yu was still furious. She was on the verge of going downstairs and arguing with the owner.

Her husband had originally bought a flat in the area so as to avoid friends, acquaintances, and his ex-wife. There wasn't a single place around there to have fun. To make matters worse, the area around the flat had turned into a building site just a few days after they had moved in, and the noise stopped them sleeping. Then they said they were building the metro, and house prices immediately skyrocketed. Shi Yu was happy for a few days because she thought that her husband really had thought ahead by becoming an engineer. She stopped complaining and, in the evenings, made soup for him as a way to make amends. After all, in the past she had criticised him a lot, mostly because they lived too far from the city centre. The cinema was over half an hour's drive away. Besides, she felt uncomfortable frequenting the same markets as those migrant worker girls. Were it not for the fact that this was the only beauty salon in this remote part of town, she would never have come, or at least she wouldn't be so worked up about it.

Zhu Xiyan stepped forwards and removed a piece of the face mask that Shi Yu hadn't wiped off her face. She showed it to Shi Yu.

'Look, all the yellow qi has been drained out.'

Shi Yu had lost her temper before, but now she didn't know what to say. Zhu Xiyan looked at her and laughed.

'Miss, go ahead and lie down. I'm going to get some ointment for you that eliminates yellow qi and can even lighten those blemishes.' She pointed to Shi Yu's face. Shi Yu hesitated, and Zhu Xiyan handed her some new clothes, saying, 'Put this on, it suits your figure. Get changed and I'll go and get the products.'

Zhu Xiyan came back carrying an aromatherapy lamp. She turned off the main light then lit the lamp. Shi Yu didn't know whether it was the aromatherapy, or because she was so tired, but she quickly fell into a deep sleep. She didn't wake up until after seven o'clock in the evening, when everyone was watching the Hong Kong news on TV. It was loud, and the sound came in from the street. They said that the Hong Kong stocks had fallen sharply, and that a second global financial crisis could be imminent. Obama was concerned about the governor of the People's Bank of China, Zhou Xiaochuan's, financial adjustment policies.

She went to the beauty salon a second time five days later. Zhu Xiyan told Shi Yu her name, and that she was born in 1983. She asked Shi Yu if she was born in the eighties too.

'Born in the eighties! You must be joking. I'm ten years older than you. Did your boss tell you to say that?'

Zhu Xiyan laughed and replied, 'She didn't. She just does the accounts and looks after her children. She doesn't tell us anything, Miss.'

Then she said that she was Hunanese and to help Shi Yu remember, she added that it was where there had been a terrible blizzard the year before. 'I'm sure you donated money. Thank you on behalf of my family.'

Shi Yu smiled and asked, 'Were you in your hometown at the time?'

'No, I was in Harbin then,' said Zhu Xiyan offhandedly.

'Where? Harbin – isn't that in the northeast?' asked Shi Yu with surprise.

'Yes, I'd found a job and the company sent me there to promote beauty products. It's so cold there, I got frostbite on my hands and feet.' To illustrate her point, she put her left hand in front of Shi Yu's face. Shi Yu saw a slender, scarred palm.

'You've been through a lot.' Shi Yu felt that this girl had had a difficult youth.

'Not really. The people there are really nice, and the food is great. We don't get to eat anything tasty at home. And the ice sculptures are like something from a fairy tale.'

Shi Yu stared at Zhu Xiyan and said, 'You don't get ice sculptures in your hometown, and it doesn't snow there. So how come there was a blizzard?'

'It wasn't in my hometown. There was a blizzard though, but we don't have those lovely ice sculptures. I'm from a small village, and it's just as cold inside the house as it is outside. The winters are torture.'

'So you came to the south, because the climate is warmer and better for your health.' Shi Yu felt satisfied with her explanation.

'Actually, no. I came here with my boyfriend. He was the best thing about going to Harbin. I made friends with his sister and that's how I met him.'

'How come you already have a boyfriend at such a young age?' Shi Yu feigned surprise. She imagined some stupid great hulk of a man, or a skinny, shriveled-up biker type.

'I'm not that young. Lots of my classmates already have children!'

'Is he in Guangdong too?' Shi Yu asked indifferently.

'He's an engineer working on Metro Line Five, actually.' She laughed slightly awkwardly.

Shi Yu laughed too, and she thought that the girl must be rather uneducated because she clearly didn't know the difference between an engineer and a workman. Seeing how happy Zhu Xiyan looked, Shi Yu thought to herself that from afar those workmen looked rather like locusts in their identical yellow uniforms and hats.

That evening, Shi Yu told her husband what had happened at the beauty salon. 'An engineer! Unless she's exaggerating to show off, she doesn't know what an engineer even is!' Shi Yu noticed that her husband hadn't reacted and added, 'They follow the metro. They go wherever they build the metro.'

Shi Yu thought about how she had berated herself earlier. The metro had been extended right up to her door, and now every time she went home, she had to hunt for a parking space. The people on the building site made a lot of noise talking and laughing as they got off work, and even made a racket when they were queueing to shower. She had gone to complain in the name of the Environmental Protection Society's campaign against noise pollution. 'The builders of Shenzhen.' That was the kind of headline she saw in the Shenzhen Special Zone Daily.

'It must be hard on the building site. I've seen them eating, huddled together, and it looked like there was nothing in their bowls but a few vegetables,' she said to Zhu Xiyan at her next appointment.

'It's not that bad at all! The food is really good. Sometimes I even go and eat there. When I'm off work, I sometimes cook for my boyfriend and he shares the food with his friends. They're always in a good mood, which cheers me up too. In any case, where his metro goes, I go too. See, you even have a beauty salon in this backwater. As long as there's a beauty salon, I can put food on the table, and my boyfriend can enjoy the soup and spicy fish heads I make for him. He's very fussy about fish – it has to be fresh.'

'Right, right...' Shi Yu laughed. 'How about this. Why don't you take me with you one day and show me your house?'

Shi Yu thought that Zhu Xiyan was a very optimistic girl. She had so little to eat that she was lean and haggard, and yet she still said that her life was easy. Shi Yu had noticed that, to save money, Zhu Xiyan bought the cheapest packed lunches from the corner shop next door. When she thought of that shabby little house on the construction site, Shi Yu even felt a twinge of sadness. It had been a long time since she had felt sympathy towards anyone, so she was happy to find that she felt something. She asked Zhu Xiyan if her life had been hard, seeing as she had left home at such a young age to work, and her family was surely too poor to pay school fees. Shi Yu kept trying to find something that would make Zhu Xiyan aware of her plight, but the girl was too dim-witted to realise it.

Zhu Xiyan laughed. 'We might have been poor, but if I had wanted to study, I could have done. I just didn't want to.'

Shi Yu suggested getting a new loyalty card, despite having failed to go through with it several times. She proposed that one requirement be that Zhu Xiyan do all her treatments. The owner was very happy with that plan and said,

'Okay, great. No problem. This private room will be reserved for you. There's a lot of special offers at the moment. We're giving away a package that lets you bring a friend to have their feet done, get their hair washed, and get a massage.'

Shi Yu slept badly and refused to be in the same room as other people. She particularly didn't want to see other women getting changed, or for others to see her. Besides, she had some odd habits, like the fact that she didn't like music. Whenever she walked in and heard that piano music, she would frown and tell them to turn it off. To her, listening to music in such a vile setting was akin to blasphemy.

'Some clients like it and tell us to put it on,' said an employee in response.

'Do they? They're just putting on airs. Do you like listening to piano music whilst you're having a pedicure or working out? It's torture! Those pretentious yuppies,' Shi Yu grumbled and went upstairs.

'You've got such a great figure, Miss! You're right not to let them see, they'd just die of jealousy. You've got such big breasts and a tiny waist! If those women see, they'll hate themselves. Even I'm jealous.'

'Don't be ridiculous.' But Shi Yu smiled to herself. So, she still had her assets. She had relied on her enviable figure to create quite a few opportunities for herself that year. She'd also snatched a husband from someone else's clutches – and not just any old husband. A rich one. He wasn't as good-looking or as cultured as Shi Yu, but that didn't matter. She didn't want culture or looks. She wanted money. Shi Yu felt that, apart from the fact that they had been married for a few years and still hadn't had children, her life was pretty much perfect.

'You're not so bad yourself,' said Shi Yu to console Zhu Xiyan. 'You're dainty and delicate.' She felt a pang of sympathy for the girl before her as she spoke. She couldn't actually think of another nice thing to say. Zhu Xiyan was thin and sallow, and had a few blemishes on her cheekbones. Her large, lively eyes were obscured by her overly-long fringe. Shi Yu started to feel sorry for this girl, who really didn't have any assets to speak of apart from her way with words and her ability to put people at ease when she spoke.

However, she was a bit presumptuous. The Environmental Protection Society called again as Shi Yu was lying on the massage bed. She barely said a word because she didn't want them to think that she did nothing all day. Zhu Xiyan suddenly bent down and spoke into the phone.

'She doesn't have time for this, she's got a meeting.'

At first, Shi Yu was indignant. She felt that Zhu Xiyan was too impudent and willful. She had even repeated dirty jokes that other clients had told her. It was as though she thought of Shi Yu as a friend, and not a client.

'Miss, if it were something important, they wouldn't put on an act like that. Besides, you're not like them.' Shi Yu didn't say anything, but she closed her eyes and thought that Zhu Xiyan was actually cute and unpretentious. People like that are few and far between these days. The people from the Environmental Protection Society always assumed airs, as though their meetings were earth-shatteringly important. Shi Yu imagined their expressions and lay back down and smiled. She was amazed that Zhu Xiyan had hit the nail on the head. It had been a long time since she had felt so happy. *She's right, those people love putting on an act*, she thought.

It seemed that wisdom could be found even amongst the least cultured people. Sometimes they could even come out with really insightful statements. Shi Yu was happy that she had found an advantage to being uneducated, and wanted to tell her husband about what she had learnt. Of course, she was also trying to flatter him, as he had worked hard to make a living since he was a young man and had never attended school. He was coarse and self-abasing. Fortunately, Shi Yu didn't like poor and pedantic scholarly types. Money was the only thing that had ever held any attraction for her. Her husband could earn a lot of money on each project and also got some work from the metro works on his doorstep.

Zhu Xiyan pretended to be angry and said, 'Miss, I wish I had a camera to record the face you just made.'

Shi Yu gave a start. 'What? Record what?'

'To film your ugly face! Your facial expression changed so much when you were speaking to them, I thought I'd have to re-apply your face mask.'

Shi Yu knew she was joking, so she replied, 'Go ahead and film me, I'll wait.' She thought it was funny. It was the kind of joke she would never make.

Zhu Xiyan still had that rather angry look on her face. *She's funny*, thought Shi Yu. *She oversteps the boundaries sometimes, but she's very interesting indeed.*

She thought about the Environmental Protection Society again as she fell asleep. What kind of organisation were they anyway? They were all bores who took themselves far too seriously. Shi Yu felt like she alone saw them for what they really were. They had never bothered to research the facts. If they weren't discussing things they'd seen online, they were arguing about agenda items from two meetings ago until they were blue in the face.

She filled out the form for the membership card as she got changed. The gold card was six thousand eight hundred yuan.

'The diamond card is over twenty thousand yuan, but you can bring your husband along for a free hair and face wash,' Zhu Xiyan offered.

'Oh, I talked to him about it, but he said that this place was just for women and there's too much female qi here, so he didn't want to come,' Shi Yu replied gratefully.

'Too much female qi? What's that about? That's disrespectful.' Zhu Xiyan pouted and continued. 'But you Guangdong folk are like that. Miss, your handwriting is so nice. Just now, another client said so too.'

'It's alright, I suppose,' Shi Yu replied indifferently. She was pleased with herself. Her husband had complimented her penmanship too. She still knew how to write beautifully on a blackboard.

During another treatment, Zhu Xiyan left to answer her phone when she was in the middle of doing Shi Yu's nails. The owner came over to help, and, embarrassed, said, 'Looks like you're too easy on her. That won't do – she'll get spoilt.'

'It's okay. She's got a date.'

'Right, but you having to wait around for her is a step too far. She should be grateful for what she's got.'

When she went downstairs, Shi Yu saw a tall man wearing glasses standing with Zhu Xiyan in the doorway. It was pouring with rain, and the droplets drummed against the eaves. There was an advert for the beauty salon behind them.

Zhu Xiyan looked different. She smiled at Shi Yu, then turned around to face the man again and continued talking. Shi Yu noticed that he was over a head taller than Zhu Xiyan. He was only about three years younger than Shi Yu.

So, Zhu Xiyan had told the truth about her boyfriend.

He really had been to university, and he really was an engineer. Shi Yu was reminded of her old school. When she was a teacher, she had paid close attention to guys like him, so he felt familiar. On the way home, Shi Yu wondered what he saw in Zhu Xiyan, especially as an engineering graduate.

Shi Yu never discussed love and marriage or anything similar with Zhu Xiyan again after that. She suddenly lost interest. Zhu Xiyan never brought it up either. Once, as she was leaving, Shi Yu was pleased to see that Zhu Xiyan was crying. She went over to comfort her, only to find that she was crying tears of joy. Zhu Xiyan's boyfriend's family had agreed to their engagement.

In the autumn, Zhu Xiyan came to Shi Yu's house to look after her. Shi Yu had had another miscarriage. She was still weak and didn't want to do anything. She wouldn't even cook and always ordered food in instead. Zhu Xiyan was dripping with sweat and looked as though she had had to make two journeys to bring everything over.

'I'll give you another ten yuan.'

'Don't worry, they've already paid me.' If it wasn't convenient for the clients to come in, or if they requested it, the salon would send someone over to them. The owner had gone with her the first time to help her carry everything, sighing, 'It's bad for business.'

Shi Yu and Zhu Xiyan had run out of things to talk about. If they did talk, it was often just one of them carrying the conversation. Shi Yu liked talking about the past, about how songs used to be better written, and how people used to care about each other. Not like now. Now, people would delete someone's number if they hadn't been in touch for a few days.

Zhu Xiyan only cared about the metro. She talked about it at length. 'I don't know if you know this, but once we were working on the metro at Liantian village by Luohu Lake and scared the villagers, because they thought we were going to dig up their ancestors' graves. They came out on the road with kitchen knives ready to fight. Luckily our people were used to that sort of thing, so they sent someone over to explain. It was fine in the end. We actually did dig up their ancestral graves after all that, but when we found the bones no one dared say anything.'

Sometimes Zhu Xiyan would do a few chores around the house once she had finished giving Shi Yu a massage. She would help Shi Yu mop the floor, clear up the stuff on the sofa, or take the rubbish out. Shi Yu always wanted to give her something as thanks. Sometimes it would be a bottle of imported spirits that cost fifty yuan. On other occasions, she would give Zhu Xiyan her old clothes.

'How come I've never seen you wear the clothes I gave you? Don't you like them?'

'I do, but I have to wear my uniform when I'm on the clock.' Shi Yu didn't say anything, but she had seen other employees wearing normal clothes at work. Another time, Shi Yu gave Zhu Xiyan an old painting for the house. It was a present she had been given years ago, before she was married. It had two angelic children on it, a boy and a girl. Zhu Xiyan said she liked it, but Shi Yu found it in the rubbish the next day.

Uncultured people are all the same; they don't appreciate nice things, Shi Yu thought to herself. She hesitated over whether to take it out, then saw that her name was written on it. She didn't feel so angry after that, because after all, it is quite bad to give someone something that has your own name on it.

Shi Yu noticed that Zhu Xiyan was working hard, so she told her to help herself to the ice cream in the freezer. As Shi Yu drank her coffee, Zhu Xiyan sat next to her wolfing down ice cream.

'Here, drink something. That stuff will make you fat if you're not careful.' Shi Yu gestured at the bowl of soup. She made it for her husband but always ate it before he got home.

'Who cares? My mum complains that I'm too thin. Parents always worry over nothing. My boyfriend says so too. He says that he'd still love me if I were a fat pig. And you've got to have some fat on you to breastfeed.'

'That's true, parents do worry over nothing. You know, when my husband and I got married, my mum said that I was a homewrecker. Parents are so old-fashioned. They don't realise that loveless marriages are what's truly shameful. Homewrecker, huh! You should have seen his first wife. She was common as muck. Hadn't even been to primary school and she was so fat.'

Shi Yu measured out twice her size with her hands. It was the first time Shi Yu had talked about it to anyone. She had been repressing it for so long.

'What do you do for a living, Miss?' Zhu Xiyan changed the subject. The other girls from the salon always asked the same question when they had nothing to say, but Shi Yu brushed them off and wouldn't even tell them her name.

'Guess.'

Zhu Xiyan thought long and hard before replying. 'You're a doctor or a teacher.' Shi Yu was surprised, but not unpleasantly so. At the very least, that meant that she seemed cultured.

'Why a teacher? Do I seem very strict?' Shi Yu pretended to be cross.

'No, no,' Zhu Xiyan said hurriedly. 'It's because you make me turn the music off. Teachers do that too. It's only white collar office workers who always say that they want to listen to Beethoven or something. It's like they just come to show off, not to get a beauty treatment. You're not a show-off, Miss.'

Shi Yu gasped. She had never thought that Zhu Xiyan could be so perceptive. That and the business with the painting made Shi Yu think that Zhu Xiyan was completely unlike other girls, and that she shouldn't be underestimated.

Zhu Xiyan brought the conversation around to the metro again.

'Once, we extended the metro to a fishing village. The fishermen had just come back from sea. When they saw that the village didn't look the same as when they had left, their faces dropped. They looked like sad little orphans. But when they found out that they would get good money for the requisitioned land, they were so happy. Otherwise, the land was useless. It was neither sea water nor fresh water and it stank. Now it's great, they're rich, and they can buy a new house and give some money to their kids so they can get married and still have some left over for retirement.'

As she was talking, Shi Yu's husband came home earlier than expected. Shi Yu smiled and stood up. She introduced him to Zhu Xiyan. 'This is my husband.'

Zhu Xiyan just nodded and didn't get up. She looked out of the window and shoveled ice cream into her mouth. Shi Yu's husband blushed, unused to having a stranger in his house. He turned to Shi Yu.

'I came back to get some clothes. I'm going away on a business trip for a few days.'

Later, when Shi Yu couldn't sleep, she nudged her husband awake. 'Isn't it weird? She looks like that, she never even finished middle school and yet her boyfriend is an engineering graduate from a good university.'

The argument happened one afternoon. At first, she didn't think anything of it when she saw Zhu Xiyan's bridal photos, until she heard another beautician say that Zhu Xiyan had got a hefty commission when Shi Yu got her gold card.

'How much did this photoshoot cost?'

When Shi Yu got married, she didn't even wear a wedding dress. She felt a little despondent.

'Four thousand eight hundred yuan, she said so herself,' said the owner. 'And some of the other clients chipped in.'

Shi Yu was furious. She felt as though Zhu Xiyan had tricked her. *I thought she was from the countryside and had given up her chance to go to school so that her younger brothers could go instead. I thought her whole family was dependent on her. I only got the gold card because I felt sorry for her, so that she could afford to put food on the table. Little did I know that she would spend it on a bridal photo shoot.*

She wasn't going to make a complaint, but all of a sudden she felt as though she'd been deceived.

The situation was past saving when she found her husband and Zhu Xiyan in bed together.

She decided to track down Zhu Xiyan to talk things

through and try to salvage what remained of her dignity. Even if he left her, she didn't want to seem like a spurned woman.

She had arranged to meet Yu Zhong from the Environmental Protection Society before she saw Zhu Xiyan. Not ten minutes into the date, he asked her to lend him some money. She even had to pay for the coffee.

Shi Yu felt like she was on the verge of a breakdown by the time Zhu Xiyan arrived.

'Seeing as you're happy, you can keep him,' Shi Yu told Zhu Xiyan. 'I don't want him anymore. I haven't wanted him for a while. I quit my job for him. I put my heart and soul into being a good housewife for him and I still couldn't hold onto him. That's all in the past, of course. I don't care about him anymore. What hurt is that you didn't just take my money. You had to do this to me, too.' Shi Yu didn't want to seem pathetic, but she couldn't help saying it.

Zhu Xiyan was like a different person in normal clothes. She laughed cruelly and said, 'Of course I took a cut. I'd been pushing it for so long and sucking up to you, and all of that costs money. The salon calculates our cut by the second. You keep your husband. I don't want your leftovers. I only slept with him for his money.'

Shi Yu felt herself tearing up, but as soon as she saw Zhu Xiyan's completely indifferent expression, she smiled coldly instead and said, 'Don't be so modest. You make a great couple. You're perfect for each other!'

Zhu Xiyan got straight to the point. 'Listen, if I hadn't taken the money then someone else would. If you hadn't gone to the salon to complain, and lost me a big chunk of my money, I wouldn't have gone after him. I can't stand people who make a bit of money and then think they're amazing.'

'You can't stand them? You're just as bad,' Shi Yu said bitingly.

Zhu Xiyan looked away. 'Anyway, I only did it for the money. I wouldn't marry just anyone. My dream was to find someone cultured. I want him to keep face and set his mind at ease, so that he can build the metro. Oh, I forgot to tell you – I'm pregnant. It's my boyfriend's, obviously. I want my son to study hard and become an engineer when he grows up, not a migrant worker. We'll take him back to Shenzhen to see the metro, and he'll be so proud of us. I know he will.'

The builders packed up and left in the middle of the night. There had been complaints about the noise, so they laid down strict rules and left quietly. Most of the neighbours didn't even wake up. It wasn't until Shi Yu went to the market after breakfast the next morning that she saw the street. Apart from the metro exit bulging out onto the road, it looked exactly the way it had the year before.

AN ATTEMPT AT EXHAUSTING
A PLACE IN PARIS

BY ANNA POOK

In mid-October 1974, Georges Perec began work on An Attempt at Exhausting a Place in Paris. *For several days he sat in cafés and bars around Saint Sulpice and observed the minutiae of everyday life: buses, people, cars, pigeons, plastic bags. His aim was to highlight the things that are often overlooked; the result is a portrait of Paris that allows the city to speak for itself.*

Forty-three years later, I set out to document another arrondissement of Paris, using the same premise as Perec, paying attention to what he referred to as the infra-ordinary. The choice of location isn't insignificant. La Chapelle is a 'quartier populaire', a melting pot, whereas Saint Sulpice was, and still is, a notably bourgeois area. The contrast between the two locations exemplifies some of the changes Paris has undergone since Perec's experience – from city to megacity.

Le Capucin is a café situated on the corner of place de la Chapelle and rue Marx Dormoy. The entrance to La Chapelle Métro is two hundred feet away at the junction of boulevard de la Chapelle, rue Faubourg Saint-Denis, rue Marx Dormoy and rue Louis Blanc. People, trains, buses and taxis converge on the crossroads of La Chapelle. There is a constant flow of traffic, pedestrian and vehicular. Frequent peaks in pollution have resulted in cars registered before 2006 being banned from circulating within the city's periphery. The population of the 18th arrondissement has increased substantially with a recent influx of refugees who have been sleeping in makeshift camps along Canal Saint-Martin and under the arches of the viaduct at Stalingrad Métro. The vast majority of these refugees are young men.

DATE: 16th January 2017
TIME: 11:07 a.m.
LOCATION: Le Capucin (café)
WEATHER: Blue sky, sunshine, biting cold

Outline of an inventory of some strictly visible things:
• Letters of the alphabet, words: 'Toilettes 0.50 cents. Merci' typed on a laminated sign taped to a door in the café, COLUCHE in red capitals on a black and white poster of the famous French clown wearing a red nose, 'ORIGINE VIANDE, France, Pays Bas', (MEAT ORIGIN, France, Holland) written in faded white chalk on a small rectangular chalkboard in the corner of the café, 'PROPRETÉ' (CLEANLINESS) printed in black capital letters on clear plastic bin bags opposite the café on place de la Chapelle – one bag is already full and tied shut, the other almost empty, 'le système est bad,' (the system is bad) tagged on the side of a Ford transit van in plum-coloured paint,

'VILLE PROPRE – anti graffiti' (CLEAN CITY – anti graffiti) on the side of a graffiti-covered truck.

- Conventional symbols: four sets of traffic lights, two no entry signs, a bus lane, a cycle lane, no parking, no stopping, a picture of a car being towed away by a lorry.
- Numbers: 35 (a bus heading in the direction of Aubervilliers), 65 (a bus heading in the direction of Gare de l'Est, 84 stitched in white thread onto a blue parka, Tirage No: 107 (Draw No: 107) on the TV screen in the café announcing the latest results of the lottery.
- Fleeting slogans: 'AB, le propreté, c'est notre métier' (AB, cleanliness is our business.) 'Grace à vous + 3000 tonnes' (Thanks to you, + 3000 tons) on the side of a refuse truck. 'La La Land, le meilleur film de l'année' (La La Land, the best film of the year) on the side of a bus. 'KOTRA, fresh and frozen logistics' printed on the flank of a lorry; 'systèmes de fenêtres, portes et façades' (window systems, doors and facades) on another.
- Ground: dark grey tarmac littered with cigarette butts, scraps of paper and broken shards of bottle-green glass.
- Stone: the curb, the buildings, the viaduct that supports the overhead tracks of the metro.

Trajectories:
- The 35 goes to Le Mairie d'Aubervilliers.
- The 65 goes to Gare de Lyon.
- A refuse truck parks on the crossroads just opposite the café then heads down rue Marx Dormoy.

Colours:
- Green man.
- Pink plastic bag.
- Two pairs of camouflage trousers.

The digital display board that announces messages from the Mairie (Town Hall) is blank.

In front of the café, a young street vendor extracts a black bundle from a Carrefour shopping bag and places it beside him on the pavement. He presses the shopping bag flat against his body and then folds it in half. Again and again he folds the shopping bag in half, until the stiff fabric is squashed into a compact square. Then he rolls it up and tucks it into the back pocket of his jeans. He kneels down and spreads his wares out on the black blanket – belts, phone covers, winter hats in grey and black. He looks left, then right, then left again.

The 302 goes left down boulevard de la Chapelle.

The 35 goes down rue du Faubourg Saint-Denis.

In the blink of an eye, the street vendor gathers up his goods and shoves them back into the Carrefour shopping bag.

A taxi with its red light on drives down rue Marx Dormoy.

The street vendor has gone.

The 302 turns right down boulevard de la Chapelle.

The metro crosses right over the viaduct.

The street vendor has returned. He extracts the black bundle from the Carrefour shopping bag and places it beside him on the pavement. He presses the shopping bag flat against his body and then folds it in half. Again and again he folds the shopping bag in half until the stiff fabric is squashed into a compact square. Then he rolls it up and tucks it into the back pocket of his jeans. He kneels down and spreads his wares out on the black blanket. He looks left, then right, then left again.

DATE: 24th January 2017
TIME: 1:18 p.m.
LOCATION: Le Capucin (café)
WEATHER: Pale grey sky, opaque

The 302 goes to La Courneuve.

The café owner smokes a cigarette on the terrace outside. He's wearing a heavy wool jumper. A royal blue apron is tied around his waist.

'Triez ou vous vivez' (Sort where you live) is written on the side of a refuse truck going down rue Marx Dormoy.

Young men in black puffer jackets walk towards the metro station, their hoods up.

Lilac and fuchsia shalwar kameez poke out from under heavy black coats. Thick-soled trainers on the women's feet.

A bin bag full of bread rolls is slung over the shoulder of a man in a black parka crossing place de la Chapelle.

A refuse truck goes up rue Marx Dormoy. 'Triez sans vous tromper' (Sort without error).

An elderly man in a beige trench coat limps along the road, a rolled up newspaper in his right hand, his brown satchel worn diagonally across his chest.

A woman in head-to-toe red stands out amongst a group of young men all wearing grey, black, navy blue and brown that are heading towards the metro station.

The street vendor has a customer. Both men are dressed

in shiny black jackets and beanie hats. The street vendor's wares are spread out before him on the black blanket – belts, phone covers, winter hats in grey and black.

A blind man crosses the street, his cane sweeping left and right. His bomber jacket is pine forest-green.

The street vendor takes a twenty euro note from his only customer and hands him back a tenner.

The customer leaves.

The metro crosses left over the viaduct.

The metro crosses right over the viaduct.

Cars: black, grey, black, black, black, grey, black, white, black.

The 65 goes to Porte de la Chapelle.

A green truck, a white van.

'MAIRIE DE PARIS. ACCUEIL ET SURVEILLANCE' (Paris Town Hall. Reception and surveillance) on the backs of two men in navy uniform walking past the café and down place de la Chapelle and away from the crowds.

The 35 goes to Aubervilliers.

A sea of people walk in the direction of the metro station: man, woman, man, man, man, man, woman, man, man, man, man, man, man, man, woman, woman, woman, man, man, man, man, man, man, man, man, man, man.

A father pulls his daughter along on his shopping trolley in the opposite direction. White bobble hat, red coat, pink boots.

The next wave of people approach the metro station, shoulders hunched, moving quickly towards the underground: man, man, man, man, man, man, woman, man, man, man, woman, woman, man, woman, man, man, man, man, man, woman, man, man, man, man, man, woman,

woman, man, man, man, man, man, man, man, man,
woman, man, man, man, man, man, man, man, man, man,
man, man, man, woman, man, man, man, man.

The 65 goes to Porte de la Chapelle.

Ground: spots of chewing gum on the pavement, cigarette butts, a lone pigeon hovering around the pedestrian crossing.

The metro crosses right over the viaduct.

The 302 goes up rue Marx Dormoy. 'Je monte, je valide' (I board, I validate.)

A film poster for 'The Boyfriend' on the side of a bus. James Franco is smiling.

The metro crosses left over the viaduct.

The metro crosses right over the viaduct.

Cars: white, grey, black, occasionally red.

The metro crosses left over the viaduct.

Two yellow postal vans turn left down rue de Jessaint.

A yellow poster for a play is displayed on place de la Chapelle. 'C'est encore mieux l'après-midi' (It's even better in the afternoon). A red stiletto, a tiny man dangling from its heel.

Flashing yellow lights of a worksite. They are digging up the road under the overhead tracks of the metro.

Man, man, man, woman, man, man, woman, woman, woman, man, man, man, man, man, man, man, man, man, man, man, man, man, man, man, man, man, man, man, man, man, woman, man, man, man, man, man, man, man, man, man, man, man, man, man, woman, man.

Stop-clock. One minute: fifty-three people go past the window.

Seventeen vehicles.

The metro crosses left over the viaduct.

The 65 goes to Porte de la Chapelle.

Yellow: a fluorescent vest tied to a bicycle frame chained to a railing by the side of the road. Fluorescent yellow gloves of the cyclist otherwise in black, two canary-yellow postal vans, the poster advertising the play, the flashing lights of the refuse truck and the worksite.

Four heavily armed CRS officers (French national police guards) stand on the corner of boulevard de la Chapelle and rue Marx Dormoy. One stands with his arms crossed. He is a human bipod, his legs wide apart.

14:17. Time to leave.

DATE: 25th January 2017
TIME: 2:18 p.m.
LOCATION: Le Capucin (café)
WEATHER: Grey sky, freezing temperatures

'Your friend not here today?' says the café owner. He is wearing the same thing as yesterday, a thick woolly jumper in grey and navy stripes and a royal blue apron tied around his waist. He has walked the length of the counter to greet me.

'No,' I reply. 'Not today.' I am usually accompanied by my friend, Rosemary, who lives a stone's throw away. Despite our efforts to be inconspicuous, it is difficult to do so in a café frequented mostly by men.

I order a hot chocolate bien chaud and sit down in my usual spot facing boulevard de la Chapelle, the crossroads and the entrance to the metro station.

The 302 turns right down boulevard de la Chapelle.

A white van with blue flashing lights but no siren has parked up by the newspaper kiosk on rue Marx Dormoy, thirty feet in front of the café.

The 35 goes to la Mairie d'Aubervilliers.

A black van with tinted windows turns left down rue de Jessaint. The sliding door is open, the grey seats inside just visible.

A man turns left down place de la Chapelle, a blue plastic crate full of bread rolls balanced on his shoulder, two plastic bags full of loaves in his right hand. I cannot see his face.

An elderly man crosses place de la Chapelle in short strides, his hands grasping a black umbrella behind his back.

A man is sitting at the table next to me. He sees me writing.

'Are you a writer?' he asks.

'Yes,' I reply.

'Have you ever been published?'

'Just a short story in England, and I helped edit an anthology that was published in the US.'

'That's great.'

'But I'm a teacher, really. I've been a teacher for fifteen years.'

'Me too. I'm a maths professor. We have the same culture,' he says, gesturing to the notes, pens and empty coffee cups covering our tables. 'The same...'

'Spirit?' I venture.

'The same spirit, yes. Literature, maths. It's the same thing.' He pulls out a school textbook from his briefcase. It has an orange cover with 'Year 5' written in the top left-hand corner.

'What age are Year 5?' I ask.

'Year 5? They're thirteen,' he says.

'Oh. I always mix them up. In England, Year 5s are only nine years old.'

'In Africa, in the country I grew up in, the numbers increase: Year 7, 8, 9, 10… In France, they decrease. It's the other way round.'

He opens the front page of his textbook and points to the list of authors 'That's me,' he says, tapping his name with his index finger before leafing through the book and placing it back on the table. 'I am proud,' he says in English, putting his hand on his heart, 'very proud.' He takes another textbook out of his briefcase. This one is pink. 'Year 4' is written in the top left-hand corner.

'Who are your favourite authors?' I ask.

'Victor Hugo, Zola, Steinbeck. *East of Eden.* The classics. Contemporary fiction too. Wole Soyinka. Do you know him? He was the recipient of the Nobel Prize. I read his book before he won the prize.' He emphasises *before*.

'What was the name of his book?'

'Aké,' he says, accentuating each letter. 'The Years of Childhood.'

I jot down the name of the book in my notepad.

'He's African, from Nigeria.'

Our conversation is interrupted by the maths professor's mobile phone which has started to ring.

'I'm going to write to you,' he says when he's finished advising his friend on the best places to park in the area. 'I don't have a business card, but I'll give you my contact details.' He takes an A4 notebook out of his briefcase and tears off a page. The squared paper reminds me of the maths books I used in school. He writes his name, mobile number and email address.

'And if you'd like to,' he says ripping out another page from his notebook and giving it to me. I write down my name and my email address and hand it back to him. His friend arrives. The maths professor introduces us. 'She's a writer,' he says.

My mobile phone rings. It's my friend Isabelle phoning from the south of France. The maths professor orders a coffee for his friend. The waiter brings it to the table and the tiny cup perches precariously on the table's edge, next to the folders, papers and textbooks.

'Don't worry,' says the maths professor to the waiter, 'I'll be careful.'

Ten minutes later my new friend gets up to leave. Before he heads out the door, he looks me in the eye and says, 'I will write to you.'

DATE: 30th January 2017
TIME: 1:08 p.m.
LOCATION: Le Capucin (café)
WEATHER: Grey skies, spitting rain

I arrive later than I'd hoped to Le Capucin. I only have an hour before I need to leave. My usual table by the window is free but there is a man on the table next to me staring blankly at his mobile phone. Most of the customers are still wearing their coats. The plastic curtain that separates the terrace from the street is covered in condensation and drops of rain. I think of the A.A. Milne poem 'Waiting at the Window'. In it a child names two raindrops James and John, and commentates as they compete in a race: first one down the window pane! There isn't a clear winner here; none of the raindrops are moving.

On the corner of place de la Chapelle and rue Marx Dormoy the street vendor has his wares spread out on a black blanket. He leans back against the black metal railings, shoulders hunched, hands in his pockets. He looks left, then right, then left again.

Just in front of the street vendor, a woman carrying a baby in a sling is waiting for somebody, rocking ever so slightly from left to right. The baby is covered in an apricot-coloured blanket. AG Courtage (AG Brokerage) is printed in white letters on the purple fabric of the woman's bag.

The theatre poster on place de la Chapelle has changed. 'Tout ce que vous voulez' (Everything you want) in white letters on a black background. Two actors, one half of their faces showing. Stéphane de Groodt and Bérénice Bejo.

The Mairie de Paris digital display board is empty, unchanged.

The 35 goes to Mairie d'Aubervilliers.

The 65 goes up rue Marx Dormoy.

I hear the springs and push-buttons of a pinball machine. In the corner of the café to my right is a pinball machine I've never noticed before. The cast of The Sopranos are painted on its side, their faces white, ghostlike, their expressions grim. I recognise two out of ten: Steve Buscemi and James Gandolfini.

A young man walks past the café in a black bobble hat with white stars. I think of the American flag. The bobble is a mixture of threads: green, black, white and pink.

The 46 goes up rue Marx Dormoy.

My neighbour gets up from his table.

The 302 turns right down boulevard de Chapelle.

The 65 goes to Gare de Lyon.

The sound of the pinball machine has stopped. Two men are lifting its front legs. As they try to repair it, they chat loudly with the café owner who is leaning against the counter.

A large yellow postal truck drives down rue de la Chapelle.

A new customer sits down on the table next to me.

The 35 goes to la Mairie d'Aubervilliers.

The 65 goes to Porte de la Chapelle.

The original occupant of the table returns.

'Oh, were you sitting here?' says my new neighbour, acknowledging the unfinished cup of coffee on the table.

'Yes, I was.'

'Well feel free to come and join me,' he says, settling in.

'I'm actually waiting for someone,' says the other man.

'Well I always sit here,' says my new neighbour. 'I don't have to tell you that but I'm telling you anyway.' He crosses his arms and orders a coffee from his seat. The other man retreats to a bigger table at the back.

An elderly lady with a shopping trolley walks past the café. The shopping trolley is white with pink, orange and red flowers like a 1970s tablecloth.

A tall man walks past eating a sandwich out of a brown paper bag.

The metro goes left over the viaduct.

The two men finish the repairs to the pinball machine. The younger of the two joins my new neighbour, who stands up and asks the owner for three sugars instead of two. I pass him the lump of sugar from my saucer. Too late. The café owner has beat me to it. He thanks me anyway.

The man with the sandwich walks past the café in the direction he just came from.

Three men in black puffer jackets with matching fur-lined hoods are sitting in the terrace. They are huddled over the coffees even though the weather is much milder than it's been in weeks.

The 65 goes down rue Marx Dormoy.

The metro crosses right over the viaduct.

It's 1:33 p.m.

It's hard to focus on what's happening outside as my neighbours are talking loudly about how to get a café business up and running.

'The Portuguese,' says the man with three sugars, 'are just like the Arabs.'

The 302 turns right down boulevard de la Chapelle.

The 35 goes to Aubervilliers.

A bus turns right up rue de Jessaint, a poster advertising the film 'The Boyfriend' on its side. James Franco is smiling.

'You have to set business up quickly. If you don't do it quickly, it means you can't afford to get it done.'

The metro crosses right over the viaduct.

The 305 goes up down rue Marx Dormoy.

A woman simultaneously eats a banana and pushes a buggy down place de la Chapelle.

The metro crosses left over the viaduct.

Two women enter the café to use the toilets. They each pay the required fifty cents.

The 35 goes up rue Marx Dormoy.

A white lorry with a blue logo 'Médecins du monde'

(Doctors of the world) goes down Place de la Chapelle and turns right onto rue Marx Dormoy.

Two girls with oversized scarves walk past carrying brown paper Primark bags.

A young man pops his head into the terrace and tries to bum a cigarette off the three men in puffer jackets. They shake their heads solemnly.

Two CRS vans park up by the crossroads of rue Marx Dormoy and boulevard de la Chapelle. Both vans are full.

The metro crosses left over the viaduct.

The street vendor walks past the café towards his usual spot, his Carrefour shopping bag in hand.

I never saw him leave.

12—MEXICO CITY

PLANES FLYING OVER A MONSTER

BY DANIEL SALDAÑA PARÍS
TRANSLATED BY PHILIP K ZIMMERMAN

I get so close to the airplane window that my face is almost touching it. We're flying over the city. I play at identifying the buildings: the World Trade Centre, formerly known as the Hotel de México; the Torre Latinoamericana in the distance, marking the border of the Centro Histórico; the Reforma 222 shopping mall, which a few years ago, before I emigrated to Canada, I would pass every day on my way to my job as an editor.

I haven't been in Mexico City for twelve months, and all I can think is that it's horrible, and I love it. This contradiction is perfectly common; all of us chilangos have felt it at one time or another when spotting the monster from afar. I think of all the times I've seen the infinite ocean – of city streets, grey houses and dirty avenues – spread itself at my feet as I sat on a plane. Every time I've landed in Mexico, I've felt this same mixture of repulsion and enchantment, this movement of attraction and rejection.

This dual impulse was felt, too, by Efraín Huerta, who in 1944 published his 'Declaración de amor' ('Declaration of Love,' namely to Mexico City) in a book that also contained one of the most beautiful and dead-on texts ever written about Mexico City, 'Declaración de odio' ('Declaration of Hatred'). I sometimes read the second poem aloud, exulted, as a way of recalling my roots: 'We declare our hatred for you perfected by the force / of feeling you more immense each day, / more bland every hour, more violent every line.'

Ten years ago exactly, I landed at Mexico City's Benito Juárez International, the airport we're approaching now. I was returning from Madrid after four years in Spain. I was a young poet, aged twenty-one, and had a grant from the Mexican government to write my first book. I had never lived in the city as an adult, but a fireproof arrogance – characteristic of young poets – made me trust blindly in the future.

It was October 2006, and I settled into a small apartment in the Colonia Roma district, which back then wasn't so ridiculously gentrified.

To enter my block – a precinct of plants and caged parakeets – you had to pass between a synagogue and a piano repair shop. The soundtrack of my life during those years was a strange mix of Jewish music and atonal experiments, like a John Zorn composition arising spontaneously from the streets. An odd architectural whim had left the short hallway between my living room, bedroom and kitchen open to the sky – roofless – and so when it rained I got wet just moving from one room to another.

I had very few belongings: an orchid taken from my mother's house, a handful of poetry books and a cafetera italiana – a moka pot. I lived on quesadillas, sex and canned beer. I'd sit in a little wooden chair in my roofless hallway, facing my orchid, and write poems on an old laptop. I knew no one; no one knew me. The Distrito Federal (which in the meantime is no longer called the Distrito Federal) was a cluster of possibilities.

Before long I got to know some other poets through the grant I had. I danced with them and fought with them, I loved them, I got drunk with them, we traded insults. The things that young poets in any city do – and that, paradoxically, make them feel unique. I felt unique listening to the piano tuner's imperfect notes as I danced in the roofless hallway of my little apartment, in my indoor rain.

I've spent two weeks in Mexico City since that landing at Benito Juárez International – since the moment when I thought, like Efraín Huerta, that I love and hate this city. Two weeks of going out every day, of coming back at dawn, drunk on electric light and intensity, smog and tequila. Two weeks in the strange parenthesis that is this visit to my birthplace after a year of living abroad again.

Jorge, Benjamín and I are lying on the roof terrace, watching the sky and talking. Every once in a while, the noise of an airplane interrupts our conversation. The district we're in, Colonia Narvarte, lies under the traffic pattern of Benito Juárez Airport. With increasing frequency after two in the afternoon, hundreds of commercial flights describe an elegant curve over Benjamín's house before taking aim at one of the ancient airport's two runways.

Three hours ago, Benjamín, Jorge and I each dropped half a dose of LSD. Now, immersed in the hallucinatory lucidity of the drug, we're conversing with a certain lethargy, interrupted from time to time by the noise of the turbines above us. It's a Sunday, resplendent and slow. It must be three or four in the afternoon.

Every time the sound of turbines cuts the sky in half, Benjamín, Jorge and I fall silent and watch and listen with all the power of our attention. The plane pokes its nose into our field of vision from the far left, which I imagine corresponds to north, and from there it glides smoothly to the far right, like a hot knife through a block of butter. For a few seconds after the plane is no longer visible from where we lie, its noise echoes. The LSD intensifies the Doppler effect, and I know all three of us – Benjamín, Jorge and I – are thinking of just that: how the sound of an airplane reveals, in an almost scientific way, the curvature of the planet and the exact size of the atmosphere above us.

A little more than a year ago, just before emigrating to Canada, I somewhat unexpectedly took on the leading role in a movie being filmed in Mexico City. I say it was unexpected because I'm not an actor, and I had never worked in the film industry before. But I agreed to act in the movie because I thought it might be an interesting experience – and because I needed the money. Of the two months the business lasted in total, four days' shooting took place in Colonia Narvarte some ten streets from Benjamín's house, where I'm lying on the roof terrace and watching the sky. The planes passing overhead during filming were a torture for the sound engineer, who each time lost important moments of a dialogue that was more or less improvised and unrepeatable. Knowing the problems this would create for the editing process, I got into the habit of shutting up whenever an airplane went by. As soon as I'd sense the hoarse sound of turbines in the distance, I'd pause, more or less naturally, and not resume the dialogue until the noise had died away. The upshot was that the director ended up filming takes of up to seventeen minutes without a cut – to the great irritation of most of the crew, who were accustomed to working in a more conservative and expeditious style. This experience made me extremely sensitive to the planes over Mexico City, planes I had been ignoring with relative success for thirty years. Ever since then I've been unable to hold a conversation in Mexico City without pausing, however briefly, at the sound of an approaching plane.

I don't know where I got the cockeyed notion that I might write for a living, but it's an impractical one to say the least. Nobody writes for a living in Mexico. Or rather some people do, but those are people I don't know and ultimately have no interest at all in knowing. To live comfortably as a writer in Mexico, you need to have a lot of opinions about soccer and politics – in a very shallow sense of the word politics, you can be sure. The rest of us Mexican writers spend our time sending pitiful emails soliciting work or applying for grants, when we're not laboring obscene hours at jobs somehow related to writing.

I didn't know any of this when I came to live in the city exactly ten years ago, eager to express in innocent verses my squalid vision of the world while listening to the music of the synagogue and the piano tuner. Back then I believed, with ridiculous fervour, that I would be the glorious exception to the norm. I'd devote myself to writing, and from my roofless hallway in Colonia Roma, I'd gradually conquer the world. Instead I ended up working ten- and eleven-hour days for a magazine, a publishing house, a festival, an independent movie.

Writing in Mexico City is like holding a conversation when you're under the takeoff and landing path of the city's airplanes: you have to shut up sometimes, to let the noise take over everything, to let the sky split in two before picking up where you left off. From 2006 to 2015 I tried to be a writer in Mexico City. The sky split in two many, many times during those years.

At first, I survived on grants. Now, in Mexico there are grants for young writers which require them to attend workshops led by their senior colleagues. These older writers are, barring some exceptions, people whose only merit is having gotten old. Literature in Mexico is a gerontocracy. The old are praised for surviving to another birthday; the young are regarded with suspicion and treated with contempt. And the workshops, in general, are places where all the edges are filed off a piece of writing, where a text is homogenised until it loses all capacity to wound or bewilder. For three years I lived off grants of this kind, confronting the workshop system with hyperbolic obstinacy.

But all grants must come to an end – it's a law of physics. When I started working as an editor at a literary magazine, I thought that it wasn't such a bad thing to be doing, all things considered. I could write a little during the slowest weeks, right after an issue had been put to bed. I could request a piece from any writer who interested me. Imagine, they were paying me to read poetry – not a bad gig overall. But this illusion was short-lived: the magazine was (and still is) a nest of vipers. Editing each issue was like dancing with hyenas. Writers close to political power dividing up an imaginary prestige and macerating in the mediocrity of a prose that aspired at best to pallid efficiency. They weren't all like that, but most were. The editor-in-chief, a well-known liberal, turned against me because I had dared to address him as 'tú' rather than 'usted' – my damned Montessori education. So, finally, I left.

Those years weren't all bad, though. I married a beautiful, intelligent woman, and we moved together to Colonia Narvarte, directly under the landing path of the airplanes. The recurrent sound of turbines became the new soundtrack of my existence, replacing the music of the synagogue and the piano tuner.

Little by little everything got twisted, my vice and my violence stoked by the hypertrophic city. I observed the growth of my alcoholism with tenderness, as others watch the maturation of a child. I became irritable, prone to excesses of wrath. I wrote a novel in the dead hours of my devastation. And then the sky split in two. I got divorced. I lost all faith in what I was doing. I had to stay silent for a time, listening to the passing airplanes.

It's very easy to idealize Mexico City. To paint it as a tourist destination for fans of Roberto Bolaño. To present its hippest neighbourhoods as epitomes of a cosmopolitanism that hasn't turned its back on tradition. All that is complete bullshit. Aside from the three or four neighbourhoods where the emerging middle class lives, Mexico City is essentially ugly. You have to embrace that ugliness, to find its charm without betraying it. You have to listen to Witold Gombrowicz, who praised the grimy immaturity of Buenos Aires – the vileness of the slums – over the brightly lit, pseudo-European boulevards.

Typical Mexico City is not the combination of blue and sienna of the Frida Kahlo house in Coyoacán but the

unpainted grey and exposed rebar of the ocean of houses
that spreads around Calzada Ignacio Zaragoza as you leave
town headed for Puebla. It's a city where there are hair
salons and pet stores that make payoffs to the drug cartels
in order to dye grey hairs and sell hamsters. Women can't
dress the way they like or take public transportation without having their asses grabbed. There are zones of extreme
poverty next to office buildings where the CEOs arrive in helicopters. There are daily protests because the government
can't fathom why people are so intent on having decent
jobs. There are whole neighbourhoods that go without water
for days. There are windy afternoons when a pungent stench
of garbage blows in from the east. Every time it rains, the
whole city floods and the storm drains spew shit. Every now
and then a dismembered corpse appears in some sector of
the city, or a body dangling from a bridge. There are human
trafficking rings that hold captive dozens of teenagers and
prostitute them with the connivance of the police. There are
hundreds of SUVs filled with armed bodyguards who control
the population by violence and with total impunity. There
are millionaires, in some neighbourhoods, who pay con-
siderable bribes to the right public official in order to have
the air traffic over the city rerouted so that the noise won't
disturb them when they're watching American TV series in
their home theatres.

In August 2015 I emigrated to Montreal because I could
no longer write in Mexico City. That wasn't the only reason,
of course, but it's the one I choose to tell about. It's impossible to find the time to write if you're working nine or ten
hours a day, and given the state of the Mexican economy,
it's impossible to survive if you're *not* working nine or ten

hours a day. In this context, writers from well-off families have more opportunities. Of course, in comparison to the country as a whole, I wasn't badly off, even if I did come from a solidly middle-class family of university professors and not one of businessmen. Female writers who come from rural areas and write in indigenous languages are condemned to a marginality infinitely greater than mine. I'm white, male, relatively heterosexual and a capitalino – a capital-dweller – in a country that's racist, criminally poor and covered with unmarked mass graves.

In the Monstrous City there always seem to be more important things to do – anything but write a book! There are parties that can't wait. There are art exhibitions where a section of the museum gets blown up. There are demonstrations which you ought to join, protesting the disappearance of dozens of people. People abducted by a UFO, perhaps, or more likely massacred by the state in collusion with the narcos. And in the dead hours there are friendships and absurd plans that end up winning me over, uprooting the idea of spending the next five hours in front of a computer. (The plan, for example, of watching the sky from a roof terrace in Colonia Narvarte at three or four in the afternoon on a Sunday, three hours after ingesting half a dose of LSD.)

Writing in Mexico City, for me, was hardly ever writing. Letting weeks pass without adding a single paragraph to the novel. Typing up commissioned pieces in two and a half hours before heading out to interminable dinners that degenerated into karaoke. Walking at dawn in search of a taxi. Listening to the airplanes overhead and thinking of the novel that I wasn't writing, that I might never write.

Nowhere have I felt so part of a community as in Mexico City. But every community has its dark underside. Noise, constant and deaf, like an airplane that's always passing and never passes, hangs over Mexico City and forces me to stay silent. And every so often this dark certainty, like the shadow of an airplane, flies over my spirit: literature is incompatible with literary people.

The effect of the LSD is fading. The afternoon too. There's a rose colour at the edge of the sky and an impossible orange in a few of the clouds. 'It's the drug,' I think, but it's also the chromatic spectrum of the air pollutants, which can convert Mexico City into one of Akira Kurosawa's *Dreams*. There are fewer airplanes now, but the three of us have stopped talking anyway. Sundays in Colonia Narvarte have always struck me as cruelly melancholic.

I say goodbye to Benjamín and Jorge and set off on my final walk home. But then I remember that my home is three thousand miles away, and so I walk aimlessly, through empty streets, until night falls.

13—TOKYO

SLOW BOAT
A Novel Extract

BY HIDEO FURUKAWA
TRANSLATED BY DAVID BOYD

I worked like a horse – I had debts to pay. I borrowed what
I needed to settle up my hospital bills, then paid my 'victims' in monthly instalments. I found jobs. Day jobs, night
jobs. Sometimes, I had three-shift days: morning, swing
and graveyard. Sleep? I wasn't sleeping much, to be honest.
On average, I probably got a little over three hours a night.
Maybe four. Just enough to keep a body moving. The only
thing I had going for me was my youth – the inexhaustible
energy of a nineteen-year-old. Nothing else. Just the stamina
to fuel me through the sleepless years to follow.

I didn't have time for rest, so I learnt to sleep deep.
Quality over quantity. Meaning 'no distractions'. Everything
had to go. Including dreams.

I had almost no dreams in my workhorse years.

Not even enough to fill a short film.

It was really strange. When I was ten or eleven, I did nothing but dream – now I was totally dry.

Life has a way of doing that – restoring balance. That's how I see it, at least.

My mom really did kick me out of the house. I moved into a small, cheap place in Shinjuku. Kami-ochiai, Ni-chome. The closest station was Nakai, on the Seibu Shinjuku Line. It was in a two-storey building several decades old. It was all wood, so I guess it had to be built after the war. Shared toilet, no bath. The sort of place where people live when they don't have money – where rent's stuck in the golden age of Godzilla. Financially, I cut every corner I could, spending next to nothing on food, almost never using electricity, never turning on the gas. I streamlined my bathing routine, which involved trips to the local bath and the coin shower (note: three minutes for the price of a coffee). I made it a priority to find jobs where meals were provided – which had the added benefit of helping me balance my diet. Clocking out of my last job for the day, I went straight home and slipped right into bed. No heat, no lights, no nothing. That's how I survived. I didn't have a phone, but my building had a line in the hallway, so I could receive calls from the outside world – as long as somebody was around to pick up. After a couple of years of hardcore work, I bought a PHS. One of my bosses (at a courier company) said I needed to get it and told me where I could find one for almost nothing. My first briquette of plastic. At long last – the cellular age!

I spent all my time making money. Wages in, damages out. Soon I was twenty – a fully-fledged adult. Not that I stopped to celebrate my entry into adult society or anything.

Outside of work, my life was a perfect blank.

My early twenties. Filled with a peace I'd never known. The calm of nearly dropping dead from overwork.

Click. The digital calendar flipped; the century ended. From 31/12/1999 to 01/01/2000. A whole lot of zeros. Some feared the date. Like the Rapture was upon us. Others celebrated. Couples dying to have 'millennium babies' sought pharmaceutical assistance to get the timing just right. Still others, partying in high-end hotel rooms, uncorked ultra-high-end champagne bottles. *Pop, pop, pop.* Even more people burrowed into underground bunkers, waiting to see if the computerised world would descend into anarchy. They really thought that, in one apocalyptic moment, bank accounts would vanish, aircraft would drop out of the sky and nuclear missiles would destroy the planet as we know it. Good old Y2K. The Japanese government didn't help, telling families: 'Be sure to stock up on mineral water and emergency food supplies.' Panic. Sheer panic. The world was in jeopardy – double jeopardy – whether it was God or computers that would eventually do us in was inconsequential.

Okay, my Y2K. For me, the collapse of the world's banks was the big fear. A matter of life and death, if you think about it. So, on 1st January, I got in line to receive my ATM oracle, like everyone else.

I hadn't bothered checking my balance in years. What was the point, right?

Then my turn came, and – what the hell – did Y2K do this? This couldn't be right.

But it was. I had been too busy working to notice that I had settled my debts... a good eighteen months back. I was in the black. The ATM was showing me a number I never saw coming.

Seven, almost eight, million yen?

That's how I entered the new millennium.

Alright. Time to face the music. I was never going to make it out of Tokyo. Two massive failures had made that abundantly clear. Guess it was just my fate. But even if it was, I'd have to fight fate on this one. Fight against my shitty karma. Granted, I'd been a shitty person. But, as human beings, we've got inalienable rights, right?

At least I had plenty of cash for my third escape attempt.

Let's think this through. Prior experience told me that any attempt to exit Tokyo ended in violence.

If I couldn't get out, I'd have to bring *out* in. Enter the Trojan Horse of Tokyo.

My master plan.

I needed a fortress – an impenetrable, impregnable lair. My own stronghold right in the heart of the city. A place with the power to keep Tokyo out – an *autonomous region*, if you will. A place to fill with all the music and smells and flavours that Tokyo can't handle. Everything Tokyo can't have. I needed a place all my own.

You might call it a business.

I had to do something, right?

To keep on fighting. With everything I had.

Not like I had anything left to lose.

March, 2000 A.D. The Power of Kate opened in Asagaya, Suginami ward.

Magazines called Kate a café. In reality, I was going for a place that defied definition; I had no interest in opening a 'café' – or any place you're supposed to spell with a cute little accent mark. But why should I care? I had misread the world my whole life. So what if the world misread me back?

All that mattered to me was that Kate had the power to

fight against Tokyo. Food and drinks were secondary – just a part of my cover. The Power of Kate. Sounds like a Hollywood romcom, doesn't it?

Where did the name come from?

From life. I needed a name when I submitted the paperwork to the broker. I clearly wrote: 'The Power of Hate (temporary).' But some bespectacled pencil-pusher misread my handwriting – and Kate was born. Why was I trying to call my place the Power of Hate? Because I hated the world with every breath of my being.

Still do.

But okay. The Power of Kate.

A quick rundown on everything that had to happen before opening. Phase I. Get a public health licence (took one day) and a fire safety certificate (two days). There were free courses for both. Next, apply for a restaurant permit – which took nearly a month. Put together tons of forms for the tax office. Then burn through loads of cash on equipment. Interior renovations, dishes, recruitment...

My only job was going to be running the place. Not cooking, not serving. So, Phase II.

Cooking: I knew a guy. No worries there.

Serving: I tracked down a few foreign waiters. Easy enough. Phase II was over in no time.

Phase III. Set up thirty or so cockroach traps on the premises. Cleanliness is everything.

Then Kate opens. On the second floor of a renovated home on Nakasugi Avenue. I gave the place everything I had – guerrilla warfare against my shitty karma. Not much later, my third girlfriend made her first appearance in the chronicle of my life.

She came from the east...

But, wait, her brother came first. I met him at a beef-bowl joint. No, not at the counter – behind it. In the kitchen. I'd been working there maybe a couple of months. Night shift. (It was one of those twenty-four-hour places.)

Watching him wrist-deep in the pickles, I had to ask: 'You been at this long? You've got the best pickles in the business.'

'Huh?'

I figured he was two or three years older than me. His close-cropped hair made him look a little thuggish.

He stared at me, picked up a loaded dish and hurled it to the floor. *SMASH!* Pickles and broken ceramic pieces everywhere.

'What the fuck kind of question is that?' he said.

'Wh–what?' I just stood there, stunned.

'Listen to me, you little shit.' He was looking me right in the eye. 'I'm not some grunt making fast food by the fucking manual. Got it?'

'Ye–yeah. I got it...'

'Here. Try this, asshole.'

He grabbed something out of the kitchen fridge. It looked a lot like foie gras. When did he make this? He'd been feeding this to the staff? Looked amazing. What was it?

'Angler liver – fresh as fuck.'

This wasn't no yellowtail.

Angler liver and daikon.

'How is it?

'...'

'Well?'

'Well... damn,' I said.

No other words for it. It was like an ambush of flavour, so

good, really good. My taste buds exploded. I looked at him and said: 'Kaboom!'

'What the hell's that supposed to mean?'

I took another bite. That was answer enough.

He started explaining: 'My family's been making sushi for three generations. My old man taught me Edo-style before I could read... I was a teenage sous chef... I can make any dish you can name. Get it?'

Pretty sure I got it.

'But...' I said.

'What, you want more?'

'Um, yeah... but...'

'But what?'

'If you're this good, why are you working at some no-name beef-bowl?'

He just looked away, coolly.

'Nowhere else I can go. I've got a record.'

'A criminal record?'

'Shut up and eat.'

That was the beginning of a deeply satisfying partnership. From then on, nearly every night, I ate what he made for the staff. Soon 'kaboom' wasn't cutting it. I had to find new adjectives. Like 'kablam' or 'kablooey'. How did he come up with all of his mind-blowing creations?

This had to be what they call 'fusion'.

He was a perfect fit for Kate. I had him on the phone maybe two seconds after I decided to open a place. It was obvious, right?

The first few months went fantastically. Kate drew in plenty of customers, and they seemed pretty satisfied. I know I was. Kate had a potent mix of exotic spices, a region-free menu and nomadic DJs (who were under explicit instructions to 'sound like anything but Tokyo'). To destroy any lingering trace of the city, I covered every surface with giant ferns. In time, the place started to look like *Jurassic Park* – minus all the killer dinos. Most critics raved about the excess of oxygen. They loved Kate. Funny. Kate had been misread again – billed as a café ahead of its time.

It was a hit.

Idiots. Tokyo thought my Trojan Horse was avant-garde? Die, Tokyo, die.

So – did my escape plan work?

Well, Kate hit a bit of a speed bump in June. A slipped disc sidelined my chef (the beef-bowl ex-con).

'Ca–can't move...' his pained voice hissed through my cell phone. 'I'm in the hospital.'

'What? Are you okay?'

'Shit no – that's why I'm in the hospital.'

'Seriously? What do we do?'

'Man up.'

'Huh? You mean ritual suicide?'

'Yeah, right. Look – Kate has to stay open, with or without me. The doctor has no idea what's wrong. All he does is giggle like a damn idiot. I can't make any promises about coming back to work. Hate to wuss out like this, but I think I have to hang up my apron.'

'CHEF!'

My brain was a total blank.

'Man up, man!'

'But suicide isn't the answer...'

'Knock it off.'

Chef was hors de combat, but he was going to make sure

Kate stayed open for business. He told me he'd already lined up a replacement, someone he trusted. Nothing for me to do but wait for said help to arrive.

Then help arrived.

It was just a few hours later. No introductions, no questions. No 'Hello', no 'Nice to meet you'. She just made a beeline for the kitchen – like she was ready to clock in.

I mean, she didn't look anything like the help I had in mind. My first thought was: strange. Kate doesn't get that many high-school girls in uniforms – and they almost never come alone. My second thought was: isn't it a little hot for a blazer?

That was all I was thinking. I mean, I thought she was a misguided customer. 'That's the kitchen! You can't–' I start to say.

But she just stared me down. Didn't say anything.

'You... you can't be back here.'

I tried to sound like I was in charge, but – on the inside – all I was thinking was: hey, she's pretty cute. Piercing eyes. Nice full body.

I guess I was checking her out.

She looked right at me and said sharply:

'Of course I can.'

She whipped her cell phone out of her skirt pocket and slapped it down on the counter like she meant business. There was a Snoopy figure dangling from the strap. Then, right in front of me, she started unbuttoning her blazer. *Pop, pop, pop.* Wh–what was she doing!? She wasn't not gonna show me her boobs or anything!? No. It was no striptease. Not even close.

She opened her blazer to reveal four streaks of metal in the lining – two on each side. Knives.

'My brother says I'm running this kitchen – starting tonight.'

'Say what?'

'Don't worry,' she said with a smile. Holy shit, she was cute.

'Just leave everything to me.'

Then she headed over to the vegetable stash, grabbed a long white daikon and got to work – reducing it to ultra-thin slices at superhuman speed. *Sssh-sssh-sssh.* Then, *ch-ch-ch-ch-chop.* She filled a bowl with water to soak the diaphanous strands.

I was speechless.

What skill. No movement was wasted.

A sight to behold.

Then, with a cool look that said 'this is nothing', she turned to me and said:

'You look like you've never seen a teenage knife girl before...'

Another smile. I was in love.

With my chef's little sister. She moved into her brother's apartment in Koenji that day. Her folks lived in Hatchobori – a neighbourhood for low-level officials... in, like, the Edo period? Everything happened so fast. Mere hours after my chef's untimely injury, she was by his side at the hospital. (She had to be initiated into the mysteries of her brother's menu before making her appearance at Kate.) Living in Koenji made it easy for her to go see him – to drop off fresh clothes, pick up dirty laundry, or ask for help with his more esoteric dishes. Chef's back problems turned out to be pretty serious – just like he predicted. He was discharged after about two weeks, but he was basically an invalid. Whenever his sister wasn't at school or on the job, she did the work of a live-in nurse.

What a sister.

All they had was each other.

'No, my dad's alive,' she said one night. She'd just finished making dinner for the staff.

'He is?' I asked, taking my first bite.

My taste buds went wild for her Kyoto-style sablefish. The others loved it, too. The Hindu inhaled his helping; the Taoist was literally tearing up; the Romanian Christian cut his fish neatly, then put it away with the silence of the Black Sea.

'Yeah, he's alive but... hmph!'

'What? What is that? Hmph?'

Had something bad happened? Sounded like it.

Was I supposed to ask? Probably not. Let it go... She was a knife-wielding teenager.

Still, I felt the temptation.

I cleared my throat. Then asked – softly: 'Is it... complicated?'

'Nope.'

Right back to work. Sharpening her trusty sashimi knife while she hummed the theme song from *Sazae-san*.

Of course, her presence in Kate wasn't sanctioned by the Governor of Tokyo. She was 'unlicensed'. Yeah. That had a nice ring to it.

Kate had to work around her schedule. We called last order early, so her morning commute to school in Kita ward wouldn't be a strain for her. Our lunch menu was limited to dishes that could be served cold or heated up in the microwave. But that didn't mean we lowered our standards. Not with her. She kept her eye on the ball. And she really knew her stuff. Me? I was just technically in charge.

Every day, after school, she hit the kitchen. By 5:30,

everything was ready to go. Then, from six, she was a school-girl possessed by the spirit of the knife.

God. What a sight.

Starting on 20th July – Ocean Day – she worked a full load. No more school. One hundred percent Knife Girl. Had summer break actually come through for once? Under summer's suspicious auspices, Kate had its second full-time chef.

During Obon, she told me, 'I was really happy to take my brother's spot...' She was wearing goggles and gripping a mini-torch. 'It got me out of Hatchobori.'

She triggered the flame and brought the surface of the crème brûlée to a crisp.

'You mean – there *was* something?'

I asked from the double-pump coffee machine.

'A lot of things...'

'A lot of things?'

No answer.

Well – it came days later. Under her breath: 'My dad did a horrible thing...' She was standing by the mixer, fine-tuning a dessert of her own creation, a black sesame *shiruko* we named 'Edgar Allan'. (By the way, this was not Kate's first homage to the Master of the Macabre. We also had a chocolate cake we called 'The Raven'.)

Taken aback, I said: 'A horrible thing?'

'Yeah... It's kinda hard to explain. I mean, he never hit me or anything. I just...'

'Yeah?'

She shook her head. 'Never mind...'

'No, never never mind,' said the eavesdropping Hindu.

'Asshole,' she said with a quick back fist.

'You're the one who's hitting people,' said the Taoist. Then she thwacked him with the handle of her sashimi knife. Only the Romanian Christian held his tongue. A wise decision. Well – he barely understood Japanese, so... the Power of Kate. One big happy family. Long live the Trojan Horse!

Then summer break came to an end. Meaning my teenage chef was back to juggling school and work – not that there was any drop in the quality of her work or whatever. But, wait, there was something I wanted to say about that summer. *It wasn't cursed.* It didn't come to a grinding halt like when I was ten or eleven. It didn't drag on forever like when I was nineteen. And that got me wondering. *Was the Power of Kate working?* It looked that way. I mean, I managed to escape Tokyo's usual havoc, for once. Without even leaving the city.

We made it through the summer. *We* did.

To be clear, the first-person plural refers to me and my Knife Girl. The tale of my third love stands alone in the annals of my history. This time around, things really began when the summer ended.

It was towards the end of September – more than two weeks after she went back to school – when she filled me in on the Hatchobori drama. It was a weirdly quiet day at Kate. One server came down with food poisoning and called in sick (eel liver was the culprit); another had to go home early (something about 'the vault of heaven'?); the last server left right on schedule – without so much as a goodbye.

She and I were the only ones around. She was making the next day's lunches, and I was – you know – doing the books.

After her knife-cleaning routine, she started to talk. I was at the counter, facing her.

'I... um...'

'Huh?'

'…'

The only noise in the room was coming from the ventilator.

'You know, I've been playing with blades ever since I was a kid…'

'Blades?' Meaning *knives*?

'Like this.' She lifted up a razor-sharp fish knife, letting it catch the light.

'In my house, they were always around. I guess I liked the way they sparkled. Legendary blades give off a really intense light… and that caught my eye, or – like – maybe hypnotised me. My dad taught me all the basics. He never stopped to think about how I was just a baby. On my third birthday, I pinned down my own eel, slit it open, gutted it, broiled it and made sushi. I had a fish knife that I used for everything until I was like five. Then I branched out into other blades: sashimi, kamagata, mukimono… I was on TV, on Junior Chef Championship, and came in second. They called me 'Girl Genius'. I was in second grade, maybe third, but I could scale a fish better than any of the middle-school kids.'

'Whoa…'

'It was child's play for me. I've lived with knives my whole life. I've come close to losing a finger so many times I lost track. When everyone else my age was holding a milk bottle, I was gripping my boning knife. This is what I was born to do. that's why my dream was… going into the family business or whatever…'

'Like, take over?'

'Not really. I mean, my brother was around, so I knew I was never going to take my dad's spot. I just thought – you know – I could open a sister shop or something. All I needed was the family name... or, like, part of it. I wanted to make my living with knives, with food. And I was serious about it. I was really, really, really into traditional Japanese cooking... Or, like, Edo-style with a modern twist. That was my dream.'

'Sounds great to me,' I said.

'To *you*!' she screamed. 'I was blind as a Bodhisattva. I totally misinterpreted what my dad was doing. I really thought he cared about me. One day, he looks me right in the eye and says, "I know what you're thinking – but forget it. This business is no place for girls. Believe me, you'll never make it!" Just thinking about it makes my blood boil. He didn't want me in the family business at all. Everything he taught me was just... supposed to make me a better house-wife! I mean, are you fucking serious!?'

'What the fuck...'

'Right, boss? Maybe he meant well, I dunno, but he swore he'd never let me get behind the counter. I lost my shit. Don't get me wrong. I know where he's coming from, I really do. It's hard for anybody to make it in that world – and the men in this line of work eat women alive... now more than ever. Before the bubble burst, Hatchobori had it all, tons of places to eat and work – but it's not like that anymore. Now it's nothing but parking lots. But where else can you go? Nihonbashi? Ningyocho? My dad knew the odds were against me. So he picked me off, like in baseball. You know? But, but... aaugh!'

'It's okay. Let it out.'

'Thanks, boss... Yeah, my dad and I collided, we collided head-on. But my brother was there and he stood up for me. He was, like, "Yeah, living by the knife is tough... but you're no softie. You're tough, you're a diehard." When my dad heard that, he went apeshit. He beat the crap out of my brother – then he disowned him, which was when my brother started having run-ins with the law.'

Now I got it.

'When my brother called and told me he hurt his back, I didn't think twice. Of course I was going to look after him. I owe him big, and I hate being at home and... and... and...'

'And?'

She ran around the counter, right up to me – knife in hand!

'... and I wanna be with you!' she said, squeezing me tight.

Huh?

'Boss–you cut right through me.'

Say what?

'You believe in me. I mean, I'm your Knife Girl, right? One hundred percent? It makes me wanna cry. Just me being here could get you in trouble. But you never even flinched...'

She's right about that. I never gave it a thought.

'I can tell you've been fighting too – with everything you've got. You're strong. And you're protecting me – like my own guardian Śakra. You don't even know it, but you saved me. Really. You gave me a chance. To fight against this idiotic world. And I'm not gonna give up. I'm not. You know I'm not.'

Knife Girl versus the World. And I thought Kate was *my* fortress.

I guess she had burnt some bridges, too.

I told her everything I wanted from her. Not as my Knife Girl. As my girl.

Love.

She was my third girlfriend. My schoolgirl chef from the east.

Fall, 2000 A.D. We went out. We went places. With phantom two thousand-yen notes stuffed in our wallets. We started in Koenji. We went to see her brother – my first chef. Then we went exploring. We shopped for food at Queen's Isetan, for clothes on Look Street. We bought shirts. A long-sleeve with mahjong tiles for me; a short-sleeve with a tarantula print for her. Then we just wandered around the area, making fun of all the second-hand stores. Steering clear of Hatchobori, driving slowly towards the core of Tokyo–Edo? We went east, to eat *monja* in Tsukishima. 'The way my grandparents see it,' she told me, 'this place isn't Edo... because it's reclaimed land or whatever. But the monja's great, right?' We headed back. We took in the view from Aioi Bridge at night. Sumida River, the Harumi Canal. We could see Koto ward in the distance. When we entered Chuo ward, we pick up the faint scent of newly-printed books.

So many sluices.

So many bridges.

That's what we saw. When we went out. When Kate was closed.

The rest of the time, we were perfectly happy in our fortress. Kate was our little universe. Our way out of Tokyo, even if we never really left.

She was the heart of our fortress. The heart of me.

USING LIFE
A Novel Extract

BY AHMED NAJI
TRANSLATED BY BENJAMIN KOERBER

Cairo's not what you'd expect from a city of its size. In spite of its teeming millions, this is a city that is hopelessly repressed.

A coalition of social, political, and religious taboos conspire to keep everything that ferments in the city's underbelly from rising to the surface. The rare puff of light or glimmer of rot that happens to simmer up from below will be snuffed out in a snap, either by the swarms of flies that patrol the city's hangouts, or the seasonal Black Cloud that seals its atmosphere, or the thick layer of dust that blankets its crumbling streets and alleyways, or the shrieks of pain from circumcised women whose husbands force them into a quickie before the metro closes at eleven.

On the surface, Cairo's residents appear as a wretched assortment of women wrapped in layers of cloth, and pitiful men whose ravenous sexual appetites go forever unfulfilled. A more penetrating view, however, reveals this city of twenty-odd million to be buzzing with shadowy gatherings of all sorts, each with its own secret rituals and languages.

The casual visitor will be unable to crack their codes, unless, by happy coincidence, he stumbles upon someone who holds the keys. Cracking the codes by yourself, or acquiring your own personal key, requires a long and toilsome journey in which you abandon yourself to the city in all its filthiness, until it becomes part of you and you become part of it.

The secret societies of the Cairenes include religious fanatics who move about in cohorts of brothers and sisters; homosexuals who organise cocktail parties and meet-and-greets in homes out in Dokki and Mohandeseen; young artists drowning in rivers of beer stretching from Zamalek to downtown; wife-swapping groups in Imbaba; street children overdosing on soda in the shadows of slums and abandoned railroad yards; hashish dealers making the rounds in the brothels of Dar al-Salam; a Church that's maintained its control and influence over its flock for centuries; bodybuilding fanatics; boxers obsessed with their fists; mendicant musicians and worn-out belly dancers in the backstreets of Faisal and the Pyramids District; gluttonous businessmen organising hunting trips to begin after midnight; junkyard dogs; foreigners who ride motorcycles in Maadi; youth committed to charity and public service in Agouza; folk singers in Shobra; S&M fans in apartments that overlook the Nile in Maadi; families begot of incest with a biological map stretching from the corniche at Rod El Farag over to Ahmed Helmi Street; fornicators with donkeys in Ezbat Antar; the men in black, defenders of security and stability; dog catchers and dog dealers roaming about in bands in the desert; private security firms in the Fifth Settlement; killers-for-hire hiding out in al-Ataba. All these secret societies grow up and mature in close geographic proximity to each other. They greet one another by sniffing each other with the tips of their noses, or by licking each other's necks, or by looking each other in the eye: each one's secret is safe with the other.

In the decade preceding the Tsunami of the Desert, the telecommunications revolution contributed to the rapid propagation of these groups, portions of some of which actually succeeded in rising to the surface. The police made a game of hunting them down and tormenting them. They would randomly expose some of their members and throw their meat to the media, which would happily take the bait, add some spices, and throw it in turn to an audience always hungry to devour the flesh of someone the police told them was sharing his wife with other men, or smoking hash at Sufi festivals. Simply lifting up the lid would leave a member of one of these groups exposed. He'd be wrenched out of the city's long intestine and left starving out in the street, easy prey for the junkyard dogs.

That's not to say life in Cairo was completely miserable. There were good times to be had year-round: some during our long summers, and quite a few during our short winters. Such times were, invariably, either days off work or days without it. They say the city never sleeps, they say it bursts at the seams. The city rotates and revolves. The city branches out. The city beats, the city bleeds.

In their places of work and worship, the people of this city swarm. They shop and scurry and go for a piss, so the Wheel of Production might go on spinning despite the traffic. That's how it all looks, if you're an eagle soaring up above. But if you're just a little mouse of a man spinning inside that Great Wheel, you never get to see the big picture.

You go to work and do your job, and might even earn a reasonable salary. If, by some great fortune, you manage to see the fruit of your labours, it still won't move you an inch. Whether you work or not, the Wheel of Production keeps on spinning, and the current carries you along.

Which brings me to the time Mona May and I went with a group of friends over to Moud's apartment in Garden City. This was after a party at Youssef Bazzi's place. We stayed up until the morning smoking hash and competing to finish a whole bottle of vodka. I remember seeing the music dissolve into monkeys that clung to the ceiling. There was a blond German tapping her leg to the beat. Erections popping around the room. A young Palestinian-American, with poor Arabic, talking a lot about racism. Smoke, cigarettes, hashish. And more smoke.

'Bassam,' said Kiko, turning to me with a totally bloodshot look. 'I've got smoke in my eyes.'

'Go easy on 'em, baby.'

I pulled a tissue over her eyes and blew gently. The German girl watched with a confused look. As I pulled the tissue away, my palm dripped with the dark freshness of Kiko's face. I planted a light kiss on her lips.

'Did you know there's a kind of sexual fetish called "licking the pupil"?' said the German girl in English.

'How exactly do you mean?'

'Yeah, I read about that once,' interjected Moud.

'That's disgusting,' objected Kiko, wrapping her arms around me.

What are your typical twenty-somethings to do in Cairo? Might they go for pupil licking? Are they into eating pussy? Do they like to suck cock, or lick dirt, or snort hash mixed with sleeping pills? Or one might ask how long it would take for any of these fetishes to lose its thrill. Are they good for life?

Everyone there had done lots of drugs, both during and after college. Yet there we all were, little islands unto ourselves, with no greater aspiration than to hang out together. We managed to stay alive by sucking our joy out of one another.

Mona May was standing next to the speakers. Her eyes were glazed over as though her soul had been sucked up by the music monkeys on the ceiling, and her body swayed to the beat.

After a while, taking drugs clearly gets old. Or they are just not enough. And if one of us ever gave in to total addiction, his life would be over in a few months: this we knew by trial and experience. Those of us left in that room were too chicken to end our lives in that or any other way, maybe because we still clung to some sort of hope, some sort of love or friendship.

For all that Cairo takes from its residents, it gives nothing in return – except, perhaps, a number of lifelong friendships that are determined more by fate than any real choice. As the saying goes, 'He who goes to Cairo will find there his equal.' There's no such thing as smoking by yourself. And the food's only got taste if you have someone to chow it down with, happily, carcinogens and all.

In this city, you'll be lucky if you can get over your sexual tension, and appreciate sex as just one of the many facets of a friendship. Otherwise, your horniness will make you a testy bitch. Kiko rubbed my back, and I felt a heat between my legs.

As dawn came up, Moud went to his room, and everyone else went home. Too lazy to head back to 6th of October City, I lay down and fell asleep on the couch. I woke up early with a slight headache, an army of ants marching in the space between my brain and my skull. I went to the bathroom and took one of the pills Moud had brought from overseas to fight hangovers. After taking a warm shower, I called Lady Spoon and agreed to breakfast at Maison Thomas in Zamalek.

On the way, the streets were clean and empty of traffic. It was a holiday: perhaps the Islamic New Year, or Victory Day, or Revolution Day, or Saltwater Catfish Day. Whatever it was, the city looked drowsy and everyone was checked out. At moments like this, I barely recognise the place. When I'm able to get from Qasr El Eyni to Zamalek in under twenty minutes, I almost feel like she's decided to warm up to me. But I know that wicked smile on her face. She's telling me, 'At any moment, I can have you stuck in traffic for over an hour, with nothing to do but sit back and feel sorry for yourself as the noise of the streets slowly sucks the life out of you.' Open veins spewing blood all over the bathroom.

I met Lady Spoon outside the restaurant. She had on a long white dress showing her arms and a bit of cleavage.

'You smell really nice,' she said, kissing me on both cheeks.

'It's Moud's cologne.'

It was her neck that made me fall for her. She's nine years older than me, but she knows how to stay youthful, exercising regularly and always eating healthy. She's pretty, cheerful, and has a successful career in advertising. Unfortunately for her, she's a Protestant and happens to love Egypt, and her chances of meeting someone with both these qualities in Cairo are slim at best. She studied overseas before spending quite a long time being terrified of getting married or settling down. Sometimes, she'd like to have children. She had been used to dating men who were older than her, but suddenly, they had stopped showing an interest. Those that did show interest didn't interest her. This was the first time that she would be dating someone younger than her, which made her embarrassed to tell her friends.

The name 'Lady Spoon' was given to her by Mona May. She saw her at a concert once wearing a pair of spoon-shaped earrings.

The same earrings she had on that day. They swayed with the movement of her hand as she sliced a loaf of bread. In spite of the dryness in my throat, I'd been smoking since I woke up this morning. Cigarettes have a different sort of taste with the morning breeze in Zamalek: something resembling bliss, desire, a softness in violet and orange.

Our breakfast was eggs, along with slices of the finest quality pork, imported from abroad. After honey, jam, and a glass of orange juice, I was back to life. As the poet says, 'You ain't you when you're hungry.' At Maison Thomas, her smile nudged me awake under a white bed.

We walked around the streets of Zamalek in the direction of her apartment. She had a thin silver bracelet around her ankle, and toenails painted red. Sometimes we would walk hand-in-hand, and sometimes with my arm around her waist. Under the shade of the trees, we laughed. We shot smiles at the officers standing guard outside different embassies, but their solemn demeanor didn't change.

I thought, 'Do I love her?'

Of course I loved her. I can't touch a woman I don't love. But then, what is love exactly? It's a relaxing of the heart, a tranquility in your soul, a warmth in your stomach. It's like any love in Cairo, always ready to disappear. A love of companionship.

In her apartment, we smoked a joint of hash. I rubbed her knee as she played around on her computer looking for an old Madonna song. I lifted her dress above her knees and slid to the floor. Nestling between her legs, I lifted up her foot and started licking her big toe. I walked my tongue in gentle taps along her leg until I reached her knee, which I pummelled with kisses.

'It tickles,' she giggled in English.

I gave her knee a parting kiss, and continued my tongue's journey up her thigh. I planted a kiss, soft as a butterfly, on her thinly-lined underwear and pulled it away with my hands. I plunged my tongue into her pussy. I drank a lot that night. I drank until I felt thirsty. I gave her a full ride with my tongue before she took me into her room, where we had slow and leisurely sex. She turned over, and I put my fingers in her mouth. Wet with her saliva, I stuck them in her pussy. Slipping and sliding. I stuck them in from behind. I grabbed her short hair and pulled it toward me. I humped her violently and then lay on top of her for a few seconds. I got out of bed and threw the condom into the trash. As I gave her a smile, the phone rang.

'Hey dude, where you at?'

'Mona. What's up? I'm in Zamalek.'

'So, you still up for a beer tonight?'

'Maybe.'

'I'm with Samira. We're going up to Muqattam Mountain.'

'So you've got a car?'

'Yeah.'

'Okay then. Why don't you come pick me up in Zamalek?'

'When?'

She climbed out of bed with a gentle smile. Sex was over now. We still had some friendship and goodwill on our faces. People were eating each other alive out there, so why couldn't we keep things civil?

'How about in an hour or so?'

'Let's make it an hour and a half. Outside Diwan Bookstore.'

'Okay.'

'Bye.'

'See you later.'

After a quick shower, I gave her a kiss and a pat on the ass, which was my way of showing gratitude, or something like that. My hair was still wet as I went out. On the way to Diwan, I whistled to myself these words: 'Okay. Bye. See you later.' I had a smoke in front of Diwan's display window, which was full of those trashy English books that sell best in airports and supermarkets – the kind that soak your mind in grease and fry your heart in oil. It won't be long before they start selling them with Kentucky Fried Chicken. I tried calling Mona, but she didn't respond. Then I caught her sticking out her head and waving at me from Samira's car. Her hair blew in the breeze, or maybe it was just the loud music spilling out of the radio. Flags fluttered along the street, the car stopped, and I hopped in.

In order to get to Muqattam Mountain, we had to pass

through the decaying remnants of Old Cairo. Oddly enough, it took us only seven minutes to get from Zamalek to Abd al-Khaliq Tharwat Street. On a typical day, it might take us a full hour and a half to get to the Azhar Bridge at the end of Abd al-Khaliq Tharwat, but on an atypical day, like that one, Cairo seemed to be liberally bestowing her gifts on all those traversing her streets.

All this emptiness was due to a lack of spare change on holidays like that day. The streets, especially downtown, had taken on a completely different appearance. Mona was wearing a long skirt of some light fabric. I stuck my head between the seats and saw she'd bunched up her skirt in her lap and was rolling a joint. I was distracted by the glow of her knees, and Samira turning up the music. Jimi Hendrix's guitar shrieked like a hen laying its first egg. I opened the window as we pass over the Azhar Bridge, and imagined I caught a whiff of cumin, pepper, and spices. As we exited the bridge and entered the Husayn District, I smelled some burnt coffee beans that, without being an expert, I could tell were of poor quality. The scent filled my nostrils. Among the tombs in the City of the Dead, the smell of liver fried in battery acid lingered like a rain cloud. We finally emerged from the torrent of odors that fills Cairo all the way to the edge of Muqattam Mountain. We went to Bar Virginia and ordered some beers.

We only talked about things that would lighten the mood: films we'd seen recently, some interesting new music, tales of the wonders and oddities recited by taxi drivers, the jesters of the city.

The sun was about to set, and Cairo was laid out before us like a grid, a two-dimensional image from Google Earth.

In the middle of this mess of satellite dishes, horrendous-looking houses, and high buildings, there appeared one of the city's old ponds. It's a small spot of water, the last that remains of the many pools left over from the Nile after it was circumcised by the Aswan High Dam. In the background there echoed the voice of Muhammad Muhyi, singing a song by Hefny Ahmed Hassan.

A gentle breeze blew. Condensation collected on the green bottles of beer. A moist handshake of appreciation between the beer and its connoisseur.

Samira was fooling around with her phone. Mona took her beer and clinked it with mine. Her smile, a lock of her hair blown by the wind, and Cairo at sunset in the background. For a few moments, I felt something resembling happiness.

MARGINS OF ERROR
A Novel Extract

BY FERRÉZ
TRANSLATED BY VICTOR MEADOWCROFT

Jacaré is running, darting quickly along narrow pathways
with crude side panels made of wood, a real labyrinth. Nails
protruding from boards gathered at the market to erect the
shacks tear at his skin. Only the cold night air and the heat
of flight prevent him from feeling the intense pain. He's
running to save his life. They're chasing him, he doesn't
know who or how many, but he knows that they want him.
Reason? As he runs, his life plays back in quick fragments
within the confused universe of his mind, his memories
race past, until they arrive at that night. Revelling, smiles,
lots of drink, a few joints. It's a party, he's buzzing and he
bumps into a guy, into the wrong guy. He cries out. In the
middle of the boards he just ran across there was a nail, and
now it's lodged in his foot. Even so, Jacaré knows he can't
stop. He wants to make it home, wants to give his mother a
kiss, wants to see her one last time, wants at the very least
to tell her he's sorry. He shouldn't have gone out, especially not alone and unarmed' Now his thoughts become

confused, he's already exhausted and disoriented. He stumbles and falls into a cesspit, his body sinks, the smell of rot makes him vomit, his vomit mixes with the filthy water he's trying desperately not to swallow. His pursuers are getting closer. He lies there with his head in the cesspit until they go past. Their footsteps get further and further away, and Jacaré feels a sense of relief; he gets up feeling disgusted, but with a faint smile at the corners of his mouth. He's met by a bit of dark pipe he could almost swear was the barrel of a gun. It's positioned level with his stomach, and Jacaré can already hear the echo of the bullet inside, inside of him. He sees a boy, twelve or thirteen at most, but he doesn't recognise the kid: it wasn't him during the altercation at the party. The boy mumbles something. Jacaré is almost frozen, but he makes out the words of his executioner:

'member the girl you kill in that crash, sangue?'

'Narigaz, Narigaz! Listen, meu.'

'Huh... I'm listening, I'm listening, I was just thinking 'bout some stuff... but, hey, were you tight with that guy who died, Matcherros?'

'No way, he was a Corinthians supporter! But you know, he was cool... well, at least he seemed that way, right? He was always wearing that jacket and played football every Saturday in the big field. He even had a team he organised himself. Everyone was surprised when he turned up dead, all covered in shit, you know? No one could understand what'd happened, but Deia, that old lady over on Rua Doze, said he was mixed up in some bullshit with the guys from Cohab. I doubt it, 'cause everything that comes out of that viper's mouth is fofoca – just mean gossip. But, anyway, he'd already fucked up with that crash. You hear about that?'

'I did, yeah, he was completely off his face and tried to overtake on the inside, right?'

'Yeah, that's exactly what went down.'

'It's real fucked up, in the end everyone who dies in this dead-end place gets put into the same category. That's why I'm saying, truta, I wanna keep studying and, God willing, mano, I wanna have a better future. Worst thing is, if you really look at the facts, you'll notice that out of all of our friends only one or two round here are really trying for anything. Take you, for example. You're wasting your time, Matcherros, you have to get with it, mano.'

'Hey Narigaz, look after your own shit, fool, 'cause I got mine sorted.'

'Yeah, I can see that. There's an empty cell over in São Luís just waiting for you, so keep doing the crap you're doing, you'll see.'

'Yo, even my old man don't talk to me like that, truta. Take care of your own shit.'

Narigaz could see his friend was agitated and decided to continue his train of thought using other friends as examples.

'It's true, just think about it, Alaor is going all out and Panetone and Amaral are busting their asses too, but the rest, mano, let's be real, are wasting their time. They should've listened to the ideas Thaíde was rapping about, you get me? 'I'm poor, but I'm not a failure.' Those guys are missing something, I dunno, maybe it's a solid grounding' They gotta wise up, yeah, 'cause if you look around, everything's evolving and our friends are just standing still, and I'm not saying that 'cause I'm any better, no way. You know there's none of that that with me, but, let's be real, cara, those guys are gonna be swallowed up by the system; while they sleep till midday and wind and grind in clubs till morning, the playboys are studying, developing, doing little courses in anything and everything.'

'Whatever, Narigaz, truth is it's just like the pastor said, this place is cursed. Didn't you hear him explain how the name Capão comes from a word for a worship ground? This place was called Capão because it was just a patch of trees in the middle of nowhere where macumbeiros came and did their witchcraft. Over time, the wickedness in this place increased. Redondo is because of the round layout of the neighbourhood. The pastor even said spirits get trapped here and go around driving people out of their minds.'

'What kind of old wives' bullshit is that, truta?! You believe that pastor? Didn't you see the scandal that kicked up at the door of his church? A woman turned up saying he killed her sister over in Paraíba and now here he was trying to play the pastor.'

'Ah, sometimes it's just a bitch's lies.'

'Forget about it, I'm gonna keep going with the idea. So you see, the playboys have more opportunities, but, in my opinion, I think we have to defeat them with our creativity, you get me? We have to destroy the sons of bitches with the thing we're best at, our gift, mano. Duda and Devair are fucking awesome painters, Alaor and Alce are sick rappers, and Amaral and Panetone are shit-hot at football. You, Matcherros, you're always drawing. But you're all wasting your time, you have to apply yourselves. Some try, others give up too easy, and what's happening is time is passing by, you get me? And nobody gets out of this shit. But go over and try share a few ideas for five minutes and you'll hear complaining for hours. Everything's messed up, cara: this guy has fathered a baby now, the other guy's dad ran off with some cow, so-and-so's father is such a son of a bitch they've started calling him a faggot, and it just gets worse. Show me now, who has the gift of being able to read a book, who have you seen round here saying they're trying to better themselves, who's studying at home, who's applying themselves? Nobody, mano, 'cause when it comes to going drinking at the weekend, everybody's up for it, but when it comes to studying... then there's nothing doing, and the future waits out in front, a long way out in front of this place.'

'That's it, mano, you're right, except for one or two, most of them really are in the shit, and then life makes them pay the price. But you can be sure, Narigaz, that if you stop to really think about it, you'll go crazy, so there's no point in keeping talking about it, you talk and talk, but in the end the one that's full of desire is you. But it's like you said, the future is waiting out in front, way out in front. It's not this place's fault, it's our minds; and the future of the playboys is just much closer to happening than ours is.'

'That's exactly what I'm trying to say, but I've been talking my ass off, right, mano? Let's go get some bread over there and then we can head over to Panetone's house.'

'I need to speak to him as well, I wanna see if he'll lend me his combat boots. Do you think he'll need them today?'

'Maybe, but he just bought some trainers, and he's crazy about them. A pair of blue Adidas, you get me?'

'Ah, I know, they're low, right? Flat-soled, like for indoor football. I think those trainers are awesome, Amaral has them in red.'

'Those are the ones. Now finish that coffee. Do you want more bread?'

'No, no, I'm good.'

A short while later, they were heading over to Panetone's house. Matcherros still had the last piece of bread in his mouth, but Narigaz had already eaten the whole roll. He didn't waste any time when it came to food. That's a habit of people who've had a troubled childhood, and it's even worse when you take into account the three sisters he competed with at the table. They reached Panetone's house and he wasn't in. So Matcherros invited Narigaz back to his place; they walked another hundred metres and were there. Matcherros' father, Lucas, was outside getting some sun, sitting on a little bench made out of crates from the market. The two of them didn't even have to take the initiative to go over and greet him, because he struck first, attacking Matcherros.

'You're fucking hilarious, you know! You want to keep those damn mutts, but you think dogs don't shit. The yard is a fucking mess, full of flies.'

Matcherros didn't even wait for Narigaz to go inside before calling out in answer to his father.

'Bullshit, it's those fucking rabbits that attract the flies and stink of shit.'

His father took a step forward and, meeting his son's eyes, asked him to repeat what he'd just said.

Matcherros was in no doubt about his father's reaction and lowered his gaze, before heading towards the kitchen. When he got there, he picked up the coffee pot, poured a bit of cold, weak coffee into a cup and drank it. Until that moment, he hadn't been aware of the presence of his uncle, Carimbê, who was lying there shirtless, looking terrible; wrinkled, with parched lips and bloodshot eyes; bald, with a few strands of hair at his nape, his boots and trousers all covered with mud and piss. He also noticed the catarrh on the pillow, saw the dentures inside a glass of water, the still-lit cigarette half-lying on the floor, the filthy ashtray and a cup of filthy coffee. Everything surrounding the man was filth. Carimbê's breathing was slow and heavy, his gaze, focused on the ceiling; he was drunk again. Narigaz also noticed the horrifying appearance of that drunkard. They both retreated to the kitchen, and Carimbê remained where he was, unmoving, uttering words that were incomprehensible to any other being. Maybe he was reliving some past event.

Glossary

Sangue – *lit.* blood; *informal* friend, associate.
Meu – *lit.* my/mine; exclamation similar to 'man' in English, used to express surprise, admiration, delight, etc., or for emphasis.
Fofoca – gossip, slander.
Mano – *informal* friend, comrade, colleague; *informal* brother.
Truta – *informal* close friend, associate.
Cara – *informal* person, similar to 'guy' or 'dude' in English.
Macumbeiro – someone who practices macumba, an Afro-Brazilian religious cult using sorcery, ritual dance and fetishes.

THE SCATTER HERE IS TOO GREAT
A Novel Extract

BY BILAL TANWEER

Before we were poor, we used to go out to some nice place to eat every week. I liked that place along the sea where I had spicy barbeque chicken. My chicken piece was so spicy that I used to get tears. But then we became poor. Though, Amma tells me I should not say we are poor. After all, we have enough to eat and drink, and have a place to sleep and we are better off than millions.

One day when I started crying, Baba told me, 'Don't cry, don't cry. Let us go to the sea on the bus.' I had not been on the bus before, so I was happy and wanted to go with Baba. Baba says that it is one and the same sea everywhere around the world, but he also says there are only very few cities that have the sea. Karachi has a sea.

Amma made me wear my nice dress-pants and put a lot of powder on me so that I would not get skin rash from the heat.

The bus did not stop. It moved and we had to sit in it while it was moving. Baba lifted me onto the bus, the conductor pulled me in and then, running, Baba also got onto the bus. The conductor was the last one to get in. It was dangerous. My heartbeat grew fast. At such times I do not feel good. Our doctor-uncle told me not to play too hard, and not to fight. Because then I become ill for a long time. And because old uncle is not here, Baba will have to pay the doctor's fee. Old uncle always used to pay our doctor's bill.

Baba paid the conductor, who had all the money in his hands. I asked Baba, 'Why doesn't the conductor keep the money in his pockets?' Baba said because there is too much of it and someone might steal it from his pocket. But why don't people steal from his hands? Baba said because he is always watching his hands. When you don't want your things to be stolen, you must always watch them. We were sitting at the back of the bus, and Baba was looking out of the window. The bus seats were red and looked dirty. I did not touch them, but I was sitting on them. There were designs on the roof with glitter on them. I closed my eyes, opened my blackboard and made those same designs in one of the rooms in my house. The big eagle, white horse with wings, lots of green hills, a big light-pink rose in the middle of the green hills, and shining gold and ruby-red colours surrounding them. It is difficult to make shiny things on blackboards, but I had a trick. I threw water on the chalk to make it shiny. The floor of the bus was dirty. It had grease-like things all over it. You should not draw dirty things on the blackboard.

The man sitting next to us leaned out of the open door, which is always open, and spat out every few minutes. I looked away. Baba did not even notice the man, who wiped his face with his sleeve after spitting.

The bus was going very fast and the wind blowing in from the windows was very hot. So I hid myself behind Baba. It was like being in a shadow. Shadows are empty places in things. The colour of shadows is also black, which is the colour of empty things. Blackboard is also black when it is empty. No one can draw shadows on blackboards because shadows keep on changing. You cannot draw changing things. But this happens, you know; you draw and you look and it has changed.

Then a fat man without a leg got on the bus. He was even fatter than Baba. He was smiling. He got on the bus and made a joke, 'Aray bhayya! Slow down! If I fall out of the bus, my wife will not wash my clothes!' Everyone smiled. The conductor also smiled. He paid the conductor in coins. The conductor gave him a discount.

The fat man without a leg looked at me and smiled and gave me a cow-toffee. It made me think of my Comrade-uncle who also brought cow-toffees for me when he came to see Baba. Baba told Amma that he was a sad man. 'He left his family and everything for his work. He keeps thinking of them, but I don't think he realizes that.' I knew he was sad because he smelled sad, like tired and sweat mixed.

The fat man without a leg was a nice man. My Comrade-uncle is also nice. He was even nicer when he lived with his family. He was tall and everyone liked him. He brought me toffees – many kinds of toffees – and biscuits. The skin under one of his eyes is black because he fought the police. He does not say his prayers. He says there is no Allah. Many people say he is sad, and without his family because of that. He shouts at those who tell him to pray. He was not like this before. He used to smile. He is a communist. That's the name of people who do not pray.

The fat man asked me my name, my school and what I would become when I grew up. I told him I will be a pilot and fly fighter planes and fight with India. He told me that fighting is not good, and told me to fly planes to carry people from one place to another. I said but those planes do not fly fast. He said they are very fast. I said but I do not like the way they looked, like eggs. I told him I did not like egg-planes. He started laughing. His stomach moved even more than Baba's when he laughed. His teeth were very dirty. He gave me the cow-toffee. Baba said I should thank him. Then Baba told the fat man about me. He said this boy is very naughty and loves to fight and beats his classmates. I said that is because they call me parrot, parrot.

Then I went to sleep. Baba put his arm around me, and I was in the shadow so the hot wind coming in through the door did not touch my face and I went to sleep.

I woke up when someone shouted.

Three thieves had come in the bus. One of them sat next to the back door, on Baba's side. The other was at the front door. And the third one stood in the middle with his gun. They all had shiny guns and their faces were covered with cloth, which kept falling away. (We all saw their faces. One of them had a thin moustache. The other had a thick, short beard; he was chewing the hair of his lower lip.) The one standing in the middle of the bus was shouting loudly. We were all scared. He said, 'Close the windows!' One window would not close. It was stuck. The thief was shouting at the man sitting next to that window asking him to shut it. I was so scared. I thought the beard-thief would shoot this man for not shutting the window. But then he told him to leave it. He also told the conductor to close the doors.

The bearded thief shouted at us, 'Whatever you have, drop it on the floor in front of you. If I find anything near anyone, I swear to God, I will fire a bullet through his head without a thought.' The thief sitting next to us stood up and started taking everyone's money. He took it first from Baba. I wanted to fight him. But I was scared. No one stood up to fight him.

The thief who was at the front sitting with the driver said to the ladies in the front compartment, 'Do not fear. You are like our mothers and sisters. We will not bother you. We do not need your money.'

When he said this, the fat man said, 'Please let us go. Aren't we like your brothers and fathers?'

The thief thought that the fat man was trying to make fun of him. He looked at him straight in his eyes, 'What did you say? Haan?' and then slapped him. It made a loud sound. He put the gun on his head, 'You find this very funny, haan? Funny, haan?' And he slapped him again. Everyone turned to see the man being slapped. It was like in class. When the teacher slapped one boy, no one spoke again.

The thieves took all the money but kept riding the bus with us. They took the money from the conductor. The conductor was watching his notes when the thief took them from him. One of the thieves took the money and put it in his bag. Everyone was looking at them doing this.

Then one thief started telling the driver where to go and how to drive, when to slow down, when to drive fast. He also hit the driver once on his head; it did not make any sound. The slaps on the fat man's face were louder. The thieves took the bus very far and after driving for a long time they told the driver to stop. And then suddenly two thieves quickly jumped out and the third thief started shouting at the bus driver and everybody else. '*If* somebody steps out, we'll shoot them straight in their head. *Nobody* comes after us. *Nobody. Understand?*' When he shouted like that I hid my face under Baba's arm.

The bus driver then drove so fast and everyone on the bus stayed quiet because we were all afraid that the thief who was shouting might shoot us from behind the bus. The bus driver stopped the bus at the sea and said it would not go any further. 'Get on other buses if you want to go anywhere.' Everyone suddenly became angry. They started to fight with him because thieves had taken their money.

Baba and I got off at the sea. The fat man without a leg was also going to the sea. He was not smiling now. His face was red. Baba had a secret pocket in his shalwar where he always hid some money. He gave a few notes to the fat man. Then he took me to the sea.

We sat on the shore and watched the waves that came so slowly. There were few people there and the wind was cool. I wanted to go on a camel ride, but I knew that Baba did not have the money for that. Baba was quiet. I felt he was drawing the night without a sun on his blackboard again. So I snuggled under his arm and said, 'Baba, let us draw even bigger camels than there are here.' I was so afraid to close my eyes because it was getting darker and I was afraid that new thieves might come. But I think it made Baba happy.

When I drew the camels, Baba said, 'Let us sit on these camels as well!' So I sat on my very, very big camel. I rode on it. And when Baba asked me, 'How does it feel riding such a big camel?' I said, 'It is like riding on waves.'

Evening came. Baba and I sat on a bench and had roasted

peanuts. Baba asked me if I was afraid of the thieves. I told him I was not. I wanted to fight them. He smiled. He told me never to fight thieves and if something like that ever happens again, 'just give them everything without saying anything.'

When we returned home, we took the bus again. This time I ran and got on the bus myself without the conductor's help. On our way, we passed that place where we used to have barbeque and where my chicken was the spiciest. I put my head on Baba's arm and he put it around me so I was in the shadow again. As I closed my eyes, I imagined a blackboard as big as the sea on which I drew a ship – a big ship moving on waves like riding a camel. And then I saw the cloth with which the thief covered his face, which kept on slipping and revealing his face. I wanted to draw a sun in the sea because it was dark and I wanted to give light to the ship, but then I fell asleep. But I remember the ship looked like an empty place, like a shadow, and the cloth was fluttering in the wind like its flag.

17—SÃO PAULO

DESESTERRO

BY SHEYLA SMANIOTO
TRANSLATED BY LAURA GARMESON

I come from a family of migrants and immigrants: my mother's family came over from Italy and my father's came from the northeast of Brazil to try to make a life in the country's financial capital.

My own migration was different, it wasn't geographical. There are only twenty kilometres separating the centre and the periphery of São Paulo, where I was born, but it took me twenty-four years to make the journey between the two, and to feel as though the city centre also belonged to me. It wasn't just a case of taking three buses. Before that, I had to understand who I was, as a woman who came from the periphery, the daughter of northeasterners and of immigrants far removed from their original culture. I had to understand that being a woman and coming from the periphery meant taking three buses in order to speak, five buses in order to be heard, and seven buses in order to be respected. There is no train for this journey. You have to set out on foot, taking step after step, and that was what I did when I was writing Desesterro.

I wrote it drawing on memories of my upbringing combined with the experience of crossing a social divide and reaching the other side. And that's what Desesterro is about: it is about the distances that we cover within ourselves to arrive at who we truly are. It is about the social distances that leave their mark upon our bodies and tell us what we can and cannot do. I don't write this aimlessly: the periphery is both far from the city and within it. As am I. I am always far from and within São Paulo.

'Come here, girl, quick. Didn't I tell you don't go about with your arms hanging at your sides, that it don't look right? And don't spread your legs like that, you look like a punk, it means you don't sit straight and people will talk. And shut that mouth, don't you know if you get a shock you gonna bite your tongue and then what? You acting like it's no big deal, you don't listen do you? Well you should know better. I ain't gonna be around forever, take that hand out your mouth you little beast, I ain't gonna be here forever and you think the world gonna treat you like I do, giving you a les-son every day? You better learn, girl, learn fast or the world gonna chew you up and spit you out. Lucky you still got Fátima looking after you. Get those knees together, quick, didn't I just say square up those feet? What you looking like that for? Listen I'll straighten you out with the plank if I have to, you hear me? Stand up straight, goddammit. Where you think you're going? The wind's coming, get inside, shut the windows, quick, and shut your mouth while you're at it, what'd I just say? Don't answer that I'm your grandma, brat! And quit talking like that, didn't I tell you things have names, savage? Don't look at me like that, goddamn, and don't get smart with me girl, you should know better. Quit your whistling, go and close the window, go on quick, little beast. If the dog gets out let the wind deal with her.

Penha's granddaughter crouches, watching the wind cavorting outside through the gap under the door, her dress lifting to leave her legs bare. The wind is rising, rising, rising, my God, it leaves nothing lying down. It strikes against the windows of the house the walls strikes fear into us too, my God, what was that banging on the door? Scrawny barks at the wall, she doesn't like the wind so she barks, shut up, brat, says Dona Penha, but the wind keeps blowing that awful wind makes Dona Penha sit her full weight down in the chair to rest once and for all, goddammit, to rest enough for a lifetime.

Penha's youngest granddaughter, the brat, seizes her chance, her only chance to do what she wants. Grandma's so still, my God, only the wind can make grandma sit so still. And the girl's so restless, my God, the girl who's always restless can finally make fun of her, with Scrawny between her legs like a leaf dancing in the wake of the wind, the two of them one blissful being, banging on windows on the door on pans with the wind answering earth, dead leaf, bone, corpse.

Grandma's still, grandma isn't moving, and the girl whirls about with the wind inside her. Grandma isn't moving in her chair, and the girl looks for the wake of the wind and finds Scrawny's tail. Grandma's barely breathing and the girl's panting corpse bone dead leaf sweat earth. Scrawny can't bear it either, running, barking, growling, beating her tail against Penha's skirt, biting Penha's shin, licking all the scraps from Penha's nails and poor Penha doesn't move. She stays in her chair, hands clutching her rosary, body poised in prayer.

Penha's granddaughter comes up to her grandma, talking nonsense. The girl with the spread legs, hand in mouth, punk-ass look. Grandma doesn't move when the girl kicks her in the shin, or when Scrawny's teeth tug on the wrinkled skin of her leg, she doesn't move when her youngest granddaughter spits on her, or when the little dog pisses on her toes, nor when her granddaughter, good idea Scrawny, when her granddaughter goes and pisses on her.

Grandma isn't breathing.

In Vilaboinha the wind raises everything the earth keeps, so Penha was used to having to shove a dead body aside to open the door, can you imagine, this wind don't even respect death. The earth there slowly chews over corpses, like a cow ruminating human flesh, holy human flesh, can you imagine, this wind can only be in league with death. Goddamn earth that don't keep nothing, listen Maria de Fátima, when I die I want to be strung up high.

The vultures come in on the heels of the wind, the vultures come and perch in the garden of corpses. They tear out one part, then they wait, and wait. Vultures are good at waiting; their eyes are on the afterlife. Penha could watch the damned things all day, all day long, goddamnit. They're the hand of God devouring what the eyes don't want to eat, the hand of God, they can only be, they have to be, it was them who took Cida. Look at them pecking away, saintly things. Look how they peck out the worms first.

At first, yes, Penha was afraid. She hid herself away in the crannies of the house, seeing grace in these eaters of wounds. Look at them pecking away, goddamnit, look at them taking an interest in rotting flesh. At first she shut herself up in the house, can you imagine, watching the creatures outside pecking away at death. Look how they chew. She throws them a severed arm, bones showing, blood, fibres. Look at them flying over to it, look at them fly.

Penha knew she was going to die this time when she went to close the window to hide the girl from sight and she heard the rattle of phlegm at the back of her throat, with no one else around, can you imagine. She set off walking round the room dragging her feet across the floor, goddamnit, would you believe it, the rattle of phlegm right here in the silence, goddamnit, the phlegm of someone else who isn't even here. Penha set off dragging her feet, can you imagine, pushing down hard on her heels to fill her other ear with sound. Goddamnit, who knew so much could be unearthed from the silence?

It wasn't Cida, Penha knew it, Cida didn't come back not even in dreams, Cida didn't cough up phlegm or spit, Cida died and she was never coming back to Vilaboinha. Just as well Penha's daughter stayed in the tree that she'd planted, the only tree in all these streets to thrive. Cida was there in the branches, in the leaves, on a quiet day when the air was still, Penha could hear her daughter's breathing in the rustling of the trees. But this phlegm, she knew the phlegm wasn't Cida.

Penha hadn't been walking long when the dog appeared at the door, Scrawny, with her tail behind her. Get gone. The dog appeared, barking at the sound of her slippers. Go on, Scrawny, go on, get. The dog didn't stop growling she didn't stop. Goddamnit, you can't just take someone's own feet away. Get out, Scrawny, out. The dog was growling Penha

was dragging her feet the dog was growling Penha was dragging the dog came closer, closer until she kicked her in the
ribs, goddamnit, who told you not to keep quiet?

Penha starts dragging her feet again, the silence buried
inside her. She keeps on dragging her feet, soothing the
earth. The girl outside and inside her. Penha drags her feet,
but the silence drags along too, turned into earth that's raised
by the wind, the wind that draws breath from the silence.
The phlegm thickens. The whispering rises. The wind inside
her tells her everything. She can't hear what it's saying, she
doesn't let it tell her, she drags her feet so she can't hear.

Her granddaughter watches her from outside, the girl with
the punk-ass legs, one eye wider than the other, feet on the
ground, still, feet finally still. The dog beside her barking, yelp-
ing, growling, goddamnit, she just don't quit growling, does
she? The girl watches her grandma, Penha doesn't try and hide
it: she keeps on dragging her feet while she can. Someone's
there, very close by, where there's nothing. That was when she
knew that this time she was heading straight for it: it must be
death, the bastard. You know full well what it was.

It had always been like this: everybody died, except Penha the
madwoman. The wind would strike against the closed door,
leaving an arm a torso a body part on the doorstep. Nothing
came for Penha. Everything has its time, they would all say,
everything has its time, they'd repeat at every opportunity,
everything has its time, goddamnit. Only Penha didn't. But
now this phlegm, now this silence all turned inside out, it
can only be death, it can only be Penha's time, it must be her.

But everything does have its time, even the wind. All day
long it brought death to their door, day in day out it tried

Penha's patience, it tried it yet again: and still it didn't come. Everything has its time, even the girl, that little devil pacing the earth outside, clearing up after the wind. And when Penha would think this must be it, the earth's breath, and when she was shaking cups maybe this is the wind, just once more, it didn't come not a whisper of wind came to bring her body to the earth, goddamnit, was it not her time?

Everything has its time. Even this goddamn wind.

Once Maria da Penha choked on a coconut shell and all and she couldn't stop coughing up everything the whole coconut shell and all, and she couldn't stop hacking with the shell and coconut and all, lungs like coconuts two little coconuts. Everyone was thumping her on the back, even using it as an excuse to whack her in the ribs, everyone was yelling spit it out woman, this girl can't even spit, and she was thinking maybe this shell and coconut pricking her throat maybe this shell and coconut stampeding inside her maybe this shell of earth lodged in her throat maybe this is death? No, it wasn't.

Penha watches, the wind won't come, it's going to end up at the knees of the girl under the sink, goddamn sullen child. Get out from under there, savage, she thinks of saying, get out before I drop a bucket on that sorry face. Instead she just huffs, shoots her a dirty look and says nothing. Fátima, the blabbermouth, Fátima doesn't shut up. She must be in league with the wind, goddamn ungrateful granddaughter, it can only be the wind inside her body pushing out all that talk. Shut that mouth before I give you one, Fátima, she thinks of saying.

Fátima doesn't stop:

– Cátia didn't run away or nothing, Gran, it's not true. What would she run away for, Granny? She went far away to help... she's got her mother and sister taken care of. Vera makes out like she ain't got no money to make people feel sorry for her, she fakes it. Cátia didn't run away, Granny, she sends everything she earns to her family. Cátia's a good girl, she ain't like the others who run away, there's not that many women who go leaving Vilaboinha behind.

Dona Penha huffs, shoots her a dirty look, and says nothing. She dries her hand on the dishcloth, nearly tearing it. Here comes blabbermouth, again with this phony excuses idea. Good people have their heart in the earth. There's also people born with the goddamn high road in their chest, keep to themselves, the quiet type, they come back at least. This goddamn Cátia's heart is outside her chest and she's still leaving saying, can you believe it, she still leaving saying she went looking for something, went to do what?, asked the heart.

– But don't you know? There's people who like making up stories – Fátima doesn't shut up.

– But God's watching everything...

– Don't go taking the Lord's name in vain, brat.

– Relax, Granny, it's okay to go around saying it.

– Well find a way to not say it, you hear me? And here let me take care of Maria. Drink your coffee, go on, before it gets cold drink your coffee. And don't go believing all those stories, blabbermouth, you even look like a blabbermouth with that loose tongue, my God. You gotta be taking care of your daughter, she's growing up and you don't even notice, you went off looking after others, dreaming of life far away.

I ain't gonna be around forever, Fátima, so you need to watch yourself, listen good to what I tell you. You're very shallow, you ain't gonna die soon, but you should know this. All this land ain't your home and every man ain't your husband, you think any man stops beating before a woman starts praying? You got your eyes fixed on something beautiful off in the distance and it means you don't see straight, idiot, just you watch yourself, you'll see, Maria de Fátima.

Grandma Penha, hips against the sink, places Scarlett on her lap, leaving Fátima quiet to the side, finally silent. She goes to take care of her granddaughter's child, small as she was, fine fair hairs sprouting from her forehead, she goes to take care of Scarlett, poor little mite, so scrunched up, so sweet. Penha feels her youngest granddaughter watching her, Penha feels the girl-turned-animal staring crouched under the sink. If she didn't know her granddaughter, strange girl, she wouldn't even have noticed. Penha looks at Scarlett, all bony elbow flesh, so teeny-tiny. Penha looks down at Scarlett Maria in her lap, she looks at the wind, she looks at the wind and, again, she sees nothing. Nothing at all.

Then there was the time when Maria da Penha cut off the very tip of her finger, go fetch that knife Maria da Penha, go on, Maria, enough laziness, she was just a hungry kid peeling mandioca root, Maria da Penha was peeling the mandioca and she ate her fingers with the knife, she cut off the very tip of her finger and she was losing blood, losing strength, losing the will, what's this that you lose with a cut what's this that stays with a cut what's this bucket of blood, is this death? Of course not, Maria da Penha, enough of

that nonsense. Go on, get back to preparing that mandioca.
Go on, you still got a whole bunch.

– Keep those legs still, girl. Quit picking at your nails, goddamn obsessive, Lord have mercy. Take that hand out your
mouth, you little devil, ain't nothing tasty about your own
flesh. You'll end up tearing the whole nail out and whining
if you get salt on it. And don't pull that face, come now.
Don't go thinking you'll be rid of me, savage, I'll come
back to grab you by the feet. You think Fátima plucks out
her lice one by one, disgusting child? Leave that wound
alone, come on, quit fooling around, you don't even look
like a child of God. And stop putting your feet on the earth,
only the Lord have mercy, d'you hear me? I ain't gonna be
around forever, everything has its time. Come here, savage. Come here, out from under the sink, lay your head
here on my arm, come on, don't pull that face. Lay your
head here, wipe that nose first. Then you'll be whining if
I don't come near you, can you believe it. Come on, devil
child, lay yourself here. Fátima, my child, everything has
its time. Here, take Scarlett, it's nearly lunchtime and the
chicken ain't gonna kill itself. What'd I say? I know it's the
last chicken, ungrateful girl, but you'll be whining if there
ain't no food. What's that in your hair, Fátima, child? Leave
it, I'll get it. Now I'm gonna repeat what I tell you, what's
that, Fátima? Take Scarlett, here, go on, and quit fooling
around. Granny's already giving you back, pretty one. What
about you, devil child? Don't stand there scratching your
head, you trying to make me itch? Then go pray and ask for
mercy, didn't I tell you to quit talking like an animal? Let
me straighten out those legs, no whining, ungrateful girl,

now go and hit the earth, go on, go take care of the windstorm, go on, girl, I don't want you around when I go kill the chicken. Go on, run, brat. Even a chicken suffers in the eyes of this little devil. Did you see that, Fátima? At that age with body hair starting to grow and she still putting bad luck on the chicken's death, did you see that? Your sister don't respect nothing, Fátima. She killed my peace when she was born. And now she won't leave me be.

What about when Penha became a young woman? She lost so much blood, my God, she lost so much blood that all her sisters, certain the little creature was going to die, burned everything she had. They hung Penha's scrawny body upside down, like a banana tree, they hung Penha's body the other way up, keep that blood inside you, come on, messy girl. The blood nearly broke her head, she could barely feel her legs, she nearly died like a chicken, dazed and dripping blood onto the earth below, look Ma, if we cut her up she'll fit in the cooking pot. Pale-faced, and everyone was saying how quiet she was in everything: it was blasphemy to die on Good Friday. As you'll see, Penha didn't die of that.

With her belly propped against the kitchen sink, Penha sees the girl running far, far, far, Penha sees the girl running as far as she can, raising the earth, then she suddenly stops short, unable to go on. When she gets close, she straightens her legs, she's still close trying to straighten up those legs, not knowing how to go on. A curse! What is it that girl keeps staring at?

Whenever she finds her youngest granddaughter staring into the distance Penha doesn't know what to do. She's tired of telling the little devil to quit drawing attention to herself. Penha doesn't know what to do with the girl: she follows her gaze, follows her gaze right up to what she can't see. Goddamnit, Penha follows her gaze even thinking: this girl sees everyone as a circus fleeing the world, can you believe it, a circus marching to its death. Penha follows her gaze, goddamnit, Penha tries to hide it: you keep running, go on, devil child!

The dance was worse. Everyone was running, trampling, rushing, Maria da Penha was breathing deeply. Everyone was running and there she was thinking she was going to burn to death. She couldn't just get up and go outside and live, not now she was pregnant, not now Toninho had left her, not now she'd been thrown out of her auntie's house. There she was believing all she had to do was wait and everyone was desperate, there was a smell of burning flesh, believing all she had to do was wait and everyone was burning, my God, there are people my God where's the fire my God lost the child my God, not even Toninho came. Let alone death.

Penha puts the chicken in the bucket, goddamnit, if we don't kill it right away the bird won't die. Maria da Penha says so. If we don't kill it right away the meat gets tough, if we don't want the blood to spoil, it won't work. Penha skewers the chicken the last chicken the chicken for the festivities she skewers it deep in the bucket, the iron of the bucket cracks, the bird screeches, but the girl lying on the ground outside pretends not to hear her grandma calling.

   – She's far away, Granny – says Fátima. – Don't worry, the girl's far away.

– What's got into you now? You want to cross me, is that it? That girl sees too far, Fátima, don't you see her eyes jumping out her head?

– Don't worry, Granny, the girl's all grown up now.

– Didn't I say the bird's blood will spoil?

– But Granny, the girl...

– Quit being stupid, Fátima, what's the story this time? Ain't no pity that helps with killing, your sister knows it, the brat, but she's pretending not to hear, that devil. If my legs were good and my hip was where it should be, if I had it in me, I'd creep up behind that girl with the plank, I'd make that brat run real far I mean real far away from my chicken. Then she'd come back to eat.

– Go on, Granny, kill the bird. The girl's all grown up. She can't turn the blood of a chicken just by looking at it. That's the kind of magic only children do.

– Be quiet, Fátima. Don't you go thinking you know this girl better than I do.

– Just drop it, Granny. She's my mother's daughter too. She's your Cida's daughter too.

What happened next, goddamn, even if we told anyone they wouldn't believe it.

The blood from her first period was nothing compared to when she lost her other child. The child was already whole in her guts, it must have been, the blood she shed was a whole person made triplets: the youngest a well, the middle one a river, the oldest pain. The child came gushing out, made her intestines hurt. She thought it was being born, this is how a child is born, this is how the belly withers, how the belly button inverts, this is how flesh turns inside out people inside hunger found, but no this was nothing. Just another way for death to forget Penha. Now there's someone with a strange sense of humour.

So there it is. Penha breaks its neck and leaves the blood all splintered goddamnit. The girl far away is startled by the chicken's death, she twists her legs, can't keep still. Let alone the earth. Her grandma starts, thinking someone's coming, she loses the chicken from the bucket, and bites her tongue with the few teeth she has. She goes running after the chicken, her hip won't let her, it's clucking, her hip is clucking and Penha stays put, goddamnit, watching the bird's final flight from a distance. The bucket rolls away.

The chicken keeps on running without a head the chicken doesn't die. The chicken's running, running, running, far, far, far, raising the earth from the streets, the chicken runs past the girl stopped dead in her tracks, past the dog, past all of them and disappears into the distance into the stuff of the earth. It isn't dead, the chicken isn't dead. Goddamnit, that stare of her granddaughter's. And now the little chicken head, lying in a pool of blood, forgotten by the sink, next to Penha's hand, now it insists on staring straight at Penha.

That was the last straw. The despair, just imagine it, of seeing the girl's eyes in that little chicken head! Goddamn granddaughter, that girl, if she wasn't Cida's child she would have given her what for. The dog's yapping goddamn mutt, useless even for gnawing bones let alone for a good pot broth. Her granddaughter runs inside the house her legs covered in earth, goddamn earth that can't even keep what belongs to it.

Dona Penha huffs. Shoots her a dirty look. And says nothing.

– Granny.

Fátima won't shut her mouth, the brat.

– Granny, I'm going to São Paulo.

18—CAIRO

THE BRIDGE

BY MONTASSER AL-QAFFASH
TRANSLATED BY GRETCHEN McCULLOUGH
WITH MOHAMED METWALLI

Since the Giza Bridge was finished, she started seeing her
apartment on the fourth floor, as if it were on the ground
floor. She was always annoyed by the honking of the cars. Yet
it was amplified when it was coming above the bridge, as if
the sounds were coming from within the apartment. She no
longer had the edge: the absence of tenants facing her, who
could watch her. Passengers in cars crossing over the bridge
could see the inside of her apartment, especially if it there
was a traffic jam, or cars were stalling on the bridge or moving slowly. She started seeing faces, gaping at her, while she
was watching television in the room by the street. She was
forced to keep the shutters ajar; then, she kept them closed
most of the day. It was hard to imagine that those days were
gone, when she didn't worry about leaving the shutters open
and was able to sit in the living room or balcony without
anyone observing her.

It was not only the problem of the passengers, but also
the sweepers, who dawdled on the job, since a fast sweep

would subject them to another round by their supervisor. Her son, Hassan, yelled at one of the sweepers for gazing at their apartment, who, nodded in agreement and looked toward the sidewalk, though he kept sweeping in the same spot. She could easily have stared them down in the hope they might understand her rage. But that would mean she would always pull a long face when she stepped onto the balcony.

She could no longer stay awake until after midnight. Dawn was the only time she could comfortably stay on the balcony – then there were only a few cars crossing the bridge and she could ponder the vast expanse beyond and view the clouds with their different shapes. Once she figured out one shape, she kept looking to find another one. Many a time, she viewed the clouds with Hassan as a little boy. She encouraged him to find many shapes – he shouldn't be satisfied with just one shape. In fact, he would find animals, birds and cartoon characters, in the clouds, and eventually would roar with laughter pointing to a cloud that looked like his aunt, with a longer chin, or bigger ears, or even a moustache. She would smile, staring at the cloud, without finding the point, knowing that he was imagining something funny. She wouldn't scold him, enjoying the notion that he was participating in her favourite game. And when his sarcasm surged about the relatives, who he imagined in the clouds, she reminded him it was time for lunch. As they left the balcony, Hassan would still be describing the tail of one of his uncles to her.

Dawn didn't last long since the bridge had risen. Soon, a barrage of faces started to gaze at her, forcing her to hide inside. Those who annoyed her most were the passengers of mini-buses and public buses, for whom peeking into the apartments opposite the bridge, especially the ones with open windows, would represent the only relief from the crowdedness and the suffocation inside the vehicles. The looks of those passengers were like predators searching for prey in the flats, which they could scrutinise and examine from every angle. She tried staying on the balcony with disinterest, but it was annoying to ignore the looks of others, besieging you, considering you a source of entertainment, while they waited. She knew her late husband would act like their son Hassan, reading the paper as usual on the balcony or sitting with his friends without thinking of the bridge. And he would repeat like Hassan: 'We live in this apartment. We're not imprisoned here.' She was convinced by all of this, but to no avail. Her expeditions to the street were rare. Every time she went out, she felt pain in her legs, and panted, as if she had walked for miles. In addition, that vast expanse which she used to enjoy and had considered part of her apartment, making it limitless, did not make her regret her rare expeditions.

When I was visiting Hassan, she prepared tea for us while we were on the balcony. She pointed to the bridge with all the stalled cars, wondering about the benefit of building it, since it didn't solve the problem of traffic. I had heard this comment from her as many times as she used to ask me if I remembered these days when I used to sit on the balcony, undisturbed. Neither me, nor any of Hassan's friends showed that we were annoyed about her repeated story of the bridge. We felt listening to her might help her bear whatever had happened to her beautiful space. We also felt her desire to linger on the balcony, distracted by the conversation with us, without having to worry about the gazing faces. We were always keen that she wouldn't hear us while we were whispering about the weird things we had seen in other apartments that we had passed on the bridge: Hassan would signal to us to stop whispering as he saw her coming toward the balcony.

She reminded me of how my mother had lamented the days when she had a view of the Pyramids from our apartment. The difference between them was that the buildings that were built in front of us, obscured the view of the Pyramids completely – none of them were visible to us at all. Yet this bridge kept the expanse after cracking it with a long fissure. Whenever she saw it, she wished to wake up one day, and find it all gone.

She surprised me one time, by remembering a story I must have told her about my mother's refusal to live in a ground floor apartment and on her insistence, despite my father's attempts to persuade her to change her mind. She vehemently agreed with my mother's decision, telling me she would have regretted it had she backed down. It was not only surprising that her comment came years later, but also that she was incensed about my father's promotion of the ground floor: indeed, she compared his stance with the bridge stretching in front of her. She thought that neither of the fathers comprehended the notion of having a wide view. Hassan commented that this is not a fair comparison. Then, she hurried to say, 'I'm just saying, for example. God bless everyone.' She smiled at me, while she entered the apartment with steady steps.

19—MANILA

SOMERSAULTS

BY JEFFREY P. YAP

From a pedestrian's perspective, the avenue was just a sea
of buildings. But for us living in it, it was something else.
The news arrived as hearsay at first, from gossip-mongers
who strutted along the arcaded sidewalks, shaded from the
sun. One of these stirrers, Bernice, closed her umbrella and
approached our shop. Our store occupied one of the mid-
rise buildings that shaped this part of the city and glowed
in neon signage once the night set in. Bernice removed her
sunglasses, placed them on our glass counter, and fanned
herself with a tabloid.

'Here, it's official. They're killing your street,' said
Bernice, showing us the newspaper and blowing air down
her red silk dress, which shimmered in the blazing afternoon. My wife Alice took a good look at the front page. The
woman pointed at the small article just below the headline.
'Train to be built soon.' What a horrid title it was – thank
God it was in small font, almost invisible to a passerby
glancing at the dailies.

Reading it further, it mentioned a ten-kilometre train above the street that would pass through the avenue, not just a street as Bernice had said, but an extended road that traversed eight cities.

'From forty-five minutes to ten minutes travel time, from point A to point B. Now that's pretty fast,' said a customer who came in with the same paper tucked under his arm. I stormed outside, just to breathe. I looked up and in front of me was a stand-alone theatre. We had about ten of these structures, all lined up in less than a kilometre. Motion pictures were shown in buildings with façades adorned with relief carvings of anahaw leaves and sometimes geometric shapes. The massive concrete one in front of our shop had details of straight and curving lines. Right at its entrance were vertical blocks lined up to form an uneven symmetry. Its signage lit up in pine-tree green at night and its billboard was surrounded by over a hundred yellow light bulbs which glared the title of the weekly Hollywood film.

Further to the right there were shops of different kinds. Next to us was a store selling sporting goods, where special basketballs were encased in glass counters and could not be dribbled unless there was a promise of purchase. A number of bookstores lined the avenue, all the way to the junction where the universities stood almost next to each other. Books were stuffed on shelves while school supplies dominated the centre aisle. Children accompanying their mothers to the store always wanted those piles of new notebooks, neat and freshly minted, with hard covers and smooth white paper in between its covers. The aroma of scented erasers was blown away by electric fans standing at every corner of the store, including the scent of intermediate pad and yellow paper. But the smell of sticky-back plastic dominated, standing vertically near the cashier counters. It was all rolled up to make the lives of sales ladies easier, so that they still had ample time for lunches of hot soups, steamed rice, and sweet and sour pork in Chinatown.

I turned my back and looked at our building, a two-story prewar structure left to survive more than three decades ago when our district was burned down and shelled, and our families were left with nothing but a structure that was almost razed to the ground. Ours was three buildings from the corner. It was spared because corner buildings were most likely to be damaged by war than mid-rises built in between two structures. We painted it off-white, including its columns and arches. The swing-out glass windows were always cleaned with moistened newspapers and it glared when the sun blazed right through it like the punch of a fist. Our signage was a bit discreet, just a little above the arches of the ground floor, saying, 'R.D. Lim Grocery' in block letters. Different from the other stores in the inner Chinatown with names like 'Double Prosperity,' 'Lucky Eight,' and 'Red Dragon Merchandise.'

My wife, who was raised in this district, was thankfully, a non-conformist and found the trend of naming a business after a value, virtue, and dragons a bit silly. She named our store after the name of her father who owned the building, which was constructed in the 1920s, back when our avenue was second only to the first class narrow street near the church and the plaza.

Alice felt a sense of doom after reading the short article on the tabloid's front page. It mentioned that the government had already approved the 1980 memorandum that the elevated train would cut straight to the inner city where our building was located. There was a photo showing the gleaming concrete like an overfed python, with a rolling train sliding above it. Below the train tracks was the street without lights, and on both sides was the sea of buildings, all war survivors, about to take on the challenge of this massive reptile that planned to take over and spew venom onto our district.

I sank into a chair behind the cashier counter. Everyone in the shop felt that these were times of uncertainty. One loyal customer who came in with his basket even asked me what was wrong. Alice, who was about to go to the stockroom, answered for me and told the man that our business, the avenue, and the community was about to face the huge snake of a train.

Because of this news, our community could no longer hide what we wanted to say about the government. We knew we couldn't fight the giant who'd made the protesters and student leaders disappear. Plans of peaceful protest were mapped out and our version of Town Hall meetings were done during downtime, when there were no customers, to discuss the problems at hand. After talking about our main agenda, we would extend our talk over coffee and express our sentiments about the failure to collect the garbage on a regular basis or why we had to give food to the Metro Com police who visited all the stores at noon time. We always gave them the canned pork and beans that were about to expire. When they returned and asked why it tasted funny, we told them that it was the natural flavour of imported beans.

Bernice heard the hiss of the smokestack near the river. It was four in the afternoon. It was time to go, she told us.

'By the way, that ice plant will be torn down by the train construction,' she added.

The ice plant laden with red bricks, a smokestack that belches thick, black fumes, and a whistle that blew every day at four in the afternoon to remind us that another day had passed; these were the structures that made the downtown distinct from the suburbs. Bernice dropped by the store and spoke about this. She even suggested that we should rally in front of the city hall and the office of public works to stop the demolition. If the ice plant would not be spared, how much more at risk was our lowly business in an equally-antique building?

I told Alice that there wouldn't be a direct hit because the train will be built in the middle of the road. She looked at me like I had dropped a crate of apples on the street. She explained to me that constructing an elevated railway in the middle of a busy intersection would threaten all the businesses that surrounded it. Of course I knew that. Who wouldn't? Even our sales girl and delivery boy understood the consequences when they heard the news.

I assured Alice that our loyal customers would keep us afloat for a few more years at least, until the market caught up again and sustained a regular flow of patrons. But she knew that demographics change when something new is introduced. This time, it wasn't just about curfew and prohibition of selling alcohol to minors – those were easy to deal with. The store was losing its buyers; the python had to be stopped.

Alice kidded me that we only had five loyal customers. She gave me a silly grin that made us laugh, at least for a moment, and I remembered that when she took over the business from her father the store was called Otis Department Store. Alice breathed life into the business that her father had bequeathed her, and she loved the building itself even more than the store. It was a structure reminiscent of a bygone era, an original façade, with neo-classical columns and pilasters that seemed out of place on an avenue where the fine clean lines of art deco structures dominated the streetscape.

When I met Alice, I knew that she liked selling general merchandise and preferred perishable items like meat and vegetables to shoes and bags. She told me that food sold better than luxury items. I had suggested that we put up a school supplies store, but she said that notebooks and pencils would not sell because we were no longer living in the heyday of Manila.

So, instead, we sold black chicken, an exotic Chinese delicacy famed for its medicinal, healing properties. We were the only store on the avenue that sold black chicken and it could not be found in markets and groceries. After several months, we had to wake up as early as five in the morning to satisfy customers banging the glass door and pleading for us to sell the poultry. We also ventured into wholesale items. Boxes of canned instant milk and luncheon meat were stacked up in our small warehouse at the back of the store, where rats almost as big as our missing cat could be found lurking in dark corners, perhaps feasting on uncooked spaghetti noodles still wrapped in its packaging.

All of these things, these minor matters in the store, prevented us from having children. Alice told me once while I was helping her arrange the canned milk on the shelf that she couldn't afford months of having another human being inside of her. The afternoon heat while tending the store could roast her and the baby. I told her, almost in a whisper, that it would be nice to have a son assisting me with the inventory or a daughter helping her mother organise the shelves. We're still young, she always told me. All of the black chickens should always be sold at the end of the day.

As I threw away a pack of spaghetti that had been eaten by a rodent, Alice reminded me that I should man the store at all times especially when she was out meeting with the suppliers. She also told me that I should increase the frequency with which I checked the inventory from three times a week to five times a week, and inspect all the corners of the store for pests lurking in the grocery items. Sometimes, I felt as though I might as well wear a blue short-sleeved polo shirt with a black-plated name tag, a pair of blue trousers, military boots, hold a baton, and walk in and out of the store.

Alice asked me for a strategy, for a plan. She told me that she had already submitted a letter of appeal to the city hall asking to reroute the railway to another street parallel to us. However, after a number of phone calls to the mayor's office, the secretary with a shrieking voice was already hanging up on us. We changed the tones of our voices and pretended to be other people, but that didn't work. Passing by the newspaper stand, the headlines screamed in our faces that the plan was final. Construction would start soon.

There was no point in cursing the national or even the local government. Alice had been repeatedly shouting 'idiot' in the store until one of the customers thought that she was referring to him. With profuse apologies, Alice held man's hands and asked for his help. How could we save the store from this so-called development? She let go of the man's hands, turned to me, and asked what I could do help her.

'I don't know how to deal with politicians,' I answered.

'I'm not asking you to talk to the mayor. Think of an alternate marketing strategy for store promotion,' Alice said.

Several ideas came to mind. I suggested that we place an advertisement on top of the school at the foot of the bridge and give out flyers. It was a strategic vantage point, and people walking along the plaza would see the name of our store 'R.D. Lim.' Why not put out another ad? 'R.D. Lim – if you want black chicken... we have it!'

'A simple advertisement won't work,' Alice said.

The woman could read minds.

'How about a huge advertisement near the church?' I asked.

'I don't think so,' she replied. 'The priest hates black chicken. Besides, have you seen the banner of that other store on top of that bank in front of the church? They have a grocery section too you know.'

'But not black chicken,' I said.

'Forget black chicken,' Alice said. 'Our customers already have more chicken than they can consume. A sale banner in front of our store will do.'

I shrugged and resorted to picking up a string of noodles left by a rat. Alice talked to one of our regular customers who had come to the store earlier asking for the black chicken to be replaced with a bar of detergent. Wishy washy. From cooking to laundry. From chicken to detergent. He always assumed that we would completely understand and immediately replace his purchase. He even requested that the laundry soap not be cut in half because he preferred it that way.

One of the reasons why the rats were so enjoying their stay at our store was because Griswald the cat had not made an appearance for a while. He had been missing in action for the last week. Alice said that we needed to find the cat so it could start catching vermin in the store again.

What Alice didn't seem to realize was that we were in the pits of downtown. Griswald had probably been slaughtered by the cooks at a nearby panciteria, and ground into meat for siopao. I told Alice the rumors about the delicacy made from cat's meat. She got offended, thinking I was accusing her race of being unhygienic, cat-eating natives.

Alice spoke with another customer, a Chinese man whose skin was like dried plum and smelled of the Tiger Balm that wafted through the store. He explained that he wanted a regular chicken because the black chicken tasted like rubber. She attended to customers like they were dominos: no matter how many the complainants were, she toppled them all with the flick of a finger by saying, 'No, I'm sorry. I can't replace that.'

Alice approached me once the complaining customers had left the store.

'What are you doing just staring at the merchandise? A customer is complaining, and I have to deal with it all by myself. Nora is getting stupider by the minute, and you have nothing better to do but stare.'

'We need air-conditioning,' I said.

'Pardon me?' she asked.

'You heard me. We need to cool this store so you stop being in a bad mood all the time.'

'Start looking for the cat! I have no time for your silly remarks!'

Walking out of the store had become my habit each time Alice and I argued. It was the most peaceful and least messy reaction that I could think of. When Alice was deranged, especially now that the store was under threat of closing shop or worse, demolition, the best solution was to let her babble endlessly until her furore subsided. Her anger, though tolerable at times, was something I had difficulty analysing. It was difficult to figure out or understand where it was coming from: it could be the threat to the business setting her off, or it could be Griswald the cat. Next to the grocery store, that cat was her only source of joy.

Looking for Griswald in the midday sun was as fun as supervising the unloading of goods from suppliers. Alice was right. The construction of the concourse and platform of the elevated train station was right in front of our store. The station would be wide enough to cover the entire inter-section of the avenue, thus turning the junction now filled with natural light into a dark pathway with very limited space for pedestrians. There was no way that the construction could be transferred elsewhere because the purpose of the mass transport was for convenience. The avenue would die.

A jeep zoomed in front of our store, almost crushing the bones of my toes. And Alice was hopeful that Griswald was still alive? Those jeepney drivers would not think twice about running over my wife's cat.

On the way to the plaza, it dawned on me that the search for Griswald was a perfect excuse to stay away from my responsibilities at the store. The inventories, stock orders, and replenishment of sold out items were so mechanical, and allotting a whole day solely for work made me want to bite my nails. Cruising downtown and its inner streets was far better than counting the boxes of canned milk. From hearing street peddlers shouting simultaneously, almost like a chorus, to marveling at the charm of the prewar buildings and two-story old houses with tiled roofs. Smelling the hopia mongo fresh from the oven and put on the tray for a free taste, walking past fellow city dwellers, skin to skin. Making my way out of the side street onto the avenue were things that I actually enjoyed, far more than the everyday routine of manning the store and staring at nothing.

The church near the plaza was drawing in people coming from the inner streets. There were green and white-striped nylon tents near the church door and a couple of vendors selling puto and bibingka. It could be another fund-raising project for the reconstruction of the church convent. Alice mentioned that some choir members had come to the store with a solicitation letter, singing their guts out. I doubt she gave them a decent amount of cash. She probably just gave them a box of canned goods that were about to expire.

I checked out one of the stalls and peered at the bibingka being tended by a young woman with a ponytail, wearing a plain white shirt, and a shin-length jean skirt. Her skin was white but not the China white that was almost yellow and caught one's eye at first glance. She was the type of woman who needed to smile in order to attract men. But the smell of melted butter and cheddar cheese on top of the bibingka made me turn around and give her a closer look.

'Would you like to sample our specialty?' she asked.

'Actually, I'm just looking for something,' I told her.

'Just one bite, Mister,' she asked me with all smiles. Her eyes brightened up when stared at.

'Jeric,' I said as she moved her hand to pop her bibingka into my mouth.

'You're looking for something?'

'Our house cat has been missing for a week,' I replied while chewing her bibingka.

'What kind of cat?' she asked.

'A macho cat. A small monster with orange stripes reaching up to the end of its tail,' I replied.

'I've seen a lot of cats around here, especially in the morning when I sweep the church's front yard,' she said.

She told me that everyone in the church called her Miss Clarisse. She was a regular church person who volunteered at the parish church for two hours every day including holidays.

'I think I've seen your cat before,' Clarisse said.

'When did you see him?' I asked.

'I saw him on the church steps two days ago and he ran towards the plaza,' she said.

She pointed directly to the bank and told me that Griswald was on its steps and rubbed its head on one of the Carrara marble pillars that supported the building.

It could be one of those cats wandering the side streets with stomachs drooping on the asphalt because it was stuffed with leftovers from the soda fountains. But I wanted to believe Clarisse so I could tell Alice that someone had actually seen Griswald. Besides, it gave me free time out of the store to interact with people other than customers who complained that our black chicken was not fresh anymore.

'Thanks, Clarisse,' I said. 'I will return tomorrow and look for him.'

'Why don't you stay for a while? The parish community will be serving snacks for everyone. You can eat more bibingka if you want,' she said.

A couple of volunteers carried tables and chairs made of rattan and placed them in the front yard of the church. As the late afternoon breeze cooled the surroundings, the food was laid on the table, and the people at the plaza started coming in. Some of the churchgoers also brought food in aluminum trays wrapped in transparent plastic. Had I known that I would be invited, I would have brought some steamed black chicken.

'Hello, sir. Hello, ma'am,' I said, smiling at people who nodded at me. 'I'm the owner of R.D. Lim Grocery!'

'Oh, the store that sells black chicken. Where exactly in the avenue again?' a woman asked.

Some people were still having difficulty figuring out the exact location of our store, so I told them that we were in front of the art deco theatre near the plaza. I intentionally left out the information that our rival, 'The Emporium', was just across the street from us.

'But your business is in danger because of that construction, eh?' the woman said.

I fell silent. Clarisse ushered the woman away from me.

I sat on the bench that faced the bank and watched the flock of pigeons descend on the roof. They flew away when they saw the three sculptures of eagles just below the building's trusses, with their wings spread like they were about to take a flight, and their eyes aimed at a destination far from the city.

'Naysayer,' I told Clarisse while pointing at the woman.

'Just ignore her. She thinks that she won't be affected by

the construction,' Clarisse said and sat beside me to eat her chicken sandwich.

'You know, I went to your store once,' Clarisse added.

'Really? What did you buy?' I asked.

'Just a few groceries – soap, shampoo, detergents, toiletries mostly,' she said.

'You never bought food from our store? You were just eager to buy cleaning aids, I suppose,' I asked.

'Anyway, what are your plans? Are you going to file a complaint to stop the construction?'

'Alice is taking care of it,' I said.

'Is she your wife?' she asked.

'Yes,' I replied.

'I think I saw her when I went to your store that day. She looks like a Hong Kong actress,' she continued, 'her skin was glowing in your dimly-lit store.'

I nearly choked hearing this. I drank a soda to clear up my throat.

'Look for me next time you visit so I can assist you,' I said.

'I will. But I wouldn't buy your store specialty,' Clarisse replied.

'Why not?'

'Fr. Perez says that black chicken is bad for the soul.'

'That's his opinion, what's yours?' I asked.

'I don't know. But don't you think it makes sense?' Clarisse said.

'It's just the colour of its feathers. It's actually sweeter than the traditional chicken,' I answered.

'Really? So how should I cook it?'

'You can roast or fry it. But it's best if you stew it,' I said.

'Like tinolang manok?'

'Yeah, just like that,' I answered.

'Wouldn't the broth look like squid ink?'

She laughed and covered her mouth with her hands. I told her that I would be back the next day and would try to bring her a steamed black chicken.

The priest finally arrived, with his immaculate robe billowing against the wind. The children ran to him while a couple of women shook his hand and guided him to his reserved seat. A plate of pancit had been prepared for him. When he was about to sit, another woman grabbed his arm and gave him an embrace that made him gasp for air.

'Are you talking about me?' asked a man whose voice was hoarse, yet audible.

'Father, this is Mr. Jeric. We're talking about the merienda, and how grateful we are that you initiated this event,' Clarisse said.

Fr. Perez gave me a forceful handshake and looked at me steadily. I think it was for over a minute. He looked at my full head of hair parted sideways, my eyes shaped like almonds, my nose – not flat but not high-bridged either, the shape of my face that's just right for my body frame, my tallness of five foot and ten inches and my brown skin that made me look like a katipunero.

How about his eyes? He was not cross-eyed, but they were so small that a mere smirk would make them disappear. The hair, receding from the top but cut about an inch long, was an indication that he had already accepted the fact that he was losing it. He was fair, like a mestizo friar from that old medieval city across town. Tall? About the height of ten small soft drink bottles stacked on top of each other.

'I heard that you're a shop owner in the avenue. To be

honest, I'm in favour of building those tracks. More people will visit downtown,' the priest said.

'But our community is not in favour of it. We're already losing customers who prefer shopping in the new commercial centres outside the city.'

'Why don't we wait it out? Let's allow the construction to roll. Then we take it from there,' he said.

The priest tapped my shoulders and walked away. The crowd was building up and I somehow felt that I was drowning in it. The more people who arrived, the more I felt the need to leave.

Clarisse sat beside the priest as I left the church. She was all prepared to serve her master – ready to pour water in his glass, squeeze calamansi on his pancit, and slice a bibingka.

Back at the store, Nora and Alice were putting up the banner 'SALE! 50% OFF ON ALL ITEMS!' in front of our store while the customers kept asking them questions about the upcoming sale.

'Any luck with Griswald?' Alice asked.

'I looked everywhere. I'll try again tomorrow morning,' I said.

'Are you serious? I need you here tomorrow. I'll ask Nora to look for Griswald,' she said.

'Can I look for the cat myself?' I asked.

I should have mastered the art of conversing with Alice. I should have told her, 'No. I'll look for Griswald tomorrow,' and that would have been that. Her interrogation should have stopped when I said no.

'Fine. Start looking for Griswald tomorrow, but you should come back early,' Alice said.

I started mimicking her as I entered the store. It had

been a tedious day of looking for a cat that did nothing but eat tuna, walk the streets, and wiggle its tail all day in the hope that passersby would find his antic adorable. Why were cats so self-centred? I wished I could tell Griswald that it was not always about him. We were busy running a business and a pet was supposed to make things better. After a long day at the store, pets should entertain their masters.

I took off my shirt and went straight to bed. I felt the heat coming out of my body like steam. I smelt of cheese-and-butter bibingka blended with the odor of the city, bathed whole day in the sun.

Time to rest, I told myself. I didn't have to convince myself that I was tired, but I still kept changing positions so I could sleep comfortably. I thought of taking a shower but that would take up too much time. I tried closing my eyes again but still, I couldn't sleep.

As I was about to doze off, Alice came in and said something that I couldn't understand. I tried to read her lips through the haze and figure out if she was telling me to get up because it was still too early for bed and we hadn't had dinner yet. Forget having dinner, forget about closing the shop. I was not hungry anymore and I was sure that the shop had already been closed for the day.

I felt that she slapped my face with a newspaper but I woke up to the smell of warm cheese and coconut shavings coming in from the window. We had been smelling all sorts of things like bunches of bananas, fish balls deep fried in rancid oil, and even the soy noodles from the restaurant a few buildings away. Alice told me to get up because some people from the city hall were downstairs and wanted to talk to us.

I grabbed my shirt and went down the stairs. The men from the city hall were in crisp white shirts and khakis, looking like tamed school boys. A letter was handed to us that was signed by the mayor. Alice read it first, her eyes squinting at the small text. She frowned for the most part and didn't finish it. She gave it to me, and I read it quickly.

'As the president of the shop owners' community, the mayor would like to seek your support and understanding on this project. It's for the best and will benefit the public,' the officer said.

'But why the avenue? Of all places?' I asked.

The officer shrugged. Perhaps the question didn't warrant an answer, or he didn't know how to respond to it.

'Why not put it underground? Just like in other countries?' Alice asked.

'Ma'am, our city is a swamp. If we start digging, it'll flood and we'd all drown,' the other officer replied.

'How about rerouting where the train would pass?' Alice said.

'That's not possible, Ma'am. Plans have already been made. And signed,' the man said.

'Can it be retracted?' I asked.

'No, sir. We're very sorry,' the other man said.

'So there's nothing you can do?' Alice asked.

The two officers bowed in defeat and left us standing and holding the letter.

I sighed and went outside. I squinted when the streetlight flickered. I looked at the signage of the theatre with its green neon light peering through the darkness of our store, which was only brightened by a number of light bulbs covered in cobwebs. I thought of going to inner downtown, where the noodles houses and burger joints were still open until late evening. Bowls of broth would be lined up on the table for the customers to see. I signalled Alice that I was going out again, this time for some fresh air to blow the cobwebs away because I couldn't sleep anymore.

Across the street from our store were tailors and clothes shops, tended by elders with tape measures around their necks. Swaths of fabric in shades of ocean blue, blood red, and moss green were displayed in a shop window. The store beside it had two mannequins: a man in white trousers, vest, and blazer, with a black tie completing the get up; and a woman in a blue polka-dot dress accented by a large red ribbon on her neckline.

The neon signs were lit up and the theatre lobbies began to smell of buttered popcorn and soda spilled on the marble floor. Couples were lining up at a ticket booth with signage that gave moviegoers the option for orchestra, loge, and balcony. Volkswagens and Jeeps raced against each other on the avenue and men hanging around outside the theatres looked at the women passing by, still in their office uniform of short skirts.

I opted to have a sandwich in a diner past the two bookstores and shoe shops. When I arrived, I saw through the glass divider that the cooks were flipping burgers in the kitchen. I sat on a bar stool and told the waiter that I wanted a cheeseburger and orange juice. The waiter was elderly, his white hair half-covered by his hat. His wrinkled face must have witnessed this avenue in its golden age, seen how it had been destroyed and then how it had flourished after the war, and was about to go downhill again in the coming months.

I asked the waiter if he knew about the train construction. He said yes, so I told him about the visit of the people from the city hall to our store. His eyes had a hint of preparation as I told him about the possibility of closing the avenue for the contractors who would be occupying the street to lay down their materials. Each post that was to be built would cover the frontage of every store and theatre, I said. By the time that the elevated railway was finished, the entire area would be blighted, I told him, and the shops might well start to lose their customers.

'Are you afraid?' he asked.

'Of what's going to happen to our store? Yes, of course,' I replied.

'No, I mean if we hold a rally,' he said.

'How? Where? Well, yes, that I'll be afraid of as well,' I told him.

He smiled and began wiping the counter. As I finished my juice and burger, I left my money on the table and waved him goodbye. When I stepped outside, there were parked Jeeps on the street that caused gridlock all the way to the end of the plaza.

There was a sense of dread going back to the store, like the feeling of Sunday nights for an office worker and the first day of school for an incoming high school student. Maybe it was because the impending rain that would flood the avenue knee-deep, or the uncertainty of what was going to happen in the coming months. I anticipated the construction of the platform right in front of our store. In the next few weeks, we would be covering our frontage with a huge plastic to prevent the dust from seeping into our groceries, and the heat of the mid-afternoon and the odour of steel and cement would be wafting through our bedroom. I was also prepared to accept Alice's frustration over our failure to convince the mayor to stop the construction.

When I arrived at the shop, I saw the sign 'Sorry, we're closed.' It wasn't even late evening yet, so I took out my keys and opened the door. When I went upstairs, Alice threw a towel at my face.

'You stink of the afternoon sun. How about taking a shower first before going to bed?' she said while she was combing her hair in front of the mirror. The glare of the fluorescent light faintly illuminated her face. She seemed far away from me, as if I couldn't reach or touch her.

'I left food on the table,' Alice said.

'I already ate at Sam's. I'm tired,' I answered.

When I woke up the next day, I felt the sweet heat of the morning sun on my skin. I hadn't slept well last night so I closed my eyes for a few minutes. When I opened them, I was gazing at a flock of pigeons flapping their wings and landing on the signage of the theatre. I wanted to put birdseed on the smooth surface of our windowpane, but Alice didn't want to see bird droppings on the glass. I had offered to clean the windows every day using old newspapers, but she said that selling chicken was more important than feeding pigeons.

Alice was cooking fried eggs again. I heard the clink of the jar as she scooped out foetid lard and dropped it on the skillet. The aroma of heated oil and egg reached our bedroom. I swear to God, if I ate another fried egg for breakfast, I would grow a beak and black feathers. She served pancakes with butter and maple syrup and crisped bacon only if she was in a good mood. If she was cranky and foul, she fried eggs.

'Breakfast!' she screamed from the kitchen.

'I'll just take a shower!' I shouted back.

I didn't hear more from her. She was probably downstairs, cleaning up and preparing for opening the store.

I couldn't help but feel giddy about leaving the store that day while I shampooed my hair and played with the soap suds. I splattered water all over the bathroom and Alice's bathrobe. The stacks of tissue papers were already dripping wet, so I grabbed the bath towel hanging behind the door and prepared to get dressed.

'Aren't you joining me for breakfast?' Alice asked.

'Coffee's fine,' I answered.

'Are you sick and tired of my fried eggs?'

'Not just the eggs,' I half-whispered.

'I can cook bacon and pancakes if you want.'

I told her that I needed to check the inventory before I left the house to look for Griswald. I was almost middle-aged, so product control in our store was like brushing my teeth or parking the car on a side street. My main task made me yawn by midday but eventually I would catch myself going ballistic over a missing can of meat loaf.

'It's good that you're constantly checking the inventory,' Alice said while she handed me a cup of coffee.

'I've been doing this every day. We have to make sure that all the items are in good condition,' I said.

'Take a closer look at that can of corned beef,' Alice said.

'What about the corned beef?' I asked.

'The label,' Alice answered. 'I can draw a better-looking cow.'

'It's easy to draw a cow,' I replied.

'You can't even draw a spoon and fork,' she said.

'Well, what about the cow? What kind of cow do you plan to draw?'

'I will draw a strong cow. I want its mouth open and its body muscled and well contoured. That cow looks weak and somber,' Alice said.

'He's sad,' I said.

'You think so?'

'He's sick and tired of being a cow. That label reminds me of those prewar photos of Filipinas that appear on tobacco labels. They're all beautiful but behind the make-up and the piña dress, they have no idea that their picture will be used for tobacco and sold everywhere.'

'So are you saying that they're idiots?' Alice asked.

'They're misled, not idiots. They probably think that it's for an art exhibit. A picture-perfect photograph is an image of the fine life that they long for. They just want to be happy.'

'Why the sudden interest in women?' she asked.

'I'm analyzing, not taking interest,' I replied.

I left the store and assured Alice that I'd be back before lunchtime with or without Griswald. She nodded and kept staring at the corned beef label. I wondered if she was serious when she said that she was planning to call the manufacturer and send them a sketch of her healthy and happy-looking cow.

The street sweepers cleaning the street wore their yellow shirts and matching red pants and bandana. I strode towards the church while the morning fog sheathed the city and the mist coming from the hose dampened my face. Since the parish was just a few metres away, I thought I might as well pay Clarisse a visit and thank her again for the hearty meal and good conversation yesterday.

The church door was open and I could see Clarisse sweeping the marble floor. I approached her whilst parting my hair on the side. It felt like approaching a college girl sitting on a cement bench under the shades of the mango tree during break time.

'The churchgoers will slip if you keep on scrubbing,' I told her.

She looked at me and wiped the trail of sweat from her face with her bare hands. She smiled. She looked away. She looked at me again and smiled with her lips closed.

'So, have you found Griswald?' she asked.

'Not yet,' I answered. 'Perhaps you could help me.'

'I'd like to help you, but I'm very busy today.'

'That can wait,' I said. 'May I invite you to breakfast?'

'I already ate,' she said. 'Cheese and pan de sal.'

'How about a proper meal at Ramon Lee's?'

'Chicken for breakfast?'

'A heavy meal. Just for today.'

Clarisse left the broom and dustpan in one corner and told me that she had to be back in an hour. Not a problem. The cook can prepare fried chicken, rice, and atsara in five minutes. I can eat fast but I wasn't sure if we had enough time to talk.

'What about your wife's cat?' she asked.

'Let's forget about the cat for now. Come on, let's eat,' I told her.

I turned back and saw Fr. Perez peering at us through the capiz-shell window of the convent. I didn't know if I should tell Clarisse that the parish priest was looking at us. I stretched my arm over her shoulders and looked at the priest, who was still staring at Clarisse. I tried to make eye contact, but his eyes were focused on Clarisse's nape.

The inner streets of the city had a life of their own and were physically different compared to the avenue where our shop and other stores were located. As Clarisse and I walked and asked each other about morning rituals and our day-to-day activities, we had the back of the buildings as our backdrop, with emergency exit ladders jutting out of the structures.

On the sidewalk were garbage bins filled with black bags still uncollected by the metro cleaners. The new government had claimed that even the pits of this district would be spic and span so that not even a fly would not dare plant its feet on the sanitised ground. But right now there were rodents bigger than Griswald. Clarisse witnessed everything but she never said a word; she didn't even ask me why we took a turn on a shorter but more decaying street. I was about to say that it didn't look like this before but I when I looked at her, she seemed to have understood what I was about to say.

Walking briskly and doing small talk in a city with cramped sidewalks proved difficult. But I was contented. At least this was a different kind of morning.

Past the narrow alley, we were pleased that we were walking to the avenue extension again. Here, the morning was sweet like the sugar cane juice sold in Chinatown nearby. One could feel the weather was just right: not too hot, not too cold. There was fog on the steps leading to the chicken restaurant. Two old women were carrying a basket on their way to the market. A young man whose skin was as brown as horse manure clanged his bell and yelled, 'Hot bread in the morning!'. A young mother, still in her house dress, dragged her son to school, while he opened his lunch box and inspected his Tetra Paked juice and sandwich wrapped in a green transparent plastic.

We ordered fried chicken and it arrived in a few minutes. It was nice to see spring chicken after so many years of selling black chicken.

Clarisse eagerly dispatched every piece of chicken into her mouth. She admitted that she was very hungry. A decade of eating cheese and pan de sal for breakfast was just not right.

'This is so embarrassing. I'm a good eater. There are so many things that you still don't know about me,' Clarisse explained while she was halfway through the basket of fried chicken.

'I think we have enough time for your stories,' I said.

'I don't think so. I've got to run after this meal,' she said.

'Eat and run?' I commented.

'So what do you do for a living aside from owning a grocery?' she asked.

'It's not really mine,' I replied.

'What do you mean it's not really yours? That's conjugal property, right?' she asked.

'My wife runs the place. I just help her,' I told her.

'So what do you do aside from helping your wife?' Clarisse asked again.

'I handle the marketing side. I also handle the inventory, logistics, and sometimes the customer complaints. My wife handles the finances and store management,' I said.

'You seem good at doing several tasks at the same time. You're like an acrobat who can do various stunts. I can imagine your body rolling forward or backward, your knees bent and your feet going over your head,' Clarisse said.

'I could perform acrobatic stunts to promote our store!' I said.

'And it will be more fun if you're holding a chicken while

doing the stunt! May I ask why you do so many things?'
she asked.

'I do it for Alice, for the store, and for the customers,'
I muttered.

'How about you? What do you do for yourself?' she asked.

I look at the ceiling and cupped my mouth with the palm
of my hand. I asked her more questions instead.

The chicken basket was almost empty when Clarisse realised that we had already been in the restaurant for almost an
hour. We left, and she suggested that we take the street parallel
to the avenue and walk all the way to University Avenue. She
told me that most of the stray cats roaming the city retreated
there because the sunlight receded behind the three-story
accessorias thus making the sidewalks cooler and a more
comfortable resting place for lost and homeless animals.
I told her that we could walk on any street that she wanted.

'The cat might be sleeping in one of those alleys,'
Clarisse said.

'Or Griswald's innards might have already been cooked
for siopao,' I blurted out.

'Don't say that. We will find your cat,' she said.

We scouted another street but there was no trace of
Griswald. Dogs sniffed the garbage thrown just below the
street sign at the corner but there was not a single cat in
sight. We turned left to another street and asked the old
woman tending a kitchenette if she had seen an overfed
orange cat but she said that her eyesight was poor. On our
way to a panciteria, I thought of making a poster, 'Have you
seen this cat?' with a photograph of Griswald going crazy over
a purple yarn. Clarisse walked purposefully and with ease,
strutting past the morning crowd.

A young boy drinking soda told us that he had seen an orange cat that was bloated from eating leftover food from restaurants on University Avenue. He pointed to an alley between a newspaper warehouse and a printing press.

'Cat world,' exclaimed the small boy.

'Are you sure, kid?' I asked.

'Yes, Mister. He's the biggest cat I've seen in that alley. His tail has an orange streak.'

'I wish I had a boy as bright as him,' I said.

We made our way to an alley shaded by two five-story buildings. The boy was right, it was a cat world. There were black-and-white cats, cats with grey-and-orange stripes, mother cats and kittens. They were like rats squirming through holes and trashcans.

But I still couldn't find Griswald. He was as fat as a butterball so it would have been impossible to miss him in the swarm of felines.

I walked behind Clarisse while she searched for Griswald. She had no idea what Griswald exactly looked like, but there she was, checking the stacks of boxes and old newspapers.

'Have you seen him yet?' she asked.

'No, not yet. We should check down the street,' I told her.

The alley was always shaded by the backs of the buildings so that even the sunlight could not permeate into it. The roof trusses of the two structures that stood across from each other met in the middle of the alley and covered this side street, which was referred to by our neighbours as an alley for ants because only small things could pass through. We could hear the printing press machines being operated behind us and the smell of newspaper ink overpowered Clarisse's perfume of fresh baby powder, which was like sweet morning dew on a flower sprinkled with cold water. I walked behind her while opening the garbage bins along the way. When we heard a cat purring under the stacks of papers, Clarisse lurched forward to the end of the shaded alley. But after rummaging through all the stacks of newspapers, Griswald was nowhere to be found.

She walked past an elderly man with a walking stick and a woman looking at her grocery bag. I was already catching my breath as I followed her. She was taking Goliath steps while I lagged a few steps behind her. I should have eaten Alice's fried eggs this morning.

As we approached the plaza, there was a group of people surrounding the fountain, holding placards and with white towels tied around their heads. One of them was the waiter who had served my burger last night. When he turned around and saw me, he showed me what was written on his placard: 'Halt the construction! Save the avenue!'

Clarisse stopped in a corner and scanned the plaza already occupied by the protesters. When we walked a little further, I saw our neighbours in the crowd shouting 'Stop the train!' all at the same time. The metro com in brown uniforms were already surrounding the group of about a hundred people, composed of shop-owners and their employees.

'Are you joining?' Clarisse asked.

For a moment, I thought about myself. Every day, for the past ten years or so, counting cans of sardines and other goods was the only thing I had really accomplished. The daily routine had become my source of comfort. Two things came to my mind, Alice and saving the store. But where was I in the equation?

I left Clarisse standing in a corner as I joined the crowd and started shouting 'Stop the construction!' The rest of the community began to mill around the plaza. The bureau of public works across the fountain was closed but we knew that there were people inside.

When Clarisse was about to enter the church, the metro com started dispersing the crowd with a water hose. The people with placards were thrown everywhere by water pressure and the rest of the protesters ran away and hid behind the arches of the buildings. I stood in the plaza and kept shouting that the giant was selfish and that his snake could not pass through our avenue.

Someone grabbed my collar from behind and dragged me into the middle of the plaza. While I was being taken away, I saw the sun perched atop the building with the three eagles watching me from their posts.

I was punched several times in the face. My head slammed against the ground with every blow. The eagle in the middle was about to fly. Its claws were large enough to pick me up and take me uptown.

Three or four of the people now kicking me in the gut and groin lifted me up and dragged me to the sidewalk. The skin of my arms and face scraped on the asphalt, which was already warm from the mid-morning sun. I felt my skin being rubbed away from my body, the abrasion of the second layer getting red, the blood gradually dripping out of it. The friction of the packed dirt against my peeled skin caused me pain. I tried to think of calmness and serenity, hospitals and nurses, hot soups and bed rest, just to veer myself away from this dread.

I was couldn't see anymore and my head was throbbing. I felt a shot of pain in my left eye. I could hear a woman's voice begging the men to stop. Was it Alice or Clarisse? The more that the woman pleaded them to lay off me, the more I got kicked and knocked, until I spat blood. Finally, I landed on the gutter.

The eagles on top of the building had left me. I tried to open my eyes to take a close look at the men, but they were nowhere to be found. I searched for the woman's voice, but no one was around.

When I tried to open my eyes, I saw Griswald approaching me. When all the men fled and left me lying on the plaza, Griswald moved closer to me and licked my face. 'My blood isn't milk,' I said, in protest, while I struggled away from the cat.

But Griswald continued licking my face and it gradually lessened the pain. Clarisse had disappeared and the rest of the protesters had left as well. My blood tasted sweet, not bitter as I expected. I got up, picked up Griswald, and walked back to our store.

The customers in our shop were spilling on to the sidewalk. Nora was talking to one of our regulars while Alice was putting two trays of black chicken in the shop window. The 'SALE! 50% OFF ON ALL ITEMS!' banner in bold, red, and capitalised letters had been unveiled. Under the shadows of the train station construction, our black chicken took centre stage, perhaps for the very last time.

It was not yet high noon, but the sun felt like midday on my wounds. I tried to wipe my sweat off my face but I screamed in pain each time I dabbed the palm of my hand on my cheeks and forehead. Nora saw me and called Alice. But she was too busy counting the remaining chicken on the table. I walked up to her and handed her Griswald.

'Here's your cat,' I said.

'My God! Your face! What happened?' she asked.

Left with no words to say, I let the blood drip from my face. Alice ran inside to get the First Aid kit and I was left outside to sell chickens and explain to the customers that my bloodied face had nothing to do with the clearance sale. Clarisse said that I could be an acrobat doing various stunts. As my body rolled forward and backward, with my knees bent and my feet over my head, I would shout, 'Clearance Sale!' until I ran out of breath and the blood trickled on
my forehead.

Every shopper who passed by our store asked what had happened to me and I told them to buy something first. Halfway through my narrative, the chickens were sold out, and Nora had to get a new batch of chicken from the freezer.

Alice was taking so long, I might as well do something good for the community. 'Free chicken for everyone! Get as many as you want!' I shouted. Everyone was getting hold of as many black chickens as they could. In the swarm of the customer's screaming and Alice's nagging, I could see myself being carried away by the eagles from plaza. I opened my arms wide enough for me to be picked up by the eagles. I saw one of them slowly descending towards me. Upon reaching the ground, the bird opened its claws and clamped the back of my shirt to lift me up and take me to a new avenue where the python could not conquer and would be killed by mere stones thrown by the people. It would be an avenue that is ours, and not under control by any power or state but ourselves.

ACKNOWLEDGEMENTS

Mr. Fix It: Troublesome Kinshasa is published by Phonome Media (August 2017).

'Mangosil' is published as part of *The Walls of Delhi* by Seven Stories Press (June 2014).

'The Water Was Drained' was first published by The River Rail (January 2018).

The Broken Doll comes from the as yet untranslated novel Сломанная кукла, published in Russian by Eksmo (2016).

'Driving in Greater Noida' was first published by Granta Online (February 2015).

'Metro Line Five' was first published by Paper Republic (November 2017).

'Planes Flying Over a Monster' was first published by Electric Literature (August 2016).

Slow Boat is published by *Pushkin Press* (March 2017)

Margins of Error is an extract from the as yet untranslated novel *Capão Pecado* published by Planeta (2nd edition, January 2017).

The Scatter Here is Too Great is published by Jonathan Cape (August 2014).

Desesterro is an extract from the as yet untranslated novel *Desesterro* published by Grupo Editorial Record (November 2015).

Using Life is published by Center for Middle Eastern Studies, The University of Texas at Austin (November 2017).

'Somersaults' was first published by *Sunday Times Magazine* (April 2017).

Kathleen McCaul Moura began her writing life in the city of
Baghdad and went on to live and work in a number of megacities;
Delhi, Mumbai, London, Sao Paulo and Rio de Janeiro. She has
published two novels and worked as a journalist for the BBC and
Al Jazeera English. Her non-fiction has appeared in publications
including *Granta*, *The London Review of Books* and the *Guardian*.
She now lives in Norwich with her four children and is studying
for a doctorate in creative writing at the University of East Anglia.

Dele Adeyemo is an architect, researcher and creative director
conducting an AHRC/CHASE PhD at the Centre for Research
Architecture at Goldsmiths, University of London where his
research explores strategies for de-colonising the production
of space. Dele is a contributing editor at *The Real Review* and
regularly writes for UK journals. Previously Dele co-founded
and for seven years directed the architecture and creative studio
Pidgin Perfect, where he innovated new culture-led approaches
to public engagement in the process of placemaking, architecture
and urban design. As part of the British Council's UK/Nigeria
season in 2015/16 whilst director at Pidgin Perfect, Dele directed
the project CreativeLagos.com, mapping the emergent creative
spaces and people that are rapidly transforming the culture of
this megalopolis.

Kunlé Adeyemi is an architect, designer and urban researcher. He
is the founder/principal of NLÉ and 2017 Aga Khan Design Critic
in Architecture at Harvard University Graduate School of Design.
His notable works include 'Makoko Floating School', an innovative
prototype floating structure located on the lagoon heart of Lagos,
Nigeria. This acclaimed project is part of an extensive research
project – 'African Water Cities' – being developed by NLÉ an
architecture, design and urbanism practice founded by Adeyemi
in 2010, focusing on developing cities and communities.

Jessica Zafra writes columns for major dailies in the Philippines, and has a dozen published collections of essays on film, literature, travel, rock music, popular culture and politics, as well as two collections of short fiction. Her work has appeared in the *New Yorker*, *Newsweek*, and *The Standard* in Hongkong. She has just written her first novel.

Richard Ali A Mutu was born in Mbandaka, Democratic Republic of the Congo, in 1988. He won the Mark Twain Award in 2009, and published his first novel, *Tabu's Nightmares*, written in French, in 2011. His novel *Mr. Fix It: Troublesome Kinshasa* was published in Lingala in 2014, and has since been translated into French as well. Ali was selected as one of the only writers working in indigenous languages for the *Africa 39* anthology, which showcased the continent's most talented writers under forty, including Chimamanda Adichie and Dinaw Mengetsu. He works as a lawyer and writer, and hosts a weekly television program about Congolese literature.

Uday Prakash, born in 1952 in the remote village of Sitapur in Madhya Pradesh, is one of contemporary Hindi literature's most important voices. After completing his master's degree with distinction, Prakash started his career as Assistant Professor in Jawaharlal Nehru University, New Delhi. He was also Assistant Professor at the Times Research Foundation, School of Social Journalism, and Professor and Head of the Department of Media and Journalism at IGNTU, Amarkantak. Prakash has worked for a range of newspapers and television sources in Delhi, all the while publishing poetry and fiction to international acclaim. His writings have been translated into all major Indian languages and Asian and European languages including German, Japanese, English, Dutch, Hungarian, Spanish, and Russian. He is the recipient of the Sahitya Akademi award—the highest literary award in India— which he returned in protest of the murder of dissenting writers by right-wing extremists. His 2013 book *The Walls of Delhi* was a finalist for the DSC Prize for South Asian Literature. Translations of his works have received prestigious awards. Also a filmmaker and a TV director, Prakash divides his time between New Delhi and Sitapur.

Diego Gerard is a writer, editor and translator based in Mexico City. He is the co-founding editor of *disONARE Magazine*.

Emily Ruth Ford is a British writer and translator living in North London. After reading English at Oxford University, she spent ten years as a journalist, working for *The Times* and *Agence France-Presse* in Shanghai, Hong Kong and New Delhi. In 2016, she left journalism to study on the MA in Creative Writing at the University of East Anglia. She won the Royal Society of Literature's V.S. Pritchett Short Story Prize in 2017 and again in 2018. In 2019 she was selected for the inaugural London Library Emerging Writers Programme. She is currently at work on a novel.

Liza Alexandrova-Zorina was born in 1984 in a little town on Cola Peninsula beyond the Arctic Circle (the setting of her prize-winning novel, *The Little Man*). She later settled in Moscow and became a prolific journalist, film-maker, popular columnist and a public activist. Liza was a finalist in two important literary competitions: the Debut Prize and the NOS Literary Prize with her novel *The Little Man*, and was also the winner of the Northern Star Prize for her collection of short stories *The Rebel*. She has six novels to her name. Some of them have been published in French, English, Arabic, Hindi, Ukrainian and Estonian.

Deepti Kapoor was born in Moradabad, in northern India. She is the author of *A Bad Character*. She lived in Delhi for many years, moved to Goa, then went back to Delhi.

Ayodele Olofintuade was born in Ibadan, but spent her younger years travelling between Lagos, Ibadan, and Abeokuta. She is the author of *Lakiriboto Chronicles: A Brief History of Badly Behaved Women* (2018) and *Eno's Story* (2010). Her short stories have been published in several online literary journals. She is an investigative journalist, and researcher, who has written papers about African Feminism. She also runs an online Feminist and Queer ezine, *9jafeminista*. Ayodele lives in a universe populated by fantastic beings and beasts.

Wu Jun grew up in Northeast China, but moved to Shenzhen after graduating and has lived there ever since. Shenzhen serves as the setting for much of her fiction, which includes the novel *We Are Not the Same Humans* and six short story collections. Her works have been published in literary magazines including *People's Literature* and *October*, as well as numerous anthologies. Wu Jun won the Chinese Novel Biennial Award in 2008 and the *Fiction Monthly* Hundred Flowers Award in 2013. Her works have also been adapted for the screen translated into English and Russian.

Anna Pook grew up in South London and lives in Paris. From 2009 to 2014, she was the resident creative writing instructor at the Left Bank bookshop, Shakespeare and Company. She received an MA in Prose Fiction from the University of East Anglia, where she was the 2014/15 recipient of the Man Booker Scholarship. Her writing has appeared in *The Mechanics' Institute Review* and *Litro Magazine*. She is working on her debut novel.

Daniel Saldaña París is an essayist, poet and novelist whose work has been translated into English, French, and Italian and anthologised, most recently in *Bogotá 39. New Voices From Latin America*, published in the UK by Oneworld. *Among Strange Victims*, his first novel, was shortlisted for the Best Translated Book Award in the US. His second novel, *Ramifications*, is forthcoming in the UK by Charco Press.

Hideo Furukawa was born in 1966 in Fukushima, and is highly regarded for the richness of his storytelling and his willingness to experiment; he changes his style with every new book. His best-known novel is the 2008 *Holy Family*, an epic work of alternate history set in northeastern Japan. He has received the Mystery Writers of Japan Award, the Japan SF Grand Prize and the Yukio Mishima award.

Ahmed Naji: writer, and criminal. Born in Mansura-Egypt (1985). His first novel *Rogers* translated into Italian. He is second novel *Using Life* was published first in 2014 in Arabic then translated to other languages. He has been accused of hurting public morals and sentenced for 2 years. He was granted the PEN/Barbey Freedom to Write Award. Now he is a fellow writer at BMI in Las Vegas where he is living with his family.

Ferréz (Reginaldo Ferreira da Silva) was born 1975. He is a Brazilian author, rapper, cultural critic and activist from the favela of Capão Redondo in São Paulo, Brazil. He is a member and leader of the literary group *Literatura Marginal* that emerged during the late 1990s and early 2000s (decade) from the urban periphery of São Paulo. He has emphasized that his writings are for the youth of the favela, and that they should feel a sense of pride in reading literature that reflects their reality and experiences.

Bilal Tanweer is a writer and translator. He was one of *Granta*'s 'New Voices' and a recipient of the PEN Translation Fund Grant for his translation of Muhammad Khalid Akhtar's *Love in Chakiwara and Other Misadventures* (Picador India, 2016). He has also translated two novels by Ibn-e Safi, *The House Fear* (Random House India, 2010). He is an Honorary Fellow of the International Writing Program at the University of Iowa. His debut novel *The Scatter Here Is Too Great* won the Shakti Bhatt First Book Prize 2014 and was a finalist for the DSC Prize for South Asian Literature 2015 and The Chautauqua Prize 2015.

Sheyla Smanioto graduated in Literary Studies from the Brazilian university Unicamp, where she then did a master's degree in Literary Theory. Her debut novel, *Desesterro*, won the SESC Prize for Literature and was a finalist for the São Paulo Prize for Literature. She participated in the anthology *Golpe: Antologia-Manifesto* (2016), organised in protest against the Temer government.

Montasser Al-Qaffash has published four collections of short stories and three novels. Among other awards, in 2014 his *At Eye Level* was granted the Sawiris Cultural Award for best short story collection.

Jeffrey Pascual Yap finished A.B. Philosophy at San Beda College, Manila and M.A. English Studies, major in Creative Writing at the University of the Philippines, Diliman. He became a fellow of national writers' workshops, taught Philippine Literature in English, and published short stories and essays in Southeast Asia. He has won awards for his adapted screenplays and travel essay in the Philippines.

Bienvenu Sene Mongaba is a Congolese writer, translator, and publisher. He directs Éditions Mabiki, which champions Congolese languages. He has written three books of fiction in Lingala and several in French. He splits his time between Kinshasa and Belgium.

An avid reader and passionate linguist with a keen academic interest in African literature, **Sara Sene** is a translator working with Italian, English, French, Spanish, and Lingala.

Jason Grunebaum is a senior lecturer in the department of South Asian Languages and Civilizations at the University of Chicago. His English translation of Uday Prakash's Hindi novel *The Girl with the Golden Parasol*, for which he was awarded a 2005 PEN Translation Fund grant, was published by Penguin India in 2008, and his translation of a trio of Prakash novellas entitled *The Walls of Delhi* was published in 2012 by UWA Press. He received a 2011 NEA Literature Fellowship for the translation, in collaboration with Ulrike Stark, of Manzoor Ahtesham's *Tale of the Missing Man*. He received a 2006 Fellowship from the American Literary Translators Association and has been awarded residencies at the Blue Mountain Center for the Arts and the Djerassi Foundation. His fiction has been published in *One Story*, *Web Conjunctions*, *Southwest Review*, and *Third Coast*. Salman Rushdie selected his 'Maria Ximenes da Costa de Carvalho Perreira' as a distinguished short story of 2007.

For twenty years, **Natasha Perova** has been the editor of the publishing house Glas. Praised by such luminaries as George Steiner and Sir Isaiah Berlin, Glas is responsible for translating overlooked Russian classics and up-and-coming Russian writers into English. Through her efforts, writers such as Sigizmund Krzhizhanovsky, Victor Pelevin, and Vladimir Sorokin are now known in the English-speaking world

Lucy Craig-McQuaide developed a love for language learning and translation whilst growing up in Belgium. She graduated from the University of Cambridge in 2017 with a degree in Chinese and now works in London in education in London.

Philip K. Zimmerman is a writer and a translator from Spanish and German. Born in Madrid, he was raised in Upstate New York. His work has been included in the Berlin International Literature Festival and the New York International Fringe Festival, and he recently completed a translation of Helene and Wolfgang Beltracchi's autobiography, *Selbstporträt (Self-Portrait)*. He lives in Munich, Germany.

David Boyd is Assistant Professor of Japanese at the University of North Carolina at Charlotte. He has translated stories by Hiroko Oyamada, Mieko Kawakami and Toh EnJoe, among others. His translation of Hideo Furukawa's *Slow Boat* (Pushkin Press) won the 2017/2018 Japan-U.S. Friendship Commission (JUSFC) Prize for the Translation of Japanese Literature.

Benjamin Koerber is Assistant Professor in the Department of African, Middle Eastern, and South Asian Languages and Literatures at Rutgers University. His work has appeared in the *Journal of Arabic Literature, Jadaliyya, Maʒazef*, and *Wasla*.

Victor Meadowcroft grew up at the foot of the Sintra Mountains in Portugal and translates from Portuguese and Spanish. He is a graduate of the MA in Literary Translation programme at the University of East Anglia and currently working on *Lisbon Tales*, an anthology of Portuguese fiction set in Lisbon, in collaboration with translator Amanda Hopkinson.

Laura Garmeson is a writer, journalist and translator from Portuguese and French. Her work has been published in the *Financial Times, The Economist, Asymptote Journal* and *3:AM Magazine*, among others. She is based in London.

Gretchen McCullough was raised in Harlingen Texas. After graduating from Brown University in 1984, she taught in Egypt, Turkey and Japan. She earned her MFA from the University of Alabama and was awarded a teaching Fulbright to Syria from 1997-1999. Her stories, essays and reviews have appeared in the *Texas Review*, *The Alaska Quarterly Review*, *The Barcelona Review*, *Archipelago*, *National Public Radio*, *Storysouth*, *Storyglossia*, *The Literary Review* and *The Common*. Translations in English and Arabic have been published in: *Nizwa*, *Banipal*, *Brooklyn Rail in Translation* and *Al-Mustaqbel*. Her bi-lingual book of short stories in English and Arabic, *Three Stories From Cairo*, translated with Mohamed Metwalli was published in July 2011 by AFAQ Publishing House, Cairo. A collection of short stories about expatriate life in Cairo, *Shahrazad's Tooth*, was also published by AFAQ in 2013. Currently, she is a Senior Lecturer in the Department of Rhetoric and Composition at the American University in Cairo.

Mohamed Metwalli won the Yussef el-Khal prize by Riyad el-Rayes Publishers in Lebanon for his poetry collection, *Once Upon a Time in* 1992. He co-founded an independent literary magazine, el-Garad in which his second volume of poems appeared, *The Story the People Tell in the Harbor*, 1998. He was selected to represent Egypt in the International Writers' Program, at the University of Iowa in 1997. Later he was Poet-in-Residence at the University of Chicago in 1998. He compiled and co-edited an anthology of Off-beat Egyptian Poetry, *Angry Voices*, published by the University of Arkansas press in 2002. He published his third collection *The Lost Promenades* in 2010 by the independent al-Ketaba al-Okhra publications. The same collection was republished by the General Egyptian Book Organization (GEBO) in 2013. *A Song by the Aegean Sea*, his latest collection of poetry, was published by Afaq Publishers, Cairo in 2015. In 2016, he was a guest poet at the *Prague Writers' Festival.*

MEGACITY

First published by Boiler House Press, 2020.
Part of the UEA Publishing Project Ltd.
International © 2020 retained by individual authors

Design and typesetting by Emily Benton Book Design

ISBN 978-1-911343-81-3